In the shadows of the chilly room, Ethan reached out and, without asking, took Jacob's bourbon and swallowed it. His black bow tie was undone and askew; one collar was up. He looked like a drunken fool.

"Good Lord, Ethan, you have lost all restraint! Is there any sense in my addressing you at this time?" Jacob stood still, watching as his brother began circling the long oak dining table. "Ethan, I must tell you something very disturbing," he began in an even tone. "There can be no retreat on this issue."

"Charge!" Ethan cried, raising an imaginary saber.

Jacob could see the drunken luster of his eyes. "Ethan," he repeated. "Your friends are watched as spies. You will be a marked man if war breaks out." Jacob spoke in haste, and there was bitterness in his words. "Why must you always bring out the basest in me?"

Ethan's mind was too foggy; he struggled to isolate one comment and understand it. "The Keyeses are spies? Stuart told you that?" How had the old man found out?

"Yes!" Jacob shook with rage. "Your friends serve Mr. Lincoln!" Turning his back in disgust, Jacob stood, facing the fireplace. Two and a half decades of frustration surged within him. The good brother, the one who must always make peace and compromise, the one who stayed home with Daddy while Ethan ran off to Harvard University.

Grabbing the wrought-iron fireplace poker, he whirled around and raised it.

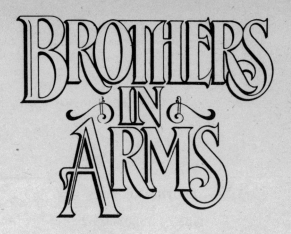

BROTHERS IN ARMS

COURTNEY BISHOP

LYNX BOOKS
New York

BROTHERS IN ARMS

ISBN: 1-55802-029-2

First Printing / December 1988

This book is published by Lynx Books, a division of Lynx Communications, Inc., 41 Madison Avenue, New York, New York, 10010. The name "Lynx" together with the logotype consisting of a stylized head of a lynx is a trademark of Lynx Communications, Inc.

Printed in the United States of America

0 9 8 7 6 5 4 3 2 1

To Patti, with love and admiration

The author wishes to thank Rick Britton for his help in ensuring the historical accuracy of the scenes presented.

BROTHERS IN ARMS

CHAPTER 1

DECEMBER, 1860

Hand-held torches, a hundred strong, shone a ghostly light on the faces of the young men carrying them down Main Street past Miller's Pharmacy and the hardware store. Chanting "Long live Virginia!" and "Down with Unionists!" in loud voices quivering from the chill air and inbred pride, the marchers welcomed the coming of the Second War for Independence, as they called it, with the same enthusiasm as their grandfathers, who had marched boldly into battle against the British less than a century before.

The One Hundred, as Charlottesville's best and brightest young men were known, marched four abreast in a military cadence. From this night forth, most of them knew that every public act—and many private ones—were to prepare them for the looming battle against Northern oppression, a battle Mr. Lincoln and his Federal bullies were fated to lose.

"For if the great God Jehovah were not on Virginia's side, surely He would not take arms against her, the oldest and richest of America's commonwealths, homeland of Washington and Jefferson, and verdant nursery of Patrick Henry!" So had said James Cabell just before the march had begun.

Such treachery on the part of God was impossible, unthinkable, reasoned the One Hundred as they wound their way toward Mr. Jefferson's university and the inevitable clash with the Unionist sympathizers they knew to be meeting there.

"It's cold, Jacob. I should've worn gloves like you

said!" Matthew Randolph shouted to his friend and mentor, the elder of the two Parson boys.

"You'll get warm bashing in some heads at the university!" someone shouted, having overheard Matthew.

"Tuck the torch in your trousers!" another suggested, and a dozen husky voices broke into laughter.

But Jacob Parson's voice was not among them. Jacob frowned as he turned the collar of his black frogged coat up against the lightly falling rain. He saw nothing humorous about their vigil; searching out violence was against his pragmatic nature. Still, he was as full blooded and proud as the next man, and taller and stronger than most. At twenty-six, he might well have been the oldest figure in the march. Something told him that their mission was a mistake; that attacking one's cousins and neighbors, in whichever cause, was inviting a retribution he preferred to avoid.

He had attended the University of Virginia only sporadically—running the Twin Pines plantation was more than a full-time occupation—but Jacob knew several of the students there and liked them. Knocking their heads together hardly seemed the most effective way to persuade them to abandon the newly elected Lincoln and his would-be cabinet of baboons and tyrants.

They marched roughly parallel to the railroad tracks of the Orange and Alexandria line. Like a lazy silver stream, the rails meandered east to west through the small city of Charlottesville. No train whistle or locomotive's roar broke the eerie silence of the night. But for the soft tapping of the evening rain, which threatened to turn to sleet any moment, the young men heard nothing but the hissing of the torch flames they held above their heads, the rhythmic scuffing of their boots against the hard mud and dirt of the street—and within, the rapid beating of their own hearts. The oaks and elms lining the quiet, narrow street seemed to scoff at them; Jacob felt their brooding, disapproving presence like a pang in his heart.

"My grandfather did not whip the British so we could fight one another," Jacob had argued when the Chesterfield twins had first asked him to join the march a week before.

"But they wouldn't stand for treason!" Noah Chesterfield had argued, and Jacob could not deny the truth in his words.

As Jacob and his brother had learned from their father at an early age in the smoky, dim light of the library at Twin Pines, the Parsons were patriots first and plantation owners second. Parsons had fought for religious and personal freedom since stepping off the ship from England in the 1700s. The gold-leafed family Bible recorded the names of Parson men who fought in 1776, and again in 1812, finally convincing Great Britain to relinquish control of her vast and cantankerous colonies. But for the riding accident that had crippled him, paralyzing him from the waist down, Jacob's father would surely have fought alongside Zachary Taylor—another Virginian— and Sam Cabell in the Mexican War of 1846–48.

Yet the passion of the zealots who surrounded Jacob troubled him, and he was moved to ask his fellow marchers a question that concerned him.

"Isn't it strange that we're willing to fight the North to be able to do and say as we please, but we won't let our own neighbors here at the university do the same?"

That question stopped the One Hundred for no longer than a moment, when several voices brought up treason and glory and Dixie. Then they were off, with or without Jacob Parson, who thought too much about things as it was.

A sudden gust of wind from the north sent blinding spikes of sleet into their confident young faces. It struck Jacob that most of the Commonwealth's greatest families were represented in this march for freedom and independence. Who could the Unionists boast of having in their ranks? A Cabell? Certainly not! A Lee, or one of the Randolph boys? Not a chance! The Unionists found their solace in the Northern sons of manufacturers, young men born and bred in Pennsylvania and Delaware and Maryland, who knew not which way to turn or whom to fight.

They came to Virginia to learn a little, to brag about their home states, and to perhaps find a Southern belle tame enough to marry and carry home to Mama and Daddy up in Pittsburgh or Dover. Jacob grew angrier each time he thought about these fine, spoiled young men who washed their hands of their fathers and turned their backs on their own homes to undertake a Southern educational experience, only to balk at it the moment controversy arose. Let them go home, back north where they belong, he thought, fuming.

By the time the marchers reached the University Hospital, a two-story white-framed building with candles flickering yellow-orange in every window, their ardor had cooled with the worsening weather. Half of the young men would have gone back home to warm fires and a hot toddy but for the shame of it. Jacob, on the contrary, had worked his way to the head of the column of four, angrier than ever at Lincolnites seeking shelter under the magnolias and oaks of Mr. Jefferson's university.

Rounding the turn in the rutted dirt lane, the One Hundred approached the twin red-brick pillars flanking the arch Thomas Jefferson had designed to welcome students to the grounds of the University of Virginia. Picking up the pace, Jacob Parson and Hart Earley, whose broad, sturdy build gave him a stature of leadership second only to Jacob's, led them up the serpentine path toward the Great Lawn and the Rotunda Building, where the rallying Unionist students were likely to have gathered. The path was muddy and treacherous, and more than one marcher slipped and fell. The usually high-spirited group proceeded with grim determination.

Once over the split fence that was built to keep out the livestock, they ducked under the covered walkway that ran down both sides of the rectangle of classrooms, residences, and open grassy land that defined the Lawn, then paused to reform. Students joined the marchers in twos and threes, cheering them on.

"Where are they?" Hart Earley asked. Jacob, too, looked from side to side, puzzled. Not a man was in sight.

"They hid from us," a high voice shouted from the middle of the pack. The crowd of young men now huddled close together for warmth and from bewilderment. "Well, I'm wet and I'm cold," Jacob heard William Wilson's boy call. "Let's hit somebody!"

Jacob raised a hand for silence, and the One Hundred and their university boosters hushed. At twenty-six, Jacob was recognized by all of them as an older and wiser man, if a bit too cautious and contemplative. Unlike most of the rest of them, Jacob no longer stood in the shadow of his father but actually managed the affairs of the family and oversaw the Parson tobacco empire himself. He had done so since his father's injury, ten years before. When Jacob spoke, it was in a commanding tone, with a low, booming voice that carried to the farthest reaches of the crowd.

"I say we send two scouts to seek out the traitors and report back to us!"

There were general shouts of agreement. Hart Earley and Isaac Morely, whose father owned the *Richmond Enquirer*, volunteered, dashing down the muddy lane and into the darkness beyond the lawn.

"Where's that brother of yours, Jacob?" Jimmy Kilpatrick called out. Kilpatrick was a broad-shouldered, narrow-minded troublemaker with no skills other than using his fists and shooting off his mouth.

Jacob twirled his moustache between his fingers in annoyance. Jimmy Kilpatrick had been promoting the idea of war with the North for more than a year. It was as if he had never heard of Dred Scott, the runaway slave ordered returned to his master from a so-called free state. Kilpatrick and his hotheaded friends ignored or belittled the compromises cooked up by President Buchanan and the Congress to guarantee slave states the right to do as they pleased within their own borders. To Jacob, this was all a reasonable Southerner could ask for. But they wanted more. Jimmy welcomed a war. He wanted to return to Albemarle County a hero and a soldier. "Maybe Ethan's leading Lincoln's forces up ahead!"

"Lincoln ain't president yet!" somebody shouted. It was true; Lincoln wouldn't take office until March.

"Nobody I know voted for him!" Kilpatrick called out, to the cheers and hoots of the others. That, too, was true. Lincoln received not one vote south of the Mason-Dixon Line; his name wasn't even on the ballot in most Southern states.

Jacob chose not to recognize Kilpatrick's jibe at Ethan, silently letting it pass. But the truth in the inquiry stuck to him like a burr. For all he knew, his brother was with the Unionist supporters at that very moment. Ethan hadn't been at home when Jacob left Twin Pines, and he had shaken his head in refusal when Jacob had asked him earlier in the day to join their march. Jacob frowned. His foolish, misguided little brother probably deserved a good whipping. While Jacob was considering what action he might be forced to take should this band of marchers get hold of his younger brother, a voice rang out in the darkness. "We found 'em!"

The shout caused chaos to overtake the waiting men. Breaking from their columns, they ran in the direction of the voice. Whooping and hollering, they raised their torches like clubs, and tripped and bumped into each other in their exuberant rush toward the target of their vigil: the jittery torch lights that appeared in the distance. Jacob rushed to get in front of them, to try to impose some discipline, but the others would have none of it; they pressed ahead, ignoring his cries. The smartly tailored young men had become a mob. Pushing and tugging, they advanced like a gigantic multilegged centipede stalking a helpless prey.

About halfway down the lawn, where a passageway opened onto a path to the library and the athletic fields, the One Hundred paused. Ahead of them, the Yankee sympathizers stood, just twenty strong, in a small circle on the steps in front of the library.

Jacob raced ahead to try to reinstate order and to look for Ethan. But a dozen husky patriots led by Jimmy Kilpatrick surged ahead of him. In a moment, torches were tossed aside, and a mêlée commenced. Fists and feet struck out blindly. Jacob stood at the perimeter of the mess, watching the fight. He yelled out in disgust to Kilpatrick as the hotheaded fool struck Hart Earley by mistake, but his cries went unnoticed.

A fist slammed into the back of Jacob's head, knocking him harshly to one side. In one swift motion, he turned and knocked his assailant down with the back of his clenched fist. Then as another stranger approached him, he lost all sense of reason and restraint, jumping into the fracas with both fists flying.

Just a minute or two after the ruckus had begun, whoops of victory went up to the somber skies. "Go tell that ape in Illinois what we done to y'all!" Jimmy Kilpatrick shouted, shaking his fist at the retreating band. Following Jacob's lead, the victors began to retrieve their soggy torches, useless now. Their voices exhilarated by the confrontation, they spoke of the yellow-bellies they had sent flying home to mama.

"Yankees is gutless!" Isaac Morely shouted to hurrahs of agreement. "It is a knowed fact!" The sleet had intensified, pricking their skin like briars, and it soon became apparent that there was nothing to do now but proceed home. The skirmish left them flushed and charged with the thrill of their victory over the small group of Lincoln sympathizers, but with the conflict over, the bone-chilling sleet began to penetrate their muddy, wet clothing. They began to walk back to their horses and buggies at the far end of town, shivering as they talked and laughed in small groups.

Jacob was stooping to pick up a torch someone had left behind when he saw the familiar silhouette in the shadow of a tall oak; the broad back, the tapering waist, the tilted head. It was Ethan, all right. Jacob, well aware of what had brought him to the university, suppressed the urge to call out to his brother. Ethan was deciding whether or not to join the Unionist cause. This was one more secret that Jacob must keep from his parents, one more unacknowledged favor owed him by his younger brother. Ethan had had the best of educations, but sometimes it seemed to Jacob that he knew very little.

The progress he himself had made was considerable. Jacob was pleased that he had succeeded in the eyes of the world. He had run Twin Pines at a profit and wielded his family's political positions with thought and foresight, helping to select senators and congressmen who voted traditional Southern positions. Unlike Ethan, who had yet to do anything more than read and discourse, Jacob was a doer, a man of the world.

Indeed, it pleased Jacob that his efforts received the attention due an eldest son, for his father took little interest in Ethan's affairs. Yet, though he ran Twin Pines with skill and insight, his father still treated Jacob as though he were sixteen, reserving his most critical attentions for his eldest's performance.

Yes, their father was far more exacting of Jacob, impressing upon him his duty to preserve and defend Twin Pines from financial and foreign foes. Jacob feared failing him perhaps even more than he feared the repercussions of the splitting of the flag or the breaking of the Lord's Commandments. Unlike his rebellious younger brother, he never opposed or corrected the old man, even when circumstances overwhelmed him. He did not complain, but silently set about accomplishing everything that was demanded of him.

It was often too much for him. But he rarely allowed himself to reflect on the fact that his father had ended his childhood in that one uncharacteristically careless moment. He had been a boy of just sixteen when a riding accident confined Charles to bed with a broken back, forcing Jacob to dress and act the part of a man.

Jacob would never have a university education or the opportunity to see the North and the world beyond Virginia's borders. He would never know the carefree years and wide-eyed, freewheeling discussion until all hours of the morning that to him epitomized his younger brother's educational experience at Harvard. With war looming so near, he might as well hope to visit the moon!

Even his mother had said as much. But she, too, had grown dependent upon Jacob's ties to Twin Pines.

Jacob had often wondered what trick of the mind allowed his mother to separate their roles so clearly in her mind. Ethan was the intellectual, much like the rabble rouser their mother's brother had been before his death of a fever in 1850.

No, Jacob reflected, she would never love him as she did the son who so reminded her of her lost family. While she indulged Ethan's whims, she expected Christian perfection from Jacob himself. He was too obviously a Parson, too glaringly his father's son. Already Jacob showed the slight paunch that would develop into the stout roundness his father displayed. Unlike Ethan, he wore a moustache and sideburns befitting a Southern gentleman.

It struck Jacob as odd that at that very moment, standing there in the freezing rain, representing opposite sides of a conflict, he and Ethan were most alike: stubborn, proud, and a little jealous of each other.

The spirited party broke up when they reached their horses and buggies. Like a group of boys caught tipping over outhouses for a lark on All Hallow's Eve, a few mumbled, "We showed 'em, huh!" and "Good goin'!" But if a Yankee army were to march into their fields and homes for real, Jacob wondered, would they prove just as ill-prepared and disorganized?

As the One Hundred headed for home, the sleet hissed and bit. Their horses shook their heads and snorted in rebellion as they were coaxed into motion. They drove away like thieves, anxious and silent.

Jacob's reverie was broken by the sudden appearance of a shadow directly in the path of his buggy. Through the mist and vertical sleet dropping like nails, he could see only ten feet ahead.

"It's your brother," the shadow called.

Jacob discerned the husky shape of Ethan, who sidestepped the slowing buggy and jumped aboard, springing like a cat. After a short silence that threatened to explode, Ethan spoke.

"You really showed that nest of spies who's who, didn't you! I bet they'll run home and join the Virginia militia tomorrow! Am I right, brother? Wasn't that the plan?"

Jacob's hands held the reins in a deathgrip. It took all his considerable composure to refrain from knocking his arrogant brother onto his pants.

"If you weren't my only living brother," he whispered through clenched teeth, his eyes fixed stonily on the mist-shrouded road ahead of the buggy, "I'd knock you straight to hell, Ethan Parson!"

Ethan threw back his head and laughed, howling like a hound. "You and what man's army, big brother?" he managed to say between hoots. "You've bent over the ledger books too long on your wide bottom to lick me in a fair fight!"

The taunt was just what Jacob had expected. It reinforced his idea of his brother: Ethan was a mischievous lad masquerading as an adult. And as a boy, what he thought about slavery and secession didn't matter one bit.

"You're a hotheaded child, Ethan," said Jacob, still looking straight into the opaque sheet of sleet and rain. "If you ever grow up, I'd be pleased to whip the tar out of you."

"I'm shivering in my boots, brother," Ethan replied. Leaning back in the seat, he covered the broad, chiseled features of his face with his hat. "Wake me when we get home, huh?"

Jacob pulled the carriage to a halt before the entrance gate to the Parson farm, ten miles east of Charlottesville on the road to Richmond. Ahead of them, atop a knoll a half-mile away, stood the large, two-story white-framed mansion that was their home. A pillared porch swept three sides of the house, and the other buildings dotted the surrounding land, which rolled and dipped before the mansion. In the mist, Twin Pines looked like an enormous doll's house, a two-story wedding cake dripping in the rain. Jacob nudged Ethan to hop out and open the gate, but Ethan merely slumped over farther, asleep.

"Some rabble rouser you make," Jacob muttered under his breath. Jumping down from the carriage, he went to open the gate. As he did so, Ethan jumped to life and grabbed the reins. Letting forth a wild "yeeha!" he whipped the tired bay, who responded by jolting past Jacob. Like the village idiot fooled yet again, Jacob stood holding the smooth wood of the gate as his brother raced down the winding half-mile-long road to the house. Jacob would have to walk now.

The cold rain ran down his neck and back in rivulets as he bent to latch the gate. How could he get even with Ethan for this?

By the time he reached the house, the manservant Alex was already awake and waiting outside the front door. One of the tallest men, black or white, that Jacob had ever seen, Alex had been the Parsons' house servant since before Jacob was born. Their return had obviously interrupted Alex's repose, for he wore not the black suit and white shirt that was his everyday attire in the big house, but the cotton trousers and work shirt which Jacob knew he preferred at night and during days of rest.

"Your brother ain't none too tired tonight," Alex said, watching Jacob's expression.

"My brother has hell to pay," Jacob mumbled, watching the manservant rumble and scratch his wiry salt-and-pepper hair as he led the bay to the stables. He felt for Alex, who liked nothing less than to be awakened from a sound sleep, "less'n Mistuh Lincoln hisself marchin' up the drive."

Deep down, he knew he would never pay Ethan back. His little brother was one of those life-blessed people who broke the rules and got away with it, more often than not. For this, Jacob hated him as much as he admired him.

Leaving his muddy boots just inside the door, Jacob tiptoed up to his bedroom, passing the hushed quiet of his parents' rooms and his sister's private domain. As he opened the door to his own room, a hiss behind him in the hall caught his attention.

There stood Ethan, stripped to the waist, toweling off the sleet and rain.

"What kept you, brother?" His blue eyes were sparkling mischievously, and the grin on his face was enough to make Jacob want to reach for his musket. Scowling, Jacob stepped wordlessly into his room. Yet so flustered was he that he closed the door on his toe, and nearly howled in pain. Wet, weary, and angry, he hopped into bed. Compared to this brother of mine, he thought, how much worse can an army of Yankees be?

CHAPTER 2

IN THE EARLY-morning light, Charles Parson fumed, tugging in frustration at the quilt and linen sheets covering his carved mahogany four-poster bed. Above the white lace of his bed shirt, his protruding neck was mottled and red, his round face bloated.

Charles was angry. He had two strapping sons, both intelligent and virile, yet neither one showed much inclination toward matrimony or the Virginia State Senate, the only two earthly institutions the old man put any faith in.

"Am I to die and leave Jacob unmarried, and young Ethan half out of his mind with Unionist fever?"

When he ranted, which was often, his color rose, and at a distance Charles appeared to be healthy enough for a man who had not taken a step in ten years. But at arm's length or closer, the burden and pain of the last decade were evident in the deep lines etched into his once-handsome face. The skin that had stretched taut across Charles's wide, arrogant face now sagged. And even though he exercised his arms daily, and followed a regime of moderation during meals, he was heavy and flaccid, and unable to do anything to remedy the situation.

The vanity he'd grown up with had gradually left him, replaced by the bitterness of age and infirmity. Again and again he dreamed of the accident and imagined a dozen different outcomes. In his bleakest moments, Charles wished to be dead. "God must have a wicked sense of humor," he once told Jacob, "to throw me off a horse I rode only that day, for ten minutes."

His dark, unruly hair had thinned and turned white. His hands shook, and the vision of his pale gray eyes was less than perfect. To a man as proud as Charles Parson, each flaw gnawed at him like a cancer, and together, they all but devoured him, eating at his faith and trust in a better future for generations of Parsons to come.

He often snapped at his wife and servants or took Jacob to task for some small infraction or indelicacy. And all the while, Charles was tortured by the conviction that he could accomplish almost anything better than they. Jacob's shortcomings particularly pained him. From Ethan, who had chosen an education in the Northern tradition, a second son with little stake in the future of Twin Pines, he expected far less.

The full burgundy skirt of Anna Parson's wool gabardine gown rustled as she turned to regard her husband. Anna knew better than to reply immediately to a question so weighted. Moving gracefully across the room, she merely smiled and squeezed his fleshy hand. At forty-six, Anna Parson was still a handsome woman, though the years of bearing and raising three children had caused her once-petite figure to fill out considerably. The chestnut waves of her hair were pulled back from Anna's face and coiled over her ears in thick tresses; the pale skin of her face and hands was soft with a rosy translucence that reflected the morning light of winter. Her blue eyes shone with a look of forbearance. "The boys will choose their paths wisely, Charles. You have taught them, remember?"

"Bah! Jacob's lost in the profits, and Ethan's lost in

the clouds. I've raised a banker and a prophet. What is to happen to Twin Pines?"

Anna ventured a smile. She loved the grand old house just as if it were a living, breathing soul. She had come to Twin Pines from Maryland as Charles's bride nearly thirty years earlier, at seventeen. It had nurtured her in her finest years, when she'd given birth to Jacob, Ethan, and Martha, raised them, nourished their bodies and spirits, and saw her husband's tobacco plantation prosper. And Twin Pines had sheltered her and Charles during this last cruel decade of immobility and pending doom. Were the house to be destroyed, she would die with it, Anna was certain. She'd even said as much to her daughter Martha.

"Not I," Martha had immediately exclaimed. "I would live happily anywhere on the continent of Europe! I could marry a prince in Paris and never look back!"

The house had an airy quality to it, largely provided by the open passageway running through the center from the broad front doors of heavy oak, past the wide staircase, sunny parlor and dining room, through the kitchen, and onto the back porch, to stand over the cellar quarters where Alex and Clara lived away from the common field bondsmen. Many a day when her children were young, Anna had watched Jacob chase his faster younger brother around and around the house and onto the porches which ringed it like a moat. As the boys squealed and wrestled, Anna had gloated, her heart full. These are my sons, she told herself. This is my house, my life.

She had been inside grander homes, such as the Stuarts', but none held the warmth of the wood as did Twin Pines. Her husband, who cherished the house as she did, would defend its honor to his death.

She had raised both boys virtually on her own, for they seldom saw their father until the riding accident had left him paralyzed ten years earlier. And she loved them deeply. Jacob, the good son, was just twenty-six and already master of the farm and grounds. But it was Ethan who was Anna's true pride. Named for her brother, a professor of religion at Harvard before his death, Ethan, at twenty-one, promised greatness of a different sort than her husband and Jacob—if he didn't get hanged before Christmas. She saw it in the spark of his blue eyes, those of her family, and in his tall bearing.

Upon his return from Boston six months earlier, the qualities that separated him from the other Parson men had become even more pronounced. The university had changed Ethan; his sympathies had developed under the influence of his companions there. Now he spoke of the institution of slavery as if it were an evil that overwhelmed any good that Jacob and the other powerful landowners of the South might accomplish. It was, in his words, the "sewage that taints the clear stream." Such talk sent Charles and his secessionist friends reaching for their muskets. Charles himself kept one loaded at his bedside, within reach. If that young baboon of a president Lincoln sent Federal troops into Virginia to prevent its secession, Charles had cried, the Parsons would fight to the death! And their slaves would stand with them!

Anna was pouring her husband a second cup of English tea when the resonant bang of the door slamming downstairs startled her, causing her to jump and spill the tea on Charles's nightshirt.

"Good God, woman, be careful!"

After wiping off the tea, she excused herself, leaving her husband to write letters to his acquaintances in Richmond and Montgomery, and hurried down the wide oak staircase to see what the commotion was all about.

As she might have guessed, Brett Tyler was the cause. Handsome, powerfully built, and with a wily countenance, the brash Tyler had pushed past Alex, himself big and powerful as an oak. The two men, one white and one black, stood glaring at each other in the entry hall.

"Don't stand there like two boys fighting over a toy," Anna snapped at them. "What is it?"

"Yessum," Alex replied. "Mistuh Tyler here got the mail from town, and Miss Martha's books fo' Christmas, and he don't be wantin' to surrender dem to me like I axe."

The anger in the tall black man's voice was apparent. He didn't like being baited in what he considered to be his house, where only the Parsons themselves held greater influence.

Tyler turned an irreverent smile to Anna. His dark eyes lacked fitting respect as they rested on her ivory features, framed by the high collar of her burgundy gown. "Jacob told me to deliver the mail to him," he said defiantly.

"I always takes in de mail," Alex countered. Again, the two men squared off.

"I'll have no violence in my house," Anna said sternly. "Give *me* the mail."

"The books is heavy," Tyler said, holding out the two bulging leather saddlebags an arm's length from her. "Weigh as much as you, I reckon."

The wicked young man's eyes were sparkling with amusement. He was obviously enjoying the scene. But she would have none of his impertinence. "Then let them drop right there," Anna ordered.

"I don't think you want me to—"

"Do as I say, Brett Tyler!"

With a shrug, Tyler let the bags fall to the hard wood floor. The sound of glass breaking brought a wide smile to his fleshy lips. Without a word of apology, he turned and left, leaving behind muddy boot prints where he had stepped.

"Dat boy de Devil in po' white skin," Alex hissed. He was still scowling as he bent over to pick up the bags and carry them into the first-floor parlor. "Won't Miss Martha be pleased to read dem new books?" Alex commented. He was happy to be in charge once again, glad to be freed of the ordeal of dealing with the sneaky white rascal. "Why she love dem books so?"

Anna Parson didn't reply. She wasn't listening. Something about the Tyler boy's manner had unnerved her. That impudent, ignorant young man acted as if he understood everything about the Parsons, as if he saw the world more clearly than either of her sons.

"Hide the books," she ordered. Alex nodded, scooping up the dozen hardbound books in his powerful arms. As he turned to leave the parlor, Martha, the Parsons' only daughter, suddenly appeared in the doorway. Her arms folded across her bosom, she looked as if she had caught the manservant and her mother doing something terrible.

"Are you two sneaking behind my back?" Martha had quite a fairy-tale princess look about her, even sleepy-eyed and wrapped in a robe and a floor-length nightgown. With her long, silken black hair, blue eyes, and a simple smile that was already melting the hearts of Albemarle County's young men, she had a quick wit and a will to match her physical comeliness, if it was often tempered by the wanderings of her imagination.

Alex assumed a blank expression as Anna told her daughter to mind her business. "Alex, you do as I say. Find a resting place for those romances now, please! And, Martha, I will not allow you to spoil your father's Christmas surprise for you. Now shoo, both of you!"

As ordered, Alex and Martha departed, and Anna was left to resume planning for the Christmas fête at Twin Pines. It would pale next to the Stuarts'—the grand Epiphany Ball early in January—but all the same, Anna wanted the affair to be festive and breathtaking, if mostly for her husband's sake. He had so little to enjoy now, passing his days in a cantankerous languor, writing sharply worded letters to politicians and the *Richmond Enquirer*. Or he would call out impossible orders to Jacob, who broke his back—and those of all the estate's bondsmen—to carry them out.

Anna remembered her husband when he was whole and well. She'd often told her children that when she'd met their father at a ball when she was sixteen, he'd looked exactly like a bust of Julius Caesar. In her mind, she still held and treasured visions of Charles as Adonis, swift and strong as a stallion, and just as willful. Yet the sweet, powerful memories were clouded now.

Her brow creased as the unbidden thought came to

her: she had married a Greek statue come to life. And now, ironically, Charles had become, like a statue, immobile and cold. As much as Anna loved him and tended devotedly to his needs, serving even his most unreasonable wishes, she yearned for the full and tender bond, the passion of their earlier years together.

Some fourteen years younger than her invalid husband, Anna Parson found that she could not sleep some nights, shameful of the blood pounding through her veins, so heavy with desire. But as a dutiful wife and companion, she could do no more than settle for the kiss on the cheek Charles gave her each night and morning, and pray that exhaustion from her daily endeavors would calm the fires within her heart.

Anna rang for her modiste, Clara. Clara, Alex's wife, tended to Anna's personal needs, and also supervised the other servants in the cooking and cleaning. The handsome colored woman came in as she always did, without making a sound or uttering a word. She wiped her hands on the apron covering her dress and looked at Anna expectantly.

"Clara, fetch the guest list and gift list for the Christmas party," Anna said. "They're in the library, I believe." Clara nodded and disappeared, returning a moment later with a small stack of papers.

"Thank you. I believe I heard the children rising. Is breakfast prepared?"

Jacob awoke grumpy and sore. In ten short hours, rheumatism seemed to have overtaken him; his right arm ached from holding his torch aloft for so long the night before, and every joint throbbed and creaked. Picking up a silver-handled mirror he kept on his bedside table, Jacob took a good look at the face reflected there. He looked older than his twenty-six years today. His gray eyes were puffy and bloodshot. There were lines creasing his forehead and running from the tips of his moustache around his mouth. His full lips were raw and red from the cold and wind that had accompanied last night's march. Even his thick brown hair had lost some of its fullness, and was perhaps receding a bit above his temples.

A knock sounded at the door, and with a sigh Jacob rested the mirror back on the bedside table and looked expectantly at the oak panels. "Yes?"

Alex entered, his bristly gray brows furrowed, his face bearing a grim expression. "Yo' daddy want to see you now," he said.

"About what?"

Jacob didn't truly expect Alex to answer—offering an opinion could be considered impudent—but he couldn't refrain from voicing his question.

Alex shrugged. "Maybe about last night," he ventured.

Jacob stood up straight and groaned, staring probingly up into Alex's bright dark eyes. "How much does he know?"

Again the colored man shrugged, then turned to leave.

Jacob brooded. Did Father know of Ethan's support of the Unionists? And if so, what did he want Jacob to do?

Five minutes later Jacob took in his breath sharply and rapped three times on his father's door.

"Come in, son!"

Each time Jacob entered the sick room, he had to fight to keep from wretching. The very air was debilitating. The mingled odors of ammonia and bourbon and flatulence shrouded the spacious rectangular room in a stuffy fog of decay and death. It was as if the heavy fetid air were crushing Jacob's father like a stone on his chest. Even the amber glow of the oil lamps at his bedside seemed somber and unpromising.

Jacob adored his father. Even now, crippled and withered and weak, he was a great man, a monumental figure in the Parson family history. To his eldest son, Charles Parson was a worthy successor to Washington and Jefferson and the other leaders of Virginia and the nation. In two decades, Charles had transformed their prosperous tobacco plantation into a gathering place for the most influential men of the state, and a home where tradition reigned, family honor was sacred, and family duty supreme.

Even now, crippled and imprisoned in his room, his father was a formidable intellectual foe. And as Jacob knew, Charles continued to receive letters and documents from the important men of the South. Jacob, too, corresponded regularly with the plantation owners of Virginia and the Carolinas, as well as with Governor Letcher and others of political prominence. He, too, had staunchly backed the campaign of Jeff Davis, advocated caution against the compromises of Buchanan and the mediocre stance taken by Lincoln's Republican party, just two years old. Yet in the political arena, he clearly stood in the shadow of the powerful Charles Parson. He had inherited a lesser perspicacity than this father, who never passed up an opportunity to expose the lack of depth of his vision.

Jacob found it downright spooky that their father knew every last detail of what went on both at Twin Pines and beyond the confines of their estate. Growing up, they had felt like hares scurrying through the grass while their father was an eagle two miles in the sky, his eye on their every movement.

Jacob often debated the issue of slavery with his father. Much to his consternation, Charles would playfully defend the abolitionists, a group he despised in real life, tearing to pieces every argument Jacob had spent hours preparing and practicing. There was simply no outwitting or beating the old man at anything, from chess to arm wrestling.

His father pointed to the crumpled handbill on his bedside table. "Read it to me," he commanded.

"Daddy, you can read it yourself," Jacob dared to say.

"Read it," his father repeated, his gray eyes smoldering. His voice and his stare were as imperious as ever, Jacob noted.

Jacob coughed to clear his throat, then began to read the printed notice:

" 'Virginia belongs to the Union!', it says in big letters." Jacob paused, nervously eyeing his father. Surely he wouldn't want him to read such trash any further. But Charles's mottled face remained an impassive mask.

"Just read it, boy, and never mind the editorializin'." His father reached for the glass of water on his bedside table, resting it on the swell of quilts and linen covering his belly once he'd taken a sip.

Jacob continued reading, feeling his collar grow tighter with each word. " 'As a legendary voice for common sense and justice in these United States, Virginia cannot heed those irresponsible voices of treason and disharmony. Our Constitution guarantees all citizens certain rights, but not among them is the questionable right to dissolve this precious Union. Come to the University Library tonight at nine o'clock to show your support for the Union, which has protected us for fourscore and four years! All peace-loving citizens of the Commonwealth are welcome!' "

"How many showed up?" Charles asked his son.

"Daddy, how should I know—?"

"How many?" His father's voice was booming now, and he nearly upset his glass of water. "Ten? Twenty? More?"

After a pause, Jacob gave in to the persistent stare. "About twenty."

"Tell me the truth, son. Was Ethan among them?"

Jacob was relieved that his father had worded the question as he had, for he wouldn't have to lie. "No, Daddy, he was not among them."

"Are you telling me the truth, son?"

"I am."

"Praise God!" Charles Parson said with a weary sigh, setting his glass once again on the small table beside his bed. Jacob ignored the prodding, jealous fear that his father might love Ethan as deeply as himself. Ethan, who had chosen to attend Harvard, who had chosen not to help run Twin Pines. His father and mother worried so about Ethan. But *what are my choices?* Jacob lamented to himself. *I have none!*

His younger brother had nothing to show for his

twenty-one years but a diploma and a shelf of books. But Ethan had traveled and lived away from the plantation. He had stood on his own two feet and lived alone, something Jacob didn't expect to have occasion to do until his father died. And even afterward, he felt sure the ghost of Charles Parson would haunt him here at Twin Pines. His father would never grant him another peaceful night of sleep. Somehow, he would always be there to remind Jacob of his stupidity.

Charles cleared his throat and straightened the sleeve of his nightshirt.

"Now, about you and that Stuart girl."

"Caitlin Stuart, Daddy." Just her name made Jacob prick up his ears. He could well imagine the dark flashing eyes and brows, the pale skin and honeyed hair. Her contrasting beauty was breathtaking.

Why then didn't his heart beat faster, and the blood in his veins boil, as they did in those French novels Martha read like Scripture? For some reason he felt little inclined to marry at this time. Running the plantation took all his strength and ingenuity. He feared marrying anyone until he could imagine a woman seated before the hearth, holding a glass of claret for him, and perhaps children laughing upstairs. But now, with war looming, that scene was out of the question.

Besides, something about her threw him. She always looked like she held a great secret she was bursting to tell but never would. She was too complicated for Jacob's taste. But how could he ever explain any of this to his father? Charles would just call it all hogwash and tell Jacob to get on with it.

The old man's anger flared. "I know her name! I want your engagement announced at the Epiphany Ball. Have you proposed to her yet?"

"Not in so many words, Daddy." Jacob felt a good deal of affection for Caitlin. Her father was influential in Albemarle County and partial to Jacob. Marriage with his daughter would add to Jacob's position of prominence. For as everyone in the county knew, George Stuart had profited handsomely from his marriage to Charlotte Hurt, inheriting over one hundred acres of prime tobacco-growing land. Jacob could not repress a certain delight in the thought of sharing that wealth, joining it to the Parsons' only slightly less considerable holdings. Naturally Jacob would comply with his father's wishes. Time would surely bring him the sense of comfort and ease he currently lacked in her presence.

"Find the words! I do not wish to feel compelled to write them on your cuffs. Propose to her, Jacob, and announce it at the ball. Agreed?"

"Yes, Daddy."

"Now get some breakfast. And tell Clara to carry a tray of tea and honeycakes up here now. Go. Go!"

Jacob descended the pine staircase to the main foyer. Heading through the open walkway to the kitchen, he relayed his father's order for breakfast, then proceeded to the dining room.

The dove-gray room was warm from the fire blazing in the six-foot brick fireplace. With a quick look at the portrait of his grandfather over the mantle, Jacob joined his mother and sister.

The carved oak table was covered with white linen and crowded with bowls of biscuits, sausage links, bacon, eggs, home-fried potatoes, grits, and gravy. As Jacob served himself, Martha turned her blue eyes to him.

"Where's Ethan? Have you two been fighting again?"

Jacob set down his knife and fork, gazing at her with mock sternness. "Am I my brother's keeper?"

"Now that you mention it, yes," their mother answered. "Join hands for grace," Anna ordered.

Just in time for the final words of the prayer beseeching the almighty God for peace on earth and life everlasting in Heaven, Ethan appeared, rubbing his eyes. Above the crisp collar of his shirt and coat, his dark hair stood in unruly, rumpled shocks. Martha sarcastically applauded, drawing her mother's attention.

"Pardon me, Mama," Ethan said softly, taking his seat. He reached wordlessly for the biscuits and gravy.

"Are you ill or just ill-mannered?" his mother inquired. But her smile was indulgent. Rarely did she chastise Ethan for his late appearance at meals.

"A letter's come for your from your Yankee friend!" Martha blurted out.

Jacob stopped eating, genuinely concerned. "From who?" he inquired.

"Whom," Ethan corrected him. "I trust you mean that Jeffrey Keyes has written to me?"

Martha nodded coyly, looking to her mother.

"Where is the letter? Or have you read it already?"

"I have not! Mother has it!" Martha cried, giggling.

Anna took advantage of the momentary silence to remind her battling children that no mail was to be opened before breakfast was completed.

"I'm done!" Ethan cried, jumping to his feet. "Where's my letter from Jeffrey?"

"It's in the library, on your father's desk," Anna said.

"Thank you, and excuse me." With a quick bow, Ethan ran from the room.

"If I behaved like that, I'd be banished to my room for the month of January!" Martha suggested.

"Little chance of that," Jacob teased, reaching for a biscuit. "You never get any mail. Do any of your friends know how to form their letters yet?"

"Jacob, shame!" Despite her stern tone, Anna was half-pleased by her children's bickering. She enjoyed spirited banter between them, as long as no one broke into tears. "Now hush and eat. Jacob, what did your father have to say?"

"Are there no secrets in this house?" Jacob wondered aloud. He was in no mood to discuss either the rally or his intentions toward Caitlin. "He said very little. He asked about the march at the university last night."

"Was there any loss of life?" Martha asked. It was an ill-kept Parson family secret that she admired the gawky new president from Kentucky and agreed with him that the nation must remain united at all costs. Yet at Twin Pines, she saw little wrong with the manner in which they treated their slaves. Families were never separated. Indeed, to Martha, Alex seemed a good deal freer than she herself was. Of course, she granted, she could not be sold or horsewhipped without a good fight.

Jacob ignored Martha's question. Standing, he faced his mother and excused himself. "Mother, I have letters to write. I'm sponsoring a meeting here next Wednesday, to discuss Virginia's plans for secession, and, in particular, how they will affect us and the surrounding counties."

"With your father's blessing?" Anna asked.

He frowned. "Of course."

Anna bowed her head, indicating her assent. Such talk inevitably led to thoughts of war and sadness and deprivation. While she approved of her son's involvement in political affairs—as she had supported her husband's—Anna feared the outcome of such planning to be for the worst.

"Will your brother be participating in the discussion?" she asked, surprising Jacob.

"He's expressed little interest, Mother. I should doubt it."

Martha giggled and mischievously asserted, "Perhaps Ethan could portray President Lincoln in a debate; all he needs is a stovepipe hat and an ax!"

"Martha, hush! Such nonsense!" said Anna Parson.

Grinning, Martha quieted herself. She liked nothing more than raising Jacob's ire. He had early taken on the role of her protector. But Martha wanted no such stifling protection. She had been on the verge of submitting to her first embrace at their own Christmas gala the year before when Jacob had snatched Chester Earley away, nearly thrashing her frightened beau. She had maintained an appropriate distance from Chester afterward, but the marble egg she'd held had failed to serve its intended purpose of cooling her palm.

In her heart, Martha cheered Ethan's rebellion, his friendship with Yankees. She glanced once at Jacob, whose red face swelled above the tight white collar of his shirt, and she was pleased. Spiting him was almost as good as riling Daddy, she figured.

"Mother!" Ethan shouted from the library. "We're having houseguests for New Year's. Jeffrey Keyes and his sister!"

Jacob sensed an involuntary stiffening of his spine. Just the mention of the Keyeses' name raised the hairs on the back of his neck. Jeffrey Keyes and his sister were devout abolitionists who had written a score of vitriolic tracts attacking slavery as an abomination before God. How could Ethan dare invite them into the Parson home? It was as if the Devil himself were coming to visit, and only Jacob recognized the Great Deceiver for who he really was.

He wouldn't allow it. He would have to explain to his father why he could not allow their visit. But then a darker, more satisfying thought struck Jacob. Suppose the Keyeses were to come after all? The bondsmen at Twin Pines were treated fairly and with respect. So far as Jacob knew, they were content. The Keyeses would discover for themselves that all Southerners were not alike, that *Uncle Tom's Cabin* was not the gospel they saw it to be. Perhaps seeing the plantation in operation would cause them to change their minds, soften their hard-edged views. Wouldn't that be a challenge? He could imagine his father relishing such a battle. Besides, Twin Pines could stand a little fireworks, especially if all the heat fell upon Ethan. So Jacob kept quiet.

Martha rose and excused herself, and Jacob listened absentmindedly to the rustle of her green satin as she left the room. She was no doubt about to plunge into one of her romances about some Parisian ballet dancers and a wicked viscount with a gypsy heart. Jacob looked across the table. It was time he raised a touchy issue with his mother: the war. She must be prepared.

"Mother, this is difficult for me to say." Jacob dreaded the intelligence that forced him to face facts squarely, ugly as they were. "You are of course aware of the current state of affairs. We in the South are outmanned four to one. The North has ten times the factories we have, and but for Charleston and New Orleans, all the important shipping harbors are under their sway." He swallowed, reaching for the silver coffee service. His mother remained calm, if reserved. "It comes down to this: If war lasts more than a year, we are lost. Victory over a number of years is impossible. Do you recognize the implications of what I'm saying, Mother?"

Anna Parson waited to reply until Clara had cleared the table and left the room. "Jacob, we have no choice. Like Daniel in the lion's den, our only strength is faith. Have you spoken to your father about this?"

"Yes, Mother. He already knows."

"And what does he advise?"

The look on her face startled Jacob. Did she actually expect Charles to deny the situation or to suggest some way of overcoming it? His mother would have to accept that for all his intellectual prowess, his father had not the physical strength to carry through any action on a practical level. "He advises . . . he says nothing, Mother. There is nothing to say." Unlike Anna, Charles Parson valued the power of reason and calculation above everything else—even faith. He had quizzed Jacob on the facts and accepted Jacob's thesis; that if a war was to be fought, the South must win quickly.

There was a long pause during which Jacob watched his mother uncomfortably. Her face wore an ivory mask of loss and pain, and in her pale blue eyes shone the light of fear.

Outside the dining-room windows Jacob watched the live oaks swaying in the cold wind. From the kitchen, he heard the shouts of two house servants arguing about whose turn it was to wash the dishes. They might well be doomed, and his mother knew it. So did Daddy.

CHAPTER 3

"MARTHA AND I will take care of those, Clara. Just set them on the table."

Clara set the candles, freshly wicked and dipped in cranberry-colored wax, on the long table in the ballroom before returning to the kitchen to see to the brass tubs of wassail that had been set there in preparation for the evening's festivities.

Everything was just as perfectly arranged as it was every year, yet as Anna took in the finery—the garlands and ribbons, and even the towering tree—it all seemed tarnished. Word had arrived in the Richmond papers that dimmed her happiness: South Carolina had seceded from the Union.

They had all been there when Jacob received the *Examiner*. It was too late to keep the news quiet until tomorrow, as she might have wished—indeed, if she had her way she would have hidden the news and the whole ugly happening from Twin Pines for eternity. Anna returned determinedly to the task at hand; she could not allow her own sense of foreboding to dampen the true spirit of the evening. It was a time of celebration, and celebrate they would. Taking two of the candles Clara had brought, she began placing them in brass holders and setting them on one of the windowsills.

Martha turned from the mantel, still holding the garland to be affixed there. "It's only South Carolina. They're a bunch of hotheads, right, Mama?"

But Anna merely smiled and surveyed her daughter's new dress. It had taken Clara and two of the other servants to clothe Martha in the white crinoline gown she now wore. The skirt fell in a cloud of full flounces, and the ruffle that followed the neckline off her shoulders, scooping low above her firm breasts, was trimmed with red grosgrain. Ethan had insisted the gown was so massive that it would be impossible to dance with her even if he wanted to. Martha certainly had definite opinions for one whose main preoccupation was with the drama of her own emotions and the finery of her dress.

Anna pulled the shawl Charles had given her years ago more tightly around her. She herself felt foolishly attractive. At Martha's prodding she had worn a satin gown of royal blue. The collar was appropriately high, the cut simple. Yet she could not suppress the feeling that all who saw her would be able to discern the scandalous feelings that crept over her in odd waves every now and again. It was unforgivable, shameful. That Charles had not been able to be a husband to her for a decade was all in the divine order of things, she firmly reminded herself. It was her cross to bear. With a deep sigh of resignation, she picked up two more candles.

Jacob and Ethan eyed each other warily in the mirror that stood at the far end of the upstairs hall. News of South Carolina's secession had arrived not half an hour ago, for the newspapers had been delayed, as was everything else during the Christmas season. But rather than discuss the matter as brothers should, they merely straightened the ties at their throats and adjusted their already impeccable waistcoats.

From the ballroom, the strains of a lively tune cut through the somber scene like a naughty child disrupting a funeral. Ethan could not help himself from tapping his foot to the rhythm; Jacob chose that moment to excuse himself, realizing that no one had told their father. *He*, at least, would openly recognize the seriousness of the situation.

Turning, Jacob raced down the hall. When he reached the doorway of his father's room, Charles looked up, surprised by his son's hurried entry. Noting the copy of the *Richmond Examiner* in Jacob's trembling hand, he sat up slowly in his bed. "Read me what the newspapers say," he said, indicating the chair by his bed.

Jacob sat, cleared his throat, and read. "At one-fifteen P.M. today, December the twentieth, eighteen sixty, an ordinance was unanimously enacted by the South Carolina legislature, dissolving the Union. Cannons were fired, church bells rung, the palmetto flag was raised, and there was general rejoicing in the streets of Charleston. One legislator said, 'Trying to prevent this natural action is no more sensible than riding a tornado after saddling it.'"

Jacob paused to gauge his father's reaction. He showed no outward sign of agitation, stroking his long sideburns thoughtfully. But his forehead and jowls had become slightly redder, and his eyes gleamed with fire. His father took a deep, raspy breath—a dying old man's breath for sure, Jacob thought—and held up a hand. "Every Southern state will join South Carolina. It will be only a matter of months, perhaps weeks. All now depends on what that lame-duck Buchanan and the log splitter do up in Washington. What's your best guess?"

Jacob's gaze and his thoughts drifted to the snow-dusted rolling hills, the red clay of central Virginia peeping up in lines and patches. It was such a beautiful scene. This farm and this earth are so beautiful, he reflected. How could they do anything to risk losing or spoiling it? "I don't see any way to avoid war, Father. Lincoln may be fair minded and peaceful, but he is a Republican." As they both knew, he was the first president elected from the newly created party. "And his constituents include abolitionists. From everything he's said, Lincoln believes in holding the Union together at all costs. If he loses the South . . . If he just lets her go, he loses the chief money crop of the nation, King Cotton. He loses the respect of the people who voted for him. He loses the heart of his own country. Foreign nations will be studying his every move with a critical eye."

"He's from Kentucky; he understands the South, I am convinced. He cannot allow it. Lincoln will send troops into Carolina, if need be, to prevent secession. I am sure of it."

Charles Parson paused. Perhaps he was admiring the analysis, but with Daddy, Jacob never knew what he truly thought until he spoke. "If you were to be president in two months but were a Virginian, as you are, what would you do, son?"

The old man was watching, alert and expectant.

"Daddy, you know I'm a Virginian first and last, but I believe in the Constitution and the Bill of Rights and the United States, too."

"You can't be all things to all people, like the log splitter's trying to be," his father contended.

Jacob swallowed hard. His mouth was dry. "Then I'd stand against the prevailing tide of opinion in the North—as I understand it to be—and I would allow the secession. I would recognize the states in whatever manner they chose and establish friendly relations, as we have with France or England at the moment. I would ignore the petty abolitionist politics of hatred and division. I would—"

"Bullshit, boy! You are dreaming!" his father shouted, his jowls shaking above his nightshirt. "You are the President of the United States . . . the *United States*! . . . and one lonesome state dares to pull out of your powerful Union. Now what do you do?"

Goaded by his father's taunts, Jacob burst forth, "I would stop them! I would send in the army. I'd crush them." He was trembling with suppressed anger.

"Exactly! *Now* you're talking like a president." The gleam in his father's eyes only increased Jacob's ire. The old man relished an argument. Verbal jousting was his favorite sport. But the arguments he relished the most were invariably those which set Jacob at a disadvantage. Each time he entered the fetid room he vowed not to be bested, and each time he left a session such as this one, he invariably felt the worse for the encounter.

"Now tell Alex I'm ready to shave and dress."

Jacob left the room without looking at his father, who

reached for the pewter pitcher and poured a glass of water, frowning.

Charles, feverish and trembling from the exercise, watched in silence as his son exited. Virginia would need men of leadership who showed not the slightest sign of weakness. The old man wanted Twin Pines to be managed by a confident, right-thinking man. Jacob had the head, but damned if he didn't lack the gumption, to Charles's continuing frustration. Well, he would have to keep at him if he was to be the leader he must be. Certainly Ethan could not be counted on. If only his second son weren't such a mystery. What drove the boy? He thought too much about things you couldn't see.

Alex was humming a spiritual in the kitchen when Jacob summoned him to his father's room. Surely the sadness of the Negro melody matched the occasion, he thought as he roamed through the open passages, inspecting the decorated rooms of the house. He breathed deeply. Away from the odor and raging criticism of his father's chamber he was once again calm and in control. When he stepped into the wide entrance to the ballroom, Jacob clapped his hands twice and raised his voice.

"This isn't a funeral. This is Christmas, the birth of our Lord. Let us rejoice! The comings and goings of sovereign states have little to do with Twin Pines this evening, am I right? No more talk of war. I forbid it! The joy of the season forbids it. The Yankees and Mr. Lincoln want war no more than did Mr. Buchanan. So let us give thanks today for peace and prosperity and give no more thought to the clouds forming on the horizon. May they blow by us without shedding a drop of rain.

"Now merry Christmas . . . and get back to work!"

Alex and the house servants cheered and hooted. Martha perked up, and even Ethan gave Jacob a frank stare, as if approving his words.

But one look told Jacob that their mother knew better; that war wreaks havoc, and conflict was heading their way with increasing certainty. Anna sat as still as a mannequin in a large stuffed chair, her embroidery in her lap.

Upon her face was an insolent look, a scowl. Jacob understood from her expression that he could never lie to her about the war, nor about anything that threatened Twin Pines and his father. She would have to forgive him for today's performance, which he offered to the servants and Martha. Such a rallying of forces, however misleading, was necessary from time to time. Right now, Jacob reasoned, morale was more important than truth. His mother ought to understand that.

Caitlin Stuart sat in silence beside her father as he stopped their buggy on the winding road approaching Twin Pines to appreciate the beauty of the scene. It was a dark night and the stars were shrouded in heavy clouds. The candles lighting every window of the Parson home blazed with a magical intensity. The glittering house on the hill stood like an emblazoned symbol of Virginia's traditions and glorious past.

"There is a blessing on this house," George Stuart said.

She understood only too well the meaning of his comment. She and Jacob Parson had always been expected to marry. Now that she was of age, Caitlin was certain Jacob would soon announce his intentions. Her father, she knew, hoped the matter would be settled quickly. He had not asked her opinion. Nor had she expected him to. So Caitlin didn't ask her father to explain himself now. He wouldn't anyway, unless he was of a mind to. That was what teaching the Socratic method at the University of Virginia Law School for so many years had done to him. If a question didn't strike him as interesting or something he himself might ask, he simply ignored it. It had taken Caitlin most of her youth to keep her temper in control, for nothing infuriated her more than being ignored, as if she were a common servant.

She *was* grateful to him for having sent her to an academy in Richmond, for few girls had the opportunity. Yet she also wondered if his motive had not been more to be rid of her than to educate her. She had once overheard Noah, her father's most trusted house servant, say that she looked too much like "Miss Susan fo' him to bear de sight." Her mother had died from scarlet fever when Caitlin was just six, and her father had been avoiding her ever since. Now, at eighteen, she had come to see him just as he was: an opinionated, powerful, proud man, unable to admit to making a mistake.

She caught herself trembling and forced her arms to remain still in the chill of the open buggy. Her father mustn't see her so nervous. Tonight she would put herself to the test for the first time, right under his nose. And her father—on the rare occasions she aroused his interest— was not the kind of man to withhold a question; if she appeared nervous, he would ask why. She smiled to herself and then erased it just as quickly. Can I do what's expected of me tonight? she wondered. Am I that brave? She risked not only life and limb, but her father's rage and the disapproval of all those around her.

Caitlin took her father's gloved hand in hers and said, "Come, Father. Let's get there before all the punch is gone."

He snapped the buggy whip, and the dappled mare trotted up the final stretch of the lane leading to Twin Pines. As he reined in before the picket fence surrounding the house, one of the Parsons' slaves raced from a corner of the yard to steady the mare as the Stuarts dismounted.

"Merry Christmas!" Caitlin called out gaily to the servant, who nodded and smiled in return. "Please see that our gifts are bought in."

"Come, girl!" her father said, leading her by the arm to the front door. A wreath of holly and spruce encircled most of the oak door. Stuart rapped on it firmly three times.

Dressed in a black morning coat, top hat, and white gloves, Alex nodded in greeting as he opened the door, and wished them both a merry Christmas.

"I left your gift in the buggy, Alex," whispered Caitlin, brushing his arm for a moment. "How's your family?"

"They fine, miss, thank you. People's in the ballroom."

"Fine, fine," said George Stuart, hurrying his daughter

inside. He was anxious to greet their hosts, and then to buttonhole Jacob. He had heard some ugly rumors about Ethan's Unionist sympathies. The matter had to be discussed.

Once inside the French doors to the pine-floored ballroom, all but bare of furniture, Caitlin ran straight to the ten-foot-high Christmas spruce, lit with scores of candles and decorated with brightly colored garlands and ribbons and delicate ornaments flashing gold and silver in the flickering light. Fires blazed in both fireplaces, and friends and neighbors were gathered in small circles in front of each, warming themselves and drinking wassail toasts. They all turned and waved or shouted, "Hello!" and "Merry Christmas!" to the Stuarts.

From where he stood near one of the tall windows, Jimmy Kilpatrick leaned toward the identical redheaded, freckled faces of Aaron and Noah Chesterfield and whispered, "Courting that Stuart girl is like planting cotton on the lawn of the White House in Washington, D.C. Ain't nothing going to come of it."

Noah jostled his brother's arm, nearly upsetting his wassail. No one who didn't know them well could tell them apart, and sometimes, when the spirit took them, they switched identities in the middle of a ball or dance to confuse the ladies they escorted. But with Caitlin Stuart they didn't dare try such a ruse.

Their eyes joined those of every eligible bachelor in the room, falling upon Caitlin with awe and desire. But for Martha Parson, Caitlin was the prettiest woman in Charlottesville. Her dark, flashing eyes, so unlike the pale blue of her father's, held a luminous intensity. Her figure was feminine and petite, her bosom alluringly hinted at by the low cut of her taffeta gown.

But not even Jimmy Kilpatrick, who had a mouth that ran way ahead of his brain, gave any serious thought to courting Caitlin. For it was well known that she had been promised to Jacob Parson, almost since birth. The marriage would wed two powerful and wealthy families, and would provide the couple with five hundred acres of tobacco fields and seventy slaves. But most important, the union would guarantee their families' place of prominence in the history of the state of Virginia. The marriage between Caitlin and Jacob was what both fathers wanted more than anything else in this world before they died. Both Jacob and Caitlin knew and understood this.

As one of the Parson field hands launched into a Virginia reel on his fiddle, shaking his head to and fro with the rhythm of the music, Caitlin spied Jacob Parson out of the side of her eye. Would he approach her tonight?

Ethan stood in the doorway leading from the ballroom into the dining room, watching as the dancers circled in front of him. He had glimpsed Caitlin Stuart and her father, and he wondered when his clay-footed brother would beg the pardon of Colonel Gooch and make his way to their side. In the shimmering white gown, Caitlin appeared all too unreal to him, a storybook princess come to life for a night.

But beyond her beauty, there was something more. Ethan had always seen in her glittering eyes an intelligence and a sensitivity out of place, like his own. Or had he just imagined it? They had never spoken about slavery or abolition, nor would they ever. He could not know if her intelligence signaled a sympathy for his view. Damn Jacob! Stepping uncertainly, testing his wits against the strength of the wassail he'd been drinking, he headed around the perimeter of the ballroom toward the refreshment table.

In a room crowded with attractive and interested young ladies, why was he drawn again and again to the one woman whose heart he could not hope to conquer? Was it that impossible challenge which drew him to her?

Ethan sipped the spiced wine in his glass. He had grown up with Caitlin Stuart visiting Twin Pines more often than any relative. He knew her mind and her spirit as he was sure his brother Jacob, blinded by his damnable, everlasting sense of duty, did not. Yet her heart was a mystery even to him.

Ethan watched his brother try again to slip away from

Colonel Gooch without being rude. What an ass you are, brother! he wanted to shout. You have a beautiful woman waiting for you, yet maintaining social graces prevents you from dropping old Gooch like a rotten egg and hurrying to her side. Sometimes his brother could be such a fool. If Caitlin were mine, he thought with a jump in his pulse, I'd be at her side before Alex had time to remove her wrap! You're too slow to grab what you want, brother.

The movement of the music and swirling dancers seemed to quicken with the strength of the wine. On a whim, Ethan started toward Caitlin, watching through a dizzying fog as her father turned from her to greet James Cabell. Halfway across the room he caught himself. He must rein in the foolishness flowing through his veins with the wine. What was he going to do, dance her into a carriage and spirit her away? Spinning on his heels, he wove his way into the kitchen.

The sweetbreads were still baking, but Ethan caught sight of an open bottle of sherry on the table. He filled a glass with the sherry, then raised his glass to Clara. He drank the liquid as if it were water, waiting for it to dull the throbbing in his loins.

Jacob stood beneath the glittering chandelier at the center of the large room, next to a long table laden with ham biscuits, cornbread, cookies, and cakes. He had finally slipped away from Colonel Gooch, who had lost one eye in the Mexican War of 1848 and cast the other on Martha ever since. He had once offered their father one hundred acres of prime tobacco fields and twenty slaves worth a thousand dollars each for her hand in marriage. Dickering with the old colonel for his daughter's hand was one of the few sports left to Charles since the accident, but fortunately for Martha, he had refused.

Jacob held a glass of bourbon in his hand and studied Caitlin. He had known her all his life, but only at that moment was he struck by the suddenness of her blossoming, like the first white dogwood flowers bursting open and scattering their scent in the air like a delicate perfume. Just last summer, she had seemed to him a child, giggling and sharing secrets with Martha as they teased the hounds with scraps of ham from the kitchen. Now, wearing a taffeta gown scooped low above her breasts, and long white gloves, Caitlin was clearly and undeniably a woman. He was mad to hesitate. If ever he were to marry her, now, before war and certain separation, *now* must be the time.

Yet even as he approached her and she turned her glowing round face toward him with a warm smile, a voice deep within Jacob's heart whispered, *Wait. Don't.* He struggled to hush the voice, grasping George Stuart's hand and shaking it with fervor. They spoke of the secession of South Carolina, the next move on President Buchanan's part, what Lincoln would do if Virginia seceded, and when the next ride of the fire-eaters—the band of armed property owners and their sons who kept a sharp eye out for runaway slaves—might take place.

Caitlin greeted him warmly, offering her gloved hand. She wasn't tall, but the brightness of her eyes attracted one's interest, and when the warmth of her smile fell full force upon him, Jacob felt suddenly too hot.

He was struck by two things: Caitlin's obvious vivacity and appeal to every man in the room, and his own feelings for her as she stood not three feet away, shimmering in the firelight. She was lovely, and he loved her, considering her a true friend and companion. And as he looked at her tonight, he knew there could be something more. He desired her, but he couldn't help fearing that their nuptial bed would be yet another proving ground where he would show himself to be inadequate. He also knew that he ought not to worry as he did; he would be the unquestioned head of their household. But the intelligence of her gaze made him fear the possibility of the criticism that might be hidden there. Jacob wondered if he would ever overcome his inhibitions regarding Caitlin.

Yet he would marry her. It was what his father and

hers wanted most. Jacob could not deny his father the satisfaction of seeing his wish fulfilled.

"Where's Martha?" Caitlin asked. She had a full voice, deep for a woman. He and Ethan had made fun of it in their younger days, but no more. It took Jacob a second to compose himself. He was being torn in two, half of him wanting to pat her rouged cheek, and the other wanting to dance all night with her, guarding her from the advances of anyone else who might want to share even a moment of her time or be the object of one of her brilliant smiles. "She's . . . she's not here," he concluded.

Caitlin laughed and turned to her father. "It's a good thing Jacob's not intending to make a career of detection."

Jacob reddened, and Dr. Stuart quickly pointed out, "The young man has a career, and a fine one."

Caitlin laughed again. "Daddy, I am well aware of Jacob's accomplishments in the tobacco business, and politics as well." She fluttered her eyelids at Jacob, acting the coquette.

At the sound of applause, two husky manservants opened the French doors and entered the ballroom, carrying Charles Parson on a decorated litter. Fully dressed in a black suit, silk blouse, and a black silk vest threaded with gold, Jacob's father seemed more a man than he did any other day of the year. But Jacob could see that the effort was costing him. He was perspiring profusely, and his hand gripped the litter more tightly than was necessary. As the old man waved and smiled at his guests, Jacob's mother hurried to stand at his side. Jacob felt his heart jump to his throat, and he had to fight back a stream of tears.

Caitlin's father was the first man to greet his host, and after the servants had set him on the floor near one fireplace, the two old friends talked quietly for several minutes, their gazes falling upon Jacob and Caitlin more than once.

"We are the subject of keen scrutiny," Caitlin noted. She saw that he was surprised by the vocabulary she sometimes used. He had no doubt forgotten that she had received a formal education in Richmond. She had learned to read at an early age and with her father's blessing, unlike Jacob's sister, who had to woo her father slowly. Ever since, she herself read too much; everyone said so. But unlike Martha, who read only romantic novels from the Continent of Europe, Caitlin preferred histories and lately, tracts arguing both sides of the current issues facing and dividing the nation. Should he bother to learn of her inclination, this evenhandedness would infuriate her father, who saw only one side to every issue—the right side. His.

She stole another glance across the room. Her father's stalwart face was animated, Mr. Parson's even more so. How quick her father was to provide her with the perfect life. He had sworn she wouldn't be denied anything once her mother had died. Yet he hadn't the slightest clue as to what would make her happy.

And what do you want, Jacob Parson? she wondered. Do you really love me? Who do you think I might be, must be? Caitlin's confusion about marrying Jacob was reflected in her gift, a volume of romantic verse by Wordsworth. She had never before seen him read poetry of any sort. Nor was she sure he would appreciate or even understand the verse. Yet she had felt a compulsion to give it to him. How foolish! But utility was not the gauge of her gift to him this Christmas; rather, she wanted to learn—she must know—if a hidden vein of lyricism stirred his soul as it did hers. Yet what would she do if it did not? She could not decline to marry him because he was unmoved by odes. Caitlin thought briefly of retrieving the gift and replacing it with another. She could give it instead to Ethan, who must have read Wordsworth at Harvard.

She realized that Jacob had said something, and she asked him to repeat it.

"You've given your father such pleasure many times, I know," Jacob said kindly. He was aware of the scent of magnolias, her perfume. "And to others, too." He might have taken her hand then, but Ethan burst into the room cradling an armful of Chinese rockets and explosives.

"Fireworks!" he called out, grinning. "Who's got matches and a bourbon?" As Jacob expected, Jimmy Kilpatrick had matches, and he and the Chesterfield twins ran to help Ethan set up the fireworks on the southern side of the hill. Some of the guests crowded to the windows, but Jacob and Caitlin lingered near their fathers, who were talking in hushed tones about war.

"Everyone's trying very hard, aren't they?" Caitlin asked.

He knew what she meant. They were all pretending that nothing had changed or would change, that parties and balls were inevitable but war was not. But just as sure as the night sky would light up with exploding fireworks, conflagrations of a different sort loomed just beyond the black horizon. Yet Jacob had made a promise not to give in to the dark insight quivering within him, not during the evening's festivities, not even to Caitlin.

"War is not yet a certainty, Caitlin. There are thirty compromises before Congress right now."

But Caitlin knew better than to believe in compromises. Compromise had failed to hold water since the Missouri Compromise of 1820, which kept slavery out of states north of Missouri, letting it stand in the Southern states where the institution was firmly entrenched. Every Southern schoolboy knew about that and all the other compromises, which only skirted an issue that could not be skirted. And sitting on her father's knee, too, asking questions that went unheeded, Caitlin had learned fast about compromises.

"When you open my present tomorrow morning . . ." She trailed off, unable to look in Jacob's eyes.

"What is it, a stick? A bag of coal?" He seldom joked. There was no time. Probably the only person Jacob could joke with was Ethan. Lord only knew why, for his younger brother went out of his way to infuriate Jacob every chance he got.

Jacob had just finished his bourbon when the first

rocket went off with a boom, roaring and sizzling into the sky for a hundred feet before fizzling out and dropping from sight. The spectators gasped and shouted their approval, and soon Ethan and his friends filled the southern sky with bursting arcs of green and red.

"It's so pretty," Caitlin said, watching through the window with Jacob at her side. "Not at all like war."

Just off the dirt road to Richmond, three miles east of Twin Pines, Brett Tyler wiped the dew off the kitchen window of his family's two-room farmhouse to see the fireworks exploding in the night sky.

"What is it?" his mother called out. A heavyset woman, Dora May Tyler wore only a worn cotton robe and a soiled men's shirt; her husband's. Her skin was tanned and wrinkled by the sun from washing outdoors and working in the small five-acre plot of Parson land that constituted their farm. Beneath her shirt, her once-firm breasts now sagged; they had never known the restraining support of a corset. Her dirty face swelled with alcohol and bitterness.

Dora May and William, Brett's father, slept on a pallet against the far wall of the room which the four Tyler children shared with their parents. All three girls were awake now, sniffing adventure.

"Some fool up at the Parson house setting off fireworks," Brett said, trying to keep his voice calm. "I'd like nothing more than to set off a dozen rockets myself," he said, thinking. "Thing is, I'd aim them *at* the great house on the hill, not away from it."

His father had been drunk since word of the secession of South Carolina reached them earlier that day. He had kin around Charleston—kin with money, or so he always said—and he took pride in their thumbing their noses at the Union. But then, William Tyler was drunk every living day of his life. This was no rare treat. He was snoring so loudly that Brett wondered if the old fool would wake up before Christmas Day had come and gone. It was possible, of course. His daddy could drink more whiskey and sleep more hours than any other man alive or dead.

The three girls, who ranged in age from twelve to nineteen, pushed to get a look out the window as the fireworks lit up the night, and Brett yielded his place to them. He had seen enough.

How foolish can the Parsons be? he wondered. Here we are about to fight a war, and they waste gunpowder like it was dirt. The Parsons and all the fine, wealthy families of the Old Dominion made him sick with anger. One on one, he was better than any of them, Saint Jacob or Ethan the Genius included. Brett could barely read enough to get by, but he could think like a fox and move like a cat. The Parson boys were house pets, pampered and soft. They wouldn't survive the war, Brett knew. But he would. He would thrive in battle. He'd win a commission and marry a rich girl with enough property to kill the surveyor stuck with trying to walk it off.

But the girls oohed and ahhed at every explosion, led by Sara, who was almost twenty and should have known better. As if the Parsons had set the whole thing up just for them. Brett glowered over his sisters' dark heads at the disgusting display. Some Christmas present from the high-and-mighty Parsons! And here his daddy had raised tobacco on land owned by the Parsons for most of his life, and all William Tyler got to show for his trouble was some rock candy and ribbons for the girls and their mother, and a bottle for the two men, as if there couldn't be anything else on earth they'd rather have. Well, the good, sweet, stinging bourbon made Daddy happy, but it did nothing for Brett. Nothing less than a gift of the farm itself, and a chance to beat the tar out of both of the Parson boys would please him. And maybe a kiss and a little more from Martha Parson, who was getting right prettier every day.

"What are you thinking, boy?" his mother asked. Dora May had come up behind him as he stood near the girls, and was watching the expression on her son's face with interest.

"I'm thinking about that house there and how I'm going to get a piece of it."

His mother laughed, a raspy cackle that racked her body. When she had regained control of her voice she said, "Ain't but one way, Brett. You marry that pretty Parson girl and prove yourself a hero. Either that or jump over the moon with Old Man Parson watching, right now."

"Brett loves Martha Parson, Brett loves Martha Parson," Abigail sang. Brett took a step toward his youngest sister and raised the back of his hand. "You wake Daddy, and then you'll be sorry." Brett glowered. Abigail didn't have to be told twice.

It amazed him that none of the girls was pregnant yet, with all the tomcatting done in Albemarle County by families both fine and not so fine. "Must be God's watching over us," he said aloud to his mother.

When he talked like that, her only son worried her. He would do better to be a simpler kind of man than he was. But she was proud of him. Brett was angrier than the rest of them put together. Ain't no way he was going to settle for the bottle—or any of the damn Parson handouts designed to numb them against the manipulations of their mighty neighbors.

"Promise me you'll be something, boy, like the Tylers once was." His mother said this with an edge to her voice that Brett rarely heard.

"You ain't given up on your dreams at all, have you, old lady?" he said, teasing her. She ruffled his hair, which she could barely reach, and smacked him a little too hard on the cheek, just to let him know she was still his mother.

"This here is one stinking Christmas," Brett said sadly, heading for his blanket and roll in the other room. "Don't nobody dream of a Christmas like this." Big as he was, he shook for a good half-minute under the blanket before he could warm himself enough to fall asleep, to dream of revenge and victory in battle.

"The fire's out," Dora May snapped at the girls. "Get to sleep."

"The fireworks is over anyway," little Abigail pointed out wistfully. Why did good things pass so quickly? she wondered.

"Why does it have to be so cold at Christmas?" Priscilla griped. Dora May slapped her. She turned away regretting her action, but she said nothing. The Tylers went to sleep with William's snoring as their only lullaby.

Alex's son Thomas was the last of the field hands to come outside to watch the fireworks. "I wish they'd set 'em off to the north so's I could follow the lights clean up to Canada," he said to his mother. Clara was risking a rebuke from Anna Parson by joining her son for a moment at the slave quarters, just west of the hill where the grand house stood like a monument.

"Wish you wouldn't talk like that, son," she said softly. "I worry for you when you talk so crazy."

"Freedom ain't crazy, Mama. I hear there's hundreds of black folks in Boston livin' free, and don't nobody try to come and take 'em back! They work hard and earn a honest wage." Thomas was almost as tall as his father, and he had inherited the same jet black coloring, rather than the lighter brown of his mother's skin. But while both his parents were house servants, Thomas had an anger to him that his mother found unsettling. He had hated working in the big house, always tiptoeing around the Parsons. When Jacob had returned him to field labor after only two weeks, he had been just as happy. His tall body felt no physical restraints in the field. Nobody had to know that every time he hacked at the weeds with his hoe he was stabbing the institution that held him in bondage.

Clara snorted. "Son, ain't you heard of Dred Scott? I did, in the house. Master Ethan say it's the law. We ain't even people in the eyes of the law. We belong to Mister Charles! Cain't be free never, nowhere! Not in my lifetime . . ."

"That's the white law!" Thomas protested.

"The only law! You got to live in this world, son, not the one in your head."

The boom of the fireworks echoed down the hill from the house, then faded, as if to punctuate Clara's words.

"Freedom not for us, Thomas. Not now. Maybe later, but not now."

Her son flashed her an angry look, a look that given to a white man at the wrong time of day could cost her son his life. "Then when, Mama? You tell me when." The impetuous young man stormed off, racing around back of the shacks where families stood huddled in the cold, awaiting the next rocket.

Clara could not tell her son—not yet—that she had just become a tie in the Underground Railroad, she and Alex both. If she told him even a word about it, all their lives wouldn't be worth a penny, let alone the thousand dollars they'd fetch up on the slave block—if they lived that long.

A candle slowly waved in the kitchen window, and seeing it, Clara ran back across the bare, snowy field and up the steps to the kitchen. Just inside the door stood Caitlin Stuart, her hands on the hips of her white gown. When Clara entered, bowing her head, Caitlin leaned near her to whisper. "Our first passenger arrives New Year's Day."

Clara's brown eyes grew wide. "So soon?"

"There's no more time for some people. Now get some more punch while I find more bourbon for Daddy and Mr. Parson." Both women hurried to their duties, a secret borne within them like a child.

After the fireworks had concluded without injury, and countless toasts had been raised and drunk, the gathered gentlemen retired to the library at the front of the house, leaving the ladies, young and old, in the ballroom. Martha and Caitlin stepped away from the large group of their friends and relatives, slipping into the smaller adjoining parlor to trade secrets.

"Did he ask? Did you say yes?" Martha asked immediately after shutting the door. The look in Caitlin's dark eyes, at once passionate and unsure, replied for her. Jacob had not asked her to marry him. But why?

They sat on a small English settee. Embarrassed to have caused her friend any undue concern, Martha reached out to take Caitlin's hand. "I don't understand my brother any better than you. Neither one of them, really. I know Jacob loves you. He always has. Why won't he just say it?"

Caitlin wondered, too. What kept Jacob, who was such a good orator, from speaking his mind about loving her?

"I know a secret," Martha whispered. Caitlin breathed sharply and looked at her friend in surprise. Was it possible that she had seen her speaking with Clara? In the flickering firelight, Martha sat half in shadow, half in light. Her expression was hard to read.

"What? Tell me!"

"I shouldn't say," Martha teased, looking away.

Caitlin slid closer on the sofa and grabbed her hand. "What? Please tell me! What!"

"He'd kill me if he knew I told you, but . . . Ethan adores you, too. I see it in his eyes." Martha became increasingly animated as she spoke with undisguised passion in her eyes. "Do you think they'll fight a duel over you? Oh, I wish they would. A duel would be so romantic. . . ."

This information took Caitlin by surprise. Raising her hands to her cheeks, she could feel the heat there. And the palms of her hands were moist. "Ethan," she managed to whisper. Since going away to that university up north, Ethan had been more an image to Caitlin than a real man, like Jacob. He appeared once in a great while at the holidays, but only briefly. And then he was gone. But never had she thought of him as a suitor. Ethan had always been too independent, the second son. It would never do.

Seeing that her friend was quite pale, Martha called to Clara for a small glass of sherry, which Caitlin drank gratefully.

"I'm sorry if I shocked you," Martha said, wiping Caitlin's brow with her handkerchief. "I thought you knew. It's so obvious to me."

Still, Caitlin could find no reassuring words. And as they sat silently on the settee, she wondered what emotions Martha had let loose from Pandora's box. It was not the clear image that inevitably came to mind when she thought of marriage to Jacob. The life that would unfold at Twin Pines once they were wed was no different from the one she lived now in her father's home. It was familiar. But Ethan. The very idea was so unthinkable that it harkened a host of unclear images and emotions. She could not ignore them; but to do otherwise meant acknowledging feelings that might never again be completely hidden. For the first time she felt uncomfortable with her lifelong friend. Caitlin wondered if the gulf now looming between them could ever be spanned by any bridge of the heart either could build.

Caitlin unconsciously cupped her hands to her face, as if drinking her confusion. What was this riot of emotions that stirred at the mention of Ethan's caring for her? They were childhood friends. If what her father had said was true, like herself, Ethan stood in opposition to his family. But to think of him courting her . . . She could not and would not.

Caitlin gradually became aware of Martha, who was staring at her unabashedly.

"People are talking, Jacob, and they'll soon do more than that. Your brother better decide now where his heart and his head belong. Here, or up north in that sinful city built by Puritans. He must decide, and you must help him, Jacob. He's your blood."

Cigar smoke filled the library, and Jacob wiped his eyes, nodding in agreement. "I'll talk to him, sir. Ethan is first and foremost a Parson and a Virginian, have no doubt about that."

Jacob imagined strangling Ethan to shut him up. Dr. Stuart smiled. But for his spectacles, he looked more like a gentleman planter than a professor of law, with his curly mane of gray hair. Caitlin had not inherited the pale blue eyes that pierced like a knife, but the doggedness of spirit was clearly something they shared.

"Now, about the fire-eaters," Dr. Stuart continued. "Can we count on you for New Year's Eve? It's important that we make a show of force, don't you agree?"

Truth told, Jacob had his doubts about slave patrols. More often than not the men tended to get drunk and start trouble, picking on some poor slave who happened to be in the wrong place at the wrong time. But he could not tell Stuart that; he would never believe the patrols he supervised would use their authority irresponsibly. Besides, Stuart himself treated his slaves with firmness. In all probability, he would not consider such behavior unnecessary. "I believe more in reasoning with the black man, in treating him fairly—"

"Sure, son . . . and I do, too! But there's time for action. Do you think John Brown would've gotten within fifty miles of Harper's Ferry if the patrols had been doing their job? No, sir! We fire-eaters will allow no such uprising here."

Jacob tried to stay calm. "But, Dr. Stuart, John Brown was mad. He accomplished nothing. The whole episode lasted a day and a night. He and his handful of fanatics were hanged within a month of their capture by Lee."

Stuart seemed peeved. "The point is that it can happen again, here. More slaves could join. Nat Turner's ghost still prowls this land."

Jacob had drunk just enough bourbon to imagine he felt Nat Turner brushing past him. He shuddered. "I hope you are wrong, sir. But I shall consider your proposal."

Stuart puffed on the long cigar and blew a ring lazily toward the ceiling. "Fine, Jacob. Now, on this other matter. Your father and I would like the affair concluded before the year is out. Is that your plan?"

Jacob gulped, taken aback. It sounded so simple when Stuart spoke of it, buttoning his life into a set compartment, neatly arranging it according to his own order. Jacob wished it were so easy for him to take things in hand.

"Sir, I have a deep regard for Caitlin. She is almost a sister to me."

Jacob thought the old man might throttle him. His blue eyes shone ice cold, and he brandished his whiskey as though it were a sword. "Banish such unmanly thoughts from your head! She's a woman. You're a man. You have no common blood. Now go for her, boy. She wants a husband and sons. She'll make you a fine wife."

Jacob blushed. He was unaccustomed to talking so frankly about such feelings. Politics, yes, but not love. To Dr. Stuart, all life was a battle you either won or lost—and you'd better have a good battle plan and lots of re-inforcements. "I had thought to formally ask for her hand at the Epiphany Ball, sir, at your home."

But Dr. Stuart smiled broadly and slapped Jacob on the back. "Well, that's fine, son. I can wait another week or two. Now let's have another drink."

Jacob passed out long before the last guests left early in the morning on Christmas Day. Although Jacob weighed a hundred and eighty pounds, Alex carried him up to bed with no more effort than a child would expend putting a puppy in a dresser drawer.

But once in bed, with Alex gone to his room in the cellar with Clara, Jacob came blearily conscious, stumbled to his feet and into the hall. Blindly he tripped and grabbed on to the railing, making his way downstairs. His progress was painfully slow, and the faces of his forefathers seemed to mock him from the gilt wooden frames lining the stairway. Peeking around the corner into the ballroom, he saw at once that it was emptied of people, and he shakily made his way to the tree. Under it, he found Caitlin's gift and impatiently tore off the wrapping. It was a book! In the weak light, he could only make out what appeared to be poetry. In a drunken haze, he flipped through the leather-bound volume without reading the verse. Wordsworth. Why had she given him a book of poems? Bewildered, his sensitive teeth aching from the bourbon, Jacob crawled up the steps and into bed, where he slept until long after noon.

CHAPTER 4

ON THE TWENTY-seventh of December, Jacob's friends and acquaintances began arriving for a meeting which Ethan described as "much ado about nothing."

"If Lincoln sends in troops, Virginia will be overrun in a week," Ethan argued, carefully watching his brother's reaction. "And if he doesn't, you don't have anything to worry about, right?"

"Are you a traitor or just a coward?" Jacob wondered aloud. Ethan just laughed and ran up the stairs to his room.

Jacob felt a sense of mission about sponsoring the meeting. Instead of terrorizing bondsmen, as Dr. Stuart's fire-eaters chose to do, or standing on the floor of the State House in Richmond making speeches about the consequences of Lincoln's election to the White House, Jacob took a practical approach to the problem, one of which he was proud. He invited a half-dozen leaders and firebrands from the One Hundred to Twin Pines to plan a strategy which would protect their way of life. They would be prepared for any action Lincoln and the Federals might take.

Alex showed each young gentleman into the paneled library, where shelves of leather-bound books lined three walls of the room from the ceiling. A roaring fire warmed them as they gathered in a semicircle in front of it. Clara circulated ham biscuits and coffee. When all the gentlemen had been served, she quickly left the library, closing the heavy door behind her.

Jacob had written an agenda to guide him through the meeting. Hart Earley, the Chesterfield twins, loudmouthed Jimmy Kilpatrick, James Cabell, and Colonel Wesley's eldest son Calvin looked at Jacob expectantly.

"When's this tobacco auction begin?" Jimmy Kilpatrick asked with his typical lack of decorum.

Jimmy had been sulking silently, chewing his bottom lip. Just twenty, Jimmy was already balding, like his father, and wore a scowl like a badge. Even his friends were hard-pressed to explain why they put up with him, and his enemies were legion. Somebody once said that if you stood Jimmy Kilpatrick's enemies shoulder to shoulder, the line would stretch from Charlottesville to the Atlantic Ocean. Still, he was the son of an important man, and he was forceful, if stupid, so he had to be heard from time to time, Jacob knew.

Jacob invited them all to take their seats. "We're in for a test of our characters, gentlemen," he began, "a test of the character of the South, and of Virginia in particular. President Buchanan leaves office in two months. The South loses a friend—"

"A lily-livered hand wringer!" Jimmy Kilpatrick interrupted. "Buchanan didn't do nothin' but stall and walk away from trouble. If he had any guts, the abolitionists would all be in prison, and we'd be left alone."

Jacob sighed, and stood patiently quiet while the others vented their anger. Aaron and Noah Chesterfield laughed nervously, giving each other short, powerful punches on the arm. They often displayed their brotherly affection in this way, and more often than not a wrestling match ensued. But today, under Jacob's serious gaze, they were quiet and well behaved.

Hart Earley, husky and blond, stood to make his point, his strong thighs threatening to burst through the confines of his trousers. His friends joked that he might crush a horse between them. For such a tall, broad-shouldered young man, he had a high-pitched laugh that punctuated his speech. "If y'all remember the panic of 'fifty-seven, when the North faced a depression and a thousand businesses lost their shirts, the cry from Washington was 'Protection!' They wanted higher tariffs—"

"And they did not get them!" James Cabell said. He, too, was agitated. Wetting his finger, he pushed back his bushy brown eyebrows. But as soon as his finger had smoothed them, they furrowed again in a continuous line of concentration. His father had died in the Mexican War, Jacob knew. And Cabell's thoughtfulness suggested that he intended to rule central Virginia as his father had done before him.

Jacob's eyes moved to Calvin Wesley, sitting next to Cabell. Also the son of a Mexican War hero, Calvin was very short and stocky, powerful enough to pick up a carriage, it was said. While Cabell was introspective and probing in discussing a problem, Calvin Wesley just wanted to know who started the trouble and where he lived. He would take care of it after that. The situation with the North was intolerable to him. Like Kilpatrick, he just wanted a villain to punch in the eye and settle the thing once and for all. Jacob was surprised he had said nothing so far.

"That's right," Earley continued. "Because we grow tobacco and cotton, we have no need of such legislation. But it demonstrates how these thirty-three states are indeed two separate unions. We have slaves. They have outlawed slavery. We grow cotton, the biggest cash crop in this nation. They cannot. We are farmers, descendants of cavaliers and soldiers. They are factory owners, whose ancestors were Puritans. Gentlemen," he concluded, "we must face the truth. The Union has already dissolved. We must recognize that fact and take action." Having said his piece, Earley sat down to the claps and cheers of the others.

Jacob alone was troubled by the sentiments expressed. After the others had quieted, he resumed speaking. "Gentlemen, there are other facts to consider before we accept as a foregone conclusion the dissolution of the Union. First, there is the likelihood of a war fought upon our soil."

"We'll chase 'em back to Boston!" Jimmy Kilpatrick broke in. "Yankees are city boys. They can't fight or stay

on a horse. Hell, we was born on horseback. I can shoot
the eye out of a pea at a hundred yards."

Jacob held up his hand to still the applause. "All I'm
saying is that there are other things to keep in mind."

"Like what? Like your brother who's forgotten where
he was born and bred?"

Jacob struggled to maintain his composure. "My
brother has nothing to do with why we are here today,"
Jacob said. To my great infuriation and regret, he added
silently. His face was flushed with anger. "But, as you
know, if war breaks out—"

"You mean when!" Jimmy Kilpatrick shouted. "We'll
be ready!"

Jacob felt ready to explode. Until he finished, he decided that no one was going to interrupt him. "Don't be
so sure, Jimmy. Just you listen to me for two minutes,"
he said angrily. "Then feel free to go about your merry
way. Never mind that any of us can take on a dozen
Yankees. The facts are these: First, the North outnum-
bers us four to one. I don't know about you, but I don't
much relish those odds. And I find the idea of our bondsmen fighting truly horrifying, or women working in the
factories to provide ammunition. Second, what if we cannot rely upon help from Europe? The ties of England and
France to the North are strong, and some say that they
will not support the slave states as a matter of policy,
regardless of how desperately they desire our cotton. Our
port cities might well be shut down within a few months
of the onset of hostilities, for the North has many times
the naval strength that we do. They could cut us off completely. Without munitions, we cannot fight."

"You're surrendering, and the war ain't begun!" Jimmy
Kilpatrick shouted. Jacob rushed him and stood an inch
from the taller man's face.

When Jacob spoke, it was in a tremulous whisper
seething with anger. "I will never surrender. I will die
first. But you, my ignorant friend, must face the world as
it is, or I shall have failed here today. And I do not accept
failure."

A tense silence of perhaps fifteen seconds was broken when Martha Parson burst into the library. She smiled, looking around at the familiar faces, then walked to the bookshelves at the far end of the room and selected two slender volumes. "I do so admire Monsieur Balzac, don't you?" She left, her perfume heavy in the air.

It took them all a moment to recover their wits, even Jacob. He would have to speak to her. To enter the library when she knew they were meeting was preposterous—if captivating, as she very well knew. Then Noah Chesterfield asked, "Your daddy lets her read? That's a mistake."

"There's no stopping that girl, whatever she wants to do," Jacob said.

"What are you suggesting we should do, Jacob?" asked Hart Earley, his eyes flashing to the French doors one last time before calling their attention back to the more serious consideration before them.

"What I'm saying is that we have to be prepared, for war and for peace. Now is the time to start putting up food. This year's crops should include a greater percentage of vegetables and root crops. As soon as the weather permits, we should prepare more fields to feed our families, and less for tobacco, which will be shipped from Richmond to New York and on to Europe. I have heard that the North will soon begin seizing all Federal property located in South Carolina. That means arsenals, forts, navy yards. I don't have to explain to you gentlemen that no Southern state will allow its sovereignty to be disregarded in such a high-handed and tyrannical manner. As there will be war, we must do what we can to improve the railroads. While they are excellent here in Virginia, they are but a haphazard mess throughout the Deep South. We must activate our militias and put all military academies on alert. Trouble could begin at any moment. And as the capital's nearest neighbor, we may well face the Union armies first."

"But we ain't governors. We ain't generals. It's not our

business to be doing these things, Jacob," argued Jimmy Kilpatrick.

Jacob eyed him and the other young men deliberately. His words had achieved their desired effect; Kilpatrick and the others were now subdued and serious. Some looked away uncomfortably under his intense scrutiny. "It is our duty. Our fathers are great and good men, but they are old. This war is not their war. It is ours."

The impact of Jacob's words was immediate. One by one, the young men nodded agreement. Jacob was right. It was up to them.

"What I ask of each of you today is that you begin telling your families and friends what we have decided to do, what we must do, and why. We must write and visit our representatives in Richmond and elsewhere to put all of these vital actions into motion. To delay even a day is to invite defeat."

Jacob had just taken a breath to continue when he froze. Standing in the open doorway was Ethan.

Ethan swept the room with his eyes, meeting the perplexed or angry gazes of the six childhood companions with a dark stare. They were so certain of the justice of their cause, when reasonable men everywhere knew it to be vile. And his brother, so concerned with doing the right and honorable thing, was acting as host to these weak-minded bigots. Well, he was not going to let them get away unscathed this time. Let them find out how differently I view things, Ethan thought to himself.

Very deliberately, Ethan raised his large hands and began to sarcastically applaud Jacob's speech. "Won't anyone join me in praising my brother's valiant call for treason?"

Instantly, Jimmy Kilpatrick rose to his feet, fire blazing in his eyes. "Ethan Parson, this is your house, too. But, so help me God, you talk like that outside these walls and I'll beat you senseless!"

Grabbing his heart theatrically, as if he'd been struck a blow, Ethan reeled, gasping for breath, before replying. "Your words alone strike terror in my heart." Then, becoming serious, he stood straight and walked up to his brother. "May I say something?"

"You already have," Jacob hissed, clenching his fists.

"Am I to understand that I cannot address a gathering of neighbors in my own home?" Ethan avoided Jacob's eyes.

"As the eldest son, this will be my home after Father passes. Right now, it is his. It will never be yours."

Ethan was staggered for a moment by the hatred in his brother's voice, and he stood in silence as Jacob stormed out of the room, disgusted. His boots echoed down the hall and into the kitchen. Not until that moment did he understand how seriously Jacob took all of his wild talk about secession and war and calling up the militia.

Ethan then turned to address the gathering. Standing before him, their broad faces betrayed their distrust. More broad-shouldered and powerful than any of them, Ethan was a puzzle to the other men in the room. Nobody could call Ethan a coward, for he had licked them all growing up. But, educated up North, in Boston of all places, Ethan would rather read than ride. He never saw things simply. Not that his brother did, either, but at least you could count on Jacob being right about most things.

"Gentlemen," he began, "I have missed a great deal of your lively discussion. I feel certain, however, that I speak for all of the Old Dominion when I thank you for your concern for her continued harmony and prosperity. . . ."

"Are you with us or against us?" Jimmy Kilpatrick asked bluntly.

"Let me speak first, and then you'll understand," Ethan replied. "The war you are all rooting for will probably take the lives of many people you love, perhaps even yourselves, for one rule of war is that lots of young men die. I have studied history, as have many of you. And it strikes me that never has a nation of farmers defeated anybody."

Jimmy Kilpatrick started toward Ethan and might have

thrown a punch, but the twins grabbed him first. "I ain't no farmer, you potato-headed fool!"

"You may think of yourselves as soldiers or warriors or horsemen or whatever. But believe me, when you're looking down the barrel of a rifle, or a cannonball explodes five feet away, you are not a soldier; you are what you have been all your life, a farmer. None of you is a professional, an academy man with West Point training. You are farmers. The North has got more men, more goods, more ships, more arms, and more money."

Ethan paused a moment, then softened his combative tone. "I know all you boys. We're friends."

"Friends," Kilpatrick hissed disdainfully.

"I just want you all to recognize the consequences of what you may be doing today. Once you move toward dissolving the Union and toward war, there will be no turning back and saying 'I'm sorry; we didn't mean it.' Once war begins, once young men like you and old men like your fathers start it, there won't be any stopping it till everything you have is gone."

"You're a dead man, Ethan Parson!" shouted Jimmy Kilpatrick, pointing his finger like a rifle.

Ethan smiled weakly, staring into his antagonist's eyes. "We're all dead men, Jimmy. That's the point."

Alex entered the library, carrying an open box of cigars, which he offered each gentleman in turn. He was accustomed to such gatherings and to the well-dressed young men in long black morning coats and starched white shirts. They strutted like peacocks around Twin Pines most times. But Alex knew enough about white folks' silences to know that the one now reigning in the room was tense and uneasy. His eye caught the gleam of Jimmy Kilpatrick's knee-high black riding boots, and he thought, For what they cost, I could buy my way to Kingdom come.

Once the young men finished their cigars, the meeting broke up in a dispirited fashion. Having walked past the closed door into the library a few times during the meeting, Alex had heard enough to realize that all the rumors of war might be more than just talk, if Mister Jacob was right about even half of what he said. After seeing the gentlemen to their mounts at the front gate, Alex hurried to the kitchen.

"This no way to celebrate a new year," he said to his wife. Clara stood and wiped her hands on her apron. Leaning her wide rear end against the pine table, she shook her head. "Talk be cheap, Alex, 'specially when it's hotheaded young men doing the talkin'."

"Mister Jacob done most of the talkin'."

A look of panic flashed in the deep, dark eyes of his wife. Soon all the field hands would know what was happening, and talk of war would be on everyone's lips. And when that happened, she knew Thomas would be among the loudest. She and Alex would be safe with the Parsons; the family had done right by them and treated them well enough. But Thomas was different. He didn't see that it could be worse on other plantations. "Chains is chains," he'd told her. "Don't matter where they put 'em on." He was aching to fly.

Clara sighed and crossed her arms over her ample bosom. She and Alex would have to make sure he didn't fly so soon that it did them *all* in. She leaned very close to him to whisper, "One day we get out of here. But not now."

Early in the morning on the last day of 1860, Martha awoke sleepily to the birds in the willow outside her window calling "Pretty! Pretty!" She smiled and stretched like a cat, twisting every which way, then opened her blue eyes to see a bright winter sun pouring in between the curtains of her windows.

Slipping out of bed, she removed her sleeping cap and shook free her long sable hair, which cascaded down her back and tickled her neck. The room was cold, for Clara had not yet made a fire, but she pulled off her sleeping gown and hurried to the full-length, freestanding oval mirror near her bed to examine herself, as she did every morning. She looked for freckles, bruises, anything that might mar the beauty of her skin. To her relief, Martha found nothing this morning.

She was not a voluptuous woman. Her breasts were small but firm, her nipples rosy buds. She liked to imagine a Gypsy crashing in through the window by the willow, swooping her into his arms without a word, and carrying her off to Paris, where they would perform musicals on the streets until a rich nobleman's son fell in love with her, forgiving her sins and spiriting her away to his chateau in the countryside where she would live forever like royalty. She waited again this morning, shivering in the chilly air, but no one crashed in through the window. The birds sang as they did most mornings. Martha quickly dressed and ran downstairs to breakfast.

When she came into the dining room, the table was already cleared. Her mother appeared from the kitchen. "Martha, it's nearly lunchtime, dear. What time did you go to sleep last night?"

Martha ran and hugged her mother, who kissed her cheek. "I don't know, Mother. I was reading—"

"One of those revolting French novels, no doubt," Anna commented reprovingly.

"They're as close as I am allowed to get to real life," Martha said, defending her novels. "As I am not allowed to live as an adult!"

"Dear, you are not an adult. It's that simple." It was not really true, of course. At seventeen, Anna herself had been married. Martha resented the reins and constraints of a family and a society that valued a young lady for her appearance and her manners only. Martha played the femme fatale beautifully; she loved being a Southern belle. But her dissatisfaction with her life would have shocked her parents and her brothers, had they learned of it.

She was ready to do something reckless, to run off to Richmond or Europe, even to lie to her parents in order to escape the bonds of Twin Pines. She lived in a world that wanted her to be a porcelain doll on a shelf, denied the flesh and blood and mind that made her real. Jacob had the plantation to run and politics to attend to. Ethan was a university graduate. As a pretty young woman, there was nothing Martha could do except crochet and dance, and if the right man came along, marry and raise a family. But she had an imagination, a vision, like Joan of Arc! Yet she faced a path that narrowed inevitably as she matured, and such constraints riled her.

"Mother, what am I to do? What is there left for me to do?"

Anna Parson was surprised by her daughter's outburst and at first answered it with buttermilk pancakes smothered in honey and a pot of tea. She glimpsed the pouting expression on Martha's pert features. She was as enchanted as everyone else by her daughter's dimpled face and shining eyes, which were an even deeper blue now because of the blue ribbons holding the curls at each side of her head. But perhaps she had done wrong by Martha to allow her to circulate so freely in her world of romance and Gallic heroes.

"Martha, dear, you are to marry, of course. There is no secret about this." Martha had known this since the cradle, yet she persisted in being obstinate and disobedient. A decade of caring for an infirm husband had planted Anna herself firmly in the grasp of a harsh reality. But Martha had yet to face trials which would tame her expansive character. Anna only hoped her daughter escaped the painful demands she felt looming.

Martha willed tears to form in her eyes, but they would not come.

"Mother, my soul yearns to do something useful outside these walls."

"When you marry, you will. You shall live in your own home and direct your own servants. But you'd better learn to behave first, or only Colonel Gooch and his one eye will have you!"

Martha took one look at her mother and burst into tears.

"I'm sorry, dear. I just don't understand you," Anna whispered, soothing her daughter. "I, for one, treasure your poetry. The boys loved your poem about tobacco,

'Ode to Nicotina.' Wasn't that the title? Your father loved it, too," said Anna, trying to pacify her daughter, who was racked with sobs. She could hear the clatter of dishes coming from the kitchen and the sound of someone humming.

"It . . . was . . . silly," she said between sobs, trying to regain her breath.

"It was lovely. It began with something about a 'bright-leafed perennial, panacea for all ills,' right?"

"Mama, stop! It was terrible!" Burying her face in her hands, Martha escaped her mother's grasp and ran up to her room.

Just after she had left, Clara peeked her head inside the dining-room door. "Is Miss Martha ill?"

Anna Parson nodded. "She is, and marriage is the cure."

Fifteen minutes later Anna brought tea and biscuits to her husband herself, rather than having Clara perform the service. Charles raised his bushy gray eyebrows in suspicion as she entered the room.

"Are you acting as a servant now? Have the Parsons come to that? Get me my pistol!"

Anna had to smile. "Charles, stop now. Drink your tea and have some of these. You eat like a bird." After setting the tray at the foot of the bed, she helped her husband to sit up, enduring the groans and complaints with a smile of forbearance. She lay the tray beside him on the bed and regarded him with serious blue eyes.

"What is it?" he asked, wheezing as he reached for the panier of biscuits. "Has Ethan ridden off to beg the baboon for a cabinet post?"

He had lost a great deal of the health and strength that carried him full force through the first five decades of his life, before the riding accident. Anna had grown accustomed to the harping jibes that had replaced his former vigor. "I suppose that is your idea of humor, dear, but no . . . it's Martha."

Charles stiffened and set down the cup of tea he had raised to his lips. "What is it? Who's hurt her?"

"She's hurt herself. . . . She's hurt me. . . . I don't know what to say or do around her, Charles. I praise her poetry, and she bursts into tears and runs away."

Charles chuckled, a deep, throaty laugh that turned into a cough. "That thing about tobacco," he said, grinning mischievously. "Silliest ditty I ever heard."

"Charles, she wants to use her mind, she told me." Anna was standing with her hands on her hips, angry at her husband for taking the matter so lightly.

"*Lose* her mind, you mean," he teased. He coughed once, spitting phlegm into a handkerchief, and turned in the four-poster to look out the window.

Anna wanted his attention back. "It's time she married." Having said it, she was surprised at her own boldness. Charles always made such family decisions. Now she turned away, looking out the window at the fallow fields and the distant blue mountains to the west of Twin Pines.

"I see. And have you any prospects in mind? Do you know of any young man who can tame a bobcat barehanded? Maybe that Kilpatrick hothead." Anna was furious. She knew he was baiting her. Charles enjoyed outraging her. Rarely did he take her feelings into consideration. When she answered her husband of twenty-eight years, it was in a tense, low voice.

"The boy is barely literate, Charles. His family has nothing but drunkards and gamblers in it! If you ask me, chasing women is what he does best, that and brawling."

"He'll give us a brood of brawlers," Charles joked.

Anna checked the retort that flew to her tongue, seeing that he wasn't serious.

"Drink your tea, dear, before it's cold."

Chuckling, Charles took a sip of the tea, immediately sputtering, so that the liquid ran down his heavy jaw and spilled onto his nightshirt. "Tell Clara to rinse the cups in clear water, will you? This tastes like lye." Then, upon seeing his wife's pained expression, he softened his voice.

"I'll tell you what, Anna. You pick out two or three acceptable candidates at the Stuarts' ball, and we'll winnow them down to one. Then we'll set a trap for the poor fool, invite him and his folks here for a visit, and before he knows it, he'll be stuck with Martha for a lifetime!"

Anna smiled despite herself. "How you talk, Charles. As if you don't worship the girl. You make the arrangements sound like warfare."

"Love *is* war, woman. Only the scars don't show."

Anna moved away from the quilted feather bed to look out the window at the dazzling winter sunlight flooding the countryside. Her husband had received correspondence from South Carolina, she knew, and it seemed that the entire state was in a fever. Virginia was sure to follow in her stead before long.

"It should always be so peaceful here," she whispered. She didn't expect Charles to answer. She knew he never gave thought to a future filled with peace. All he had to look forward to was "a peace which passeth understanding." Death. It shamed Anna to admit it, but for her, too, his passing would mean a serenity she could not currently foresee.

Martha had composed herself, and after washing away the tears which stained her face, she lay on the bed daydreaming about the course her life might take. What did she want to happen? Whom did she want to marry? And did she want to marry at all?

Yes, she answered firmly. I want to marry. But whom? One by one she listed and pictured in her mind all the eligible young suitors she knew. Half of them were easily dismissed as homely or awkward or stupid. A third knew less than even she did about romance or anything else, and who wanted such an ignorant husband? And the remaining young men excited her less than anticipating an evening trapped with Mama and her contemporaries around the embroidery table.

She was simply not in love.

"Very well," she said aloud, as the heroines in French

novels often did while alone and in despair, "I shall fall in love!"

But how? In the books she read, the heroine made some great mistake. She ran away from home and wandered penniless and hungry through the countryside, or she ran off with a faithless Gypsy peddler who broke her heart after instructing her in the ways of love. But Gypsies were rarely seen in Virginia, unless you counted the mulatto ragseller and blade sharpener who occasionally passed by in a wagon. And he was old and smelly and had a belly like a watermelon.

No, he would not do at all. No one would. Martha next imagined a young man just like herself, only broad shouldered and handsome, as she was petite and pretty.

An image of Brett Tyler flashed through her mind, and suddenly she felt chilled and vulnerable, as if she had been found standing naked before the mirror in her room. Why did that insolent young man make her blood run cold? What did it mean? Daddy always said the Tylers were dumb as dirt and twice as plentiful. But Brett was different. Even Daddy had to admit that he was not stupid. But his hard, square-jawed face and leering grin haunted her, and Martha could not say why. With a deep sigh she took up her ink pen, her hand trembling. She would write about her predicament to Caitlin Stuart, who was full of uncommonly sound advice. She held the pen in midair. How oddly Caitlin had reacted the night of their Christmas Eve gala. But any heroine with two men in love with her would do the same thing, she supposed. With a sigh she hoped was deeply heartfelt, Martha set her pen to the paper and began writing.

CHAPTER 5

JACOB SAT AT his father's mahogany desk in the solitude of the library, laying out plans for the coming year's planting. Besides tobacco, the Parsons also raised sheep, pigs, cattle, chickens, ducks, and geese. And then there were the turkeys who really were stupid enough to raise their heads to drink the rain until they drowned. Jacob had seen a tom do it once, and after that he never let the birds roam free when the weather was sour. Daddy joked once that the Tylers had descended from wild turkeys, but Ethan said he figured it might be the other way around.

Jacob also planned two corn crops, the first of which would begin late in February, if the weather was kind. And he must make provisions for potatoes, sweet and not, and a host of vegetables which Clara stewed and canned by the gallon. Nothing had to be done yet to the apple orchard located up in the hills to the west of the house; the trees would not bud for another month and a half.

Like most of the estate owners he knew, Jacob gave consideration to the slaves who worked the land, for there was no denying they worked harder when they were happy. Each black family had a quarter-acre lot of their own to grow what they wished, on their own time. They were bound, of course, to offer their yield first to Jacob. But he paid a fair price, and there was little dickering or hard feelings between him and the bondsmen. No one questioned the system, least of all Jacob, who cherished tradition and order.

But unlike many of his neighbors, who worried that a

black man with money was too much like a rabbit free of the hutch, Jacob also paid the field hands for the water-melon, pumpkins, and pigs they produced. This left the slaves money with which to buy sugar, coffee, wheat flour, clothing, and unfortunately, whiskey.

It was a sight to behold when one of the bondsmen got out his harmonica, and the drunken Negroes led the slave quarters in a wild dance, jumping and spinning to a rhythm Jacob could never have imagined on his own, a rhythm other owners feared, calling it "the beat of jungle drums." It was the only time Jacob saw them unguarded, with joy animating their faces so customarily worn as masks of little emotion. And even that they would keep from him if they could.

Jacob—like his younger brother, who had studied slavery as a subject at Harvard—was not altogether con-vinced that he and the other slaveholders of the South, who held four million men, women, and children in bondage, had really rescued them from certain death in the wilds of the jungle. If Ethan was even halfway cor-rect, the Negro in Africa had had a society operating for a thousand years more. They fought no more often than did the white men of Europe and America.

After lunch, Jacob had a brief chat with his father before the elder Parson's afternoon nap. It was late afternoon when he wandered back into the library to discover his brother poised over the estate books, the records of everything im-portant that had happened at Twin Pines.

Ethan let out a low whistle when he caught sight of Jacob, and arched his eyebrows. "I had no idea we were so wealthy," he said, looking.

Jacob strode across the room to the desk. "I had no idea you cared," he responded, reaching around Ethan to slam shut the heavy ledger. "Do you wish to give it to the abolitionists, or directly to the Negroes themselves?"

Ethan broke into a hearty laugh, his blue eyes flash-ing. "Why, brother, I must admit that in my absence you have developed a keen sense of irony. No," he said, step-ping away from the desk to go over to a window, "I was merely wondering if there would be something left for me, when that day comes."

Jacob's ire rose. "I manage well enough. There will be something for you. Are you planning to establish residency in Boston?"

"No, brother, this is my home. I need something to do. What do you suggest?"

Jacob looked up at his brother's broad frame in surprise. In his own way, Ethan was asking for his guidance. He wanted to be a part of Twin Pines again. But there was no room for him. Jacob felt a flash of regret, then pushed it aside.

"I'll talk to Father. He'll think of something." Jacob could think of nothing else to say.

Ethan clasped his hands behind his back, poised in front of the window. "Believe it or not, I missed this red earth and these blue mountains while I was away. And it's cold up there, fiercely cold. People freeze to death in the street."

Jacob was shocked. "Why didn't you find them and bring them inside?"

Smiling sadly, Ethan shook his head. "The city is too big for that. Full of strangers. Nobody knows anybody else. It's not like Twin Pines, Jacob."

"It sounds like Hell to me," Jacob snapped, then regretted it. It sounded as though he was blaming Ethan for the shortcomings of Boston.

Ethan shrugged. In a way, Jacob spoke the truth. He'd never felt fully engaged in anything in Boston other than his studies. The politics and sights of the city itself had held little appeal for him. It was rather the people he met, such as the Keyeses, and the broadening effect their views had had on him. It had been liberating, enlightening. Yet he had never wished to make his home in the North, but rather to carry all he learned home to Twin Pines. "You'll like the Keyeses, Jacob, if you can forgive them their sentiments about slavery."

Jacob's eyes widened. There was little chance that he would forgive their criticism aimed at the institution that was at the basis of their livelihood. But he had every hope that he would soon see the pair of Yankees eat their words damning slavery. "So long as they don't insult Daddy or the family, they're welcome here. You know that, Ethan."

The brief truce was interrupted by Alex, who entered the library with a letter in his hand. "For you, Mister Ethan," he said, handing the envelope to him. Jacob recognized it as another Unionist call to arms, and watched as Ethan tore it open and read the tract. Alex left just as Ethan mentioned that he would be attending a "meeting in town" that evening.

"Ethan, you cannot go. The men involved will be hanged one day. If Virginia secedes, the kind of talk to be undertaken at that meeting will be treason!" Jacob was livid with anger, his fingers gripping the edge of the desk.

Ethan appeared unperturbed. Jacob almost envied his brother's panache as he slid the envelope smoothly inside his coat and calmly said, "Virginia remains in the Union at this moment, and as a citizen of the Commonwealth, I am free to go where I please whenever I please." He started to leave, but Jacob blocked his way.

"Ethan, it's New Year's Eve. There will be all kinds of trouble tonight. I'm begging you not to go."

"I have to go, Jacob. Just as you have to stay." Ethan brushed against Jacob's shoulder as he walked past, and Jacob recognized the physical power his brother possessed. Even as he wondered irritably why Ethan should go out of his way to cause trouble, a pang of envy shot through Jacob. Would he himself do the same if he possessed Ethan's education and gumption?

Soberly, Jacob returned to the desk to study the accounts, estimating how much seed and corn to buy and when and what to expect in payment for the tobacco and other cash crops raised at Twin Pines. But it was difficult to concentrate; he found himself troubled by Ethan's intransigence.

Had he been a more superstitious fellow, Jacob would have heeded his premonition that his younger brother would not welcome in the year 1861 unscathed, much as the nation itself appeared headed in the same direction. Shivering, he stood and tossed more wood onto the fire, but the room remained too chilly for comfort.

Fireworks, bonfires, and the random firing of rifles and muskets announced the passing of midnight to Ethan and his horse, Star. The brown mare shied and whinnied with each report.

The meeting had gone much as Ethan had anticipated. He and a handful of Unionists had gathered at the university chapel under candlelight to write a petition to their state and federal representatives, asking that they refrain from undertaking any rash actions—such as seizing the federal arsenal of weapons and ammunition in Richmond—until Mr. Lincoln assumed the duties of the office of the presidency and set policy.

Ethan patted the neck of his mare soothingly. He had felt very much alone in the small group; just six students had shown up, all of them from Pennsylvania and Delaware. A year or two younger than he, they came from different worlds. For one thing, their families supported their politics. They were heroes at home, not outcasts. With no firsthand experience with slavery, they saw it as a pure evil, a system designed by the Devil and run by his minions.

Ethan knew better. However fundamentally wrong the institution, many good men and women were entangled within its economic and social webs, and could not easily free themselves from its constraints. The handful of men, but a year or two younger than he, looked to him as a wise and worldly older brother. It was a role he wearied of playing at these meetings. It had not escaped him that in this weariness, he and Jacob shared a common view.

They all viewed Lincoln as a mystery man who might well allow a peaceful secession, figuring it to be short-lived. While arguing good-naturedly over the wording of the petition, Ethan reminded them of Lincoln's speech of two years earlier, when he'd run unsuccessfully against

Stephen Douglas for the Senate. Lincoln had said that "no house divided against itself can stand."

"That's just politics," Samuel Clarke, a boy from Philadelphia, had said, and the others had agreed.

Ethan wasn't so sure. What they did agree upon was that the attitude of the typical Virginia landowner was an invitation to disaster and strife. All this they wrote in a letter to Governor Letcher of Virginia, and to their representatives in Washington, D.C.

Ethan shivered with the cool, clear chill of the night. It was after midnight. A waxing moon illuminated his way with a pale but steady light. If he met no untoward interference, he expected to be home and in bed before two A.M. The narrow dirt road from Charlottesville was uncommonly quiet; he had not passed a soul for more than an hour.

Ethan's mare balked as a shout sounded from just ahead, followed by the sound of a single pistol shot ringing out. Some lonesome reveler who'd had too much to drink, Ethan reasoned, so he spurred his horse to hurry by. Rounding a bend in the road, he was surprised by two men on horseback, one poised at each side of the road. Across the saddle of one rider lay a musket. Both men wore heavy coats and wide-brimmed hats.

"Hold up!" one of the pair called out. His voice was gruff. Ethan reined in the mare. He had no choice. He stood no chance of repelling the pair if they wanted to rob him; he carried only a hunting rifle, and that was secured in the scabbard near his right hand. Overhead, a chilly wind creaked through the still trees.

"State your business," the man with the gun demanded. He was tall and lean, unknown to Ethan, and he spoke with an untutored country drawl. His face was hidden under a slouch hat farmers typically wore to keep the sun off their faces. It was too dark to make out any other details.

Ethan considered breaking behind the man who had no weapon, but he wasn't sure he could make it by without giving either man a clear shot. "I'm Ethan Parson," he said clearly into the night. "My business is getting home. Who are you?"

The man with the drawn musket whistled in response. "We done caught us a big 'un," he said to the other man, a shorter, heavier fellow who cackled with anticipation. "You been helping runaways, Mr. Ethan 'God-a-mighty Hisself' Parson?"

Ethan bristled at the man's insolence. If need be, he could get off a clean shot at the big-mouth before the man could aim that ungainly weapon. "Are you one of Stuart's fire-eaters?" Ethan asked. In the woods nearby, an owl hooted. Ethan shivered, a cold sweat breaking on his brow.

"If we is?"

Ethan took a deep breath. He wasn't sure how to handle these two. Perhaps he could butt them off or talk them out of trouble. "I have no business with you. I am headed home." Ethan spurred Star, and the brown mare jumped and started forward skittishly. Both men moved to cut him off, and two more riders appeared from behind a willow near the road. Four of them! Ethan's mouth went dry.

"Git down off the horse." The tall man gestured sharply with his musket.

He spoke in a deep, gruff voice for a skinny fellow, but Ethan did not recognize it. "It's too far to walk from here," Ethan replied, struggling to keep his voice smooth and calm. "Horse theft is a serious crime, you boys know." Two horses ridden by the strangers whinnied and shied, as if sensing gunfire.

"Git down from that horse before I shoot it." The man drew a pistol before Ethan had time to react.

Slowly, Ethan leaned his weight to the left and dismounted, keeping a tight grip on the reins. What would happen if he slapped his horse on the flank and dove for cover? Would they really kill him? It didn't seem possible, so near Twin Pines. He stood no chance of escaping from four men on horseback, that much was clear. "You don't sound drunk," Ethan said, trying to sound them out.

What were they after? "Why are you doing this? You're all in trouble here—"

"No, you in trouble, Parson. Git that straight. You the onliest one in trouble!" The hatred in the man's voice was so pure and raw that Ethan began to fear for his life. His heart raced; his palms were clammy, and he was shivering. What could he do? If he reached for the rifle, one of them would kill him for sure and claim it was a fair fight. Ethan began to pray silently. *Hail Mary, full of grace . . .*

"How many niggers you set free to prey on innocent white girls?" the man asked in a tone that allowed no answer. "Is that what you want for that sister of yours, some buck on top of her in the barn, while you watch?"

Ethan couldn't stand for much more of such filthy talk. They were provoking him, he knew, but he could not ignore their despicable words; the insult was too great. At least he would die with honor and go to Heaven with righteous anger in his heart. Inching his hand over the top of the saddle, he felt for the stock of the rifle. He had to do something now.

Brett Tyler was whistling a sailor's tune, "Any Port in a Storm," as he rose east along the dirt road from Charlottesville, wondering why all men didn't get and stay drunk every day of the year. For him, the answer was simple. He couldn't afford it. Great thing about New Year's Eve was that strangers would buy you a drink without making you listen to some weepy talk about a lost love first.

And speaking of love, Tyler thought, I must save or steal the two dollars to woo that busty Crawford wench with the bad teeth.

Then a gun went off with a pow that shook Tyler nearly sober in half a second. He spurred his mount, checking his musket and pistol as he rode.

The five men heard the approach of another rider at almost the same instant. Fearing it might be another fire-eater, Ethan yanked on the reins. Shielding himself from the line of fire with his mare, he struggled to climb up and onto the frightened horse.

The galloping rider came to a dead halt just ten feet shy of Ethan, cursing him soundly. "You boys picked one hell of a spot for a picnic!" Brett Tyler called out, grinning. In a second, he had taken in the scene and knew he had to do something. "I could've run you down like a squirrel, Ethan." Leaning forward on his saddle, he asked, "You plannin' on meetin' Mr. Lincoln here?"

For once, Tyler's brashness was welcome. "I'm just trying to get home in one piece," he told Tyler in a trembling voice. All six men were on horseback now. Tyler kicked his horse and joined Ethan.

"I was aiming for the same thing. Trouble, boys?"

"Keep to your own self, Tyler. We got no fight with you."

Tyler let out a whoop. "Taylor Shiflett, you tick's ass. What you doin' scarin' the piss out of a fine gentleman like Mr. Parson here? Didn't your pappy raise you with one ounce of surviving sense? Now shoo, boys. Go home." Tyler spurred his horse, and one of the four moved aside to let him by. But when Ethan followed, the skinny man Tyler knew as a Shiflett yanked at Ethan's reins, frightening his mare and causing her to rear. Ethan was thrown off and fell with a thud onto the frozen ground.

The four troublemakers whooped it up. "He kin talk but he cain't ride," one man said, cackling like a hen.

Tyler turned back to face them. "You had your fun and prob'ly broke his back," he said. "If he's crippled like his daddy, you'll be in stripes for a spell."

Cursing, Taylor Shiflett dismounted and made for Ethan, who had sat up and was trying to get his wind back. With no warning, he hit Ethan with his fist, knocking him flat to the ground.

Tyler drew his pistol and jumped off his horse before Shiflett could hit Ethan again.

From the corner of his eye, Tyler saw the motion of

a man reaching for his rifle. Without turning, he fired, and the man cried out and fell from his horse. The two men who were still mounted froze in their saddles, watching Tyler's every move, their companion's cries echoing in the darkness.

"Git on or I'll shoot you," Tyler said quietly to the pair. After a tense moment, they turned and rode away.

"Bastards!" Shiflett yelled at the retreating silhouettes.

"Take your friend and git now," Tyler ordered, pointing his rifle at Shiflett's chest. The man Tyler had shot was still groaning in the shadows at the side of the road.

Shiflett spun and kicked Ethan full force in the head with a thunk like that of a pumpkin dropping onto a bare wooden floor. Tyler hit Shiflett across the side of the face with his five-pound dragon pistol. The skinny man ducked too late, and the force of the blow knocked him over. He reached for his own gun and waved it unsteadily at Tyler.

"Drop it," Tyler said once. He had to hand it to the runt. It wasn't often a man took a blow like that without blacking out.

Shiflett was grinning like a demon. He took no more than one step toward Tyler before the bullet hit him in the thigh. He spun and fell, rolling on the ground and screaming in agony, his cries mingling with those of the other man, who had not ceased yelling since Tyler's first ball hit him. He didn't even look up at the sound of the second shot.

"We got us a chorus of woes here, Ethan," Tyler said, holstering his pistol. The Parson boy was out cold and bleeding from the mouth and nose. It took him a few minutes to heave Ethan atop the horse, where he tied him across his saddle like a corpse. Then Tyler wound Ethan's reins around his free hand and mounted his own horse. "You pitiful Parsons can't find your way to the outhouse and back, can you?" He gently kicked his horse and told him to take it slow and easy.

"Your friends be back for you, my guess is," Tyler called back to the two men writhing in the moonlight.

"That, or you two freeze to death." He set off at a slow trot, checking often to be certain that the fool Parson boy hadn't tumbled off and broken open what was left of his head.

The sound of the two horses on the road up to the house sent the terror of Judgment Day through Alex and his son, Thomas. Hidden in the woodpile beside Thomas's cabin, where they both stood watch, was the first black man headed north to freedom that they had ever seen. His name was William, and he shook so with fear that the woodpile itself was atremble.

"Stay here, son," Alex told Thomas. Thomas was too terrified to move anyway. Visions of him and his father hanging from the nearest tall oak flashed through his head again and again.

Alex walked resolutely up the hill toward the Parson house, wondering if tonight would be his time to meet Jesus face to face. Whoever waited for him at the house had to be trouble. Nothing good and holy happened after midnight.

Alex's blood pumped thick and hot when he caught sight of that devilish Tyler boy leading a dead man on a mount behind him. Breaking into a trot, the tall black man reached Tyler just as he was struggling to untie the body from the second horse.

"You done kill a man?" Alex asked, confronting Tyler from a few feet away. "Why you bring him here?"

Without replying, Tyler grabbed the fallen man by the hair and raised his head. With a gasp of horror, Alex recognized the face.

"He ain't dead?" Alex pulled Ethan up and off the horse easily, stopping Tyler in his tracks.

"Pick up the horse, too, while you're at it," Tyler joked, amazed at what a feat of strength he had seen. "He'll be all right, I 'spect. He met some boys who don't approve of Ethan's fondness for Mr. Lincoln."

Alex scowled as he carried Ethan up the path to the front door.

"You're welcome!" Tyler shouted as the front door opened, a ray of light flashed, and the door slammed shut. He was about to go home when he saw a light flickering upstairs in the corner room, which he knew was Martha's. Suddenly, he wasn't in a hurry to get home.

In another minute, when a lamp was lighted in the kitchen, Tyler dismounted and tied his horse to the fence at the west side of the lawn. I owe Miss Martha an explanation, he thought, smiling mischievously to himself.

Tyler walked around the outside of the fifteen-room house and entered through the back door without knocking. The light of the lamp fell upon Ethan Parson, whose broad frame lay still on the heavy pine table just long enough to hold him. Martha Parson stood above him in a dazed manner until Alex made a low comment. Snapping her head quickly from Ethan to Brett to Alex, she clutched the neck of her robe tightly closed at her throat and hurried to get more fresh water from the kitchen pump.

"What you doin' here?" Alex snapped at Tyler, moving toward him menacingly. "Git!"

Tyler sidestepped the towering house servant and spoke instead to Martha. "Your brother was jumped on the road back from town by some boys on slave patrol. They must've mistook him for Alex here."

Martha looked confused. Seeing her brother so badly hurt had sent her into shock. It was like walking through a bad dream. She handed a wet cloth to Alex, who said, "What did you do, help them?"

Tyler laughed. "No, I wouldn't hardly call shootin' two of 'em help."

Martha grabbed her brother's hand to hide her shock, and spoke soothingly into his ear as Alex washed away the blood. "You saved Ethan's life," she told Brett without looking at him."

"That's the truth." Tyler watched her closely, captivated by the whiteness of her skin. There were no hands like hers in the Tyler household.

"I don't believe you. Lyin's as much a habit as cheatin'

to you Tylers," muttered Alex, his nostrils flaring with rage. "You done this—" Remembering that Miss Martha was present, he clamped his mouth shut. He was the most trusted bondsman on Twin Pines, but ordinarily even he did not speak so freely in front of the Parsons.

"Alex, hush now," Martha said softly. "Why would he beat my brother and then take the trouble to bring him here? Use your head."

Alex concentrated his energies upon repairing the damage done to Ethan's face, dabbing at the cuts with a warm cloth to still the bleeding. He would have to awaken Clara; an herb poultice would speed the healing along. Keeping his eyes carefully averted, he worked quickly. He had overstepped his bounds, sure and certain, but it galled him that Miss Martha would talk to him like that in front of Tyler trash. How could she believe one word coming out of that demon's mouth?

Tyler crossed his arms over his chest and studied Martha. Dressed only in a floor-length sleeping gown and robe, her dark curls tucked into a nightcap, she looked to him too beautiful to be real. If he touched her, surely she would vanish. It was her paleness as much as her lovely features that captivated him. He'd known many women, but none with the wild, unbridled look she turned on him without even knowing it was there.

She turned to face him, and their eyes locked for a second. Martha turned away first, blushing furiously. She was pretending to help Alex, but Tyler caught the searing rush of blood and the heat on her face, and inside his pants he stiffened.

To Tyler she represented a land he would never be allowed to enter. Yet she had seen him. She had spoken to him. She had noticed him.

Tyler left the house, whistling to himself.

Dora May woke as he entered the shack. "That you?" she called to Tyler.

"No," Brett hissed, "it's President Lincoln hisself. You under arrest, old woman."

Dora May sat up, whispering harshly above her husband's rumbling snore. "You in trouble?"

Brett shook his head, knowing it was too dark for her to see.

"Cain't hear your head rattle, boy," she snapped.

"No, I ain't in trouble," he snapped. "I'm in . . . I'm in the moon, Mama."

His mother cursed under her breath. "Don't talk like that, boy. They'll put you away. Now git some sleep 'fore mornin'."

Brett lay on his pallet, but sleep would not come. Each time he closed his eyes, Martha danced into view, her white dressing gown rippling and flowing like a river. In the brilliant depth of her blue eyes shone a fire.

"And I hold the torch," he whispered smugly to himself.

Thomas could wait no longer for word from his father. The lights in the big house concerned him, but he was certain if there were any danger, his father would warn him somehow.

Following through with what he and Alex had agreed to do, he rapped with his knuckle on the woodpile. Peering out like a hunted rabbit, the agile black who called himself William carefully crawled out and hurried inside Thomas's cabin after him. Cold as the winter weather was, the shack offered everything the runaway prayed to find at each stop along "the Railroad": bread, water, a fire, and a blanket.

"How you goin' make it north without freezin' to death?" Thomas was not joking. The temperature was in the twenties, and he himself was cold all the time, even with the fire and roof and four walls. And he doubted it got any better between Virginia and Canada, which must be some thousand miles north.

"I make it," the man swore. He wasn't large or strong, at least in appearance, but there was something of the fox in his facial features. His dark eyes constantly darted this way and that, as if reacting to noises Thomas could not hear.

"Where you stop next?" Thomas asked, wondering if he himself was hardy enough to attempt such a journey. Maybe in the spring.

"Cain't say for sure. I stays with good folk in Washington, D.C., soon as I gits there."

"Colored folk?"

"White."

Thomas raised his eyebrows, his eyes wide and doubting. "You trust white folk?"

William nodded. "Got no choice. I got to."

Thomas slowly nodded his head. He knew what William meant: It was trust them or die a slave. The thought of both made his blood boil. "Where you runnin' to finally?"

"Toronto, Canada," William said. The way he spoke, Thomas figured it was down the road a good, long piece. "All men is free in Canada, black and white."

"How you gonna find the way? Follow the railroad tracks?"

William looked at Thomas as if he must be joking.

"The white men watches the trains too close. I follows the Drinkin' Gourd. Up in the sky. Didn't your daddy teach you the stars? The stars lead north. You jes walk at 'em."

Thomas could understand how you could walk toward a light on a hill in front of you, but how could you follow a star a million miles up in the sky?

"You been real kind," William said. "I be gone 'fore daybreak."

Thomas nodded. That was the bargain. "My mama wrapped some biscuits in this for you." He handed William something in a bandanna.

The runaway looked away suddenly, staring at the plank wall as though he could see through it to the hillside beyond the cabin. He must have thought he'd heard the horses of a slave patrol nearby. "Canada a big country. Bigger than two Virginias."

In the flickering firelight, Thomas's tall muscular frame tensed, and his eyes glistened with an angry determination. When he'd learned about his parents' involvement with the Underground Railroad, he'd laughed out loud. "How's a bunch a nigger slaves gonna get each other free, Mama?" But now he saw. And he knew he'd get away, too. But his mama had been right; he had to keep a low profile if he didn't want them all to end up hangin' from a tree. He'd kept his tongue on Twin Pines for twenty-five years; he could wait another few months. But not much longer.

They shook hands firmly. William's hand was so cold that it sent a chill through Thomas's body.

Thomas slept fitfully. An hour before dawn, he awoke and looked toward the fire, now dead. The area William had occupied in front of it was empty. He was gone.

"That's one," he said to himself, closing his eyes. Keep nearby, Lord, he prayed. I'll be needin' you.

CHAPTER 6

JACOB LIFTED HIS head from the book he was reading, a military history of Napoleon, and listened to the sudden bustle in the entrance hallway of the house. At first he was perplexed by the sounds of greetings and of bags being deposited. Then it came to him. Of course. How stupid of him to forget.

Since childhood, Caitlin had come to Twin Pines to visit Martha for a few days every season. But her timing this year was oddly embarrassing. The visit would last only a day or two, for she would have to return to Stuart Hall in time for the final preparations for their Epiphany

Ball. Jacob couldn't help but wonder if Dr. Stuart had allowed the brief visit with some ulterior purpose in mind.

Jacob swallowed. Closing the volume, he rose and went to greet her.

Charles chuckled, rubbing his legs to get some circulation going. "I, for one, am glad to see her under the same roof with Jacob at any time. It's a good sign, don't you agree?"

Anna yielded to her husband with a nod, but harbored other suspicions and had done so since the Christmas Eve gala, when she had caught Caitlin looking at Ethan in a manner that ought to have been reserved for her eldest son. She could see no good coming from such sentiments, and dreaded another meeting that might nurture them.

When her husband had finished stimulating his immobile legs, he sat back with a groan, his signal that she should replace the bedclothes. She responded by spreading the linen and quilts evenly over him before descending to the parlor, where Jacob and Martha were entertaining Caitlin. Only the Lord himself knew where Ethan might be, and for once, Anna was relieved by his absence.

A moment later, as she entered the parlor, she was doubly relieved to see that Jacob and Caitlin were seated together on the settee, while Martha perched next to them on one of the wingback chairs. Caitlin looked radiant as usual, in a blue gown of shirred wool. One look at her son reassured her that he was appropriately impressed.

To Anna's astonishment, no sooner had she sat down in a chair opposite them than Caitlin began apologizing for Ethan's ill treatment by the fire-eaters. Anna hastened to dismiss her apology. "It was hardly your doing, dear."

"I appreciate your kindness, ma'am," Caitlin replied, "but Daddy stirs up the kind of hate that leads to such ugly events. I do apologize for my father's intemperance in this regard."

Jacob thought it extraordinary that a daughter would

dare say such a thing with or without her father's assent. He bet that old Dr. Stuart would give the girl a good tongue-lashing if he ever found out. Again, Jacob was puzzled: What prompted her to act with such brazenness? Yet he admired her courage. He would find it a task to cross a man as stubborn in his views as George Stuart. How could he ever hope to understand such a woman?

Caitlin passed the remainder of the first day of her visit with Martha. Lively as Martha was, she had few friends, and little occasion to visit in Albemarle County. She cherished Caitlin as one does that special soul who listens without judging or laughing cruelly. Through the afternoon, and hidden away in Martha's room after supper, they discussed their unfulfilled passions. Or rather, Martha did. Caitlin allowed Martha to speak undisturbed. She was shocked by her friend's undisguised interest in Brett Tyler, but for the most part kept her opinion to herself. She didn't have the clarity of soul to condemn Martha's feelings, nor to express her own passions.

Later on, as Martha lay reading in her bed, Caitlin excused herself and hurried downstairs and into the kitchen. There she found Clara, who was awaiting her. Caitlin took the biscuits Clara offered her, then spoke hurriedly, in a hushed tone. "A second passenger is en route from South Carolina. Expect him tonight or tomorrow."

A minute later Caitlin entered Martha's spacious bedroom and gladly surrendered the biscuit to Martha, who confessed to being "famished."

"Love makes me hungry," she confessed to Caitlin. "Just reading about it, I mean," she added, checking her friend's serious face for a reaction. Caitlin failed to notice the veiled reference to Brett Tyler. Instead, her dark eyes took on a distant glow as she visualized the scene that would take place in the slave quarters when a young black man on the run from slavery would softly rap on Thomas's door and pray that the right person answered.

Caitlin added a few silent prayers to the ones she and Martha said together, kneeling side by side, and after she retired to the guest room she always occupied, next to Martha's, she was unable to get to sleep until long after the moon had risen high in the nighttime sky.

The conversation at the breakfast table the following morning was light and cheerful. Ice, along with Clara's herb poultices, had helped to reduce the swelling in Ethan's face. What surprised him most about the beating—besides the pain which still lingered—was that no one except Martha was interested in Brett Tyler's role in the drama. His father had not mentioned a word to him about it, while Jacob used the event to berate him for attending the meeting in the first place, as though that ignorant fool of a fire-eater had been justified in giving him a beating. His mother limited her interest to his health, asking Clara to press his wounds with poultices several times a day more than was necessary.

And then there was Caitlin. She hadn't said a word to him, about his beating or anything else.

Jacob, on the other hand, seemed particularly animated by Caitlin's presence. "These last two days with Ethan's swollen jaw shut tight as a drum have proved to be a positive asset to Twin Pines and to the Southern cause in general," Jacob joked, watching Caitlin for a response. She smiled, quickly turning her attention to Ethan, who met her gaze evenly. He seemed to have missed his brother's jest completely, a failure that irked Jacob to no end.

After breakfast, Jacob hurried to attend to the affairs of the estate, and Anna joined her husband upstairs. Martha suggested that she and Caitlin go riding, but Caitlin begged off, saying it was too cold. Martha hurried away, perturbed. Caitlin felt badly as she watched her friend leave the dining room, offended, to do some needlework in the parlor. But she did not feel up to another of Martha's passionate sessions of sharing secrets. Her own were too many and too dangerous.

So it was that midmorning Caitlin came upon Ethan reading in the library. He sat in a leather chair, his chin resting in the palm of his hand. The faraway look on his face was accented by the bruise on his left cheek and the cuts that scarred his temple and forehead. It struck Caitlin as doubtfully wistful.

"What are you reading?" she asked. The volume was small and looked oddly familiar.

"Wordsworth," he replied, raising his eyes to meet hers. She must have started. "What is it?" he asked. "Does Wordsworth frighten you? Surely not. He's a nature lover, you know."

Caitlin nodded, slipping into the chair next to his. "I know Mr. Wordsworth's verse quite well," she ventured. A log in the fire popped, and she jumped nervously, then colored as she heard Ethan chuckle. "I did not realize you were a poetry lover," he said.

She hesitated before saying anything more. Why did she have the impression that they were not discussing Wordsworth or poetry, but something else? The hall clock chimed the quarter-hour. A pot dropped in the kitchen, and after the clatter subsided, Caitlin heard Clara berating a house girl, her melodic voice surprisingly sharp. "I enjoy a good poem, as I do a ride in the country or the odor of the magnolia blossoms in June."

Ethan set down the book of verse and pivoted in the chair to face her squarely. In her blue dress and shawl, she appeared small next to him, delicate. But all women did. "I must ask you about the performance you gave yesterday. My brother and mother speak of nothing else."

She felt her blood rise. "Performance? You mean the apology?" He nodded. She looked away, toward the fire and the shelves on the east wall of the library. "It was something I had to do."

"For your father?" he inquired.

"No! For me." She said this with no pride, but rather in an embarrassed manner. "As I'm sure you know, my father would hardly approve of what I said."

"And if he were to know?"

She faced him again, her brown eyes flaring. "Do you enjoy prosecuting me? Is there nothing else to speak of but fathers and daughters and their mutual duties?"

Ethan was taken aback by the vehemence of Caitlin's response. He ought to beg her pardon, he knew. But he couldn't, for her anger became her. Instead, he nodded to her as a fencing opponent might when granting *"Touché!"* to his adversary for a particularly well executed thrust.

She stood and stepped to one of the bookcases where, her back to him, she examined the cover of a book. "You enjoy Shakespeare?" Ethan asked.

She spoke without turning around, and he watched her back, the wool shawl over her shoulders, the combs that restrained her blond hair, for some sign of her disposition. "My father says that a well-read man knows the Bible, Shakespeare, and Blackstone."

Ethan laughed. "Spoken like the attorney he is. But you don't much resemble a well-read man to me."

Caitlin froze at his jest; his implication was clear. She returned the leather-bound volume of *Romeo and Juliet* to its place on the shelf and walked wordlessly toward the hallway. She left the room in some agitation, bumping bluntly into Anna Parson, who drew back and looked from her to Ethan questioningly. With an embarrassed curtsy, Caitlin excused herself and hurried upstairs to her room. Anna looked at Ethan. "Your father would like to see you," she told him with no hint of emotion. When he failed to rise from the chair, she added, "Now."

His father looked well today, better than usual, in fact. Clad in a nightshirt of Irish linen and lace that Anna had given him for Christmas, he looked presentable, and the coughing that had been plaguing him seemed to have let up, however temporarily, perhaps due to the dryness that accompanied the prolonged chill of winter.

The old man bristled. "You might as well be dead, owing a debt to Tyler. More than likely that scoundrel arranged the entire affair himself. Doesn't his arrival at just the critical moment seem fishy? Think about it, son."

Ethan tried to contain himself. He should have known this was coming sooner or later. "Daddy, he shot two men. Their families could be after him right now. They could have shot him dead. But for Tyler, I could be dead—"

Ethan's father pounded the bedside table emphatically with the palm of his hand. It was a politician's gesture, and Charles wielded it well. "Son, that's nonsense. He is using you and your gullibility to get into the Parson family's good graces. I cannot allow it. Surely you see that."

"Daddy," Ethan said softly, struggling to keep a rein on his anger, "you are dead wrong. It was our Lord who brought him down that road, not the Devil."

Charles Parson snorted derisively. "Ethan, Beelzebub himself would have to roll in the pigsty for a week to stink like your hero's daddy does every day of the week."

Ethan raised his voice, overcome with frustration. "Brett Tyler saved my life. His daddy is not involved, and neither are you. Give the man his due!"

"His due! Son, that rapscallion is due the same respect I pay a copperhead!"

"You are old and sick and foolish!" Ethan shouted. His father winced and flushed. For a moment, he was unable to speak, shaking and stirring as if to rise from the bed. Ethan could not take back the punishing words, nor could he beg the old man's forgiveness. What would it take to command his father's respect? "I'm not Jacob!" he shouted, catching his father unguarded.

"And you never shall be him!" screamed Charles. His haggard voice sickened Ethan more than it frightened him. "How much more will you shame us?"

Ethan stormed from his father's room before he could say anything else he might regret. He ran down the stairs and outside to the curing barn, nestled in a hollow near a stand of magnolias. Storming into the now-empty outbuilding, Ethan slammed the wide door shut and leaned against it to catch his breath. To think he had levied such insults in defense of a rogue who—but for his kindness on the eve of the new year—had never shown Ethan or his family anything but contempt. But he knew that Tyler was but the focus of the deeper, more far-reaching arguments that separated him from Jacob and his father.

A rush of footsteps on the path from the house tore Ethan from his thoughts. Opening the door a crack, Ethan saw a flutter of blue from the side of his eye. Caitlin Stuart. Peeking around the door of the outbuilding, he watched as she hurried toward the slave quarters, a bundle hidden in her crossed arms. Ministering to some sick field hand, he figured.

More from curiosity than concern, he followed her at a distance and saw her pause outside Thomas's cabin and rap on the door three times. Ethan ducked behind a tree as the cabin door opened and she entered. Rather than embarrass her comforting a slave on someone else's property, he stood by the oak, idly watching fair-weather clouds rush by, driven by a steady north wind. He was chilled and about to give up the vigil, when he heard a door squeak. Sure enough, it was Thomas's, and Caitlin emerged from the small cabin, carrying nothing. He waited until she was but a few feet away from him before jumping out in front of her.

He was laughing when he said, "Boo!" but the terror in her eyes as she jumped back, nearly losing her balance, made him regret the joke.

"Ethan Parson, you should be shot!" she cried, regaining her composure. "Are you spying on me?" Her look of apprehension was genuine. How much does he suspect? she wondered.

Ethan stopped grinning. "I saw you going down there. Is one of the hands sick?"

"Yes," she said quickly. "It's Thomas. He has a fever." Her eyes darted up the oak from which Ethan had accosted her, and she watched the branches bend in the north wind. Ethan had seen such shiftiness in debates a

Harvard; often it betrayed a lie. But why would she lie to him? Ethan regarded her with new interest.

"Well, I trust he's better now," he said. He would not confront her now, when she was so skittish. "It seems all you do is tend to the sick and battered."

"You Parsons see to it that there are plenty enough!" she replied, smiling. He could see that she was relieved not to be cross-examined.

Together, they walked back to the house, and once inside, had Clara serve them some fresh-baked biscuits and ham with tea in the parlor. They chewed the biscuits in silence, each studying the other.

Ethan had no right to imagine Caitlin a kindred soul, yet it bothered him that she would tell him a lie when he was turning his back upon his own family in order to heed the truth. She was looking down into her teacup, obviously flustered, had not been herself around him since her arrival, in fact. He suspected that she understood his sympathies, if she did not agree. Her apology, that scene in the library . . . Obviously her opinions were strong. Perhaps too strong for the daughter of Dr. Stuart.

He continued to gaze at her averted eyes and pale face. Of course he had no evidence, but he surmised that Caitlin was smuggling books to the slaves, an act punishable by a jail sentence in Virginia. Why did she not tell him? Was it possible that she did not understand that he, too, defied the society that surrounded them? That he would not judge her harshly, as others might?

Caitlin could not bear to remain under his penetrating gaze for another moment. The effect he was having on her was too strong. She was still shivering from the shock of his tall form jumping out before her like a reproachful spirit. She must not reveal even the slightest hint of what she had been doing, not even to Ethan. The aid that she and Clara's family were offering was too precious. Exposure of their secret would lead to their sale. Not even the Parsons could put up with such betrayal on the part of their bondsmen.

Clara entered the parlor, laughing to herself as she

watched them. There sat two people as alike as two slices of the same loaf of bread, and they couldn't find one word to say to each other. She shook her head, bending to replenish the tea service with steaming hot water, but said nothing.

Inside his cabin, Thomas was in a quandary. "You want to go back?" he asked the man again.

The tall, sturdy black man slowly nodded. "I cain't go no further. My feet too tired and my heart ain't in it. I'm goin' back to my mama." He swatched at his sleeve, a stubborn set to his chin.

Thomas looked at the man in speechless anger. Here he was, helping the man get what he himself wanted most, and the damn fool wouldn't take it. "But you go back now, they maybe cut off a foot."

The runaway shook his head vigorously. "Master Tyson ain't cruel. I go back now, he welcome me. But I wait another week, he gonna whip my ass bad."

Nothing Thomas said could sway the man. Here he sat, holding provisions for a week, food Miss Caitlin herself had risked her safety to bring to the man, and the fool was too scared to go any farther. "Whereabouts your family up north?"

"My cousin in Philadelphia."

"Then go there! You be free! The man won't find you there." Thomas was running out of sympathy; he just wanted the man to leave. "You threatenin' all our lives, you turn tail and go back now. The man want to know where you been and who you talk to. What you gonna tell him?"

"I don't say nothin'. I jes' got to git home." He rested his strong callused hands stubbornly on his hips. "I's too cold and tired to carry on."

Thomas had an idea. "Jes' wait till dark. You spotted 'round here an' one of the slave patrols string you up sure."

The runaway gulped. He would stay put. For now.

At dusk Thomas slipped quietly in the back door of

Twin Pines and tapped his mother on the shoulder. Ordinarily he didn't come into the main house unless summoned by the Parsons, but Jacob was still in town drilling the militia, and Miss Anna was always up with Mister Charles at this time, or in the parlor sewing. He risked no reproof from the others.

"Tell Daddy we got us one scared nigger in my house." Clara didn't acknowledge what he'd said, but he knew his mother had heard. Thomas hurried back to the slave quarters.

Within fifteen minutes of his visit, Alex's imposing black figure filled the doorway of his son's cabin. He shut the door behind him. "You going north or not?" he asked the man directly.

The runaway slowly shook his head, shivering. "It's too far. I ain't got no chance. Word's out on me already. I worth a thousand dollars to the man. . . ."

Without saying a word, Alex reached into his coat pocket and pulled out a pistol. He drew a bead on the man's heart. Thomas gasped. "Now you listen to me. They's a million of us wants to be free and cain't git there yet. You can. And now you try to tell me you too *afraid*? Well, Mr. Runaway Slave, I got to do my duty and shoot you dead here and now." Unblinking, Alex cocked the pistol.

The runaway's sturdy frame shook violently. "You cain't kill me! You sposed to help me!"

"And you sposed to be gettin' yo'self free. So git with it, man! Don't be wastin' my time and riskin' my family's life for nothin'!"

For a minute, Thomas feared the man would prove too weak, that he might force his father to pull the trigger. But in a rush of emotion, the runaway hid his face in his hands and wept. Alex released the hammer on the pistol. "You gonna make it. I see it in your eyes. Fear ain't nothin' but your travelin' companion, am I right?"

Thomas was amazed to see the black man renew his conviction.

"Keep him warm till he go," Alex whispered to him. Thomas nodded in agreement.

* * *

Jacob rode home on the same dirt road that had been the scene of Ethan's beating just days before. After three hours of drilling and marching and leading the men of his volunteer regiment, the Albemarle Rifles, Jacob felt capable of taking on a rampaging gang of troublemakers single-handedly. He was proud of his men, who were without exception fine horsemen and exceptional shots, and the discipline they showed gave him hope that an army of the South was more than a pipe dream. Drilling beside them in a field adjoining the university were the Monticello Guard, university students. They, too, looked good, and moved as a unit in cadence to the shouted orders of their captain.

Upon returning to Twin Pines, he greeted his mother and retired to the library to plan his regiment's next military exercise. It was the first evening in a long time that Jacob Parson came home with his heart full and his mind at ease.

But just above Jacob's room of quiet retreat, Martha Parson and Caitlin Stuart stood vigil over another dangerous situation: the uncertain hearts that fluttered within their bosoms.

"I must put the rascal out of my mind. It is simply a matter of will," Martha said. She concentrated, gritting her teeth. Then, after a moment's struggle, she collapsed into laughter, crying, "I must be mad! He's a Tyler! They're plain as dirt!"

Caitlin was genuinely worried for her friend. While she herself felt ashamed of the powerfully inappropriate emotions Ethan evoked in her, at least he was a gentleman. But to cast an eye upon a Tyler! She had to talk some sense into Martha.

"You're feeling the first stirrings of desire," she explained, ignoring the warmth that often ignited her own secret parts. "But you must overrule your heart with your head. That's why God placed us in dominion over the animals. We rule our passions."

Martha grinned, tilting her head mischievously. "What if I don't want to control this passion? What if I want to surrender to it?"

Caitlin drew back, aghast at what she had just heard. "Don't talk that way! Such thoughts would kill your mama and daddy. Why, your daddy would sooner marry you off to a rooster than to that Tyler scamp, and you know it!" Martha jumped from the bed and danced a waltz around her four-poster bed as Caitlin watched, wondering what devilment she was under.

"He makes my blood warm, like wine," Martha sang, running in circles.

"Martha Parson, you stop talking nonsense this minute! The Tylers have bad blood, and that's that. You set your sights on someone else, on that Earley boy or Noah Chesterfield and—"

Martha stopped her dance to glare good-naturedly at Caitlin. "You are a guest in my house and my dearest friend. I won't have you acting like my mama!"

Blushing, Caitlin returned to her guest bedroom and flung herself on the bed. She beat the feather pillows with her fists, tears leaking from her eyes. Why was she trying to bring some sense to her dear friend when she herself seemed destined for perdition? It ws just as well that her stay was brief—she was leaving the following afternoon—for the torment of her future was overwhelming.

Martha slept poorly, awakening often to the vision of strange faces in her window and threatening shadows gathering at her bedside. She finally sat up in bed, lit a candle, and immersed herself in the verse of Victor Hugo.

CHAPTER 7

FOUR DAYS INTO the new year of 1861, which dawned with gloom and bitter winter weather, Jeffrey and Julia Keyes arrived by carriage from the Charlottesville train depot. The entire Parson family, with the exception of Charles, gathered on the steps of Twin Pines to meet them.

Ethan blew into his hands and flexed them for warmth. He felt uncomfortably jittery. There, beyond the yard and the gate, the Keyeses' carriage was advancing up the curving lane toward them. At last, Julia and Jeffrey are here, he thought. It was their first visit to Virginia, he knew. Before now, the Keyeses had seen only free black men; no bondsmen. It suddenly struck Ethan as an odd perspective. Soon they would see what he had been telling them for years, that all Southerners were not alike, and that slavery bred uncomfortable bedfellows.

He noticed Jacob watching him closely. Try not to look so miserable, brother. You may like the Yankees despite yourself. "Our first guests from the North in years," he commented to no one in particular as the carriage came to a stop.

"And our last, no doubt," Jacob added, pulling the collar of his coat around his neck. He scowled at the black buggy as if expecting Lincoln himself to emerge. What gall to invite moralizing Yankees to their home during such times. Sometimes he wondered what, besides spite, motivated his little brother. He looked at Ethan, whose chiseled face bore an expression of restrained anticipation, ready to break into a grin at the sight of the Northerners. It infuriated Jacob. What had he done to deserve this dishonor? Were their father well, he would not allow it, Jacob reasoned; and neither should he. In a moment, the driver, a bondsman dressed in livery, would open the door and assist the unwelcome guests in stepping down. Very well, Jacob sighed, I shall play the genial host, provided they don't insult us. He had to admit, he was at least a little intrigued by the visit.

Anna Parson hugged herself against the cold beneath her shawl. She was shivering, and her breath made brief clouds in the frigid air before disappearing. "Mother, you should wait inside," Jacob told her. But Anna merely leaned forward to get a glimpse of Ethan's friends. They were the first guests at Twin Pines from Boston since her brother Gerald had visited fifteen years ago, when Charles was still whole and well. The memory saddened her. She took pride in Ethan's education at Harvard, which reminded her of Gerald. If Jeffrey Keyes had shared her son's experience there, if he had helped foster the independence and rebelliousness which characterized Ethan, permitting him an escape from the bitterness enshrouding Charles—and ever more frequently Jacob—he and his sister were genuinely welcome, in Anna's thoughts.

"Perhaps this visit will be educational," she commented to Jacob, but his countenance remained stiff and unyielding.

"Yes," he replied dryly, slapping his gloves together, "perhaps we shall heal the rift between North and South."

"Such bitterness does not suit you, Jacob," Anna scolded.

Jacob sank more deeply into his own thoughts.

Martha was eager to see what the Keyeses would look and talk like. She had heard that Yankees dressed in clothes appropriate for funerals at all times and that having fun was thought sinful in Boston. She herself had endured a good dose of that medicine, Martha thought, for no one would take the pounding in her heart seriously. Perhaps the Keyeses would. She was willing to embrace them as kindred spirits. Perhaps Julia would be her companion now that Caitlin had gone home. "Is she beautiful?" she asked Ethan.

Clara pushed back the curtain at the parlor window and watched impassively as the black carriage came to a halt and the driver descended to open the carriage door. The brother and sister from Boston were bound to be trouble. She and Alex and Thomas were in enough danger already, as Christ Himself knew. Clara hoped the white folks would be leaving soon.

"Yankees!" she muttered. "That's all we be needin'. Meddlin', sniffin' around folks from up north. Pooh!"

Stepping out of the carriage first was Jeffrey Keyes, a slender young man, elegantly dressed in a gray suit and carrying a cane and top hat. He nodded at the Parsons, turned back to the carriage, and extended his hand to his sister. Julia's beauty radiated from the quilt bundled around her for the chilly journey from town, and became even more striking as she stepped down from the carriage. At twenty-one, she was a good four or five inches taller than most women, and more serious looking.

Ethan hurried in front of Alex to greet the pair, and Jacob and his mother watched from the steps as they exchanged handshakes and hurried questions.

"Well, let's come inside before we freeze to death from this draft," Anna suggested. "Alex, please see to the guests' luggage."

Stepping into Twin Pines, Jeffrey Keyes took in the clock and bright pine of the front hall with the same intelligent curiosity with which he'd viewed the grounds from the entrance. Sighing dramatically, he exclaimed, "So this is the Parsonage!"

Jacob refused to acknowledge the remark, though it was obvious Ethan thought it quite clever. He noted with satisfaction that Keyes's handshake was weak and brief, the sign of a weak-willed man, and that their guest had a head cold. Jeffrey Keyes's sister, however, alarmed Jacob.

Julia Keyes was an auburn-haired beauty with thick locks that curled about her face and shone brightly even in the gray light of the wintry day. Her emerald eyes sparkled when she curtsied. Jacob sensed a sincerity in her greeting totally absent from her brother's. For one so tall, she was remarkably pretty. The long hand she had offered was alarmingly warm to the touch.

Once he was introduced to Martha, Jeffrey Keyes immediately began to describe their rail journey from Boston in great detail. Jacob took his mother's arm, having noted that Ethan was seeing to Julia Keyes, and listened with interest as Jeffrey told Martha of the riots they had witnessed in Baltimore and the war hysteria throughout the North.

After Jeffrey and Julia had settled in their rooms and changed from their traveling costumes, they joined the Parsons in the parlor for tea. Jeffrey Keyes described with alarming glee the North's preparations for war. "The North owns and operates seven of every ten miles of railroad track and four of every five factories. They outman the South four to one, unless you count the slaves." He turned pointedly toward Jacob. "Do you count the slaves?"

Without looking, Ethan could sense Jacob stiffening. He turned to face his friend with a look that told him he had better tread more carefully. Taking a gulp of his steaming tea, he set about trying to establish the conversation on a less personal level. "I doubt seriously that any bondsmen will fight for the South," he ventured, wondering what his brother's reaction would be.

"Bondsmen. Is that what you call slaves down here? It sounds so much more genteel, doesn't it, Julia?" Jeffrey asked his sister.

Julia was well aware of the crude offense her brother was leveling at their hosts. He was a lovable fool but, especially in such sensitive circumstances, a fool nonetheless. It was time to change the topic of discussion. "Your brother has described the beauty of Twin Pines to us so accurately that I feel as if I've been here before," she said, gracefully addressing Jacob.

There was a honey to her voice that soothed over the indignity of Jeffrey's observations.

"I could live nowhere else," Jacob said honestly.

"Where else have you been?" Jeffrey asked quickly. "Have you seen Rome in the spring? Or Florence at dawn in the autumn? The light there is ethereal, sent down from Heaven above."

"You believe in Heaven, then?" Jacob was bold enough to inquire.

Jeffrey seemed taken aback. "It was but a figure of speech . . ."

"Then you do not believe in Heaven—"

Anna turned sharply toward her son. "Jacob, where are your manners? Let's show our guests the rest of the house before we inquire deeply into their religion, shall we?"

Jacob accepted his mother's intercession gracefully and led the tour of the house. The Keyeses seemed most impressed by the Parson family portraits hung on the stairway wall, and the view from their rooms.

"It is breathtaking." Julia sighed, unable to take her eyes off the blue peaks standing like great teeth to the west.

"The Blue Ridge Mountains are very old," Jacob explained as the others continued the tour downstairs. "They have been worn down by time and the elements." He found himself to be very nervous, alone with the beautiful young woman. It wasn't quite proper, though certainly nothing indecorous had taken place.

"Still, there's a magnificence to them. They appear to be blue," she observed.

Jacob had to smile. "Daddy says it's because they're trying to swallow the sky."

Julia nodded. "I should like to meet your father."

Charles Parson took an immediate dislike to Jeffrey Keyes, whose lacquered hair and narrow eyes personified Charles's worst imaginings of the untrustworthy Yankee. After a moment of awkward silence, Charles inquired about their journey and their impressions of Virginia. Jacob could see that his father felt ill at ease, confined to his bed amidst the roomful of young people perched easily around him.

"I find Virginia beautiful," Julia exclaimed. "I've been to the Berkshires, naturally, but your Blue Ridge Mountains are so . . . How shall I put it? They're welcoming!" She smiled, pleased to find the right word.

Even his father seemed to be captivated by the radiance of her smile, Jacob noted. And a moment later he paid her the ultimate compliment, saying, "You should have been born in Virginia, young lady. Then you'd be damn near perfect." Julia blushed, but everyone laughed, pleased to see Charles in such good cheer.

"Of course, Maryland lies in turmoil," Jeffrey added, looking at Charles as if he were to blame.

"Maryland can't decide if she's Southern or not," Charles explained gruffly. "My guess is, she'll follow Virginia's lead. What do you say, Jacob?"

Surprised to be addressed, Jacob quickly agreed with his father.

As the others spoke, Ethan had been leaning against the wall next to one of the windows. These gatherings in his father's room inevitably made him feel ill at ease, and he was particularly so now. Father had not mentioned their argument of two days earlier, and neither had he, remaining silent in the background.

Now, he automatically started to say something, for he was less sure of Maryland's Southern sympathies, but he caught himself and backed down. Jacob would agree with their father's every word, and that was all the old man wanted. He would listen to no other arguments, certainly not from his second son.

Anna signaled that it was time for the visitors to leave her husband's room.

"Why is it that every time a good argument gets cooking, my wife intervenes to douse the flames?" griped Charles. He nodded good-bye to the Keyeses, asking Jacob to remain behind when all the others had left. The last one out, Ethan paused at the door questioningly, but

Charles ignored his interest. When the door had closed, Charles reached for the humidor of Virginia cigars kept in a cedar box at his bedside, then addressed his son in a conspiratorial tone as he smelled the rich brown cigar and bit the tip off.

"Son, watch the skinny little rat like a hawk. He smells like a spy to me."

So his father shared his opinion of Jeffrey Keyes. "I can't very well tie a cow bell to his ankle, Father. He is our guest."

"Just see that he doesn't spend much time alone with Ethan. Your brother is easily influenced, and his opinions about the institution have left him unbalanced." The old man snickered, shooting Jacob a rheumy glare. "That Keyes girl could get just about anything she wants from a man, eh? You suppose she and Ethan are spoken for?"

Jacob felt suddenly unsettled. "He hasn't said a word to me to indicate—"

His father heaved back his head and laughed, dismissing Jacob's words with a gesture of his flaccid hand. "Shoot, son, it ain't what Ethan says that counts, it's what he don't say! You ought to know that by now. I'd say he's sweet on her. We must ensure that it does not come to pass." Charles was a little taken with her himself, but that didn't lessen the inacceptability of the matter. "You haven't forgotten about your duty at the Stuarts' ball?"

How could he have forgotten something that preyed on his mind daily? "I have not forgotten, Daddy."

"Good. Fine. Now, go see to your brother. And watch that Lucifer Keyes like a hawk, eh?"

Jacob left his father's room doubly disturbed. He had already determined that he would monitor that glib rogue Keyes's movements to whatever extent possible, but disliked the filial duty that now made his own initiative but another responsibility to his father.

Furthermore, the notion of Julia Keyes marrying Ethan all but made his stomach turn. In these times, it would be unthinkable. They made a handsome couple. Too handsome. And they had spoken with animation upon her arrival. They seemed to like each other a good deal. There was something about this that troubled Jacob.

Jacob excused himself early from the dinner table and sought refuge in the library. He set about studying plantation accounts, but the figures swam in his head like the meaningless hieroglyphics he had seen in one of Ethan's textbooks.

He heard the door to the library open and looked up, expecting to see Ethan or Alex, but certainly not Julia Keyes. The cut of her gray dress was simple, the skirt not so full as those Martha usually wore. She smiled radiantly. Jacob swallowed and rose to his feet with difficulty.

"Miss Keyes, are you lost?"

She stepped into the room, taking in the leather volumes and dusty smell of old books, and shook her head. "I came to apologize for my brother. This journey we have undertaken is, at best, awkward. You see, my brother is a fervent abolitionist. Coming here, he feels like Daniel in the lion's den."

"Then you have read the Old Testament?" Jacob inquired playfully.

Julia Keyes nodded. "Our mother was very religious. It's upon such grounds that we oppose your institution."

"But Paul himself upholds slavery, telling slaves to serve their masters."

She acknowledged this with a nod, then quietly said, "Shakespeare wrote that the Devil himself could cite scripture for his purpose."

Jacob turned red. She was learned and intelligent, and brazen enough to compare him to the Devil in his own home.

But Julia was quick to explain. "I meant no offense. I only wished to say that the Scripture is a mystery to us, and that our interpretations are colored by our times."

Jacob accepted her apology with a nod. "Many would argue with you, but I shall not. What do you intend to do on your visit?" His eyes locked upon Julia's neck, graceful as a swan's.

Jacob was relieved when Martha appeared in the

doorway, in a breathless splash of white and ribbons, flashing Jacob and Julia a bright look. Her artful cunning was a trait he lacked completely when in the company of women. And just how cunning was Miss Keyes? Jacob wondered.

"Ethan says we are all to report to the parlor for charades. There, my duty is done." Martha nodded to them and disappeared.

"Is there any creature on God's earth more infuriating than a seventeen-year-old sister?" Jacob wondered aloud.

"I find her captivating. Ethan says she reads French novels. I must say, I am surprised you approve."

There it was again. Direct, yet without offense. "I do not, but she argues, and I suppose she's right about this if nothing else. It is the one vice we allow her." He paused, and Julia smiled graciously, gesturing toward the hallway. "Shall we?" Jacob said. Taking Julia's hand in the crook of his arm, he led her across the broad hallway and into the parlor. A fire blazed in the hearth on the west wall, and two lamps had been lighted. The touch of her on his arm was exquisite; her face was long and slender, but delicate, smooth, and unlined. Julia Keyes has never done a day of women's work in her life, Jacob surmised. The Keyeses were obviously a family of some means. He ought to hate her for her views, yet he could not bring himself to despise or even to dislike her.

Ethan had already warned his family how "devastatingly proficient" Jeffrey and Julia were at charades, and Martha insisted that the brother and sister be split up, one on each team. Thus, Julia, Jacob, and Martha opposed Ethan, Jeffrey, and Anna.

Anna was delighted by the gaiety of the evening. It had been some time since her family had seemed truly festive. Even Jacob had lost some of the hardness he'd recently displayed. She had expected the Keyeses to be dour and tight-lipped, as had been other Yankees. Instead, she found the girl enchanting, and Jeffrey amusing, if thoughtlessly overbearing.

The first round passed quickly, with both teams reduced to helpless laughter at Martha's attempt to portray "Spare the rod, spoil the child." Ethan joked that they could play till doomsday and no mortal would ever figure out what she was up to. It almost made Anna forget the somber duties that awaited her in her husband's room this evening and every evening until his passing.

As the second round began, Jacob leaned his ear to Jeffrey's lips to hear the book title they had chosen for him to portray. Anna, seeing his face turn quite pale, leaned forward and asked if he was all right.

"Mother, did you approve this choice?" he asked, his voice trembling with anger.

She admitted that she did not know what the chosen title was, and glanced in consternation from Ethan to Jeffrey.

"It *is* just a book, after all," Ethan suggested smugly.

"*Uncle Tom's Cabin* is *not* a book. It is a disgrace!" Jacob stormed out of the room. And so ended the first evening of the Keyeses' visit.

Julia Keyes lingered outside the door to the room the Parsons had prepared for her, whispering to her brother in strident tones.

"You'll jeopardize everything with such stupid tricks!" she hissed.

Her brother reacted as if struck. "But did you see how Ethan stood up for us?"

"For you, you mean. And at what price? Jacob despises you already. If you don't contain yourself, we shall have missed an important opportunity to advance the cause."

Julia watched her brother as he shielded his candle with his hand and strode down the hall to his own chamber. Jeffrey still judged all Southerners as being as ignorant as those portrayed in the books he read. *Uncle Tom's Cabin*, indeed. He was often foolish, but his passions were well placed, and he was exposed to many influential friends and political societies from which she, as a woman, was barred. She knew her brother well; he would not go too far if she could help it.

Jacob, however, was a puzzle. He was obviously distrustful of her every move, yet she sensed a kind, generous side to him. Something in her stirred at the thought of Ethan's smaller, older bother. His serious face and piercing eyes belied a frightened little boy she suspected lay hidden within the man. That could prove an asset.

With some effort, she turned her thoughts to Ethan, who was, after all, the object of their visit.

The pain kept Charles awake most of the night. "It's that damn Keyes," he moaned to Anna.

Anna hushed her husband. "It's your back, dear, not our guests. Shall I give you something for the pain?"

"No, no more laudanum. I'm man enough to endure pain. Just explain to me why on God's green earth we have two spies from Boston—"

"Charles! Stop talking such nonsense! They're here at Ethan's invitation, and we shall receive them graciously. Shall I roll you over?"

Charles grunted his assent, and with a good deal of effort, found a more comfortable position. His snores were a lullaby to Anna.

Perhaps he was right about Jeffrey Keyes. Why would he insult his hosts so flagrantly if not to send a message to Ethan that such were their beliefs? Anna feared what Ethan might do under their influence. She worried, too, that the Keyeses might be right, that perhaps slavery *was* an evil and that she and her family risked an eternity in perdition for their transgressions.

Anna retired to her own chamber, falling into an uneasy slumber. Very late that night, she prayed for the safety of her family as well as for the redemption of their souls.

Very early the next morning, Jacob rode off into town. He didn't like the idea of leaving Ethan and Jeffrey Keyes alone all day with no supervision, but he couldn't deny it was a pleasure to leave behind the smirking face of Jeffrey, who seemed to have come to Twin Pines solely to gall Jacob. But the wide-eyed beauty of his sister's face lingered in his mind.

He tightened his grip on the reins. It was time to send some wires to South Carolina and Alabama to learn what moves, if any, the Federals had made to prevent the states from seizing the arsenals of weapons and munitions they held. He also carried a poster announcing the weekly meeting of his militia, the Albemarle Rifles, "due to the emergency situation in neighboring states."

"What shall we wear to the ball tomorrow? It is simply *the* social event of the new year." Martha emerged from her closet, nearly buried in the folds of the three gowns hanging from her arms. With a bright look at Julia, who sat on one edge of her bed, Martha said, "I do hope there will be talk of war . . . so long as the men don't become so animated that they ignore us!"

Martha had dominated Julia's time from the moment both had arisen. Julia was amused by Martha's endless fascination with her dress and speech. She had never known anyone quite so naive, but the girl's passionate nature was enchanting. Of course, she would not wish to possess Martha's naive sense of romanticism—one that seemed to be encouraged by the plantation system, which raised its women in such a fantasy world of privilege and isolation.

Her own ungainly height had always made her feel uncomfortable with the sort of primping and coquetry that was Martha's main source of amusement. She preferred to be of practical use, to be of purpose to the world. Yet she was not immune to the charm of her young acquaintance's ways, nor ignorant of the true enthusiasm that shone in her every move. Martha's heart was in the right place. Perhaps in time she could be brought to a deeper understanding of the world around her.

* * *

Ethan declined Jeffrey's request that he lead him on a tour of the slave quarters, "to see how slaves really live."

"This is not a zoological garden, Jeffrey," he explained patiently. "It's their home."

"Not by choice," Keyes countered.

Ethan forced himself to remain quiet as Alex served their coffee. Once he had left the room he commented tersely, "The bondsmen on Twin Pines have some privacy, too."

All through breakfast Jeffrey harangued Ethan until eventually Ethan relented. Donning their coats, and Jeffrey his walking stick, they went out into the cold morning air.

The dozen wooden cabins housing the thirty slaves who worked the plantation were identical. It struck Jeffrey as significant that the Negroes' shacks were down in a hollow, not visible from the grand manor house in which he stood. Southerners must have planned their homes that way. The pine cabins were set in two rows, constructed with lumber provided by the Parsons but built by the slaves themselves. Behind the cabins each family had a garden plot of their own, though they wouldn't be planted for a month or so yet.

Jeffrey closed his gray broadcloth jacket over his shirt and eyed the weed-covered squares of earth in surprise. "They're required to give the produce to you?" he asked.

Ethan shook his head. It seemed his friend simply would not believe the field hands might be treated fairly. "No, we buy it at a fair market price, or someone else does. Or the family keeps it." He crossed his arms over his broad chest. "Why do you ask only negative questions?"

At that time of year when the weather did not permit them to work the fields, the bondsmen's days were occupied with such chores as repairing the equipment, chopping wood, and maintaining the grounds. Several men were working on the hillside not far from the cabins, clearing brush that had fallen from the trees during recent storms. Jeffrey approached them, Ethan following reluctantly behind him.

Keyes was not surprised by the deference shown the owner's son by the slaves. But when he tried to probe their feelings toward slavery and Twin Pines, no one would talk to him.

"I might as well ask a stone," Keyes said, exasperated.

"Jeffrey, you cannot expect them to utter a word of truth to you," Ethan explained patiently. "You're a stranger, a Northerner—just the kind of man they are taught to fear and mistrust."

The somber faces of the bondsmen revealed nothing at all.

As they were walking back through the row of cabins toward the serpentine path that led up the hillside to the house, Jeffrey sprung the trap, clumsy as the device was.

"Ethan, my sister and I have come not just to extend our greetings to you and your family. As do you, we recognize the difficulty of our visit at a time when such gestures are so dangerous." Jeffrey paused to twirl the cane he carried, as if to draw Ethan's concentration from the gravity of his words. "We have come to ask your help in a just cause, a cause I know you support in your heart."

Ethan felt his heart pounding like a hammer against the anvil of his chest. "What do you mean, Jeffrey?" he asked quietly.

Keyes steered them up the path. He appeared cold and uncomfortable as they walked for several minutes before he replied. "I mean we . . . the abolitionist cause . . . we need information. If there is to be a war, and everyone agrees that there is, information will be as vital as munitions, don't you agree?"

As his friend spoke, Ethan stared straight ahead at the house that had been his home for twenty-one years. Did Jeffrey know the birds would be singing, that the sky would be clear, and the mountains in view when he tested their four-year friendship? How long had Keyes planned for this moment?

"Think of your unique position," Jeffrey continued. "Your brother directs Albemarle County's militia. He's sure to receive a commission. Your father is privy to the thoughts and intents of the great minds of the South. You can serve justice in a great way, Ethan." He stopped and faced Ethan directly. "Will you?"

Ethan had known this moment would arrive. Yet he felt like Caesar as Brutus raised the knife. Ethan could think of no words strong enough to suit his purpose, of no rationale for his desire to strike out at the slight, grimacing figure standing beside him. He was not yet prepared for this overture. Jacob was right, he thought, I am a child in an adult's world.

Ethan could not explain the anger that rose in his throat. For four trying years away from Virginia, this man had been his best friend. Jeffrey had often ridiculed Southern attitudes in Ethan's presence. Their debates had been passionate. Ethan agreed with his friend's basic premise: Slavery was wrong. But the intricacies of ending the institution were not as simplistic as Jeffrey might like to believe.

Yet there he stood, an expectant smile on his lips, awaiting Ethan's acceptance of the devil's bargain. Ethan felt trapped. He disliked the way the trap had been sprung, with he the prey. The sensation of being caught overwhelmed whatever call to brotherhood Jeffrey might raise, however positive the end.

He turned a sardonic smile on his friend. "Really, Jeffrey! Proposing that I spy on my own family just a day after you arrive at our home. Are you mad?" He continued up the stone path, frowning at the sound of Jeffrey's boots crunching on the serpentine path behind him.

"Think about it, Ethan."

Inside, Ethan brushed past Alex and ascended the staircase, two steps at a time. The door to his room slammed. Alex shook his head and looked at his wife.

"Trouble," Clara said with a knowing look. Jeffrey entered the kitchen a moment later. Alex and Clara responded taciturnly to his greeting, watching the young man as he tugged on his gray coat and passed through to the wide passageway in Ethan's wake.

"That boy leave a trail of ooze like a snail, only wider," Alex observed.

"He be a guest, like the girl. You keep your opinion to yo'self, old man."

Alex winked at his wife. "Till we get downstair, huh? That girl from Boston got the longest neck I ever did see!"

"Mister Jacob notice, too." Clara pushed past her husband, who towered a foot above her, to get out the biscuit pan for the next morning's breakfast.

"I be glad when they go back to Boston," he said, looking at his wife as she reached on tiptoes, unable to quite reach the shelf where the blue-and-white china cups were stored.

"Then it be dull 'round here, and you be complainin' about that. Give me a hand." Alex reached over her easily. It would be foolishness to mention their real fear—that their next passenger might arrive while the guests were still at Twin Pines.

The knock at the door of his room startled Ethan. Taking a deep breath, he brushed back his unruly brown hair and opened the door.

Jeffrey Keyes stood in the hallway with a questioning look on his lean face. "I've come to apologize, Ethan. I didn't respect your sense of tradition or loyalty. I am sorry. Will you forgive me?" He stuck out his hand and formed a small, uncertain smile.

Ethan stood at a crossroads. Regardless of the path he chose now—and indeed he must choose one—his life would never be the same. If he forgave Jeffrey, he knew the proposal would be repeated, that he would be called upon again to betray his family. But if not, he risked losing the only two friends he garnered in his four years of life beyond the fields of Twin Pines; he risked losing his own sense of justice and pride.

Ethan extended his hand. "You must never ask me again what you asked me today. Do you understand?"

Jeffrey's handshake struck Ethan as moist and powerless. "I'll never ask you again, Ethan. Honest."

Ethan failed to notice the precise language of Jeffrey's promise, or that he swore an oath which applied solely to himself and not to his sister Julia.

CHAPTER 8

JACOB RETURNED FOR dinner with dire news. "Buchanan's secretary of war, Floyd, a Virginian, has resigned his post. He opposes the sending of Federal troops and ships south to protect the U.S. government property. Can you blame him?"

Julia set down her glass of claret and regarded her brother discreetly. Jeffrey Keyes appeared agitated, poised to enter an argument. But she caught his eye in time, forcing him into an unspoken promise of restraint.

"Perhaps our guests from Boston side with Buchanan on this issue," Jacob ventured as Alex served the glazed ham.

Julia smiled enigmatically. "Perhaps, but we are not about to spoil a lovely meal with war talk, are we, Jeffrey?" She was satisfied that he limited his response to a shake of his head. He would play the silent partner for this evening. Jeffrey had told her of his discussion with Ethan, of course. And while Ethan's reaction was regrettable, it was only understandable. She could see that it would take some time, here in the home of his family, for Ethan to come to terms with the decision she felt he had already made in his heart.

The look that passed between them was not lost upon Jacob. He was suspicious of Jeffrey's sudden possession of conversational manners, feeling certain it had not been self-imposed. Jeffrey had not the wherewithal. What had happened today between brother and sister? he wondered. He cast an eye on Ethan, who clasped both hands around his glass of wine. His ham was all but untouched, and he wore an uncharacteristically somber expression.

Anna had instructed Clara to prepare a traditional Southern meal for their guests. Ham, beans, corn bread, and gravy filled the table, and once Jacob had said grace, Alex served the meal, and they all ate with gusto.

"No grits?" Jeffrey asked.

"Grits!" Martha cried. "Grits are for breakfast."

She wondered just how ignorant he could be. If the Keyeses, who were from Boston, could make such a remark, perhaps the inhabitants of Paris, France, underneath all their elegance and charm and worldly ways, might be stupid, too. The thought saddened her, and she ate little.

"I should think you'd have an appetite after trying on every gown you own all day long," Anna teased her only daughter.

Martha bit her lip and lowered her blue eyes, wishing tears to come. Yet secretly she liked the attention; it encouraged her strongly held feeling of being a victim in her own home.

"I quite enjoyed our time together," Julia noted. "Martha has quite a good grasp of French for someone who has never formally studied it."

"Or anything else," Ethan added, playfully tweaking his sister's arm. Martha smiled. She had been pleased to spend the day with Julia, who had plied her with questions all afternoon. What she didn't mention was the unusual nature of some of Julia's questions, such as how the slaves who misbehaved were "corrected," and who saw to it that they didn't steal from the family. Martha had considered the questions rude. Her answers had been guarded. But Julia Keyes had only asked more, refusing to take a hint any girl in Albemarle Country wouldn't have missed if she were deaf and blind. Yankees are persistent, she had concluded, and had left it at that.

After dinner they all adjourned to the parlor, where discussion soon turned to the Stuarts' Epiphany Ball, which would take place the following evening. Jacob explained to the Keyeses that Dr. Stuart was a well-respected man in central Virginia, as well as a wealthy one.

"Wealth seems to mean a good deal down here," Jeffrey observed blithely, raising an eyebrow. He sipped at the coffee in his cup innocently, as if the remark had not been meant to insult his hosts.

"My observation is that Boston is no different, Jeffrey," Ethan countered with a dark look at his friend. "Any historian worth his salt would tell you that every society has its wealthy and its poor, and both despise each other. The wealthy respect the wealthier, and the poor respect no one."

When he had finished, Jeffrey took a moment to lower his head in mock surrender. "I stand . . . or rather, I sit corrected. I must admit that we in Boston have a healthy regard for money, too, although we come by it somewhat differently."

Jacob stirred in his chair and cleared his throat. He could not remain silent any longer. "You mean you don't earn it from the labor of slaves, is that what you wish to say?" He fumed, setting down his cup so emphatically that some coffee spilled on the table.

Anna looked up sharply from her needlepoint. "Jacob! I'm sure Mr. Keyes meant no such thing."

"Perhaps my brother defends men like Dr. Stuart so staunchly for more personal reasons," Ethan suggested. He failed to notice the fleeting look of embarrassment his brother shot toward Julia Keyes, and the color that rose in his face as he folded his hands in his lap.

"What do you mean, Ethan?" Anna asked. The Keyeses, too, turned their attention to Ethan.

He laughed. "I just meant Caitlin Stuart, Mother, nothing more. Has everyone in this family lost his sense of humor?"

"Not I!" Martha cried, giggling.

Her guileless exclamation had a cheering effect, and Jeffrey and Jacob were able to carry on their conversations civilly.

When Jeffrey challenged Ethan to a chess match, Ethan eagerly accepted, relieved to break up the awkward gathering. Anna agreed to monitor the match, to ensure that neither player took too long to make a move. She went into the kitchen to get the small hourglass that emptied itself of sand in three minutes. Jacob and the two young ladies adjourned to the library to read and write letters as Clara cleared the cups and saucers from the well-lighted parlor.

In the rich orange light of the fireplace, Julia Keyes looked to Jacob more like an apparition than a real human being; too pale, too lovely to be genuine.

She spoke to him, and he had to ask her indulgence, for he wasn't listening, so lost in his contemplation of her was he.

"To whom are you writing?" she repeated. "You seem to write a great number of letters."

Her manner suggested that she was teasing him.

"Every Southern landowner considers himself an important citizen of his state or dominion, as I do. I write letters to inform and to be informed," Jacob explained coolly. He had no idea whether or not to trust her. He knew only that he feared what might happen if he did.

An argument drew Martha from the library to the parlor, where it was insisted that she replace her mother, who was retiring.

"But I don't know the rules," Martha protested.

"That's all right, for your brother breaks them all anyway," Jeffrey said.

Anna peeked her head inside the library to say good night. "We are really quite pleased that you've come," she said to Julia.

She had had her doubts about the wisdom of Ethan's invitation. But once the guests had arrived at Twin Pines, it mattered little to her how foolish or selfish they were. They had brought with them a liveliness that had reached even her husband.

But the Keyeses did present a special challenge. Anna

suspected that their visit was more than just a social call. Her instincts told her that Jeffrey had come with a more grave intent, perhaps to lure Ethan back to Boston. He could serve their cause so poignantly. It was this suspected but unproven "use" of Ethan which disturbed Anna.

Jacob stood and kissed his mother on the cheek. "Please tell Father I'll stop by to say good night later."

"I hope he is asleep, but I shall tell him, if not." She left them unchaperoned, in the glow of the library's fire.

"We ought to join the others," Jacob said.

"You are full of oughts for a young man," Julia noted. The bold manner in which she studied his every move had Jacob flustered. He couldn't walk without thinking which foot to put forward next.

"I came here expecting to find Ethan's brother a farmer; a plain, simple man who loved the land. Instead I find you." She said this as if troubled by Jacob's presence. If so, this put them on equal ground.

"I love this land," he said softly, with great conviction.

"Oh, I know. I can see that. But you are anything but simple. You will take some deciphering, Jacob Parson."

The implication of her simple statement seemed to flutter in the air between them. Suddenly the room was warm, and his head was muddled.

"May I call you Julia?" he asked.

She took a step nearer. They were now at arm's length, before the fire.

"Do. I shall call you . . . Jake." She smiled at his grimace, quickly adding, "I am joking. Jacob, of course. Always Jacob."

They were so near that the magnolia-and-honey scent of her perfume and the gleam in her green eyes filled his senses to overflowing. Had he ever been so near anyone or anything so perfect?

For a fleeting moment he pushed aside the pang of conscience, the sense of duty that told him to back off from this woman, to resist her charms. For that one moment he thought of Caitlin. Why had he never felt for her the stirrings that now held him in such breathless awe? But then he thought of nothing except the fullness of Julia Keyes's lips.

Jacob bent to cover her mouth with his.

"He kissed me! *Aaah!*"

Startled by Martha's cry, they broke apart. Jacob touched her arm, then jerked it away. "I . . . I'm sorry. I did not mean . . ."

Julia would not look at him, but turned quickly away. "We must see to Martha." But he had seen the flush on her cheeks.

When they reached the door to the hallway, they met Ethan, who in a glance took in the expression on their faces.

Ethan's mind ran riot with conflicting emotions: jealousy, that Julia should find his brother attractive; suspicion, that she might be prying information from him to use in an abolitionist tract, an act that would greatly embarrass Jacob. In his wildest dreams, Ethan never imagined catching his brother stealing a kiss from a young lady, especially a Yankee from Boston! In an odd way, it made him think better of Jacob, and he let go of some of the anger he had been holding against Jeffrey.

"What's happened?" Jacob asked. He seemed not to know what to do with his hands, as though they might be guilty of some dishonorable action on their own. He clamped them firmly behind his back.

Ethan shrugged as though the ruckus were nothing, fighting back an onrush of darker emotions. "For the first time ever, Jeffrey actually beat me at chess. When he realized what he had done, he called out, 'Checkmate' and kissed Martha on the cheek." He did not mention that he was furious with Jeffrey for behaving so abominably all evening. But he felt constrained by the ever-present knowledge that he had invited them, and he alone was responsible for their actions. He had to present the best face possible to his family, especially to Jacob. Ethan found himself in the uncomfortable position of defending Jeffrey.

But when Jeffrey Keyes came to the hallway where they stood in the shadows, the look on his face turned Jacob's concern to anger. For in Keyes's cloudy eyes lurked an ugly desire, a cool, rational lust: the look of the cruel slave buyer at auction. It was a look Jacob knew and detested.

"Where is she?" Jacob asked.

"Fled to the safety of her Parisian domain, no doubt." Ethan replied.

Jacob detected bourbon on his brother's breath. Was that Keyes's influence, also? If so, the man would have to leave, soon. But, Jacob's mind ran on, if he left, so would Julia.

"Excuse me." Jacob left the trio standing in the shadowy hallway near the foot of the stairs.

Upstairs, Jacob knocked twice on his sister's door. "Martha, it's me, Jacob."

She was slow to open the door. Jacob quickly saw why; she had been crying.

"Did he hurt you?"

Martha turned away. She wore the evening dress she had so proudly displayed for Julia, but her long sleeping gown lay across her bed. The fire in the hearth blazed and crackled.

"He kissed me! It was awful!"

Jacob wasn't certain how to react. He stood silently just inside the door. His gaze landed on the porcelain figurines crowding the cabinet standing against the wall behind her. The shelves where Martha stored her childhood treasures suddenly seemed precious to Jacob. His sister had been kissed by a man. Soon she would marry and leave Twin Pines. "What happened, Martha?"

She had always wanted to be kissed as the heroines of her novels were. But to be kissed in such a manner! She spun and faced Jacob, her eyes filled with tears. "The man is . . . is . . . reptilian!"

He regarded her soberly. "You're right, sister! Keyes is a snake. I've a good mind to send him packing."

"But what of Julia?" Martha asked. "Can she stay here without him?"

Jacob coughed, lowering his eyes. "I meant the pair of them, of course."

As Jacob left his sister's room, the gentle odors of Martha's soap and perfume blended with the wood smoke from the fire. In his mind it was the essence of his little sister, an essence he would never forget.

Downstairs, Ethan, Jeffrey, and Julia had settled onto the large sofa in the parlor. Their conversation suddenly ceased when Jacob entered the room.

"I apologize for my sister," he said, unable to look at Jeffrey. The dandy infuriated Jacob. He had no use for a man who acted thoughtlessly. He doubted Jeffrey was capable of doing a good day's work. "You startled her."

Keyes held out his small hands in a gesture of peace. "It's perfectly understandable. I was overcome with joy."

Julia leaned across Ethan, who sat between her and her brother, to squeeze Jeffrey's hand. It was an unusual gesture. Was she congratulating him for accepting Jacob's apology in such a gentlemanly fashion? The bond between Julia and her rogue brother pained Jacob. What had they been discussing with Ethan in the five minutes that he spent upstairs in Martha's room?

"Tell us more about the Epiphany Ball," Julia said, turning serenely to Jacob. "Is this another great tradition in Virginia? I've never heard of such a thing."

Jacob cleared his throat and found a chair near the door. The whole scene struck him as staged, from the silence to Julia's question. But he had no choice but to play along.

"The Epiphany celebrates the baptism of the infant Jesus and the visit of the three wise men to Bethlehem," Jacob began. Julia's eyes were wide with interest, but both Ethan and Jeffrey looked sleepy and uninterested. "It's also called the Twelfth Day, and its eve, Twelfth Night."

"Shakespeare wrote a play about it," Julia added. "*Twelfth Night*."

"My sister has read a great deal."

Of that Jacob had no doubt. For all his four years of study, Jacob felt sure Julia knew more than her brother. Did her learning embarrass him somehow?

"For as long as I know," Jacob continued, "Dr. Stuart has been hosting a ball on the night of the sixth. Some people recognize the religious aspect of the festivities, but nowadays many just come to dance and to feast."

"Which are you?" Julia asked.

Jacob blushed at the boldness of her questions. "I lead the prayers, with Dr. Stuart, as Father did, when he was able. But small gifts are also exchanged, and people dance the night away, too."

"And do you do that also?" she inquired.

Jacob could not form a response; she was much too direct for his taste, perhaps in order to cover the awkwardness of their encounter in the library.

Soon afterward he found it convenient to bid them all good night. Their conversation grew animated just moments after he left. As he ascended to the second floor, he felt as isolated as the hollow echoing of his boots on the wooden stairway.

Jacob lay awake in bed listening to the sounds of the Keyeses and Ethan in the hallway outside his door. He was relieved that Ethan spent more time bidding Jeffrey a pleasant night's rest than he did his sister.

Once the house had grown quiet, he closed his eyes but was unable to fall asleep. For beyond the fields of Twin Pines, the world appeared bleak and destined for chaos.

CHAPTER 9

ANNA PARSON AND Clara gathered early in the dining room to count and document the silver, as they did once a month at Charles's insistence. With Clara's help, Anna dutifully checked the silver piece by piece. As Clara identified and counted each piece, Anna wrote it down, repeating the name of each item.

Charles was certain that one day before he died, someone, slave or free, would swindle them of one of the Parson family heirlooms, either the portraits, the silver, or the plantation itself. "Keep records!" While his words were wasted on Ethan and Martha, Anna and Jacob heeded his advice.

"Two waiters, twenty-four teaspoons, three ladles, twenty-four large spoons, one coffeepot, two pitchers, twelve gold spoons . . ." On and on the list went. Finally, Anna heard the clock chime seven. "It's nearly time for breakfast, Clara. We'll complete the list later." With so much real work to do—Anna was weeks behind on her needlework, as was Martha—she had little energy to devote to Charles's goose chases. For the most part, the bondsmen were honest and devoted. No piece had ever turned up missing. But as master of the estate, her husband had to be obeyed.

After breakfast, Jacob sat in the library, figuring expenses, paying bills, and planning what best to do with the Parson savings. Beside the letters and papers on top of the desk was the latest issue of the *Southern Agriculturalist*, which he consulted regularly. Tobacco was still a profitable enterprise, but with war looming, food and manufactured goods promised to be dear. Jacob laid his plans, organizing his rough notes on the estate's needs into categories:

> *To Buy in Town: Hoes—6. Spades—6. Handles—12. Harnesses—2.*
> *Ask mother about crockery, candles, and sewing thread.*
> *Talk to Miller about new metal oven, tin roaster.*
> *Steel grist mill? Ask Daddy.*
> *Ten-gallon can of coal gas!*
> *Molasses and salt for Negroes.*
> *Sugar.*

Then he broke off the rambling list and found his mother's, which detailed needs for the kitchen and household. Jacob would have to figure the price of each item and total it before writing a draft to the storekeeper in Charlottesville. He found Anna's list, which read: *soda water, quinine, castor oil, coats and curtains, thermometer, whip.*

To what was there, Jacob added, *bourbon, ale, wine.*

Jacob smiled, pleased to be in control. He pushed away from the desk. It was time to rouse the field hands; the animals in the barn needed food and attention. He hoped that his family could become accustomed to the flavor of mutton, because he didn't see what else they might be eating once war broke out and supplies grew scarce.

Martha sighed. She was growing tired of sewing. It would be hours before they could start preparing for the ball, and the clear, crisp winter scene beckoned from beyond the parlor window. Ethan and Jeffrey were already outside, on a walking tour of the grounds. Dropping her needlework beside her on the settee, she exclaimed, "Julia! Come! I'll show you the prettiest horses in the known world!"

How could Julia resist? "I've not had much experience," she admitted. "I've only been on a horse twice in my life."

Martha turned wide blue eyes on Julia. It was the funniest thing she had had ever heard. "At last, something I do better than you." She giggled. "Don't worry. We'll find you a quiet old mare even your brother would ride back to Boston."

They quickly changed into riding clothes, which lacked the cumbersome hoops of their everyday gowns. While Julia did not own a riding habit, and Martha's were much too small for her, she owned several dresses without hoops, and wore one of those.

They made their way quickly to the stables, where Martha asked for two horses to be prepared. "I want something frisky," she said. "And something lazy for Miss Julia."

When two mares had been saddled, bridled, and brought to Miss Martha and her friend, two astonished stable hands had to help Julia climb onto the saddle. Martha, too, was amazed. They set off from the barn at a trot, Martha moving in cadence with her mare, while Julia bounced up and down awkwardly in the saddle.

They rode west on the path that cut through the slave quarters, passing a few black faces, women with young babies who had not yet fully returned to working, before reaching the broad, open tobacco fields lying fallow in the January frost. Suddenly Martha reined in the snorting brown mare, signaling Julia to halt.

"Let's ride in the other direction." With Martha's assistance, Julia was able to turn her horse and ride east, once again passing the bondsmen who paused in their chores to watch the two ladies trot past again, continuing on past the great house and gardens and outbuildings of Twin Pines. Soon they rode along at a gentle pace toward the east on the dirt road that led to Richmond.

When they approached two small, unpainted buildings that Martha casually identified as the Tyler farm, Julia's bewilderment gave way to an uneasy understanding. Earlier in the day, Martha had confided to Julia her fascination with Brett Tyler. Julia had listened with interest as Martha described the ignorant brute as she might an unschooled, but brave hero from a novel.

Julia yearned to warn her off, yet knew that she had no business doing so. She trusted society's conventions and Tyler's poverty to break her of the spell of mystery and heroism he seemed to cast over Martha. She was enchanted by Martha, both amused and appalled by the girl's passion for Brett Tyler. It was nothing more than a schoolgirl romance that could never amount to anything, even a heartache. Surely she would forget him at that night's Epiphany Ball, when no doubt a dozen suitors would surround her, vying for her smile and a word of encouragement.

Yet the passion which showed in Martha's flushed cheeks and high spirits stirred Julia's thoughts of Jacob, surely as impossible a romance as Martha's. Julia knew that she and Jacob were worlds apart. Neither of them could ever live in the other's sphere of comfort. She was not usually given to this sort of feeling. Yet Jacob had kissed her, as she had wanted him to. It had not been at all unpleasant, far from it. And that was dangerous. She could grow to like such attentions.

The Tyler farm consisted of nothing more than the small shack where the family lived, a few cows and chickens, a barn that had all but collapsed, and a plowed field of a few square acres. Generations of Tylers had lived and died there, and until now, none of them had made any kind of mark upon the Parsons. Julia found it difficult to believe that a hero could hail from such surroundings.

She rubbed her gloved hands against her arms. The heavy fabric of the cloak covering her dress was insufficient to protect her against the January chill. But she didn't mention her discomfort. If she was going to have any influence with Martha later, she had to bide her time and please the girl now, while she had the chance. Once she had left Twin Pines, and their relationship revolved solely around epistles, Julia would be in control. But here and now, face to face, she had to heed Martha's desires or risk losing her influence over the girl.

A tall, husky man appeared at the door to the barn with a bucket of milk in each hand. Brett Tyler. Seeing them, he stopped short and grinned like a fox. A girl younger than he, one of his sisters perhaps, came out of the barn behind him holding eggs in the fold of her skirt. Upon catching sight of Martha and Julia, she ran to the house and disappeared inside. Brett Tyler set down the buckets of milk. Julia sensed his strength immediately. He looked capable of pulling Martha from her horse and ravishing her right there on the frozen ground. He also looked as if he might well desire to do so. Broad backed and tough looking, he turned a crooked smile on them that made Julia want to head in the other direction immediately.

Tyler swaggered toward them. "Morning, ladies," he said in a gruff, husky voice. Julia thought he emphasized the word "ladies" as though he were mocking them. "What brings you to the Tyler estate on this fine day? Don't you have a ball to dress for?"

His smile showed fine white teeth, but Julia could think of nothing but the fox trying to charm the hens before the slaughter. He was far too unschooled and crude to please her. He probably reeked of manure and cheap whiskey. She found him repugnant, not at all like Ethan— or Jacob.

Martha tossed her dark head. "Our affairs are none of your concern, Brett Tyler. Isn't Jacob expecting you to deliver a buck sheep to us today?" She knew that he was, for her brother had mentioned it at breakfast.

Tyler slapped his forehead. "Why, ma'am, I plum forgot. You see, we have so many fine sheep and goats and cattle here that I can't keep track of all of 'em. I reckon I'd best git me a mess of slaves, like your daddy, don't you think?"

Martha was furious. "Why, everyone knows you couldn't afford a one-armed boy with half a mind, let alone a real field hand!"

That was just the reaction Tyler had hoped for. He

liked to see Martha angry. Her color rose, her blue eyes sparkled. She had spirit. It made him want to tame her.

"I believe Mr. Tyler is having his way with us," Julia said. Her horse moved restlessly, nearly causing her to slip off. Tyler made no move toward her, so Martha trotted next to her to help her regain her seat.

"No, I am not . . . but I'd surely like to, that I would!" Tyler said, his eyes burning into Martha's.

The front door to the Tyler farmhouse creaked open to reveal an older woman wearing a worn dress and an apron. Julia cringed. The way the woman glared at Martha and her, it seemed as if she might reach for a shotgun and blast them. She stood silently by the door for a moment, then closed it and disappeared from view.

"And how are the mighty Parsons?" Brett asked. "Is that manly brother of yours healed from his whipping on the road?"

Julia could see that Martha had taken offense at the words he used. But she knew of the service Brett Tyler had done Ethan. Martha would have to ignore the insult. "Yes, thanks to you, and to Clara's care, Ethan is fine. We owe you a great debt."

Tyler smiled, stepping so close to Martha's horse that she could smell the musty odors of the barn on his clothes. "You can repay that debt all by yourself. You know you can."

Julia watched terrified as, without warning, he reached out and grabbed Martha's boot, squeezing her ankle.

"You are hurting me, Brett Tyler!" Martha protested.

Julia wanted to intervene but couldn't maneuver her mare, who had found some grass to nuzzle by the fence.

"Not like I'm goin' to hurt you," Tyler hissed. The look of intensity on his face frightened Martha. She was no match for this man, despite the upper hand society had graced her with. Tyler played games with his own rules in operation. She had to accept them or flee.

Martha smacked the mare with her reins and pulled to turn the mount. As she did so, Tyler freed his grip on her boot, and the sudden release unbalanced her, causing her to nearly spill from the saddle. Far from being concerned, Tyler whooped, doubling over in laughter.

"Come on!" Martha shouted to Julia. Tyler turned next to Julia, who had been trying unsuccessfully to kick her horse into action. Without saying a thing, he slapped the mare hard on the rump, and she bolted. Julia managed to keep from falling by holding on to the reins, and Martha quickly moved her own mare to cut off and calm the frightened horse; the maneuver was not easy.

"Brett Tyler, you are a bastard!" Martha swore. She turned her horse and guided Julia's west, in the direction from which they had come, toward the Parson house. Shaking with fear, Martha struggled to keep her seat. How dare he! she thought. If I told Jacob, he would kill Brett Tyler this very day!

Martha did not turn to see Brett run to the fence that marked his family's property, but she heard him clearly when he yelled, "I am not a bastard! And one day you'll want me!" he shouted.

The long ride back to Twin Pines was silent, but for a stinging wind and the snorting of the horses.

When Brett entered the farmhouse, his mother and father sat at the kitchen table, waiting for him. What now? he wondered. "Daddy, don't hit me. I ain't in the mood." Far from the brash, confident demeanor he put forth in front of the rest of the world, he was quiet and sullen at home. Most times, he wanted only to be left alone. Brett wanted a father he could respect; instead, there sat William Tyler, drunk.

"I sent the girls out to the barn," his mother said.

"I seen 'em," he said. He shot them a quick glance, then went to the washbasin, poured some water into it, and rubbed his face and hands with it. Finally, he turned back toward them, drying his hands with his shirt. "What is it?"

"Set," his daddy said. He was a leathery snake of a man, lean and fast for a man in his fifties. When he hit somebody, they felt it. Brett could easily kill the old drunk in a fair fight, but William Tyler never fought fair in his life, drunk or sober. Brett felt only loathing for him—and sometimes fear.

Grudgingly, he pulled a chair up to the table and sat down without looking at his parents. "What?" he finally snapped.

"You got a ball to go to? What's yer goddamn hurry?" His father was angry.

Dora May reached out to calm him, and surprisingly, he let her rub his arm. "We seen you with the Parson girl," she ventured. "She sweet on you?"

Brett rolled his eyes. So *that* was what this was for. "You two givin' advice on courtin' now? Ain't that like the Devil preachin' a sermon on Sunday—"

William Tyler jumped to his feet and raised his hand in a flash. Brett leaned back to dodge the attack, but his mother intervened, begging William to stop.

"Button that lip and listen to your mama," his father ordered. "Git me a drink!"

Dora May did as he asked. It was her idea, naturally, kissin' up to the goddamn Parsons! She talked to her son as she found a clean mug and a half-empty bottle of bourbon, which she set in front of her husband. "Brett, we was thinkin'. Since that girl's sweet on you, and you done save her brother's life and all, it don't seem too much to ask that you treat her nice and maybe . . ."

Brett shoved away from the table and got to his feet. "Mama, you're dreamin'! If you think I will ever be welcomed into that high and mighty family, you are out of your mind! They hate my guts now, even after I saved Ethan. I told you both before. Onliest way I ever amount to anything is through war, if it comes. If I make a name for myself, if I win a battle or shoot the right man, I can be somebody. But that's the onliest way!" He stormed from the table, grabbing his musket from where it rested by the door, and plunged into the frigid air outside. His sisters saw him from the yard. Wrapped in shawls too thin for the chill air, they danced in circles, teasing him about Martha. One look shut them up.

Without knowing where he was going, Brett stuck one hand deep into his pants pockets and walked west, cradling the musket in his arms.

Jeffrey Keyes had steered Ethan to the far side of a tobacco curing barn, out of sight of the house. "My sister and I are moving to Washington, D.C., for the time being," he revealed. "We are needed there, by the cause. The personal sacrifice is something we are both willing to make. But, Ethan, it's people like yourself who will determine the success of our endeavors."

Ethan reflected that in the four years that he had known Jeffrey, he'd learned little of how the Keyeses secured an income. Jeffrey had mentioned that their parents were dead, but Ethan knew nothing more than that. Perhaps one of their family's enterprises drew them to the young capital.

"Are you saying that you and Julia are employed by the government in Washington?" Ethan was stunned.

Jeffrey tossed his head back and laughed. "No, no, my friend. Our investments in several ironworks foundries in Boston and New York should more than triple, provided there's a war, and material is needed, which it will be. No, I mean only that we shall do our duty as requested—"

"By whom?" Ethan asked. "Who asked you to move to Washington?"

A short, husky bondsman came out of the curing barn, surprising them both.

"What on earth were you doing in there?" Ethan asked the man irritably.

"Mister Jacob tol' me to patch de walls, so I done it," the man explained. "Ev'body else sick."

"Well for Christ's sake, make some noise the next time you're working in the area," Ethan snapped, immediately regretting his words. A few of the hands had been taken ill with influenza. No doubt his mother was making arrangements to have proper care administered, but the influenza always struck with a vengeance. He hoped there would be no loss of life. His eyes followed the bonds-man's retreating form with sympathy.

As the slave strolled toward the cow barn, Jeffrey asked, "Do you think there is any chance the man over-heard us?"

"Perhaps, but it doesn't matter," Ethan said in a weary voice. Jeffrey's secrets were wearing on his nerves. "He only talks to other bondsmen, and nobody listens to them."

Jeffrey took a breath and pushed on. "What I need to know, Ethan, is this: Will you meet with Julia and me in the capital from time to time, if we so desire?"

Ethan stiffened, looking away. "You mean to pass along information I've gained from my father and brother? Jeffrey, think of what you're asking me to do!"

Ethan fancied himself above all else a moral being, but he could not betray his family, not at any cost to his own sense of justice. The decision shook him.

Jeffrey stepped in front of Ethan, facing him directly. "Ethan, I have made a promise to you, and I shall keep it. I am not asking you to *do* anything for us. But I am asking you to examine your own soul." Ethan started to speak, but Jeffrey put him off with a wave of his walking stick. "Please do me the courtesy of hearing me out. Ethan, the time is near to decide what is right and what is wrong. We both know how evil an institution slavery is. Julia and I both feel strongly that we must do all we can to destroy it. The coming war will provide us that opportunity. You do see that, don't you?"

Ethan glared him. What was there to say? The time would no doubt come when he would have to face up to the dictates of his conscience. But when the moment came, it would be *his* decision, and he would act in a manner he found to be acceptable. He refused to have his friend-ship manipulated, his family's hospitality abused.

Pushing his friend aside, Ethan strode away, marching past the outbuildings and the family home, heading east as if to turn his back on everything that the owners of Twin Pines had built. He walked along the road to Richmond, blind to the view offered by the bare fields and red earth, until in the distance a lone figure appeared. A man walking toward him paused at the top of a small hill that descended into the flat farmland that comprised the best of the Parsons' tobacco fields. Ethan recognized him as Brett Tyler and waved a hand in greeting; he would never again despise the man who had saved his life, a Tyler or not. The man ignored him. Raising a musket, he fired up into an oak. A second later, a squirrel fell from the tree. Tyler raised his fist and shook it in Ethan's direction, as if warning him away.

Ethan was puzzling over the threatening gesture when Jeffrey caught up to him, breathing heavily. "Who on earth is that scoundrel? And what is he up to? Will he shoot us next?"

Ethan did not reply, but instead accelerated his pace, hoping to catch up to Tyler and ask him what he meant by the defiant gesture. But as Ethan strode toward him, Tyler bent to retrieve the dead squirrel, then disappeared over the rise, as if swallowed up by the horizon.

"What a queer fish that fellow is," Jeffrey commented, blowing into his hands. "I must get back to the house and warm up. Are you coming?"

Ethan stood his ground, puzzled and upset by Tyler's appearance. Then a chill overtook him, and reluctantly he turned, cast a murderous look at Jeffrey, and began walking back toward the house. Smoke poured from the kitchen chimney. Ordinarily it was a sign of welcome, but to Ethan the whorls of smoke now seemed dark and hopeless.

"You will give me an answer soon, won't you, Ethan? All I ask is that we remain friends, no matter what. I know you'll do what is right," Jeffrey hastened to add. Ethan kept a grip on his anger and ignored his friend, who shivered as their boots cuffed the narrow road with a hollow, martial sound.

William Tyler looked out the window of his frame house and saw the lights in the mansion on the hill glittering in the dimming light of late afternoon. He held a bottle in his hand and waved it toward the Parson house as if it were a club that could fell the entire family that had stoled the Tylers' farm right out from under his daddy. "Lookit 'em all, fine and gay. We could've been like that if we'd a gone on to Kalina. But no, my daddy had to make 'is his own way here. So here we is, nobodies and nothin', livin' nowhere."

Dora May tried to steer her husband toward the table, but he shooed her away. "You got to keep away from them Parsons. Their kind is doomed. They gonna all die out long afore the Tylers. You see . . ." He tilted his head back and raised the bottle unsteadily to his lips to finish the bourbon. Then belching, he stumbled back, crashing into the table. Dora May helped him to a chair.

He sat down clumsily, dropping the empty bottle, and stared bleary eyed into the other room where Brett and the girls sat under the light of a solitary candle, playing poker with a deck missing a half-dozen cards. They were betting with matchsticks.

"When I'm a hero in the army," Brett was telling his sisters, "I'm gonna have me three decks of cards and double my wages every payday. I'm gonna send y'all new gowns and jewelry like you was princesses. You'll see. And I'll do it all by myself, don't nobody gonna help me." He dealt a new hand, and the game continued.

William turned away in disgust. "The boy's jes' like his grandpa. Don't nothin' come of neither of 'em."

Dora May soothed her husband, wondering what would happen to her son and who would beat the dream of prosperity out of him. She only prayed that it wouldn't be the Parson girl, for that would spoil him on love forever, and she did not want that.

CHAPTER 10

ETHAN MADE THE sign of the cross, muttered a brief prayer, and tapped on the door to his father's room. When there was no answer, he opened the door softly. His father was lying on the feather bed, his mouth open, sleeping peacefully.

Uncharacteristically, he had what looked to be two or three days' growth of facial hair, tough gray stubble that somehow suited the tough old fox. It was unlike him—he'd instructed Alex to shave him daily—and Ethan looked more closely at his father. The skin around Charles's neck sagged, forming a fold at the collar of his shirt. His coloring seemed no redder or paler than usual.

Drawn to the sleeping figure, Ethan entered the room stealthily. It contained a good deal of his father's spirit. Now useless items such as his riding boots, his crop, and his favorite musket stood ready and polished against the wall just inside the door.

Only in your dreams, Ethan thought, will you ride the hounds or hunt deer again, Daddy. The thought saddened him. As a boy, he'd stood in awe of his father; he'd feared him greatly. Ethan recalled his father as a distant, disapproving almighty, who always coaxed Jacob and him outdoors to the stables or woods. "You read too damn much, boy!" his father had scolded again and again.

Only his father's injury and his mother's intransigence had allowed Ethan to attend Harvard University. He had always claimed that "no Parson need leave the Commonwealth of Virginia for any legitimate reason," and that "only a confidence man or a traitor" would seek his fortune beyond the red clay and gold-leafed tobacco of Twin Pines.

The memory cast a sudden pall over Ethan; he felt chilled. Tiptoeing to the fireplace, he added a log to the fire and stirred it with a poker. His father snorted, twitching his nose, but remained asleep.

It might almost be better if he never awoke, thought Ethan, if he were to remain unaware of the trials I will face. The conceit raised a guilt within him that stung his heart. The old man twitched again, like a dog chasing a coon in his dream. Could his father be dreaming of a chase right now, as Ethan watched? He hurriedly left the room, the sharp odor of his father's unwashed body in his nostrils like a poison.

Ethan went to the stables, where he asked a hand to saddle Midnight. The spirited black mare was his preferred mount, and pulling his coat around him, Ethan tied a knitted scarf around his neck, pushed down his broad-brimmed hat, and spurred the mare. She jumped forward, eager to stretch her legs in the cold.

He rode east, past the fallow fields and stands of oak and loblolly pine. Unhurried and alone, they advanced; the weather was bitter cold, and bondsmen and masters alike remained indoors; a day of rest had been granted the bondsmen in honor of the Epiphany.

Ethan liked the feel of Midnight's warm flank beneath his thighs. Bending low, he raced the wind for a quarter-mile. Midnight snorted, her breath visible as she stretched out.

They thundered down the hard dirt road and soon came to the rise overlooking the Tyler farm. Ethan could not help feeling uncomfortable, and he eased into a trot as they passed the ramshackle, unpainted buildings. Smoke poured from the chimney of the Tyler house. They must all be inside, Ethan surmised. An eerie silence pervaded the property. Only the wind rustling branches in the trees broke the quiet.

Chilled but dissatisfied, Ethan rode on, spurring the mare. He put a gloved hand to his cheek to check for frostbite and smelled the stiff, old leather of the glove. His sense of feeling was still good. He was safe. Five miles farther east on the winding road, Ethan noticed a small figure on horseback perhaps a half-mile away, approaching him in the gathering shadows that would soon deepen into evening. Intrigued, he kept a steady eye on the form, and soon, it coalesced into Caitlin Stuart. Riding sidesaddle, she wore a heavy wool coat, a wool riding skirt, and on her head, a bright green bonnet tied gently under her neck. Her face was bright red, her cheeks aglow. He thought he saw her smile—was she pleased to meet him?—but then she looked down, adjusting her grip on the reins.

His greeting was muted. She had taken him by surprise. "You're far from home, and on the very afternoon of your ball."

Caitlin took in her breath and bent forward to pat the neck of her mount. "I wanted to breathe some fresh air. And I have, perhaps too much. I had not realized I had ridden so far." Her voice had a honeyed power to it, yet there was nothing coy or false about it. He could not help wondering if Jacob truly appreciated her qualities, or even recognized them.

He shrugged, watching her carefully. Were her eyes always so liquid brown and dreamy? Unaware of why he did so, perhaps because of her sincerity, her absolute lack of affectation or pretense, he spoke his mind to her. "There's nothing for me to do at home. I'm utterly useless at Twin Pines."

Caitlin frowned; her eyes deepened to an even darker brown as she turned her head. "What foolish talk, Ethan. You have a university education. You can do anything. Teach, write, travel . . ."

"Yes, but here I'm worth less than a sound field hand." He held up a hand to forestall her reply. "I am not being morose, Caitlin. It is a fact. At least a field hand has a task to do that's his own—repairing a broken wheel or tanning a hide. Nothing I do here is worthwhile." He looked down at the ruts in the frozen road, then added something that greatly surprised himself. "I am considering leaving."

This information seemed to jolt Caitlin. She sat perfectly straight in the saddle, ignoring her steed's play for attention. "Have you told anyone?" Her voice was soft and unsure, a tone he had never heard her use.

"I've told you."

For a moment their eyes met, like souls embraced, as Ethan would later describe it. He was fully aware of the depth of their unspoken exchange, yet he felt bound by an inertia, a weakness he recognized too clearly in himself lately. He said nothing more, for suddenly he wasn't certain who Caitlin really was, deep down, even in that exquisite second of recognition and attraction.

Caitlin turned away first. She appeared to be uneasy and tugged at her gloves. Smoothing her skirt, she nodded toward the Blue Ridge Mountains, hidden in the clouds to the west. "There's snow in those clouds."

Ethan felt relieved that she had changed the topic. He followed her gaze, watching the heavy gray clouds scudding by, barely visible in the darkness of evening. "Likely," he agreed softly.

"I must go now," she said, unwilling to look him in the eye. "It's much too late. Daddy will begin to worry."

They parted with a tip of the hat and a nod. Long after the cold had chilled him to the bone, he sat, watching her receding figure.

Three hours later, a trio of enclosed carriages stood ready outside the front entrance to Twin Pines to drive the Parsons and their guests to Stuart Hall, eight miles up the Richmond Road.

As Anna emerged from the house into the bitter cold of the January night, she paused to pray for her husband, to give thanks for the blessings bestowed on her by her sons and daughter. Seeing them dressed so splendidly, her sons handsome in their black morning coats and top hats, Martha a thing of beauty in a white lace dress trimmed in red, with a bonnet to match, Anna felt a great surge of pride.

Charles was too weak to make the journey to Stuart Hall. The influenza had hit him with a vengeance earlier in the evening, and his temperature had soared. Anna hesitated to leave him, but he had insisted, and Clara had promised not to leave his side until she returned. Secretly, she was relieved. She could not still the warm rushes that surged over her at the thought of an evening free of Charles's harangues and coughing spells. Firmly closing her wrap around her, she took the hand Jacob offered her and allowed him to help her into the carriage.

Behind her and Jacob, Martha and Julia sat in a second enclosed carriage, and Ethan and Jeffrey Keyes shared the last.

"Someone ought to determine a method of heating these things," Jeffrey complained. "Do that, Ethan, and we'd all be rich!"

Ethan did not answer. He found that he could no longer feel at ease in Jeffrey's presence. It had occurred to him after their conversations that Jeffrey was making a fool of him to advance his own ends. His friend's convictions had grown beyond the idealism that had characterized their many debates at Harvard. As Jeffrey himself had stated, he and his sister would no doubt profit from the conflict through their ironworks foundries. Jeffrey did not seem to recognize that he himself had everything to lose. He turned away and stared stonily out the small window at the side of the carriage.

The green satin of Julia's uncharacteristically low-cut gown contrasted strikingly to Martha's white silk and Belgian lace. Dressed in their finery, the two young women found the narrow seat uncomfortable, their voluminous hoop skirts overlapping awkwardly. "Do girls in Boston dress like this?" Martha asked. She imagined them more regal.

Julia laughed. "For balls, yes. But most wear more demure clothing, day to day."

The jostling of the carriage tossed them to and fro,

and Martha struggled to right herself without disturbing her gown. "Daddy says Yankees know how to make money, but Southerners know how to spend it."

Julia had to agree. "You lead a genteel life, unlike ours in Boston. Of course, Jeffrey and I attend meetings much more often than balls, so what I say is somewhat colored."

"Jacob thinks you're beautiful—" Martha covered her mouth with her white-gloved hands, catching herself. It was this kind of remark that often came back to haunt her, especially when it concerned one of her brothers. But she had spoken without thinking, and it was too late now. "Please don't tell him I said that. He's supposed to marry Caitlin Stuart."

Julia straightened in the hard seat. Or perhaps it was the turn of her auburn head. But Martha realized that she had jolted her companion.

"Did I say something foolish?" Martha asked, trying to make light of what she'd said. "I'm told by my brothers that I have a gift for doing such things."

"No, not at all," Julia said at last, but she seemed distant. "Tell me all about the Stuarts," she requested. "He's a university professor and a leader of the slave patrols, is that correct?"

Once again, Martha found herself in the uncomfortable position of answering questions she'd rather not be asked. Why didn't Yankees have the manners so deeply ingrained in Southern ladies and gentlemen? Martha was taught never to ask a question to which she didn't already know the answer. "Dr. Stuart is a strong supporter of secession, yes," she began somewhat hesitantly. "Caitlin is just beautiful! I believe every young man in the state would fight a duel for her hand if the winner could be guaranteed the prize. But she would never stand for such bloodshed," she added lightly.

"Would you?"

"Oh, yes, I should be honored."

Julia nodded seriously, then asked, "Are duels still fought here? They are outlawed in Massachusetts."

A bump in the road sent them both flying. They landed hard, gasping, as the driver called out apologies from up front.

"There are duels fought every day of the week somewhere in the South. Daddy says it's the only way for a man to uphold the family honor sometimes."

"It seems rather foolish to me," Julia had the nerve to say. "Suppose the liar wins. What does that prove?"

Martha's notions were at once hilarious and frightful to Julia. They illustrated only too well the failure of the South to advance with the times. The North was the setting of great change; industrialization had forced change. More and more people worked not on farms but in factories. It seemed to her that even her brief glimpse into the Southern mind revealed a stubborn resistance to change. History would not tolerate it, as the coming conflict would prove.

Martha was a perfect example, defending a medieval means of settling disputes as if it were honorable and not deplorable. She turned to her companion, who had stuck her head out of the carriage to wish upon a star, and said, "You people of Virginia live on as if chivalry and the Round Table were not long dead."

"But they're not dead," Martha protested. "Daddy says Sir Walter Scott is the South's favorite writer because he's the only man who knew how a lady should be treated."

Julia raised an eyebrow but stifled her rebuttal. They rode in silence the rest of the way.

Anna waited until the carriage was just minutes away from the graceful, curving drive that led from the main road to the Stuarts' balconied porch before saying what she knew she must. "Jacob, your father wishes to know: Are you going to ask Caitlin to marry you tonight?"

He had known she would ask, that as Father's proxy she must ask. Jacob nodded. "I fully intend to, Mother, though I cannot venture what she will say."

Anna Parson took her son's gloved hand and smiled.

"Why, she'll say yes, of course. What girl wouldn't? We were concerned. You seemed to be hesitating."

"It's the talk of war, Mother. I've so much planning to do, besides my duties with the militia."

"I see, dear." Anna still worried, though. And she would continue to fret until the announcement was made and the ceremony concluded. Only when Jacob and his bride had left in a flower-festooned carriage for their honeymoon abroad would she relax.

She had often pictured her elder son's wedding day. But another darker picture developed in Anna's mind. She would rather not have imagined the scene, but like Charles and her sons, Anna was blessed and cursed with insight and imagination. Her world was about to tilt on its axis— just as it had been turned upside down by Charles's accident ten years ago—and when that happened, only the strong would cling to the earth and survive. The current talk of war reminded her of the Second Coming, and of the cataclysms of Revelations. If Caitlin Stuart and Jacob were to wed soon, she could look upon it as a sign of blessing. She fervently hoped that tonight's ball would hasten the arrival of that splendid event. As their carriage slowed to a halt, she prayed for it.

Jeffrey Keyes was overcome by the opulence of Stuart Hall as seen from the road. "The man must be very wealthy," Keyes commented as he and Ethan climbed down from the carriage.

"Actually, it was Stuart's wife," Ethan explained. "Her family has owned this part of the country since English rule, I believe."

Jeffrey cocked a red eyebrow. "And his daughter is sole heir?"

"Will be, Jeffrey," Ethan said. "Dr. Stuart is far from dead, as you will see."

Dr. Stuart and Caitlin stood just inside the door, greeting guests. Ethan's gaze lighted first on Caitlin. She wore a gown of deepest rose that accentuated the paleness of her face and golden hair. Her expression as she greeted him was composed, portraying none of the awkwardness of that afternoon. Next to her, her father's congenial expression of welcome masked almost—but not completely, he noticed—the sternness that had always characterized his robust, combative features.

Dr. Stuart welcomed the rest of the Parsons, greeted the Keyes with a warm bow and sharp eye, and pulled Jacob aside to whisper something in his ear.

"Do you suppose he's telling Jacob to keep a close watch on Lincoln's spies?" Jeffrey said with a grin, as Jacob nodded in response to Dr. Stuart's whispered comments.

Ethan shook his head. "I suspect it has more to do with Caitlin's hand. You see, Dr. Stuart very much wants Caitlin to marry my brother. So does our father. Everyone expects it of them." Ethan felt a chill. He forced himself to speak evenly of Caitlin's marriage to Jacob, though were the ceremony to take place that very day, it would dull the beat of his heart forever. Like a half-drunk man hunting a wounded bobcat at night, he felt exposed and inclined to take a risk.

Chandeliers lit the circular entrance hall brightly. The curving marble staircase that led to the second floor was trimmed in garlands, and candles blazed from every nook. The Parsons and their two guests followed a white-gloved servant up the sweeping staircase and into the Stuarts' immense ballroom, where a waltz was under way.

"There must be a hundred people here," Jeffrey calculated, searching the room.

"Dr. Stuart knows everyone," Ethan said.

Dozens of elegant couples dressed in silk gowns and morning suits danced the waltz to music provided by three men playing violins. Servants in black coats and ties served rolled sweet wafers, pecan pastries, and champagne from silver trays gleaming like stars in the candlelight.

Martha immediately yielded herself to the romance of the scene. This was but the second time she'd been permitted to attend the Stuarts' Epiphany Ball, and she was determined to be swept away by it.

"Oh, I shall dance my feet off tonight and disappear

with the first man who asks," she confided to Caitlin, who had joined her friend and Julia for a toast once all the guests had arrived.

They had barely had time to sip their punch when Dr. Stuart stood and signaled the musicians to halt. The waltzing couples watched Dr. Stuart with polite interest as he raised a glass and called for quiet.

"Friends and guests! We augur in eighteen sixty-one in peace and harmony, steeled in the knowledge that together we will face and vanquish all foes, and at any cost, protect and preserve what is ours, through justice and in the will of our Lord. Now enjoy yourselves." But Stuart raised a cautioning finger. "But not too much, for as we learn in Corinthians, 'Every man that striveth for mastery is temperate in all things.' "

Jeffrey Keyes had listened to the speech with interest from where he stood by the refreshments. Applause and shouts of encouragement greeted Stuart's remarks when he had finished. Only Jeffrey seemed to notice that immediately after giving the speech their host dropped the happy expression on his face. Indeed, Stuart seemed irked, even angry. He made his way through the crowd of guests to Jacob, whom he took forcefully by the arm, and led away. Continuing his perusal of the room, Jeffrey saw that Anna Parson had joined a group of women who sat near the fireplace, while Martha and Julia had become the center of a growing crowd of eager men.

Sipping his bourbon, he thought about Stuart's speech. The man spoke and acted with the great certainty of one who possessed a written guarantee of God's will. And all these Southern fools shared his views to a greater or lesser extent; they were so wrong and yet so convinced that they were right. All but Ethan. Jeffrey smiled smugly to himself as he considered riling the holier-than-thou Dr. Stuart, and challenging his God-given assumptions with hard, ugly facts about the North's industrial might and manpower. But he reluctantly dismissed the idea. As Julia had quite forcefully impressed upon him, they had come not to debate, but to observe.

Ethan appeared at his elbow and extended his left hand, which held a glass of bourbon. "Well, Jeffrey, this is how we celebrate in Virginia. Is it at all what you had pictured?"

Jeffrey was mildly surprised to see Ethan alone beside him. He had barely spoken a word to him during the ride from Twin Pines. Ethan must have many friends in the room. Or perhaps his association with Julia and him set him at odds with some of his fellow countrymen. It would not do to mention it, of course. Jeffrey ran a hand through his red hair. Without answering Ethan's question, he gestured across the room. "Your mother seems to be enjoying herself."

Ethan nodded to the semicircle of low couches, where Anna sat with a half-dozen women. He thought her younger looking than many of the other matrons. "She and the others are all, no doubt, complaining about sons like me who drink too much, work too little, and marry too late." He sipped the bourbon and made a face of pleasure. "Yessuh!"

"The war will change all of that!" Jeffrey declared.

Ethan noticed that Keyes had a way of stating his opinions as though they were facts. He lowered his glass. "What do you mean?"

"They will be killed, many of these women's valiant, foolish sons. Except you, of course." Jeffrey smirked, indicating a jest, but Ethan merely scowled, far from amused. The comment was identical to one he himself had made quite recently, to the gathering of Jacob's friends at Twin Pines. It was one thing to face the ugly realities of war, but quite another for an outsider to joke about one's childhood friends dying. Again he recalled his own words to Jacob's gathering of patriots. But he had meant to shock and awaken them, not to mock them. In reality, the death of any one of them would be a blow that he would feel deeply.

Ethan looked soberly at his companion and felt disgusted by the look of self-satisfaction he saw on his face. It was almost as if Jeffrey would be secretly pleased by such deaths, which would confirm his view of history and the vain chivalry exhibited by Southern gentlemen.

"Your thoughts have taken a sardonic cast tonight, friend," Ethan said. His own thoughts were quite grim as he looked out on the men and women swaying in happy oblivion to the violin music. "This is a ball, Jeffrey. Don't you dance?"

Keyes laughed, a hallow bark. "I would dance with your sister, but I fear I cannot compete with the fine young men of Virginia."

The music faded to silence, marking the end of the waltz. After a burst of applause, the thirsty dancers made for the refreshment tables, where black-jacketed servants wearing white gloves served their needs.

Ethan and Jeffrey stepped away from the tables and continued to look about the ballroom.

"Our sisters seem lost to us for the evening," Jeffrey commented. Admirers formed a solid, buzzing circle around Martha and Julia, holding their drinks and laughing uproariously at all they said.

Ethan had never seen Julia in such a situation. Jeffrey looked on in obvious approval; he must be pleased to see his sister captivating an audience of the South's best and brightest. Yet Ethan had his reservations as to whether her behavior was genuine. In Boston, she had always acted with reserve in social settings.

"Tell me honestly, Jeffrey. Is Julia pursuing my brother with her heart or her head?"

Ethan's question struck Keyes as perfectly ordinary. "Julia's heart is a mystery to me."

Ethan had his answer. He must warn Jacob.

Jeffrey was looking toward the doorway through which Dr. Stuart and Jacob had disappeared a good half hour earlier. "What do you suppose that foxy old firebrand is talking to your brother about?" he asked.

"*Dr.* Stuart," Ethan replied, using the term with a respect which he hoped would eventually rub off on Jeffrey, "is most likely urging my brother to propose marriage to Caitlin."

Keyes sniffed conflict. "*You* want her, don't you?"

Ethan evaded his gaze. "Don't be silly, Jeffrey. She's been promised to Jacob since they were three."

"And that is *exactly* why you want her, my good friend."

"No! That's not it at all." Ethan quickly lowered his voice as he realized that a small circle of young ladies had turned at the sound of their argument and were now scrutinizing them. They whispered to each other, no doubt sure that the heart of the argument between him and Jeffrey concerned one of them. "Jeffrey, you annoy me tonight. I do not wish to speak of this or anything else."

Ethan quickly—too quickly—drank another bourbon. The lights blurred, the melodic intonation of the voices around him alternately soured and hushed. Then the violins began another waltz, and he simply had to dance. But with whom? As couples once again spun around the room, his gaze landed on one, and the answer to his question was clear. Ethan blithely cut in front of Noah Chesterfield and took Caitlin Stuart's hands in his.

The distress was obvious in her features, but through the haze that had swept him unstoppably toward her, he thought he detected some other emotion.

"Ethan Parson, you are intoxicated!" she cried. "What will Daddy think?"

"Caitlin, I have never before seen or held such a beautiful creature as you. I treasure you as I would a living work of art, a—"

"Ethan!" Her face was scarlet, and she tried to draw away from him as gracefully as possible. But Ethan clung to her hand desperately and would not let her go.

Caitlin felt her father's disapproving eyes on them like dagger points. From the side of her eye, she saw Jacob, too, watching them, glaring. This was impossible! She had promised herself that when Jacob asked for her hand, as she felt certain he would that evening, she would respond with grace and the true desire to know him and make the best of their marriage. She had sworn to herself that she would keep her distance from Ethan, had managed with only some difficulty so far. But now, the touch of his hand at the small of her back . . . She had to resist.

"If I had a fan, I'd knock some sense into your head, Ethan Parson!" But she knew her words lacked the conviction she had hoped to convey.

His head spinning, Ethan led her around the floor in a dizzying whirl, oblivious to the couples and envious singles watching them. Caitlin laughed as Ethan flung her in front of him as if she were a rag doll or an extension of himself. His enthusiasm took her breath away.

"I want to dance with you till the war is over!" he said, looking down on her.

"What war?" The light in her brown eyes flashed at him like stars sending signals, and Ethan knew in that giddy, pleasurable moment that she must be his, damn the consequences. The bourbon eased his guilt, and as the music subsided, he determined that he would tell Jacob soon, that very night.

"You are different tonight, Ethan," Caitlin commented breathlessly, her chest heaving. He appeared intense and far too serious. She glanced nervously toward the doorway, where her father and Jacob still stood watching them attentively, disapprovingly. But Caitlin let him gaze deeply into her eyes for a moment before stepping back to place some distance between them. "Surely you must know you have attracted attention to us with your actions. Is such the influence of your friends from Boston?"

"No, it's not the Keyeses. It's the key to my heart," he said, punning, "and you hold it."

Caitlin blushed and lowered her head.

"I must talk with Jacob tonight," he confided, searching her eyes for confirmation.

She raised her head, meeting his eyes with hers. And in that moment, she knew her life had irrevocably changed. She nodded and said, "Then I must tell Daddy."

Ethan heaved a sigh of relief. "We are in for quite an evening, Miss Stuart."

Her face lost all trace of amusement. "Indeed we are, Mr. Parson."

CHAPTER 11

JACOB HAD ONLY twice before been invited into Dr. Stuart's private library, which housed more books than did many university libraries. In each case, he had been frank, urging Jacob to propose to his daughter without tarrying. Now the professor made one last appeal.

"Jacob, I respect your father immensely. And I respect you and what you've accomplished in the management of Twin Pines as well," he began. They each held a bourbon and lighted cigar and sat in leather chairs near the fireplace. "But, Jacob, I must express to you my concerns, which are three."

Here it comes, Jacob thought. Will I leave this room in Dr. Stuart's good graces, or despised by one of the most powerful men in Albemarle County?

"First, I must understand your intentions toward my daughter. Do you intend to marry her? Because if not, there are a dozen other young hounds sniffin' around her skirts, acceptable suitors. I'll choose second best and let it go at that."

Jacob wasn't sure how to begin. His duty was clear. Yet his affections had been confused by the visit of the Keyeses, and he was no longer sure of his feelings toward Caitlin. He frowned at the image of Ethan, drunken and foolish, sweeping Caitlin around the room. It had galled him; Ethan knew it was scandalous. In all likelihood, he had done it precisely to embarrass him.

"Second," Dr. Stuart went on, breaking into Jacob's thoughts. "Are you going to rein in that brother of yours?

The boy is a menace, Jacob. You must see that. His ingratitude to your parents tears at my heart. I can ill imagine what it must be doing to your father to see his second son cavorting with abolitionists and Northern agitators. You must send him to Europe immediately."

"Are you referring to the Keyeses?" Dr. Stuart chose his words carefully, and Jacob knew he had used that particular word with special intent.

Stuart nodded, puffing on the cigar. He blew a spiraling ring of blue-gray smoke toward the high ceiling, taking that moment to let the gravity of his charge sink in. "Jacob, I am sorry to say that I have written confirmation from sources in Washington describing the Keyeses as agents under the employ of Mr. Lincoln."

"I find that difficult to believe," Jacob was bold enough to say. While he did not trust Jeffrey, he found the professor's accusations unbelievably harsh.

"If war breaks out, they will be hung as spies, mark my words."

"Both of them? You are certain?"

"Sure as rain is wet and cottonballs white." Stuart could see that what he had said came as a blow to Jacob. "I could mislead you and say all is well, Jacob, but I don't sense you would want that. The war may well begin soon, and on our own soil, some say, or in Maryland. Boys like yourself will be dying for the cause, if it comes to that. You're a brave young man. I know you'll fight to keep Virginia free. At this very moment," he went on, waving his cigar like a baton, "Federal troops are en route to Charleston. A battle will likely ensue, and war will follow, I am quite certain. History has been leading us down this dangerous road for fifty years. Jacob, we cannot allow anything, even what we believe to be friendship, to interfere with our preservation and our family's security, now can we?"

Jacob said nothing. He admired Dr. Stuart. In all likelihood what he said was true . . . of Jeffrey. But of Julia? Perhaps what he had read merely indicated that they supported abolition, which of course they did on moral grounds. That hardly made them spies. He tried to explain.

"No, son, you are not listening! They are in the employ of enemy forces—"

"Doctor, with all respect, we have no enemies at this time, except perhaps intolerance and fear. We are not at war. I, too, reserve many suspicions of Jeffrey Keyes. But the Keyeses are my brother's friends. They are here by his request—"

Dr. Stuart jumped to his feet. "He was duped, Jacob! That is my point! The boy isn't sharp like you!"

"Yessir, he is sharp, but not like me!" Jacob cried, standing face to face with Dr. Stuart. His aggressiveness had surprised the older man, who took a step back and held his cigar at arm's length.

"I do not believe that Ethan is the dupe of any cause. Whatever he does, he does of his own free will. The Keyeses are guests in our home and will be treated as such until they leave Twin Pines. While I personally dislike and distrust Mr. Keyes, I will not have him mistreated or abused in my father's home. So long as Virginia is not at war with any foreign or domestic enemies, which she is not at this time, I consider this entire discussion presumptive and premature. Good night, sir." Jacob rose to leave, setting the unsmoked cigar in a brass ashtray beside the chair. He held the bourbon in his trembling hand.

Stuart rose also. "Jacob, at least discuss this very delicate matter with your father. Charles will see it my way. You must send the Keyeses packing. And in the meantime, you must keep them away from your brother. For all we know, he may already be poisoned by them."

"Good night, Doctor." Jacob was too furious to trust himself to speak.

"And what of my daughter?" the professor pressed in a belligerent tone.

Jacob inhaled deeply. "I intend to ask for your daughter's hand in marriage tonight. I trust that you approve. Good night, sir."

He shut the door quietly, pausing just outside to get

his temper back under control. What had made him act with such disrespect? He had never before confronted Dr. Stuart on any issue; he even agreed with much of what he had said. The Keyeses were spies. The statement drove through his mind like a sledgehammer. He had sensed it, had not wanted to admit it. All evening he had been stealing glances at Julia. Like a sparkling emerald in her green gown, she had attracted the attentions of every man in the room. And then Caitlin had spun before him in Ethan's arms, and he had wanted her, too.

Closing his eyes, he heaved a deep sigh and found himself trembling head to foot, as if facing a firing squad. When he opened them, there stood Ethan, his head to a side and his eyes glazed, grinning sheepishly.

"We must talk, Jacob," he said.

"Yes," said Jacob, grabbing his brother's arm and leading him into the empty dining room.

In the shadows of the chilly room dominated by an immense oak dining table twenty feet long and flanked by as many chairs, Jacob was about to begin his lecture when Ethan reached out and, without asking, took Jacob's bourbon and swallowed it. The dark wood paneling cast a funereal light on them. Ethan's black bow tie was undone and askew; one collar was up. He looked like a drunken fool.

"Good Lord, Ethan, you have lost all restraint! Is there any sense in my addressing you at this time or shall we adjourn until the morning?"

Ethan burst out laughing, shifting his weight unsteadily from foot to foot in a manner that startled and upset Jacob. He had certainly said nothing humorous.

"Jacob," Ethan began, circling the long table as if he and his brother were playing tag, "why do you always speak to me as though you were running for the Senate and I were some poor farmer like the Tylers? Why?"

Jacob stood still, watching as his brother continued around the long expanse of oak. "Ethan, I must tell you something very disturbing," he began in an even tone. "There can be no retreat from this issue."

"Charge!" Ethan cried. Raising an imaginary saber, he stumbled around the table at a faster pace. In the light of the fireplace, Jacob could see the drunken luster of his brother's eyes, which sparkled as if filled with champagne.

"Ethan," Jacob repeated. "Ethan, your friends are watched as spies. You will be a marked man if war breaks out, and I must marry Caitlin Stuart or risk infuriating the doctor even further." Jacob spoke in haste, and there was bitterness in his words. "Why must you always bring out the basest in me?" he asked his weaving, hiccuping brother.

Ethan correctly interpreted his brother's outburst as one of pain and frustration, not simply anger. His mind too foggy to follow all that his brother had said, Ethan struggled to isolate one comment and understand it. "The Keyeses are spies? Stuart told you that?" How had the old man found out?

"Yes!" Jacob shook with rage. "Your friends serve Mr. Lincoln!"

Ethan tried to step closer to his brother but tripped on the leg of a chair and caught himself with his hands on the edge of the table.

Turning his back in disgust, Jacob stood facing the fireplace. Two and a half decades of frustration and bewilderment surged within him. The good brother, the big brother, the one who must always make peace and compromise, the one who stayed home with Daddy while Ethan ran off to Harvard.

In that terrible moment the Devil seized control. Jacob grabbed the wrought-iron fireplace poker, whirled around, and raised it.

His brother stood slumped over the table, hanging his head. His starched white shirt was bunched and misshapen where it protruded from his black morning coat; his brown hair stood wildly on his head. Jacob stood frozen, until the cold bite of the metal in his hand awoke him. He lowered the poker and set it back with a clatter.

Ethan slowly lifted his head and turned. "Stoking the fire? Of course. Every time I fail you or embarrass the family, you do something useful." Ethan's face was a mask of sadness and pain. He slurred the words at his brother. "You can't marry Caitlin. I am. She wants me, not you. Even Jeffrey can see that. And Julia is using you. I don't know how . . ."

The blows hit Jacob one after another like a fist to the chin: Caitlin didn't want him; Julia's affections were a pretense. He was left once again with nothing and no one to trust and believe in except his parents and Twin Pines. Could it be true, all that his brother had said? Or was Ethan too drunk to know what he was saying?

Jacob couldn't think straight. He felt as if someone had reached in and yanked out his heart and pumped his head full of smoke. Turning from Ethan, he exited the dining room. He ran through the kitchen and past the startled servants, reaching for the door.

Outside, the night was clear and cold, and the stars and crescent moon cast a pale, bloodless light on the house and grounds. He placed his hand against a magnolia trunk to steady himself against the whirl of emotions that spun within him. He was at once relieved and intensely embarrassed. He did not want to marry Caitlin, not really. Yet to be insulted and supplanted by his little brother was more than he could bear. How could he hold his head up in church or at the militia drills? He would forever be talked about as Caitlin Stuart's scorned suitor, the one she cast aside to marry his younger brother.

The jealousy he felt was molten; the surge of ugly emotion brought back the feel of the poker in his hand. Jacob let out a shaky breath, but the evil emotions would not leave him. He wondered if he would ever feel anything but anger or envy for his brother; at times such as this evening, he was all but consumed by it. Were his brother to die tomorrow, he was not sure he could weep at the young fool's funeral.

Jacob was struck by a sense of foreboding, a sense that he would have the chance someday to determine which of them could swallow the bitter medicine of life with the surest stomach. Perhaps that would be the test that would show him whether the love he once felt for Ethan was forever dead, or just wounded.

Again, he breathed deeply, welcoming the cold air in his lungs. What Ethan had said cast all of Jacob's convictions into doubt. If indeed Julia were playing him for a fool and he had not discerned the deception, how could he ever trust himself again, in business as well as love? And if Caitlin, who had known Jacob all his life, preferred Ethan over him, what did that say about his own character? He looked up at the hundreds of stars dotting the sky, and imagined himself the tiniest and smallest of them, a dying body casting its last faint light toward Earth.

His solemn reverie was broken by the squeak of the door and the sound of footsteps on the stairs behind him. Assuming it must be a servant on an errand, he did not turn around.

"Jacob, your brother told me what was said."

Jacob stiffened. Caitlin's soothing voice only pained him now. Her voice was trembling, but he couldn't tell if it was from the cold or her own sentiments.

"He should not have spoken for me," she continued, "not in such an ungentlemanly manner. I can only attribute his behavior to the bourbon my father serves. It is unpardonable."

Her words were spoken with heartfelt emotion. Jacob slowly turned to face her. She had wrapped a shawl around her bare shoulders, but she was shaking. "You are cold. Go back inside," he said.

"Only once you've told me the truth."

"What truth?" he spat. "That my brother leads a charmed life while I am doomed to unhappiness? That I am a fool, with you as well as others? Is that the truth you speak of?" He was so bitter that he almost ran off, leaving her remonstrating with the wind and the trees.

"Jacob Parson, stop talking like a boy! You are a leader in this part of Virginia, and you know it! My father values no one's opinion more than yours."

"Do you love Ethan?"

Caitlin's hands flew to her cheeks, and her mouth opened. She tried to speak, but no words emerged. Tears filled her eyes. This confrontation wasn't easy or pleasant for either of them, Jacob realized. The steam of their breaths hung in the cold air, dissipating clouds of loss. The still silence of the night was almost unbearable, unnatural.

She stepped close to him, tentatively reaching out to take his hand. "Jacob, I am so sorry."

"We'll die of the cold if we don't—" he began.

She put her finger to his lips. "I must explain. I shall always love you."

"As a brother," he added curtly.

She framed his face with her gloved hands, directing his eyes to meet hers. "As a friend," she told him. "As a wife perhaps. I should justifiably be proud to become Mrs. Jacob Parson. Any girl in Albemarle County would be proud. But I have a heart, too, and it is filled and torn apart at the same time, by the same man."

"Ethan."

"No one expected this less than I, Jacob. You must believe that. I've barely seen him these past four years. It's the implied treachery of it all—"

"No one could call you treacherous, Caitlin."

She sighed deeply, shutting her eyes for a moment. "People will view it as treachery and deceit. It pleases me to know that you understand the truth. Before I would hurt you or destroy your ambitions, I'd lay down and die."

"I don't want that," Jacob was quick to say. "Not yet," he added, teasing.

Caitlin flung back her head and laughed, so that the curls of her hair danced about her face and shoulders. "Oh, God bless you, Jacob Parson. Can you forgive me? And your brother?"

He broke free of her gently and firmly and turned to face the broad fields that stretched as far as the eye could see to the south and west. In the stark clarity of the win ter's night, the stars appeared to twinkle and wink. The moon shone like a beacon, bathing them in a silver light. Trying to slow his pounding heart, he stroked his moustache and pressed into service all the willpower his twenty-six years had nurtured.

"I believe I can," he said softly. "I know I should. You have done nothing wrong, Caitlin."

"Nor has your brother." She spoke diffidently, uncertainly.

Jacob said nothing.

"You won't punish him?" Her voice trembled.

Jacob was not unaware that he had a good deal of influence in central Virginia. His word, like her father's, could ruin a man's career and future. Yet he could not. "I suspect he's punished himself enough."

Jacob spun and took Caitlin's hands in his. She seemed small and vulnerable, her face bathed in the ethereal beauty of the moonlight. "Don't ask for my blessing, not yet."

She shook her head. "I ask only that you don't hate us."

Once again he was called upon to be the stable, accepting force. Once again, he would put his own feelings aside to let others live freely. It was impossible for him to do otherwise. Jacob released her left hand and shook the other broadly, as if sealing a business agreement. There was something comical in the gesture, but Caitlin's laugh was uncertain.

"Done," he said.

Shivering, they ran up the stairs and into the Stuarts' bustling kitchen.

When Caitlin and Jacob rejoined the couples and elders in the ballroom, Ethan was nowhere in sight. All eyes turned toward them expectantly. Dr. Stuart studied them with an intensity that might have blinded lesser mortals. But Jacob and Caitlin held up under the scrutiny. Jacob left her side to get a drink, giving Caitlin the opportunity to approach her father. They spoke solemnly together in a corner of the room for a few minutes, and Jacob noted that Dr. Stuart seemed shaken and sad. Trying to gauge the expression behind the professor's spectacles, Jacob, too, felt a deep sadness. The relationship between them, between their families, would never be quite the same.

Jacob froze as Caitlin asked the guests for silence. The tension in the air leaped from person to person. What would she say?

"I've learned a song, a Scottish ballad which is a favorite of my father's. I should like to sing it now."

After a moment of scattered applause, the crowd quieted, and she began to sing the words to a haunting melody:

> "Now all that men could do,
> And all is done in vain,
> My love, my native land, adieu,
> For I must cross the main, my dear,
> For I must cross the main.
>
> He turned him right and round again,
> Upon the Irish shore,
> He gave his bridle reins a shake,
> Said adieu for evermore, my dear,
> Adieu for evermore.
>
> The soldier from the war returns,
> The sailor from the main,
> But I have parted from my love,
> Never to meet again, my dear,
> Never to meet again.
>
> When day is gone and night is come,
> And folk are bound to sleep,
> I'll think on him that's far away,
> The lee-land night and weep, my dear,
> The lee-land night and weep."

When she had finished, the silence was pregnant. "Oh, come. It wasn't that bad!" Caitlin cried, upon which everyone clapped and cheered. She had touched them with the sad ballad.

Jacob looked around the hulking figure of Jimmy Kilpatrick and gazed across the room toward Dr. Stuart. But he had left the room. He turned toward the man before him, who was staggering under the weight of too many bourbons in his belly.

"How brave of her to sing that song," Jacob said.

Jimmy looked blank. "What do you mean?"

Fleetingly, he glanced toward Caitlin as she accepted congratulations from admirers, though when she smiled her eyes reflected her father's sober expression. "To come into this room of friends and neighbors scared to death about what might happen next and sing a sad song about war and love!"

"Too sad for my taste," said Jimmy, reaching for the ham biscuits.

Then the room quieted again as Caitlin introduced, "Miss Julia Keyes, our guest from Boston."

"I have no singing voice," Julia admitted. "Rather, this is a poem. I learned it especially for this occasion." Clearing her throat, she began her recitation:

"What will you do, my love, when I am going,
With white sail flowing,
The sea beyond?

What will you do, my love, when waves divide us
And friends may chide us
For being fond?

Tho' waves divide us and friends be chiding,
In faith abiding,
I shall still be true!

And I'll pray for thee on stormy ocean,
In deep devotion,
That's what I'll do!

What would you do, love, if distant tidings
Thy fond confidings
Should undermine;

And I abiding beneath sultry skies
Should think other eyes
Were bright as thine?

Oh, name it not! Tho' guilt and shame
Were on thy name,
I'd still be true!

But that heart of thine, should another share it,
I could not bear it,
What would I do?

What would you do, love, when home returning,
With hopes high burning,
With wealth for you—

If my bark that bounded o'er foreign foam
Should be lost near home—
Oh, what would you do?

So thou were spared I'd bless the morrow
In want and sorrow
That left me you.

And I'd welcome thee from the wasting billow
My heart thy pillow.
That would do."

The applause and appreciation were immediate. In choosing a poem by one of their contemporaries, Mary Chestnut, from Richmond, Julia had proved herself capable of understanding what many called "the Southern heart." It could be mournful or joyous, as Ethan explained to Jeffrey in the doorway, but it was always romantic and grand and harkened to the past. The poem had struck just the right note. Julia was, for the moment, almost one of them.

"I can perform, too," Martha declared, approaching her brother and Jeffrey, pouting. All of her admirers had rushed to congratulate Julia, as had Jacob.

"What are you going to do, read to yourself from Byron's *Don Juan* without moving your lips? Or sew a ribbon on a bonnet?"

Her brother's glee only added to Martha's irritation, as did the smile on Jeffrey's lips at Ethan's taunt. Martha slipped from the room to "escape further insult," as she put it to them.

Five young men in formal attire followed Martha, offering her sweets and punch. Somewhat mollified, she scooped up her skirts and settled into a stuffed chair in a smaller parlor adjoining the ballroom. Family portraits adorned the walls, paintings of dour, heavyset figures dressed in black.

"Why are they all frowning at us?" Martha asked her beaus. She was bored with them, this common handful of boys pretending to be men, who thought they wanted to marry her. If they only knew me, Martha thought.

Rising to her feet, Martha whirled around the room in the arms of an imaginary beau. "I want a Gypsy to carry me away from all this," she exclaimed. "For I have a Gypsy heart!"

Then she stopped suddenly and dismissed all of them, oblivious to their wide-eyed stares. "Go on, shoo, the lot of you. Go!"

Abashed, the young men left Martha alone to brood. She thought hatefully of Julia Keyes, who had won over a room of Martha's friends with some silly poem about the sea. Poo! She could do better. She ought to stand up and read to them from one of the "obscene" poems of Baudelaire, which she had found among Ethan's books. She bit her lip and picked at her hairpins. Within five minutes she desired other company, however. She had calmed herself to the point that she could rejoin the music and the dancers in the ballroom, where, as she saw when she reappeared in the enormous room, Jeffrey Keyes and Ethan stood by themselves in the corner farthest from the violins.

"Why are the songs and poems so damn sad?" Jeffrey asked.

Ethan, who had sobered up a bit, tried to explain. "We're romantic! No matter how cruel the past, it looks better to us as we get older. We even recall wars and famines fondly, as times of great heroism and sacrifice. Southerners see themselves as the new chosen people, if you will."

Jeffrey tipped an imaginary hat. "I won't, but I shall let it pass for now."

Jacob had waited for ten minutes to shake Julia's hand.

"Come now. We're better acquainted than that," she said, offering her cheek. Blushing deeply, Jacob brushed his lips against her cheek. Her perfume and body warmth rose to strike him like divine revelation. He did not notice the awestruck looks given Jacob by the other young men gathered around Julia, or the jealousy flashing in the eyes of the other young ladies now unattended by beaus. Jacob knew only that he wanted this woman, reason and Ethan's warnings be damned.

After a round of raucous toasts had been offered, and the musicians had begun a Virginia reel, Ethan and Caitlin slipped away to the smaller, adjoining parlor. Caitlin's dark brows were furrowed when she sat down on a low overstuffed chair. If he knew her father at all, Ethan thought to himself, he had given her a difficult time. More than likely he would not accept the match.

"I told Father that I could not marry Jacob," she hurried to tell him.

Ethan relaxed, but only for a moment. Leaning forward to take her hand, he asked, "Did you tell him why?"

"I intimated, yes." The hesitant look in her brown eyes confirmed his suspicion; she had not been able to tell him. She looked anxiously toward the door before continuing. "Ethan, it is too soon for the entire truth to come out. The truth has great power, but we must save it for a time when it can make a difference. Daddy is dead set against you right now."

Letting her hand drop, Ethan sat back on his chair. "Your father and everyone else in the Commonwealth of Virginia."

"Not everyone."

Her voice was low, and there was a tinge of hurt in it. Ethan looked earnestly into her beautiful brown eyes. "Yes, of course. Except you—" He bent toward her slowly. "—my love."

Caitlin sank into the sensation of his mouth tasting hers. Curling her arms around his neck, she responded to his embrace. Then, remembering where they were, she pulled away. Looking deeply into his eyes, she told him, "This is the happiest I've ever been, Ethan. I don't know how, or when, but this will all be worked out in time." Her words held great conviction, her smile was sincere and strong.

Ethan hugged her again quickly. "It shall work out, you are absolutely right, my love." She laughed with him. Yet as they left the parlor to return to the ballroom, Ethan wondered what their chances really were. Her father was a formidable adversary, and he would oppose her choice to marry him with all the forces at his disposal. He could only hope that when the time came, Caitlin would have the courage to defy him. Even as they had embraced, he had felt that she possessed an inner circle of secrets to which even he was barred. He could only hope that one day she would ask him to enter that circle.

"Do you know why I love this library, Jacob?"

Dr. Stuart had ushered him into the library for one last "brief discussion." Jacob dreaded it, knowing that Stuart despised Ethan, and was disappointed in him.

"The books and the quiet, I suppose," he replied hesitantly. The strains of the Virginia reel were barely audible in the paneled, book-lined room.

Stuart shook his head. "No, I love it because in here I can speak the truth, unvarnished and untainted by popular opinion or social delicacy. That's what I want to do now, Jacob, to speak the truth." He reached for a box on the table next to his leather chair and offered Jacob a cigar.

Jacob declined. The ridiculous nature of the meeting was beginning to dawn on him. In one evening he had lost Caitlin Stuart to his own brother and discovered that he had fallen in love with a Yankee spy. What could Dr. Stuart possibly tell him that would challenge this? he wondered.

"You're smiling. Good. That's the spirit." Guilt sent a deep blush across Jacob's face. "I have spoken with my daughter, and while I am deeply disappointed, and fail to understand the sense of your decision not to marry, I won't make any demands, upon her or upon you. However, you must see that the Keyeses cannot be allowed to remain at Twin Pines for a moment longer. Their presence is an insult to both you and your father. Jacob, those two are known Yankee agents. If Virginia were to secede tomorrow, they might well be held for trial. And you shelter them in your home! This cannot go on."

Dr. Stuart was red faced and boiling with anger as he faced the young man he so wanted for a son-in-law. Jacob had disappointed him severely on this Feast of the Epiphany, the happiest of the Christian holidays but for Christmas itself. On this one point, at least, Jacob had to agree. He had to send the Keyeses packing, and soon.

"They shall be gone within the week, Doctor. Our family will have no further dealings with them," Jacob swore. He was at war with his emotions, but he could not ignore the impossibility of their current situation. Jeffrey—and Julia—would have to leave.

Dr. Stuart smiled. Rising from his chair, he said, "I knew you would see it my way, Jacob. You can hardly welcome into your home known agents—"

"You have made your point, sir, and I have yielded. Mother is no doubt tired, and she will soon begin worrying about Father." Jacob had to control the urge to tear a row of books from the shelves and throw them around the room.

When they shook hands at the door, Dr. Stuart cast a questioning look on him, which Jacob steadfastly ignored. He was not going to reveal Caitlin's attachment to Ethan before she, as well as he himself, was ready.

Though the music continued, Jacob soon found and persuaded his family and their guests that it was the time to depart. He had just enough time to whisper in Julia's ear a warning about her brother. She looked alarmed, her green eyes widening with fear.

She surprised him by replying, "My brother is a stranger to me in affairs of the heart. So far as I know, he has none."

Jacob thought that she must be joking, but the stark seriousness of her face soon persuaded him to believe her. Perhaps she did not know what he was up to. Perhaps.

As they were waiting for their greatcoats and wraps at the door, Jacob leaned over and spoke quietly to Jeffrey. "You must do me the favor of returning to Boston within the week. I hope you agree."

Jeffrey looked startled and blank; his narrow face was stiff with bewilderment. For a moment he absorbed Jacob's invitation that he and his sister leave, and all its implications. "We shall leave two days hence, if you so desire it. We should have had to leave soon in any event. My work demands that we reside in the nation's capital for the near future."

The words ran through Jacob like a saw. "What work is that, may I ask?" he said, taking his greatcoat from the house servant and slipping it on.

"My sister and I are seeking to make investments in companies likely to prosper in the coming conflict. You see . . ."

"I should rather not see!" Jacob hissed, placing a steely grip on Keyes's elbow. "You will leave the day after tomorrow."

Keyes rubbed his elbow much of the way back to Twin Pines, and although Julia questioned him repeatedly, he would not tell his sister what had transpired between Jacob and him. "Your Southern gentleman has turned into a mad dog! We are leaving the day after tomorrow."

Julia was wise enough to agree with him. But her heart, like so many of those around her at Twin Pines, was in conflict with itself, and like a house divided, could not so endure for long.

CHAPTER 12

THE DAY FOLLOWING the Epiphany Ball dawned overcast and chilly, with a wind from the east promising a cold rain. Jacob instructed the slaves to repair harnesses and gear and to tend to the plows and animals, in preparation for the first planting, which would take place in another month's time.

The Parsons often passed such dreary winter days playing charades, sewing, and reading. But the strain of their presence at Twin Pines prompted the Keyeses to pass the day in their rooms, and the rest of the family settled into solitary activity.

After spending the morning at her embroidery table, Martha had had enough solitude. So after the midday meal, she joined Julia in her room. Martha was secretly pleased that Julia would soon be gone. While she teased her new friend about her success at the Epiphany Ball, she had been envious of Julia's abilities to recite with such great emotion—and with such great success. But she did realize that with Julia's parting she would be losing a link with a world away from Twin Pines. And she had soon launched into a stream of enthusiastic questions, forgiving Julia for stealing her beaus the night before.

"Tell me about Washington," Martha pleaded. "What's it like?"

Julia was delighted to talk about her new home, deciding to skirt the issues of politics and war, which she judged to be of secondary importance to Martha.

"Well, thousands of people live there, including the president, and all members of Congress, while it is in session."

"Are there many stores and shops?"

Julia nodded. "Certainly more than here, although I am told Richmond has some fine shops. Why do you ask? Do you want to visit us? You are welcome, of course. Just give us a week or two to get settled."

Martha grabbed a pillow and threw it across the room. "Daddy would never let me go!" she exclaimed. "Jacob would tie me to an oak first."

Julia had to laugh. But glimpsing the hurt expression on Martha's face, she quickly recovered herself and smiled. "I do hope that one day you will be allowed to visit. We would welcome the chance to repay your hospitality. Perhaps one day your brother himself may visit the capital."

Martha froze in shock. "Jacob! In the land of the enemy!"

Julia shook her head. "No, no, Martha. Ethan. I was talking about Ethan."

Martha flopped onto the bed. "Daddy's just about ready to ship Ethan off to Europe for the duration of the war, I heard Mama say." Then Martha grabbed her throat, as if to swallow the words she had just spoken. "Promise you won't tell anyone I told you that! I'm not sure Ethan knows, or what he'd do if he knew I had told you."

Julia moved her hand to her heart and promised. "Actually, Europe is a lovely continent."

Martha asked more, especially about France, and the afternoon passed in the buzz of conversation.

* * *

In the quiet of his room, Ethan pondered his situation. Jeffrey and Julia would be leaving the next day. He wished they had already parted, that they had never come. What would he do? Their visit had not helped clarify where his loyalties lay, but merely confused him. Why, when faced with Jeffrey's taunts, did he defend a family that would not accept him as he was? Once the Keyeses were gone, he would still face the same dilemmas.

And their visit had affected not only him. He remembered Jacob and the look in his cool gray eyes when Julia had offered him her cheek at the Epiphany Ball. He found the image more than a little disturbing.

Charles Parson was puffing on a cigar so intently that Anna opened the bedroom window a crack more, and stood breathing in the cold, fresh air.

"They will be gone tomorrow, Charles. Won't you at least wish them a pleasant journey?"

Charles looked at his wife as if she had just suggested he fly a balloon to Washington to argue his case before Congress. "Woman, I sincerely hope the carriage overturns and that young spy from Boston is pinned under a horse's rump for the remainder of the year. And as for that sneaking girl—"

"Charles, you mind yourself! Jacob says there is no reason to suspect the girl of anything."

Charles spat out a bit of tobacco. "No reason! She's his blood, that's the reason."

Anna returned to her high-backed armchair near his bed. He looked so old today, and distorted by the pent-up steam that never found sufficient release. "Casting such judgments serves no purpose here, Charles," she said calmly. "We still have the plantation, the slaves, the house."

"Yes, for now. But the war hasn't begun yet, woman. Just wait. Wait till Federal troops arrive in Charleston at Sumter, and fighting breaks out. People just like our guests the Keyeses will be swinging from the trees like moss, I tell you."

Anna looked at her husband sharply. "Charles, since your accident, you paint a grotesque portrait of the human race. Shame on you."

"That's right, cut off the head of the messenger. You're as bad as the Pharoahs."

"If you'd spend more time reading the Good Book and applying your mind to it, and less time abusing its glory, your path to Heaven would be a straighter one and I would worry less." Anna was angered by her husband's false view of the world; it was one that had become more and more derogatory over the past decade of his sickness.

"Lo, and they harass and put to death another prophet," moaned Charles. "The fact is, we're headed for Hell in a handbasket, and you know it. There's talk already in Montgomery of a confederacy of all Southern states, with our own president and congress and laws. I have read about assassination plots against Lincoln, and but for the Sixth Commandment, I would applaud such an act of patriotism."

"Charles Parson, shame on you! He's a man, as you are, and he deserves to live his allotted threescore and ten."

"He's a devil and a coward," Charles snapped.

Anna saw that there would be no reasoning with him today, and she left him to fume and smoke in silence.

She prayed daily for a miracle to restore to him the use of his legs, knowing that she was so moved by selfish concerns for her own well-being and sanity. She had put up with his unyielding demands for ten long years, and on days such as this she sought escape from his putrid room as quickly as possible.

More than anything, she prayed that he was wrong about Mr. Lincoln and the war. But that prayer, too, seemed to go unanswered with the dawn of each new and inflammatory day.

In the kitchen, she snapped at Clara for no reason, then apologized. Clara remained silent as she watched Anna storm silently to the larder to see what, if anything, needed to be ordered from Charlottesville. She had seen

the same look on her mistress's face before, and she knew
Charles Parson lay at the bottom of her peevishness.

"I pray for the master, too," she said. Anna squeezed
her hand, allowing the hot tears to slip down her cheeks.

The influenza epidemic continued to lay low many of
the field hands, male and female, and on the day before
the Keyeses departure, Anna, Martha, and Julia assisted
Clara and the other house servants to deliver soup and
bread to the stricken bondsmen.

Jeffrey had told Julia of his tour of the quarters with
Ethan, but it was her first time inside any of the cabins
that faced each other in a double row. She found it ironic
that it was the last day of their visit to Twin Pines that
she finally had occasion to see the terrible institution for
herself, without intervening eyes.

Carrying two bowls of soup and a small loaf of bread,
she rapped at the unpainted plank door of the first slave
cabin she came to. When no one answered the knock, she
slowly opened the door. In the dim light of the cabin,
almost hidden by a worn quilt, lay a black man and
woman, in their thirties, she guessed. Julia smiled, but
the fright in their eyes remained.

"I have brought you soup and bread from Miss Anna.
Are you better?" Julia asked.

The woman nodded once slowly, but the man gave no
sign of understanding her. Their unbroken, wide-eyed
gaze was unnerving. She looked around her, appalled,
failing to notice the cleanliness and many personal effects
the black couple guarded. To her, the shack was a prison
cell, pure and simple, an inhumane trap set for an innocent quarry. "May I bring you anything else?" she asked.
Again, only the woman moved, shaking her head in refusal as the man coughed, hacking and gasping for breath.
They were frightened of her. She felt foolish standing before people she so wanted to help, feeling as if the gulf
between them was vast and immutable. They might as
well have stood on the moon, for all the good she had
done them.

Quickly she bowed her head and left them, shutting the door against the cold wind. It irked her to think that conversation between herself and a slave was out of the question. Would the heart of a slave always remain a mystery to her, like a book locked away in a vault she could see but could never hope to enter?

As she crossed to the next cabin, there were tears of frustration in Julia's eyes at the thought of these field hands who had nothing, and who might be sold like mules at any time. During one of their first conversations together, Martha had explained to her that the Parsons had never sold anyone, or broken up a family, but that did not lessen the sadness of their plight, nor the difficulty of her own immediate task. Why, when she had their best interests in mind, did they retreat from her?

She was amazed at the ease Martha displayed in the slaves' presence, and at the relative comfort they showed her in return. She knew all of the slaves by name, and approached her visits to the cabins as nothing more than calls of mercy bestowed by her kindness. It was proof in and of itself of the kindness of their family in difficult times. When Julia mentioned the "inherent evil of an institution such as slavery," Martha was confused about her use of the word "institution." She viewed slavery not as an institution at all, but as the way that whites and blacks had always interacted, and always would interact.

From her brother, Julia had learned of Caitlin Stuart's involvement in the Underground Railroad, which was now in its tenth year of operation. She was pleased, for Caitlin appealed to her; she sensed a strength to the woman. But more importantly, Jeffrey had indicated that Caitlin held a certain influence over Ethan. Perhaps he, too, might become involved, and that made their visit a success, regardless of what Ethan had told Jeffrey about not betraying his family and home. For as everyone knew, love would conquer even the most strongly constructed defenses.

The only troubling aspect to her first journey south of the nation's capital was that of her unresolved feelings for

Jacob. As a slaveowner and overseer of the estate, he should be anathema to her. He was responsible for the acquisition and discipline of their slaves. He must have administered punishments to the field hands.

Yet instead of despising him for it, she found herself trying to understand him. She was troubled by the recurring feeling that one day she and Jacob would meet at a boundary that neither could cross with impunity, and one would cause the other's death. She had awakened the night before in a cold sweat after dreaming of Jacob. Wearing only a nightshirt, he had beckoned to her to ride behind him on a giant steed twenty hands high, and after she had straddled the beast, it had run with such a fury and speed that she was thrown off. Jacob saw her fall, in her dream, but he would not slow the horse to see to her safety. And in his eyes shone a secret desire to see her injured.

She rarely placed much faith in dreams and visions, but she wondered how much of the dream was nonsense, and how much a portent. Julia could not even guess, and had said not a word of it to anyone, especially not to Jeffrey. For a weak man, he was able to prey upon the weaknesses of others with the insatiable appetite of a scavenger bird.

Clara was haggard and irritable. The influenza had laid Alex low for the better part of a week. His towering body was racked by chest-rattling coughs. He slept fitfully, shaking with chills and, a moment later, burning with a fever. Clara, a confident nurse, wasn't sure whether to purge him, bleed him, or just let him be. She fed him nothing but tea and biscuits with honey, the only solid food Alex could keep down.

Thomas peeked in several times a day to see how his father was doing, and always left the cellar of the great house looking morose. Out of sympathy, Jacob gave Thomas a good deal of free time, a luxury afforded few slaves, for as most Southerners believed and said, "an idle slave is a dangerous slave." The bondsmen themselves turned the motto on its head and joshed each other by saying "an idle slave is six feet under," and "a happy slave live in Canada."

The influenza epidemic slowed the Underground Railroad, where runaways and their helpers alike suffered in great numbers. The journey north to freedom was difficult enough; few men could make it, no matter how great their desire to live free. The illness and the wet, bone-chilling weather of early January served to slow the pace of life at Twin Pines. In the rich tobacco fields of the Tidewater region, nearer to Chesapeake Bay and the James River, the kinder ocean breezes warmed the winter laborer to a tolerable degree. But at Twin Pines, under the shadow of the Blue Ridge Mountains, the wind seemed to dip down directly from Canada. "The hawk," they called it. "The hawk is out today!"

The evening before the Keyeses' departure passed quietly. Anna did her best to make the guests feel comfortable, but Jacob's stony silence and Ethan's sniping did little to help. After dinner, she suggested that they play charades, but her proposition was met with no enthusiasm. Julia and Jeffrey retired to their rooms and packed, while Jacob and Ethan found themselves drawn to the library. Martha, who had finally grown weary of trying to elicit accurate and detailed information about life in the city of Washington, withdrew to her room to read a romance, where at least the characters spoke to one another, even if it was to argue or lay down the gauntlet.

In the library, Jacob pored over the accounts ledger, tapping himself on the forehead with the graphite pencil as he reflected on the figures. Ethan pulled a volume of Sir Walter Scott down from the shelves and settled into the chair before the fire. He tried to lose himself in the tale of Ivanhoe, but the knight's sense of chivalry irritated him. He preferred a man of action, particularly when romance was concerned. Closing the book in his lap, he gazed distractedly into the fire, giving himself over to the thoughts that had been preoccupying him all afternoon. The Keyeses' behavior toward him had marked him painfully and indelibly. Their boldness astounded him, yet his anger had begun to cool. Walking in their boots, would he have behaved differently? Truthfully, Ethan knew that had he still been within the pleasant confines of his rooms at Harvard, he would have responded with less hostility, however much their secrets excluded and wounded him. It was a puzzle he still had to solve; he must sort through and understand his emotions before he committed himself to any action.

When he looked up, Jacob was watching him closely. The older brother set down his pencil and rubbed his eyes. Ethan took advantage of the moment. Perhaps Jacob would be willing to hear what he had to say on another topic that was of concern to him.

Ethan chose to be brief and direct. "Jacob, I was aware of Julia's behavior toward you last night. As far as I can determine, she was not playacting. I half believe the girl's gone and fallen in love with you, difficult as that may be to conceive.

"Still," he went on, enjoying Jacob's discomfort, "stranger things have happened. We have a president who apparently resembles an ape so closely that his wife is often fooled when the circus comes to town." Ethan enjoyed his joke immensely, but Jacob had stopped listening after hearing the words "in love with you." He never expected to hear those words directed at him by his brother, who, more than he, had the fiery nature to attract such passion. He hardly knew what to do, if anything. Ethan noticed Jacob's doubt and realized with apprehension that his brother might actually fall prey to Julia's wiles. "And if you were to go to her, brother, and tell her how you feel, what then, eh?" His voice was thick with a biting cynicism. "Hell, the war can't last longer than a decade or two. You'll still be a young man of fifty, eh?"

Jacob could not bear to see his brother act this way. He refused to be rankled by his comments, and refused to have his feelings for Julia toyed with. But much as he hated to admit it, the Keyeses were no joking matter. He closed the ledger and looked across the room to where

Ethan was sitting before the fire. When he spoke it was with measured intensity. "Ethan, the Keyeses are not to be trusted. I don't care what they say or do. They are in the employ of our enemy." He held up a hand to cut off Ethan's protest. "Yes, I know that we are not actually at war with anyone at the moment, but war is inevitable. Please remember that they have crossed the line of decent behavior by invading our home in the guise of friendship in order to persuade you to join their cause, betray your family and society—"

"For the greater good!" Ethan shouted, shaking a fist in the air.

"For whose greater good? Not mine. Not Daddy's or Mama's. And not Martha's or yours! Far as I can see, theirs is the only greater good with which they are concerned."

Ethan jumped up and crossed the library to face Jacob across their father's formidable mahogany desk. "And what of Alex and Clara and Thomas and all the slaves? What of *their* greater good? Do you honestly believe they agree with you?" Ethan sounded weary. Jeffrey's betrayal had taken its toll.

Jacob thought a moment. "I am certain they would agree that what the Keyeses did was in bad taste, no matter what the end. As for your implication about whose side they would fight on, I am positive they would fight like you and I to defend our home. Twin Pines is their home, too."

"No, Jacob. Don't you see? They have no home, that's the point! They don't own anything; they are owned themselves. They may despise Jeffrey or think him a fool, but in their hearts, they know he is right about one thing, brother. Slavery must stop, and it must stop now."

Ethan hurried from the library, and in a moment, Jacob heard the tinkle of the bourbon decanter in the parlor. Ethan was drinking too much, and Jacob felt sure the Keyeses had aggravated the bad habit. His mind buzzing, Jacob tried to return to the ledger but found that the figures flew off the pages and past his eyes like tiny, shy birds.

Ethan was surprised to see Julia Keyes enter the parlor. It was late, he was tired, and she looked eager to talk. Very well. But she would pay the price if she tried to pressure him. He was one step away from telling her what he thought of her tactics and her brother's execrable behavior over the last week.

"Have you a secret message for me?" he asked, sipping at the sweet, burning liquid.

Julia laughed, trying to make light of what she knew was intended as a barb. "I came to thank you and to apologize."

"Again?"

She nodded. "We have tried your patience and put you in conflict with your family—"

"And everything I hold dear, don't forget."

He had been drinking. Julia tried to gauge the level of seriousness to his words. "I am sorry. But, Ethan, surely you understand why we came and why we had to ask you to help us. Without you, without your assistance and information, the chain we have formed from Boston to New York to Baltimore to Washington and farther south will be broken. People will die. The war will last longer, and more will suffer. That's why I must ask for your help." She paused. "Caitlin Stuart is with us. Won't you join us?"

Her plea struck Ethan as ill timed and presumptuous. "How dare you mention her name!" He looked around the room in shock.

There was no end to Julia's treachery. She would not stop at her manipulation of his brother, but must use Caitlin to achieve her ends as well. She could not leave Twin Pines gracefully, but must approach him against his wishes; even her brother had honored his wishes in that regard. "You could ruin her name with loose talk such as that. Didn't they teach you that before they sent you to spy on me and my family?"

Julia looked at him, puzzled. Was it possible that he didn't know of Caitlin's work? With a smile of understanding, she took another step toward him. There was no reasoning with him now. "All the same, I am sorry, Ethan. I am leaving our Washington address on a slip of paper on the dresser in my room."

"Fine. I will read it and eat it for breakfast."

She turned to leave, only to meet Jacob in the doorway. They almost bumped into each other.

"Are you leaving us?" he asked in an unnatural tone.

"Yes. I suppose it's none too soon for the Parsons," she said, unable to restrain herself.

Jacob drew back, stung by her remark. He knew he should not trust her, that he should look forward to getting rid of her and her brother. Yet quite illogically, he wanted their last evening to be sweet. "I'm so sorry you have that impression, Miss Keyes. It's just that the timing of the visit was a bit . . . trying, shall we say?"

Julia had to smile. He was at once so pretentious and alluring. In a more manly, hearty way, he reminded her of certain gentlemen she had met while traveling in Europe, men of honor who would rather drown on a ship than risk the embarrassment of calling out for help. "Oh, Jacob!" She ran past him and up the stairs, sobbing.

From the couch, Ethan clapped three times. "Bravo, brother. You have moved her to tears. I never would have thought it was possible. Drink?"

Jacob turned away in disgust. It was the curse of his position of leadership in the family that he could never trade places with his brother and behave irresponsibly. For if he could, he would run up the steps two at a time to Julia's room, sweeping her off her feet as he kissed her furiously, damning everything that existed outside their embrace.

But that was just a dream, and a bad one at that. He turned to his brother. "Good night, Ethan. Put the bottle away."

"Aye, Captain," Ethan replied. "Putting away the bottle, Cap. Aye, sir." After Jacob had left, he poured and

drank another bourbon neatly, and let the heat and diz-
ziness wash over him like the first warm breeze of spring.
He even raised his glass to drink a toast to Jacob but
choked on it. His laughter echoed down the hall and
passed through Jacob's heart like a keen.

Martha was sitting in bed, reading by the light of a
single candle when Jeffrey entered her room. He wore a
floor-length gown, a stocking cap, and on his feet, woolen
slippers with curled toes. The scrawny young man looked
at once so foolish and so lascivious that Martha wasn't
sure whether laughing or screaming was called for. She
did both.

"I must see you, you exquisite creature," he whispered, hurrying to her bedside and trying to put a clammy
hand over her mouth. She slapped him, appalled, and he
retreated. "Just pull up your gown and give me a glimpse
of heaven, then, hmm?"

Martha thought he must be mad. But should she call
out?

Before she could decide what action to take, Keyes left
her as suddenly as he appeared, blowing a kiss and wink-
ing before closing the door.

When he had gone, she shook for a moment, from
suppressed rage, muffling the sound by biting her pillow.
She despised Jeffrey so! But what should she do? Ethan
would merely laugh at her, as he had the night Jeffrey had
kissed her. And she feared confiding in Jacob, for he had
been in such a huff the past few days.

Martha slept poorly that night, dreaming of Brett Tyler, who rode into Twin Pines on a white whirlwind and
whisked her from her bed. Suddenly they were alone in a
strange room. Her clothes had fallen off, and he stood
shaving in front of a full-length oval mirror, like hers.
When she stood to see herself in the glass, there was no
reflection. She had disappeared.

Martha awoke shivering and got out of bed to place
another log on the fire. The shadows in the room frightened her, and she found getting back to sleep difficult. It

struck her that maybe this was one way of measuring how grown up a person was; by how much sleep they lost.

CHAPTER 13

THE KEYESES' FINAL morning at Twin Pines dawned sunny and cold. The household was alive with the bustle of servants preparing breakfast as well as for the departure of the trying guests.

Martha awoke feeling tired and out of sorts. Sitting up in her bed, she recalled her dream of the night before and, picking up the small silver-handled mirror by her bed, she checked her reflection to assure herself that she had not, in fact, disappeared. As she rose, taking off her sleeping cap and letting her hair tumble down over her shoulders, she decided that Jeffrey's exploits of last night would remain unknown by the rest of the household. Her mother and Jacob would merely insist that her activities be even more closely supervised than they already were.

For his part, Jeffrey awoke in a fine mood, lighthearted even, and he whistled as he directed the final packing of his clothes, books, and toiletries. Julia stopped by his room early; he could tell by her behavior that she was suspicious of him. She was doubly insistent that they leave without any more scenes, and if at all possible, without Ethan dead set against helping them. The cause, she reminded him. That was important. Friendships came and went, but the cause endured. But as his sister left to prepare her own toilet and bags, Jeffrey was struck with the impression that her words had been aimed as much at herself as toward him.

Ethan awoke to the slamming of trunk lids and the scraping of boots across bare pine floors. Even the scratch of the pen across paper in his brother's room next to his own irritated the pounding of his head. Rolling out of bed, he stood woozily at attention, tilting this way and that until he came fully awake. His mouth was dry, and his naturally curly hair was a tousled mess. He rubbed his eyes and, after splashing some icy water from the basin on his face, pulled on his black wool trousers and a shirt of white linen.

It was with great relief that he anticipated seeing off his guests. They should never have come.

Breakfast would do him good, provided Clara hadn't made pancakes and syrup. One whiff of her sweet syrup and he would erupt like Vesuvius, he knew.

In the room next to Ethan's, Jacob reread the letter sitting on his desk.

> *Julia,*
> *I wish you and your brother a safe journey. Your visit may not have been all that you had hoped, but at least you and Jeffrey have taken the time to see the South before you continue to condemn it. Perhaps one day, in quieter times, I will visit Boston.*
> *It has been my deep and sincere pleasure to act as your host. Godspeed.*
>
> > *Sincerely,*
> > *Jacob Parson*

He wondered if the tone of the letter was too reserved. Should he leave out the line about condemning the South? After some contemplation, he decided to leave it as it was, and to give it to her as she climbed into the coupé; that would leave her no time to protest or react in his presence. Then, unless she wrote to him, her reaction would be a mystery to him forever. Yes, that was best. Leave the final resolution of the matter to her. For his own good, he had already written Julia as merely a footnote in the history text of his life. Of her disappearance from the drama forever, he was certain.

Jacob dressed with a heavy heart. In the end he had

enjoyed the challenge of having the Keyeses at Twin Pines. He did not accept the agitation they provoked in his family, and that in his heart was no less disturbing. But their visit had awakened him to other worlds, other possibilities, however impossible for him to explore at present.

Charles Parson rang the bell, and Anna appeared in the doorway.

"Have those two spies left yet?" he asked.

"Hush, husband! I swear you've not said one kind word since their arrival." She went to the bed to fluff his pillow and help him sit up straight in bed. His groans of discomfort went through her like bullets, but she did not let him see the effect of his infirmity on her. "Charles, you must behave yourself and keep your boys' noses pointed in the right direction," she urged.

Charles sniffed. His once wavy hair had been inherited by both his sons. His was thinning and gray now, but he still ran his fingers through it as if it were a luxurious mane. "Which reminds me." He held up a letter. "Stuart tells me Jacob and Caitlin will not wed. Do you mind telling me why? And why the hell must I hear this from him and not from you or my own son?"

Anna paused and looked at him in surprise. Jacob hadn't mentioned anything to her. But she put her own questions aside; Charles was looking dangerously flushed. She tried to calm him, offering a cup of tea. "Charles, I had no idea. I'm sure Jacob will explain if you—"

"You're damn right he will! I've already sent Alex to find him."

A moment later, a knock sounded at the door, and Jacob entered, Alex behind him.

"Alex, go toss that scrawny spy out the door," Charles snapped, without acknowledging Jacob.

Alex had lost weight from the influenza, and he still felt weak. The air in the room made him feel dizzy. "Yes, Mister Charles." He turned quickly to leave.

"Alex, you will do no such thing," Anna said, dismissing him with a wave of her small hand. Once Alex had shut the door behind him, she turned sternly to her husband. "You must try to contain yourself in front of the servants, please, Charles. Giving such orders. You'll confuse Alex, and he won't know what to do." Casting a stern eye of reproof on her husband, she left him and Jacob alone, closing the door softly behind her.

"Why aren't you and the Stuart girl marrying? What has suddenly rendered you unable to fulfill your obligations as a husband?" His father spoke with rancor, and his voice carried powerfully. "You better have a damn good reason, son."

Jacob fumbled for the words to begin. Folding his hands behind his back, he looked briefly at his father, but could not bring himself to hold the penetrating hawklike gaze. Why did he feel like a failure? "Father, I regret causing you any pain," he began.

"Never mind me. What about Caitlin Stuart?" His father reached for and lighted a cigar, puffing contentedly as Jacob talked.

Jacob quickly responded to the question, facing his father square on. "We came to an . . . an understanding of sorts."

Charles raised his bushy gray eyebrows expectantly. "And? What is this secret understanding?"

Jacob sighed wearily and sat in the high-backed armchair his mother preferred. "I don't love her, Daddy, not as a husband loves a wife. She feels the same."

Charles blew a ring of smoke toward the ceiling and thought for a moment. "There is someone else, then," he concluded. "One of the Chesterfield boys, I bet. Their daddy owns half of Richmond. I knew it."

"It is neither Noah nor Aaron. It doesn't matter who, does it?"

Charles coughed. "Matters to me, son. What scoundrel cheated us out of what's ours and what's best? That Kilpatrick pup? The boy has the morals of a snake."

"Father, forgive me, but I am not prepared to discuss this further. Kindly grant me the respect due—"

"Respect! What's got into you, Jacob?"

For an excruciating moment, Jacob considered taunting his father, who could no longer whip a healthy sixty-year-old man, let alone Jacob. But he caught himself, took a breath and counted to five, then blew out the hateful air. Bowing his head, Jacob quietly asked for his father's forgiveness.

Charles waved his hand over his son's bowed figure. "You are forgiven, Jacob. Just tell me the truth." He looked expectantly at his son.

Jacob never raised his eyes. Resolutely he walked out of the room, closing the door gently behind him.

Jacob retreated to his room and closed the door. He could neither read nor rest. He couldn't think. For twenty minutes, he paced the room like a beast in a cage. He was indeed trapped. As his thoughts flew from his father and Dr. Stuart to Ethan and Caitlin and Julia and all their roles in his life, he paced faster and faster and still came to no conclusion that would leave him in peace. Finally he tired of the rote motion. Taking a deep breath, he prepared himself to go downstairs and face the Keyeses—and his brother.

After having washed the honey from her damp hair, Martha left the bath to return to her room. She started as she bumped into Jeffrey Keyes, who apparently had been lounging outside the door to the bath. She cringed, her blue eyes flashing. Clutching her dressing gown tightly around her throat, she stepped to the side and tried to walk by him without incident. He would not allow her free passage but blocked her way.

"Miss Parson, I apologize for my behavior last evening. I was—"

"Apology accepted. Good-bye." She tried to get by on the other side.

Keyes leaned an arm against the wall to halt her.

"Do you realize where you are? If I scream," she threatened, "Alex or Jacob will wring your neck in a heartbeat, you slicked-down banty rooster! Now let me by!"

Smiling, Keyes relented, stepping to the side and allowing Martha to pass. "I like your sauce," he called to her.

Martha locked the door to her room and lay on her bed, sobbing. How could she bring herself to face him once more to say good-bye?

She took longer than usual to dress, and chose a plain high-necked gown, a shawl, and a bonnet. Her face was barely visible, and her figure only to be guessed at.

Alex couldn't wait for the Keyeses to leave. Mr. Keyes struck him as the kind of man who could keep a secret for about ten minutes. His snooping made him nervous. All white folks did. He respected the Parsons well enough. But he could hang three times over if the wrong white folks learned of his involvement in the Underground Railroad. He shuddered to think of what would happen to Clara and Thomas, to all of them.

Alex looked at the floor when he saw Jeffrey Keyes approaching him. He had peeked in earlier to see what progress was being made in getting the man out of "his" house, and had been shocked to see that Keyes owned more creams and lotions than Miss Martha. What did that fine Mr. Creams want from him now?

"How do they treat you?" Keyes asked again. Alex continued to pile their luggage just outside the front door in preparation for the arrival of the carriage from the stables.

"Fine, sir. We have you loaded and ready in five minute, sir."

Keyes nodded, surveying the landscape of the plantation one last time. He had to admit to being impressed. Though stark in a light frost, Twin Pines was serene and vast, and from all Ethan had told him, productive and profitable—but at the cost of thirty lives lived in poverty and the ignominy of slavery. No matter how elegant, the Parson estate was to Jeffrey a blot on any landscape.

"We're alone now," he whispered to Alex. They both glanced about, to confirm that no one else was in earshot.

"Yessuh," Alex said. Unsure of what Keyes wanted him to say or do, he put on a wide-eyed look of innocent ignorance that seemed to work well with pushy folks.

"Do they beat you? Starve you? Threaten to sell you? What?"

Keyes's crazy questions angered Alex. I am a man, thought Alex, and don't nobody treat me like a stray dog. This is my home, too. He hankered to grab the little runt by his collar and the seat of his pants and toss him out the door.

"No, suh," he said. "They treat me right."

Keyes raised his russet eyebrows melodramatically, a gesture that questioned the authenticity of what he had just been told. Lying was such a deeply ingrained habit in the slave, Keyes sadly concluded, that the big old house slave the Parsons so patronizingly called "Alex" couldn't tell the truth from a falsehood if you paid him for it. "I sympathize with your struggle," Jeffrey concluded.

Alex was bewildered. What in Heaven that white man talkin' 'bout now?

In a moment, Ethan joined them, bleary eyed and testy. Without smiling or greeting either man poised at the front door, he commented, "A cold day to travel."

The frost was just yielding its grip over the earth. The air seemed so clear that the wood smoke from the chimneys carried in the breeze like a line of thick white clouds.

"But a beautiful one," Keyes replied. "As you must remember, we don't often have days such as this in Boston," he said. "The factories send up a good deal of smoke, more than ever now. Homes, too. There's a constant haze over the Charles."

Jeffrey fingered his leather travel gloves nervously, wondering why Ethan didn't take the opportunity to say something significant. In thirty minutes, they might be lost to each other forever. And all because Ethan could not follow the dictates of his conscience. It was this blasted close contact with his family and its tainted traditions that held him back.

Alex left them at the door. Lifting Miss Julia's trunk,

he carried it easily to the carriage and heaved it onto the rack.

Jeffrey kept looking at Ethan askance, hoping to catch his eye, but Ethan kept a steady gaze on the carriage, as if willing it to depart.

"Have you nothing to say to me?" Keyes finally asked him, opening his palms in a pleading gesture. He could wait no longer.

Ethan looked straight ahead. "I wish you a pleasant journey, Jeffrey. Look after Julia. Don't stop for any fire-eaters along the way."

Ethan's reference struck Jeffrey as an odd and threatening farewell. Is that what Ethan wished, that he and Julia should be beaten and humiliated by a band of wahoos on the road to Richmond?

The silence between the two old friends coalesced into a presence, a shadow that stood between them and blocked their view of each other. Standing face to face, they failed to recognize the bond of friendship as it once was, and as it was now. Each honestly thought he would never speak to the other again.

Jacob's resolve to ignore Julia until she had mounted the carriage melted the moment he saw her in the hallway. She held a small travel bag and a book, and was trying to tie her bonnet under her chin. Balancing both the bag and the book, she couldn't tie the ribbon.

Jacob hurried to hold the items for her.

"You are a gentleman in the Southern tradition," she said.

Jacob wasn't sure if she was complimenting him or not, and he feared his face showed his confusion.

"I like the way you treat a lady," she continued. "In Boston, men are slower to act. Kindnesses are considered more thoroughly before they are performed. You seem kind from instinct."

Jacob could feel himself color, much against his will. Would she always make him feel seventeen? "I guess I am. All Southern men are."

"Not that what's-his-name Tyler, the one Martha dreams about," she said, figuring Jacob must know all about him.

Jacob looked searchingly into her dazzling green eyes. What was she speaking of? Had Brett acted with impropriety toward Martha? He had heard Martha mention the hooligan's name, but he had never supposed she thought seriously of him. If Julia was even one-tenth correct, he faced a wicked battle to dissuade his sister from any interest in Tyler while not setting him up as some kind of romantic rebel-hero.

"I'm sorry. I should not have said anything," she quickly said, distraught by the thunderous look on his face. Was she destined to irritate the entire Parson family forever?

Jacob walked her downstairs and into the front hallway, where Ethan and Jeffrey stood just inside the door. She almost wished they had sneaked off in the night like thieves, sparing everyone the embarrassment of the current situation. Not even Ethan seemed willing to extend himself to make peace, however fragile it might be.

Alex waved from the drive, beyond the picket fence. "Ready!" he shouted.

As the foursome paused awkwardly in the open doorway, Anna Parson emerged from the parlor carrying an embroidered piece of fabric in her hands. She smiled as she approached them.

"I have brought a farewell gift," she said, handing a one-foot-square piece of cloth to Julia, who took it uncertainly.

Examining the gift, Julia covered her mouth, struck by the charm of it. The others drew near to see it.

"What is it?" Jeffrey asked, looking over his sister's shoulder. Julia held up an embroidered portrait of the Twin Pines mansion, complete with smoking fireplaces and clouds in the sky.

"Thank you so much for your hospitality," Julia said. "I shall treasure this."

"Where is Martha?" Anna wondered aloud, looking

at the stairs. "She ought to be here. You must pardon
that girl's manners sometimes, or the lack of them, I
should say."

"Perhaps she's not well," Jeffrey ventured.

Jacob cast a look that could back a bigger man than
Keyes out the door and down the walk. He hoped to Hell
Jeffrey had done nothing further to upset his sister.

Julia stepped in to fill the awkward silence. "We've
already said our good-byes, Martha and I. She's a lovely
girl. Good-bye!"

After Anna had released it, Jacob accepted Julia's extended hand firmly in his. Their eyes met and locked for
a moment, and in a heavy mist of implications he offered
his arm and walked with her to the waiting carriage, followed by Anna, Ethan, and Jeffrey.

"In different times, under different circumstances . . . ,"
Jacob began, fumbling for words to express his feelings.
A reawakened piece of his sleeping heart would return to
a dissatisfied slumber when she left. But it had to be, he
thought bitterly.

"Nothing would have happened," Julia finished. Her
green eyes filled, perhaps in response to the chilly wind
tousling her auburn hair. "We are meant to part like this,
I suppose. Everything on this green earth turns out as it
must."

Jacob stirred, shuffling his feet. He let go of her hand,
watching helplessly as she turned and climbed into the
coupé.

Jeffrey mounted the step and climbed into the coupé
beside his sister. He and Ethan had said little, for there
was little to say.

The clatter of the carriage creaking off on the frozen
dirt road heading east was the emptiest sound Jacob could
ever recall hearing.

Anna took Jacob's arm, and together they began walking to the house, Ethan beside them. "What a lovely pair
of friends you have, Ethan. I am only sorry our situation
does not permit their staying longer."

But Ethan seemed genuinely pleased to see them go;

his manner was more jovial and lighthearted. "Now we can all breathe again," he said ambiguously, then ran up the stairs ahead of them and disappeared inside.

"Why would he say a dreadful thing like that?" Anna asked Jacob, who shrugged.

"Ask him, Mama," Jacob replied softly. "It's cold. Let's get inside." The carriage was out of view by the time they had climbed the steps and reached the door. Alex ran up from the fence and opened the door for Jacob and his mother.

Inside, the house seemed quieter than it had ever been. Jacob found it so still in the library that he could not concentrate. Eventually he gave up, walking down to the barns to spur the field hands out of their lethargy. There was plenty of time before spring, when the hard work began again, but there was no good in allowing them to get too lazy.

That night, eight of the field hands crowded in Thomas's cabin to gamble on poker and drink moonshine. Warmed by the heat of the liquor and the raging fire on the hearth, they gathered on the floor to laugh and curse their fate and trade gossip, just as their women often did over the laundry tub or while hoeing the garden.

"Dat woman do want me bad." Thomas was barely listening; he had heard that short, nearly bald field hand say the same thing for as long as he could remember. He bragged about seducing every unmarried black woman in the county. "Dey all wants Coleman!"

He was relieved when the deep voice of Big Edward told Coleman to shut up and play. And gradually the potent moonshine worked its magic on Coleman, as it had already on Thomas, and he grew quiet, his eyelids drooped, and in a minute he was fast asleep on the floor.

Thomas clapped his hands for the moonshine, but Old Peter, who looked to be seventy years of age, though he was but in his fifties, refused to surrender the "nectar," as he called it. "When I'm finished, boy, then you get it," he told Thomas.

"Hey, this my cabin you abusin' yo' ole self in, Ole Peter!" he reminded the man with the bottle. "Surrender!"

Sometime later they abandoned all pretense of playing poker—nobody knew whose deal it was or who owed what—and they hunkered down to finish the moonshine.

"Then we go outside and watch the moon shine," Thomas said seriously, and every man in his cabin broke out laughing, even Coleman. Their husky laughter carried clear up to the house and beyond.

Clara awoke with the first rap at her door, knowing something was wrong. Somebody was hurt. Her eyes widened when she opened the door, and she raised her hand to her mouth, gasping.

"Thomas!" Blood had seeped through the cotton of his shirt, soaking all of his upper arm. She stared at the enormous man who was supporting him, her eyes wide with fear. "What happened, Big Edward? What you fool boys been doin'?"

Big Edward stepped into the cellar and helped Thomas to lie on the table there. He started to open his mouth, but Clara ran over to him and slapped him on the face, then did the same to her son.

"Ow! Mama, that hurts! I'm already bleedin' half to death! Ain't that enough for you?"

With that Clara relaxed somewhat; he would be all right. But the stern expression set on her face remained. Turning again to Big Edward, she said, "You better tell me what happened, and now."

It appeared that their poker game had turned into a competition between Big Edward and another of the field hands, who went by the Christian name of Robert. At first they had wanted to see which of them could lift the heaviest cow in the barn and toss her out the barn door, but Thomas had convinced them against the action; they could easily be sold for such nonsense.

Clara tended to her son while Big Edward explained, cleaning and binding her son's wound, and keeping a careful eye to see that the bleeding had stopped. The Par-

sons had never sold any of their bondsmen, but she was
glad Thomas had put the fear into the others. Such foolishness could endanger their usefulness as a stop on the
Railroad.

What had happened then, Big Edward went on to explain, was that in the spirit of their argument, he had
flashed a knife. The others had scrambled behind a small
table as he and Robert had grappled with each other,
knocking over Thomas's chair and rolling across the floor
toward the fire. It was when Thomas shouted for them
to stop and leaned in to grab Big Edward's arm that the
knife struck him.

Clara worked silently as she listened. Big Edward
stood sheepishly next to her, apologizing, but all she said
to him was "Go home. Cut anybody again and I tell Mister Jacob; understand me?" He sheepishly nodded and
stumbled home. For thirty minutes she scolded Thomas.
But she knew that it was time for him to get out of Twin
Pines. "Tonight is God's warnin', son," she said. "You
got to leave Twin Pines 'fore you die here."

Thomas nodded. "And you come, too, you and
Daddy. All of us be free up north."

She took his hand silently in hers. I can't lose you,
boy, not at any price to myself, she thought. She let him
sleep that night with her in their rooms under the great
house, piling so many quilts and blankets on Thomas that
Alex complained.

"You ain't gonna freeze to death, old man," she whispered to Alex. "Go asleep." She sat up most of the night,
rocking in a chair Miss Anna had given her years ago
after it had worn out. She had repaired it, and now it was
hers. She liked to rock, moving at her own speed, her
mind humming. Just before dawn, she fell into a dreamless sleep.

CHAPTER 14

CAITLIN STUART RETURNED to visit two weeks later. Her presence offered Martha the opportunity to ride unchaperoned by one of her brothers, and on the afternoon of Caitlin's arrival, the two young ladies took advantage of the thaw, and rode at an easy pace through the tobacco fields east of the estate house.

Caitlin immediately guessed what Martha was up to and didn't approve of the game. Toying with a poor, desperate man like Brett Tyler was dangerous, especially for someone as protected and isolated as Martha. She was shocked by Martha's flirtation.

"I hope we're turning back soon," Caitlin called ahead, but Martha gave no reply. Their horses climbed the small rise just before the Tyler farm and halted at command. Martha wanted to have a look around.

"It's almost spring," Martha said, her eyes roaming the ramshackle buildings. She half expected Brett to jump out of a haystack, and was disappointed when he didn't. Where was he?

Caitlin wondered how to persuade her friend to head back toward home when she noticed a slender black man slipping out of the Tyler barn. A quick look toward Martha told Caitlin that she had seen him, too.

"Thomas!" Martha exclaimed under her breath. "What on earth . . ." They continued to watch as he ran past a hay wagon and around a stand of oaks before circling back to the road where they waited. When he saw them, the look on his face was of shock—and fear.

"We've caught him at something," Martha said. Again she turned her attention to the barn as the creaky door swung open. The eldest Tyler daughter, Sara, appeared in the light, buttoning her cotton blouse.

Caitlin took in her breath sharply, while Martha blushed, nearly losing her balance and slipping off her horse. Thomas approached them at a quick gait, tipping his straw hat as they passed.

Martha stopped him.

"Thomas, shame on you!"

Repulsed as she was, in Martha's mind, Thomas's reprehensible actions were tied to the wild and vulgar flights of fancy she read about in her novels from the Continent. Martha had grown up with Thomas. She had never before given a thought to him as a romantic hero. Now, in a way, his abandon encouraged hers. But she wanted Caitlin's support, and, leaning near her to whisper, Martha asked for her promise of silence.

Caitlin reluctantly nodded her assent. "But I must say, you are playing with fire, young man." Thomas responded to her warning with a look full of belligerence, and Martha, too, looked at her reprovingly. Martha did have a point, Caitlin knew. Thomas belonged to the Parsons, not the Stuarts. But such vile acts as the one Thomas and the Tyler girl had no doubt undertaken threatened the fabric of Southern society, she reasoned. Much as she disapproved of slavery and believed that every human being ought to live free, what Thomas did in the barn with the Tyler girl was still wrong. They were not married, nor would they ever be. As far as she was concerned they were behaving like rutting animals.

Caitlin was shocked at Martha's lack of firmness with Thomas. She ought to have scolded him and let him know that Jacob would soon be dealing with him. Now who only knew what liberties he might take. Caitlin began to understand the Parsons' disapproval and prayed that Martha's imagination would lead her no further down the road to sin and perdition.

She was cold and wanted to go back to Twin Pines, but Martha was pressing Thomas about something.

"Where are the rest of the Tylers, Thomas? You must know!"

The young black man slunk one step back from her and looked at the ground. Why she want to know where that white trash at? "Don't know," he told her, his eyes still lowered. "Girl say they gone and can I help her in the barn, and next I know, she takin' off her clothes and—"

"That will do, Thomas!" Martha said. "You must have chores to do back at Twin Pines. I suggest you tend to them."

Nodding, Thomas took off down the road at a trot. Martha smiled, pleased by the discovery. Perhaps her own desires were human and forgivable—except to her family, of course.

Caitlin was very disturbed by the unfolding of events, and wished nothing more but to return to Twin Pines. But fate lay on the side of the troublemakers that day, and just as they were tugging at the reins to turn their horses around, the door to the unpainted Tyler house opened, and Brett appeared. The day had warmed, and the cool breeze relented. Brett wore only an open shirt. Picking up an ax leaning against the house, he began to chop some wood piled at the side of the house.

The sight of his chest incapacitated Martha. Raising one hand dramatically to her bosom, she asked, "Isn't he magnificent?"

"Like a beast in the jungle," Caitlin said in a dry tone, but Martha wasn't listening.

The muscles in Tyler's arms were as cords of steel, and his back rippled as he raised and swung the ax. Woodchips leaped in an arc, and the sharp thunk of the ax went through Martha like a gunshot. "Oh, if only he would see me here," she fretted.

But Caitlin wasn't fooled. "I'm sure he has seen us," she said. "His sister probably told him we were here. This spectacle is all for you, Martha. Let's go back to the house." She reined in the small mare with determination and kicked her, the hooves clattering on the hard road. Sure enough, Tyler looked up at the sound to see Martha watching him. He set down the ax, grinning, and she blushed but could not look away. Her breath caught in her throat as he motioned to her, as if to say, "What do you think? Do you approve?"

With his cocky stance and defiant stare, he was taunting her, daring her. But the intense fire in his eyes was too frightening. She could not accept his challenge. Martha raced away like a heroine in one of the romances she so enjoyed, passing the trotting Caitlin as if she were standing still. She arrived at Twin Pines breathless, her heart racing and her thighs tight against the heat she felt there. Nothing she did could erase from her memory the picture of Brett Tyler chopping wood.

The strained silence at the dinner table became unbearable that evening. Martha was not as glib or cheerful as usual, Ethan noted, and Jacob would look at neither Caitlin nor him. After the stuffed squab had been served, he was moved to say something, praying that Caitlin would keep quiet and let him bear the brunt of any attack.

"Mother, Jacob, Martha: I have news."

No opening could have sounded more ominous to Jacob. Setting down his fork, he glanced at Caitlin. Her eyes were downcast. In a high-collared gown of chestnut brown, she seemed smaller than ever to him.

He looked to Ethan. He, too, looked serious, but there was an infuriating smugness to his features. He was going to announce his intention.

"Should Father hear this first?" Jacob asked sharply.

Ethan smiled sadly. "I wish that it could be so, but no. It must be you who breaks the news to him."

Martha could not contain herself. "You're going to marry Caitlin! When? Here?" But her excitement at the prospect of gaining a sister-in-law as well as a confidante was not shared.

"Martha, please, let Ethan talk," her mother said sternly.

At least his mother had the decency to recognize the

gravity of the situation. Jacob forced himself to chew and swallow his squab as he listened to his brother.

"I have proposed marriage to Miss Stuart," Ethan began, "and she has accepted." His voice quivered with tension. "Her father has not yet given his permission, and as you well know, I have not asked Father yet. . . ."

"You should!" Jacob said. "You should have asked him before telling us."

"Jacob, you know what he'll say!"

"Then listen. Heed him. He's your father!"

"I cannot!" Ethan caught his breath, trying to calm his racing heart. His mother's eyes were like a doe's, soft and sad. At least she understood what he was doing. He had known it would be too much to expect of Jacob. "I shall tell Father of our desire—"

"You mean ask him," Jacob insisted, his hands clenched before him.

"No, we have decided to marry, with God's blessing alone, if need be," Ethan said softly. Caitlin would not raise her eyes, which remained focused on her lap. "Jacob, I ask you to inform Father, and to ask if he will see me regarding this matter."

Jacob pushed away from the table and stood, his face heated by anger. "I shall ask, to prevent any further embarrassment. But I can assure you that he will be devastated by your callousness. Have you chosen a date?"

Ethan shook his head. "We shall wait until the war is over, if there is one. If not, we shall marry here in the summer."

"Here, at Twin Pines?" Anna asked. "Surely Dr. Stuart sanctions the marriage of his only daughter."

Ethan kept his seat. "You know very well that he will not give us permission to marry. Very likely, Caitlin will lose everything, unless her father has a change of heart."

"And where will you live?" Jacob shouted, growing angrier. "What will you do?"

Ethan took a few long seconds to formulate his reply. He felt especially the weight of his mother's eyes on him

She, more than anyone, would feel his absence. "Most likely, we shall move to Washington or Baltimore—"

"Or Boston?" Jacob's question was more an accusation. Jacob thumped his forehead with the heel of his hand, circling the table.

"Stop! Please stop!" Caitlin shouted. "This is my fault!" Bursting into tears, she fled the table and ran from the dining room. Her footsteps on the stairs were rapid-fire clicks.

Martha, who had watched wide-eyed and silent through the entire discussion, felt moved to speak. "Jacob, they're only following the dictates of their hearts."

But Jacob would have none of it. "You hush and go upstairs. This is none of your concern, Martha."

Flushed, Martha jumped to her feet and walked angrily from the dining room, the candles flickering in her wake. They could hear her run up the stairs and slam the door to her room.

Jacob was about to say more when the bell Charles kept at his bedside rang decisively. Jacob raced from the room, scooting by Clara, who was hustling up the stairs, and whipped open the door to his father's room. Charles sat smoking a cigar in bed, a half-dozen newspapers spread on the quilt before him.

"You read these?" he asked Jacob.

Breathlessly, Jacob closed the door and took a seat by the bed, shaking his head slowly. "Daddy, your sense of timing . . . ," Jacob began.

Clara knocked at the door and entered. Charles waved his hand and told her to go away. "Tell the Missus I ain't gone to the Devil yet!"

Then, turning his red, heavyset face on Jacob, he went on. "The *Sentinel* reports that two Federal arsenals and Fort Marion at Saint Augustine, Florida, were seized by Secessionist forces without a struggle. Old Man Buchanan is caving in. Hell, he may give us everything we want before that ape from Illinois takes the oath of office!" Charles laughed delightedly, breaking into a deep, raspy cough. Jacob jumped to his side, but his father held up a hand. "I'm fine, son," he managed to say, his breathing a bit easier. "Better every day."

"I know, Daddy, I know." Jacob spoke softly, encouraging his father's lie. As he watched him, he knew with certainty that his father would die before the war was played out.

His father's newly found willingness to believe the headline writers surprised Jacob. It shocked him to think that his father trusted the hopelessly optimistic predictions of the Southern press, which either did not want war or wanted it to begin and end in a week. His father had always been a man who read past the headlines.

Charles chuckled, regaining his voice. "That fool Buchanan has proposed we try the Missouri Compromise again, as if it hasn't failed once already! How's that for original thinking?"

Jacob shrugged. His mind was spinning, and he felt bone tired. First, Caitlin and Ethan wanted to elope and live up north, and now his father thought there would be no war.

"The best is yet to come, son," Charles said eagerly. He picked up another newspaper. "Mississippi has voted to join South Carolina and secede. Isn't that promising news? The state militia chased off the ship Buchanan sent to reinforce Sumter, in Charleston Harbor. It's one good thing after another." He looked expectantly at his son, but Jacob remained glum. "What's wrong with you, boy? Constipated? See Clara. She'll fix you up."

"No, sir, it isn't that." Jacob paused, taking a deep breath. "Daddy, you must believe as I do that Lincoln won't stand for secession. He's said as much twenty times over. He'll raise troops and march them right through our front yard, right on down to Charleston, if need be." He stood and began pacing as he spoke. "And he has the manpower. He can raise a hundred thousand men with one stroke of the pen, as commander in chief."

Charles puffed on his cigar, listening with a thoughtful look on his lined face. "Tell me more, Herodotus."

"Father, I don't have to be the Father of History to

see writing on the wall. These little victories don't amount to spit, and you know it. What are you up to?"

Charles smiled, his face alive with pleasure. "Why, I'm testing the wisdom of my favorite son, and he just passed the test. You're nobody's fool, son."

"Don't be so sure," Jacob muttered. Had not Caitlin Stuart chosen Ethan over him? Yet his heart swelled with pride to hear his father praise him so.

"What are you talking about, Jacob?"

Jacob felt himself squirming as his father eyed him like a bug on a pin. "Daddy, Ethan has asked your permission to marry."

The cigar in his father's mouth almost fell out. "Unless it's one of those Tyler tarts, I'm pleased as punch," Charles said, delighted. But looking closer at Jacob's drawn face, he became worried. "Am I not?"

Jacob cupped his hands and carefully kept his eyes focused on his father's. "It's Caitlin Stuart, sir. He wishes to marry her. With your permission, I have no objection."

"What? Your own brother stole the girl, and you say 'fine, take her, you have my blessing'? Are you mad?"

There was nothing Jacob could say. He would have to let his father vent his spleen, then try to talk some sense.

"What were you doing while they were courting, counting beans in the kitchen? Are you a man or not?" The old man puffed furiously on the cigar, sending plumes of smoke curling around the ceiling. The red in his face deepened. He would not look at Jacob, who patiently waited for a chance to explain. Again, he must pay the price for Ethan's rebellion.

"Daddy, it's a *fait accompli*."

"Don't throw French at me, son," his father scolded. "That's your brother's trick. When did you learn of this?"

Jacob nodded toward the door. "Just now."

The significance of his words had sunk in. Charles looked at him thoughtfully. "He asked you, not me. What did you say?"

Jacob would have a difficult time explaining the logic

of this approach. "I said I would talk to you, to lay the groundwork."

Charles blew out smoke, breathing a disdainful *poo!* "You should've slapped him out the door and through the barn! I would've."

Jacob sighed, his shoulders drooping. "Daddy, I will not fight about this. I've already come to peace with it. Now the matter is up to you." He stood to go.

"Wait," his father said. "What are their plans? Are they going to live in the White House with Ethan's friend, Lincoln?"

Jacob was pleased to see his father regain his equilibrium as well as his wit. "They speak of living in the North, yes sir."

Charles nodded. "I see."

When Jacob left the room, he found his mother waiting in the upstairs hall. She looked up at him expectantly. "It's like persuading an Old Testament prophet to come into the city for the fair," Jacob whispered, and she nodded in understanding.

"I'll talk to him," she whispered. She carried a tray of biscuits, jam, and honey. "Go on, now. Go see to things."

Jacob left her and walked around the house, too much torn asunder by the emotions of the day to carry on meaningful work. He finally retreated to the library, studying the *Planter's Guide* and making copious notes in the estate journal, a record Jacob kept both for practical reasons and for posterity.

As he lay in bed reading Ovid's *Metamorphoses*, Ethan wondered what sort of choices he and Caitlin would be forced to make in their future. Certainly their decision to marry set them outside the good graces of their families and acquaintances.

Ethan was startled by the creak of a door opening farther down the hall. Curious, he listened closely as someone tiptoed by his door and slipped quietly down the stairs. The pocket watch on the table next to his bed read ten o'clock.

Intrigued, he got out of bed and slipped on a robe and his boots. Outside his room, the house was dark and cold. The stillness of the night was poignant. It saddened Ethan to be up and about when only cats and owls stirred. It only emphasized his feeling of isolation. He crept downstairs just in time to hear the door in the kitchen close.

A faint odor of ham lingered in the air. Ethan peeked out the kitchen window and saw a shadowy figure in a dress and a heavy cape scurrying down the path toward the slave quarters. From the size of the form, it might have been Martha or Caitlin.

Then he snapped his fingers. "Of course!" It was no doubt Caitlin on another mission of mercy, taking food to an injured field hand. One of the bondsmen must have hurt himself earlier today, and perhaps Jacob had deprived him of dinner to punish him for his own foolishness.

But then, in a flash, he recalled Julia's words to him the night before her departure. *Caitlin Stuart is with us.* He had assumed she was maligning Caitlin to some personal end, but perhaps there had been some truth to what she said.

Ethan stepped away from the door and leaned against the pine table. Very well, he thought, I can wait to see what the great secret is. He rummaged through the bread box and found a small loaf to eat and sat at the kitchen table. A pleasant sense of excitement surged through him, chasing away the heavy desire to sleep.

A package concealed in her arms, Caitlin ran down the moonlit serpentine path, past the barns and gardens, to Thomas's cabin. As arranged, she rapped three times on the door. Clara opened it and ushered her inside.

Caitlin was surprised to find not a man but a young black woman before her, huddled in blankets on the floor near the fire. She looked to be sixteen or seventeen years old, and the neck that protruded from the quilt was slender and long. Brown eyes great with fright had focused on Caitlin upon her entrance. Clara must have prepared her for the presence of a white person, yet it was obvious that she was terrified.

Caitlin quickly handed Clara the package. "It's a wrap, gloves, and a bonnet," she explained. Clara blessed her and gave the bundle to the young woman.

Caitlin then reached into her cape pockets and, one at a time, removed four ham biscuits. These she held out to the black girl herself. It took thirty seconds for the girl to reach for the food.

Thomas sat on his bed in the other corner, studying the every move of the visitor. She was scareder than hell of Miss Caitlin, but she'd make it, like the others. He understood the runaway's fear. Miss Caitlin had acted none too kindly to him when she and Miss Martha had caught him cattin' with the Tyler girl. But though Miss Caitlin had said nothing to the Parsons, as promised, he had seen the look of disapproval. Well, to hell with them all. Sara had been there that day, and she had been warm and ready every time he'd stolen away to see her since then.

Clara spoke softly and surely. "This girl runnin' from a master in South Carolina who beat her and take advantage of her ever' chance he get. She never been nowhere before, and she scared she ain't gonna be able to find her way. I told her 'bout the stars but she don't get it."

Caitlin waited for more explanations, but Clara fell silent. The flickering firelight cast long ghostly shadows on the bare wall.

Caitlin then understood what Clara was hinting at. "She wants someone to go with her," Caitlin said slowly to Clara.

Clara nodded. "She got family in Philadelphia. They hide her, git her work," Clara explained. The trip would not be easy. Caitlin would be lucky to get there herself without hindrance. Sentiment against the South in parts of western Virginia and the capital was growing, and suspicion of both Northerners and Southerners was strong. Accompanying the woman on a train seemed out of the question.

Nor could she provide the runaway with maps or other geographic documentation. For as Caitlin well knew, only one slave in a hundred could read and write his name. It was illegal in slave states to teach a slave to read and write. As Charles Parson himself said, men who could read and write possessed a dangerous freedom. Such men were not slaves anymore, no matter what kind of bonds you placed them in. For the written word provided much in the way of temptation to rebel.

Clara turned to the girl. "My boy take you to the next station. I tell Mister Jacob he sick. He believe me. Once you in Washington, you ask for the Keyeses of Capitol Hill, understand me."

The girl nodded shyly.

"Perhaps she should stay here for a while," Caitlin ventured. "She appears too tired to go on."

Clara shook her head, vehemently. "No, ma'am. Longer she stay, closer her master get. He stop and axe every white folk he see till he find her. She got to git now."

So Caitlin was left wondering what else she could do, feeling as ill at ease in Thomas's bare chilly cabin as she felt in the enormous and lovely house on the hill, a world away.

The girl whispered something but could not look at Caitlin. "She say 'thank you,' " Clara explained, putting an arm around the girl's thin shoulders.

Caitlin opened the kitchen door and was about to shut it quietly behind her when the whispered "Hello!" took away her breath.

"Ethan!" she gasped. "Thank God it's you," she whispered, the fear still bright in her eyes. She shut the door and removed her cape shakily.

Ethan smiled, then stood back to examine her. One look confirmed his suspicion: Julia had been right. "I've caught you," he said, trying to keep his tone light. When she blanched, he stopped smiling and asked seriously, "What is it?"

His concern touched her. She had known this moment would come. Now she was faced with the truth and whether she ought to share it with him fully. Her heart raced, and she could feel a tightness in her throat. The dangerous words would have to fight to get out.

Ethan's blue eyes searched for the source of her reluctance, and he began to sense that Caitlin's struggle over whether or not to divulge her secret was greater than he had imagined. Just as he was about to envelop her in his arms, she held up a gloved hand and motioned him to sit down, then sat beside him at the table. As she spoke, she removed her gloves, rolling them between her palms. Only occasionally did she look up to register his reactions.

"I went to Thomas's cabin with food and clothing for a runaway from South Carolina," she began, her voice trembling. She wished that she had told him before. He would be hurt by her secrecy, particularly now when they were together embarking on a path that isolated them from their peers. "Her master beat and . . . accosted her. Thomas is to accompany her to the next stop."

When she looked at him, Ethan had tears in his eyes. He wiped them away quickly with the sleeves of his robe.

"Are you angry?" she asked softly. She reached out a hand to hold his; he took it and shook his head.

Laughing, he caught her in his arms and spun her around the room. "I am almost relieved, odd as that may seem. Don't you see, Caitlin? I will help! Together we'll contribute to the effort. We'll be a part of something vital and dangerous, and correct. Both of us." He took her face in his hands and devoured her beauty and passion with his eyes. "Caitlin, I am not angry. I am delirious."

He covered her mouth with his and kissed her gently and longingly, inhaling her sweet scent. "If we're caught, we could be banished or sent to jail," she whispered, still holding him close.

Ethan smiled. "Jail a Parson? As Daddy might say, 'Never! Not till the moon and the earth collide!' I love you, Caitlin Margaret Stuart!"

"You go upstairs now," she urged him in a hushed

tone. "I'll follow in a few minutes, in case anyone awakens. Go now!" She pushed him away with all her might, barely able to move him. Listening, she heard him bang his shin on the table beside the stairs and utter a quiet oath. This made her smile, and at a time when she was about to turn her back on her father and all that she had come to know, she was happiest.

All through the night she felt Ethan's strong hands on her face. She dreamed of their wedding again and again. But the scene was dark and lonely; it included only her and Ethan. Where were their families and friends? "Only a dream," she muttered to herself, awakening once after midnight.

The house was quiet. An owl hooted in a tree near her window. Caitlin could not get back to sleep until the owl stopped taunting her.

CHAPTER 15

OVER THE NEXT three months, in addition to notes about planting and the running of the estate, the entries in Jacob's daily journal recorded one remarkable and ominous event after another. He became aware that in an important sense, he was recording history.

> 12 Feb, 1861
> Former U.S. Senator Jeff Davis was elected first president of the Confederate States of America (CSA), consisting of South Carolina, Mississippi, Georgia, Florida, Louisiana, Texas, and Alabama. Daddy says he's weak and won't stand up to the Yankees but will run from them. All the newspapers spell INVASION

and WAR in letters big enough to read across the barn-yard.

7 March

Lincoln is sworn in as president and challenges South to come home or face the consequences. Daddy says it doesn't take a genius to know he means to invade us, soon. Militia drills twice a week now, and planting has begun. The timing could not be worse. Fields are listed and ground laid out in rows for tobacco, corn, cash crops. March corn sown. Field hands plowing, cutting wood, hauling mud and manure as if the Yankees were just over the next rise. The sight of the bondsmen hoeing together in their white cotton blouses stirs something in me. All horses and oxen healthy for once. Only two hands sick.

10 March

Saw Thatcher's Comet, ice ball in the sky, Ethan says. Makes no sense to me how a ball of ice could light up at night. Letter from Julia Keyes today, asking me to pray for peace. Peace isn't in our hands, Daddy likes to say, and he's right. All we desire is to be left alone. Virginia resists Secessionist demands. Once we join the Confederate States living next door to the capital of the North, we'll have war for sure. Daddy says South should have shipped cotton to Europe and not held it ransom for England's help versus Lincoln. Seems last year's record crop has supplied all of Europe twice over with fabric. Wasted all the goodwill it took a century to build. Plow broke again. Slaves cannot handle it. Back to hoes. Lincoln refuses to accept Crittenden Compromise allowing the institution in territories not yet states.

6 April

Virginia two days ago rejected secession again. They've got their heads up their tails in Richmond.

Lincoln's going to throw them all in jail or hang them before they wake up. We shall see. Tobacco looks good.

April 13
Aaron Chesterfield rode all night to tell us: CSA troops under Beauregard fired upon Fort Sumter in South Carolina. Federal troops surrendered after thirty hours of bombardment. Yankee troops sailed away, but war is inevitable. Lincoln can't turn tail and hide when rebel troops blast one of his forts, even if it is on sacred Carolina soil. Ethan seems morose about it. I drill the militia every other day. Uniforms look sharp but too much gold braid for my taste.

19 April
Lincoln has called 75,000 men to arms for 90 days, the papers report. Ninety-Day Wonders, the soldiers are called. Virginia joins North Carolina, Tennessee, and Arkansas in the Confederate cause. There's talk of General Scott's invading Virginia by early summer. Tobacco crop best ever. Ethan won't talk to anybody about anything, least of all me. But I need him to watch over things while I go to Richmond and see about a commission in the Confederate Army. Daddy has already written to the Confederate Congress in Montgomery asking for my commission as major.

April tortured Ethan, flaunting her beauty and fecundity at a time when he felt stunted and barren. After Caitlin's return to Stuart Hall, Ethan withdrew completely from the ominous events of the day, taking his meals in his room and refusing to open his door to anyone except Alex or Clara. He gritted his teeth when he heard Martha call him "the hermit." Ethan ached to be a part of the Parson family and to contribute something of value at Twin Pines. But he had discovered that his conscience was a more complicated master than he had thought. It would not allow him to pretend that all was fine, yet neither could he reveal to his family the whole truth. Not until both he and Caitlin were fully prepared to face the consequences. His spirit sank with each passing day, and the situation alarmed his family.

With Jacob so often away in Richmond, and Charles incapacitated, it was up to Ethan to run the estate and guide the field hands, who took advantage of every absence to lapse into indifference. Weeds grew in the tobacco rows while the slaves's own crops were well-tended and weeded. Ethan went through the motions of carrying out Jacob's written orders, checking off each one as he accomplished it, but as soon as he turned his back, the bondsmen returned to their own interests. Ethan could not bring himself to punish them, and the bondsmen were sure that kind Mister Ethan would not beat them or even tell Jacob half of what they failed to achieve. Jacob inevitably returned in a rage, threatened all the bondsmen with the sale of their family or the seizure of their crops, and then relented once they returned to their field work at Twin Pines with their former vigor.

Ethan and Caitlin corresponded almost daily. Their letters burned with reflections upon the renewal of spring and the blossoming of their love. They wrote little about politics or war or their conflict with their families.

He cherished the sunshine and milder weather, and read and reread the heartfelt verse he and Caitlin exchanged. Still, he brooded continually about his future and Caitlin's. Many days he firmly decided to ride off to Baltimore, from whence they could sail to Europe. But he knew this would provide no more peace than his current inactivity.

Caitlin pleaded with him to give her more time to persuade her father to acknowledge their love and accept their union. He respected her wishes, but knew that Dr. Stuart would never sanction their marriage, nor would he accept their political views. Caitlin had not yet exposed either to him, and Ethan became increasingly frustrated with their silence vis-à-vis the professor.

They had seen each other only twice, both times to aid runaways who passed through Twin Pines. While his work did something to assuage his soul and reaffirm his sense of right, overall he remained disheartened. He knew that one day, perhaps soon, fighting would erupt. And when it did, regardless of which side he chose, regardless of which uniform he wore, he would never take a deep, clear breath of air again. He wrote to Caitlin:

> If I fight for the South, I betray you, those who support you, the just cause of our beliefs, and the bondsmen themselves. Yet if I fight for the North, my family and friends will curse my name. My nightmare is that one day Jacob will be called upon to hang me.

One night he rose at midnight to walk through the fragrant flower gardens. As he breathed in the rich scent of roses and white lilac, he dreamed of an easy solution, praying for a clear path to open before him.

The Keyeses sent weekly epistles urging Ethan to *take the bold step*, and to *do what is right*. Their words cost the Keyeses nothing, and might cost him everything, but this inactivity was killing him. His boots crunched on the path as he made his way around and around the garden. Unarmed and dazed, he labored to take each new breath, fearing that one day his own inertia would be the death of him.

Caitlin, on the other hand, urged his patience in preparing her father for their marriage. She was unsure that she could leave her home without coming to terms with him. And she was satisfied with the aid she provided the Underground Railroad, while Ethan, for some reason, felt he could do more.

He considered the possibilities over and over again. Then it came to him, and he felt the invisible beast pressing against his chest was released. He knew what he had to do. Returning to the house, he went quietly up to his room and began a letter to Jeffrey.

One day in mid-May, just days before the voters of Virginia would ratify their legislature's Act of Secession

from the Union, Jacob returned from training his militia
in Richmond to find the estate in chaos. Bondsmen were
either hoeing their own small plots of land or nowhere to
be seen when he rode up on the chestnut gelding he fa-
vored.

Alex read the murder in Jacob's eyes as he greeted him
before the picket fence and took the reins of the gelding.
He braced himself. Mister Jacob would be in a fine temper. But instead of gathering the field hands together for
a tongue-lashing, Jacob stood, taking stock of the plantation, brass buttons of his militia uniform gleaming in
the sunlight. Then he ran inside the house and up the
stairs, kicking in the door to Ethan's room.

Ethan lay on his bed, Lord Byron's *Don Juan* in his
hands. "You might have knocked," he managed to say
after the shock of his door's collapsing had subsided. "It
wasn't locked."

"Get up and do something!" Jacob screamed at him.
He shook his fists in the air. "This plantation is falling to
ruin while you sit here reading poetry like you're at Harvard. You must put the university behind you, Ethan, and
think of your future. You have but two choices."

Jacob stormed to the open window. "Out there are
two hundred acres of prime tobacco, for which Europe is
willing to pay most any price." Jacob was struggling to
keep his rage under control. "This land alone is worth
two hundred thousand dollars. Are you willing to let it
fall from our grasp? I think perhaps you are. I couldn't
ever let Twin Pines go, not to save my soul from perdition. Because I am a Parson. This land *is* me. But you,
Ethan," he hissed, as if his brother's name were a curse.
"You are different. You go away to Boston and return
home a stranger. Well, no more. You will either assume
an active role in our household, or you will leave. And
you will decide now!"

Drawn by Jacob's ire and the crash of the door, Ethan
looked up to see Martha and her mother standing in the
open doorway. He seemed surprisingly at ease, as if he
had been expecting the scene. Clearing his throat, he set

down the book and addressed all of them. "Mother, Jacob, dear little sister," Ethan began, speaking softly, "I have reached a decision about my future, and I am certain it is best for all of us."

Anna grabbed her daughter's hand for support, afraid she might swoon.

"I cannot remain here when my conscience dictates otherwise," Ethan continued. Jacob stared out the window at the green and flowering fields stretching toward the misty blue mountains on the horizon.

"You are leaving," Jacob said evenly, barely opening his mouth, "to return to Boston, no doubt." He felt so foolish, wearing a Virginia uniform and arguing with his brother who chose to support his enemy, his family's enemy, and now, with secession a fact, his country's enemy.

"What are you saying, son?" Anna asked, tightening her grip of Martha's hand.

Ethan turned to them. "Mother, this plantation isn't mine. It's Jacob's. It's true. He owns every inch of it when—" He didn't finish the sentence, but they all knew he meant "when Daddy dies." "No, Mama, it's true. I'm not saying this to be spiteful, but Twin Pines will one day belong to Jacob, not to me."

"And if something happens to me in this war?" Jacob asked, exasperated. "Have you ever thought about that? Who will run the plantation then? Martha? Alex?"

Ethan smiled, amused by Jacob's insinuations. Walking over to his mother, he took her hand and kissed it. "Mama, your firstborn worries about everything and everybody except himself." He addressed Jacob in all seriousness. "Jacob, if you and I die in this war, Mama and Daddy are perfectly capable of hiring an overseer to run the plantation. They shall have to when we leave anyway."

"But, Ethan, you belong here. Your family duty comes first!" Jacob shouted.

"My first duty is to God and my conscience," Ethan replied, his eyes meeting Jacob's steely gray gaze steadily.

"To everything, there is a season, Jacob. It is now the season of my farewell."

"But what of your own flesh and blood, what of the spirits of three generations of Parsons who died to build this land? How can you say no?" Jacob was racked with pain and doubt. He turned again toward the window. "I never thought I'd live to see this day."

Ethan could think of nothing to say. Martha and Anna withdrew, perhaps hoping that now that the yelling had ceased, the brothers might come to terms. Could Ethan really leave them and Twin Pines knowing that with a war brewing, he might never be able to return?

Jacob sighed deeply. "What must I do to make you stay?"

He looked at Jacob earnestly. "Free the slaves. Then hire them back at decent wages."

"Hah! You are mad!" Jacob walked out of his brother's room, tripping over an edge of the toppled door, and went downstairs to the refuge of the library.

Ethan summoned Alex to set the door back on its hinges.

"Mister Jacob is might angry with you," Alex said, bending his long torso to replace the hinges and hammer in the pins. "Your daddy, too."

"Alex, every man south of Baltimore hates me. But I cannot do otherwise. I'm here on earth to accomplish something good, to make a change. Surely you can understand that." Ethan was surprised to find himself explaining his sentiments to Alex; he had never done so before.

Yet Alex, too, seemed angry with him. "Goin' 'gainst your family is a bad thing to do, Mister Ethan," Alex concluded, nodding sternly before he turned to leave.

"Unless they're wrong," Ethan replied, about to shut the repaired door. "Then it's the only thing to do."

Charles Parson had heard enough of the yelling across the hall to surmise what had happened. The very idea of Ethan's leaving the house at such a time of crisis and family need was impossible. He sent Alex to bring his younger son to him immediately.

To calm his anger, he reached into the cedar humidor at his bedside and withdrew a rolled cigar. He sniffed it, found it wanting in flavor, and chose another. The shaking in his hands was another annoyance that ill health and age had conspired to plague Charles with. He was a man who would have been happy to be eternally thirty-five or forty, with the two boys underfoot, still terrified of his bellow, and every bondsman on the estate jumping when he said to.

And Anna! What a woman she had been twenty years ago. A small, busty, bustling presence wherever she went, Anna Parson had deftly learned in the first year of marriage how and when to withdraw from her husband's side at just the right moment. She never interrupted a political discussion about who the next governor of the Commonwealth should be with talk of a sick child or a dry well. She saw to the problem herself, warning any transgressors or slackers that they would have Charles to deal with if they didn't "hop to and get busy!"

He'd had a magic about him then. Charles knew it, and so did everyone around him. Like the knight-hero of Sir Walter Scott's novel, he could not be beaten, and he would ultimately triumph in his quest for power and wealth.

Charles struck the match and lighted the cigar. It was one of Stuart's, and Charles could taste the sun and the smoke in it. "Where is that boy?" he muttered to himself, coughing. But it had been so for some time. Ethan didn't hurry to obey him, as Jacob did. Falling off that gelding, taking a fence he had jumped fifty times before—that one stupid act had taken away his power and left him with a mind and a voice and little else. He would never accept his impotence, never.

A knock at the door drew his attention. Ethan entered his father's room with his head high and his shoulders back, as his father himself had taught him. Although he knew in his heart that his decision was right, Ethan knew that his father could convince Beelzebub himself to put away his past differences and pitch in to help the Parson flame retain its fire.

He had avoided his father's chamber since he had announced his intention to marry, weeks earlier, and now he was moved by the old man's weak and broken appearance, and by the realization that he might not see him alive again, once he left Twin Pines.

Charles grunted in disgust, burying his head in the newspapers scattered around his bed. "If you're talking, I can't hear you, boy."

Ethan sat in the stuffed chair nearest the bed. His father's bedside table was a jumble of cigar butts, pens, papers, and books. With all that knowledge, why hadn't his father's moral horizons widened? They were as hemmed in as was Twin Pines by the mountains to the west and other plantations to the east, toward Tidewater.

"Daddy, I'm no saint, but I must do what's right. That's all I am saying."

Why have I come here for this final showdown? Ethan asked himself. I can't beat the Old Man now and never could. There was little hope of establishing an understanding. He knew that his father would not yield to him, that he would make no gesture of affection or acceptance.

"Right! Is deserting your own family to live among strangers doing what's right? And what about your engagement to that Stuart girl? What about that?"

His father was glaring at him. Ethan sat forward in the chair. "This has always been one of your tactics, to throw off your opponent by interjecting irrelevant arguments, is that not right, Father?" He struggled unsuccessfully to retain his composure. "We shall marry at the war's end, which God willing will not be too long."

"Bah! Once the fighting begins, boy, it will take Lincoln a year just to get all the uniforms back and accounted for. Don't you know that seventy-five thousand armed men are on their way here even now? And against my advice, the capital of the Confederacy is moving to Richmond in May, just to rub the Yankees' noses in it.

Lincoln won't cotton to that, I bet. Hell, this war could last your lifetime and mine!"

His father had managed, as usual, to turn the argument away from him and onto war and the ever-blessed Confederacy. Even in disgrace, he did not apparently deserve true recognition in his father's eyes. This outburst troubled him, however, for Ethan recognized his father's acuity in politics. If he knew what he was talking about, all those who said that war would be over within the year were fools. Still, that couldn't change his mind about slavery. "Daddy, I have told Jacob what I will tell you. I cannot remain here as long as our slaves remain in bondage."

Without saying a word, Charles reached for his well-worn copy of the Bible and flipped through it. He cleared his throat. "The apostle Paul said this, son, not me. And was he not a holy man?"

"Yes, but he was a man, Father, not a god!" Ethan exclaimed.

Charles read: " 'Slaves, obey thy master.' Now what could be clearer?"

Ethan jumped to his feet. "Father, slavery has been an evil institution for a thousand years. Longevity does not make it right, only powerful."

"Son, it is a historical fact that all great societies . . . ancient Greece, Elizabethan England, Emperor Charlemagne's France . . . they all employed slaves. Cotton and tobacco are the lifeblood of the South, you know that? Without slaves, that blood dries up, and we all die. Is that what you want?"

Ethan shook his head vigorously. "No, no, no! What I want is change, progress. Nearly every civilized country on earth has abolished slavery except us! We are barbarians in the eyes of the world."

"Barbarians! Son, your grandfather tamed this land when no one else dared to. Now Twin Pines is a productive and valuable plantation. But without hands to work it, it will soon revert to woods and meadows. Is that what you want?" he repeated.

The sickly face was unrelenting and stubborn. Ethan discovered his hands clenched into fists at his side. Why did he try to explain himself to his father, he wondered. He never listened. "All I am saying, Father, is that it's time . . . No, it's too late! The South must join the nineteenth century and abolish slavery. Why can't you lead that fight?"

"Well, son, that's easy. Because I don't believe it. We treat our bondsmen fairly. They are like family. I have never split up a family or beaten a man—"

"But you have taken their land and confiscated their personal crops as punishment. And you have confined them in the smokehouse with only water to drink for days at a time. Have you not?"

Charles regarded his son steadily. Seeming not in the least perturbed by his accusations, he reached for another cigar. "But, Ethan, they misbehaved. The bondsmen know the rules. And those who choose to disregard them bring those rather mild punishments upon themselves, do they not?"

Ethan was exasperated. "Father, for someone who sees the world so clearly, you have one gigantic blind spot: slavery. It simply is not right for one man to own another."

"But their daddies and grandaddies were slaves, too. They haven't known anything but the life of a slave. It's just the way things are to them."

"Is that why so many of them are running north to freedom? Is that why Nat Turner led a rebellion thirty years ago?"

Charles waved his unlit cigar in front of his face. "Nat Turner! Don't mention the murderer! His band of cutthroats killed sixty men, women, and children!"

Ethan held up his hands and cupped them, desperate to make himself heard. "No man deserves to live and die in chains. Men are not cattle, Daddy, regardless of what the Supreme Court says."

Charles paused to strike a match, raising it to the cigar and drawing short puffs to light it. Ethan exhaled, a dark expression clouding his face as he regarded his father's impressive features. Sitting back down in the chair next to the bed, he wondered if his arguments had swayed his father at all. Now, as always, he displayed the immutable and godlike self-assurance and pride of a statue, such as those honoring Washington and Jefferson by the courthouse. But his decrepit physical condition made it obvious that he was indeed but a man. And Ethan vowed that his father should recognize that fact.

Charles blew a smoke ring which twirled toward the ceiling. "You have some good points, son, I must admit. If I had been born into a wealthy Boston family, like most of the abolitionists, I'd probably spew the same tripe you do. But what I don't understand is how you came to be one of them. Why, by the time those two spies from Boston left, you hated them as much as I did when I first set eyes on them."

Ethan shook his head. Ah, yes. The old man had spotted his Achilles heel with characteristic accuracy. Was he gifted with insight or simply bedeviled? But he would not be had so easily. "No, sir, I do not hate them. I respect their views, if I was disappointed by their behavior."

He had to admit that the Keyeses' visit had all but killed their friendship. Certainly he and Jeffrey would never be at ease with one another again. While Jeffrey's politics agreed with his own, his lack of moral and emotional sensitivity had been repulsive. One thing he had learned from Jeffrey's visit, Ethan reflected, was that in the South friendship and underhandedness traveled different roads. Ethan again wondered if joining them in the nation's capital was the right decision. The Keyeses were certain that it was; he was awaiting final word from them before leaving. However, the legacy of their visit made him uneasy with their judgment. But was that necessarily bad? He must think first for himself.

Ethan realized that his father had said something. "Excuse me, Father?"

His father flashed his devilish grin. "I said, for a Yankee, she's a fine-looking woman."

Ethan jumped to his feet. "Father, you are not listening to me. I will marry Caitlin Stuart! I am not going to Boston, not now. And I do not wish to court Julia Keyes. If anyone does, it's Jacob. Ask him about her!"

Ethan left the room relieved to escape the stale, cigar-filled air and the lingering aromas of illness and medicines. Storming down the stairs, he dashed outside to the front porch to clear his head. Leaning on the fence was Brett Tyler, smiling wickedly as the Devil himself.

"Tyler, what do you want?" Ethan glared down at the man, who wore trousers of worn cotton and a heavy shirt. His overture of goodwill had been rejected by Tyler following the New Year's incident, and he was in no mood to repeat the gesture.

"Good day to you, Ethan! I have business with your brother."

Ethan narrowed his eyes. "What manner of business?"

Tyler laughed. "You his secretary now? I heard you was leavin' to join Mr. Lincoln's cabinet, Ethan. Is that true?"

Ethan glared at him, which only brought out a harsh laugh from the poorly dressed troublemaker.

"I'll see if Jacob's available." Ethan turned to go back inside.

"Tell him the fate of the South depends upon it," said Tyler, never losing his foxlike grin.

Tyler waited patiently, hoping to catch a glimpse of Martha, but when the door opened a second time it was Miss Anna, carrying a trowel and a basket. She descended the side steps and passed Tyler without acknowledging him, then proceeded to the flower beds. Crocus and daffodils grew everywhere, and the azalea bushes bloomed with an explosion of pink and scarlet flowers.

She inhaled deeply and sighed, for there was more than the scent of azaleas and roses in the breeze. The musky odor of Brett Tyler hit her like a foul wind from the swamp. Why did he plague the Parsons, first rescuing Ethan and now sniffing around Twin Pines like a hound? She wondered how to get rid of him. Perhaps he would be killed in the war and die a hero. She was not proud of the thought, but it would solve the problem he posed to the Parsons. Martha was displaying dangerous signs of poor judgment where the rogue was concerned. Anna had overheard Clara make mention of Martha chasing after "that Tyler trash." Anna had been so angry and upset that she mentioned the matter to Jacob. But they could see no effective action to take. They couldn't very well lock Martha in her room for perpetuity.

For the moment, perhaps the best action to take was none at all. So she decided to let Martha get a glimpse of the dirty wretch as he really was, hoping that a taste would be more than enough to scare her away.

Apparently Tyler did not know the meaning of the word *unwelcome*. She glared at him again. He was a vile man. Martha must see that for herself.

Blithely indifferent to the countenance and judgment of Miss Anna, Brett Tyler kept his eyes on the front door to Twin Pines. Why don't Martha come to join her mother? he wondered. She has to! He had played his hand too soon at their last meeting and too roughly. If he were to suit her, Tyler reasoned, he would have to behave himself. He vowed that he would.

This yearning was an unfamiliar emotion. He had had his share of women, but never hankered for any particular one. But Martha Parson, unlike the Stuart girl, who would never look beyond his standing in society and his sun-browned forearms, looked at Tyler where it mattered: in the eyes. She was a wild one, he could see it. He knew he must appear as rough and unbroken as a wild stallion to her. She was scared—and intrigued. Marrying her would be like finagling a priceless jewel from a wealthy old family that didn't want to give it. No, the way Miss Anna was looking at him, they surely didn't want to give it. But he would outsmart them—over time.

If I am the hawk, Tyler reckoned, Martha's the willing prey. He had to see her, now! The low black iron fence before him stood like a prison wall. He would rather have leaped over it and knocked on the door until Jacob or his sister came out. But instead he waited, hands in his pockets, humming a ballad and checking the windows of the upper floor for a glimpse of her.

The front door opened, and Jacob appeared on the porch. "What is it?" he asked tersely.

You arrogant bastard, I'll not let you off that easily. Tyler cupped a hand to his ear. "I cain't yell this across the yard."

Frowning, Jacob walked down the steps and approached the gate where Tyler leaned nonchalantly.

"I want to join the militia, the Albemarle Rifles, under your command." Tyler spoke in a direct and rapid-fire speech as he had practiced.

Jacob shook his head. "What would I do with you? We already have a boy to tend to the animals. And a cook."

Tyler stiffened, rising to his full height. He was both broader at the shoulder and taller than Jacob. "I saved your brother's life."

"You did what any decent man would have done—"

"But you wasn't there, I was. Your brother'd be six feet under now if it wasn't for me."

Jacob stood back and looked toward the garden. His mother seemed not to have heard. So the sly hooligan was going to trade upon the incident, to use it as collateral to cause the family woe. "What do you want?"

"I want to be your personal aide."

Tyler stared at Jacob with intense, dark eyes that seemed to threaten violence as the next step.

"I already have an orderly. Can you read?"

Tyler nodded. "I can ride and shoot best of any man in the county," he said proudly.

"That's only the twelfth time I've heard that in the last two days. It's easy enough to make such assertions."

Tyler swung around toward his horse and grabbed a musket from the saddle. "Point to anything and I'll hit it," he challenged quietly.

Jacob saw a chance to silence this ignorant rabble rouser. He pointed up in the sky at a circling raven. The bird was at least two hundred feet in the sky and the sun was blinding.

Tyler raised the gun and squeezed off a shot. It took a second for the shot to hit the bird, scattering feathers, before it began to drop. "There's better eatin' than crow," Tyler said, keeping his eye on the tumbling bird.

Jacob looked at Tyler, who tossed the musket to him. "You hit one."

Jacob looked up. He could barely see the circling birds. He raised the weapon but knew he would be unable to hit his target. Lowering the gun, he handed it back to Tyler. "Yankees fire back," he reminded him.

"Not when they're dead."

Jacob tried another tack to discourage him. "There's more to the militia than shooting birds and Yankees," he began, testing the effect of his words upon Tyler. "There's discipline, drilling, formations, strategy—"

"I leave that to you. Just point me to the target, and it's hit. I want to march with you in battle, that's all I'm saying. You owe me the chance."

The manner in which Tyler spoke and moved suggested a bully, a man who could talk a better fight than he could carry out. But Tyler could shoot and ride. And according to Ethan, he could handle himself with skill when outnumbered. These were valuable traits in a warrior.

It was true: The Parsons had never repaid him the debt of saving Ethan's life last New Year's Eve. Still, Jacob disliked being cornered. The rascal was too sly and self-serving for comfort. "I'll accept you as a volunteer under my command," he told Tyler, grimacing as the rogue let out a whoop. "But cross me once or disobey a single order," he added crossly, "and you'll be disciplined the same as any other soldier in the regiment. Understood?"

Tyler didn't reply. That was another of his habits that drove Jacob wild—the man wouldn't answer a direct question. "I know you heard me, Tyler. Now heed me."

But Tyler wasn't even looking at him. Jacob turned

his head to see Martha on the front porch, talking to their mother. Once she caught sight of Tyler, she froze. Anna had to call her daughter's name twice to break the spell. Martha scampered down the steps to help her bring in the flowers. Jacob could not recall when he'd seen her move so quickly around the house.

When she and her mother had disappeared inside the house, Tyler turned his attention to Jacob and asked, "What's the pay?"

Jacob snorted. Naturally money would be his greatest concern. "Thirteen dollars a month. Ever dream of such wealth? Want to change your mind?"

Tyler turned a dissatisfied look on Jacob. "I hear Lincoln's paying twice that for his soldiers. Maybe I ought to join his army."

"They aren't defending their homes, they're invading ours." Jacob turned back toward the house. "Do you have any more business with me?"

Tyler cast a glance at Martha's room. "Not with you."

"Then git. Don't you Tylers ever do any work?"

Tyler placed his musket in its sheath and jumped aboard the big brown mare he rode. "When do I join up?"

Jacob glared at him. "Do you think I'm holding some sort of ceremony to induct you into the militia? You've already joined up, raven killer. Be at the university gates Wednesday at four P.M."

Tyler nodded. "I don't get into town much."

"You will."

He tipped his hat and rode off, pushing the mare at a good pace. Jacob had to admit that he rode tall and straight in the saddle, despite his lack of breeding. He frowned. An uneasy feeling had settled over him. He had been blackmailed by that scoundrel, plain and simple, and he feared that he would live to rue the day. Jacob tried to shake off the bad feelings and returned to the house to see to the accounts.

He would not be able to get a good night's sleep until they found an overseer to run the plantation in his absence. But the question remained: Whom could they hire?

The most capable men would be joining the war effort. He would have to begin looking immediately.

CHAPTER 16

CHARLES PARSON PROVED to be correct. Jacob read in the newspapers that on the twenty-third of May, the capital of the eleven-state confederacy would be moved from Montgomery to Richmond, just seventy miles from Charlottesville.

Much to the relief of the family, Ethan had made no immediate move to leave Twin Pines following his declaration of intent. Occasionally he even helped to oversee the work of the field hands.

Ethan's sympathies were well-known to the bondsmen, who trusted no white man further than they could see. But he was kind to them in the fields, allowing them frequent rests when the days grew hot, as they did in May. Sometimes he even let them return to their cabins to tend their own plots of land.

None of this was lost on Jacob, who found two or three major mistakes in Ethan's performance almost every day.

"They won't respect you if you're not tough," Jacob argued. "Can't you see that?"

He had contained his criticism through the better part of their supper of creamed sweetbreads with sherry. But the cost to the family of his laziness continued to rankle him, and as the plum pudding was served, he began to lay into Ethan for coddling the bondsmen.

"They do not truly respect us in any event. And they will not until they are set free. Can't you see that?"

Martha looked at her brothers in fascination. She had

heard and read so much about the pending war with the North, and she almost welcomed the drama of conflict. I shall be a famous nurse, she decided, and resolved to begin learning about the care and treatment of the ill.

Anna welcomed the change in reading habits, but wasn't fond of the idea of Martha tending hundreds of injured men far from their sweethearts at home.

On the twenty-seventh of May, word arrived from Richmond that a battle had been fought two days before in Alexandria, Virginia, just ten miles from the White House. Blood had been shed on both sides. Jacob had already reported that Richmond was taking on the appearance of a city at war. Thousands of militiamen in scores of different uniforms slept in warehouses, public buildings, and in tents pitched throughout the city.

After all the tension and dread of the past months, there was a sense in the Parson home that war might truly come, and they could spend their energy in useful activity rather than in fretting. Both Jacob and his father agreed that neither side had a suitable strategy. Union General Scott's so-called Anaconda plan of cutting off shipped supplies to the South and starving her into submission might take far too long to be palatable to Northern politicians, perhaps years. Anna listened impatiently to her husband and son speak of war with such enthusiasm. From all she heard and read, all the Southern states wanted, in the words of their new president, Jefferson Davis, was "to be left alone." But as Charles so vociferously and incessantly raged, Lincoln steadfastly swore to quell "the insurrection," as he termed the secession of one-third of the Union. And now that men had died on Virginia's soil, there would be no turning back.

"It's time to fish or cut bait," Jacob said to Ethan. They were alone in the library drinking coffee, and the mood was somber. "You have not left, nor do you contribute usefully here. Ethan, what are your plans?"

How odd that his brother had chosen that moment to

ask. It had taken three weeks for the Keyeses to respond to his correspondence. He had received word from them the day before, and just hours earlier Ethan had agreed to accompany a runaway bondsman to Washington, where the Keyeses would see to his welfare. Jacob had no inkling of this. He was probably still hoping that Ethan would remain at Twin Pines to oversee the plantation in Jacob's absence. The blow would be considerable, he knew, but there was no other course.

The fulfillment of working in harmony with his moral views made it worth the grave risk he was taking, making the task only more attractive. Caitlin had accepted his need to leave Twin Pines; she understood his need to act, to *do* something. She herself would remain at Stuart Hall for the present.

After his first courier assignment, he expected others, and Julia had written that he was welcome to join her in publishing the abolitionist newsletter she wrote and distributed, *The Drinking Gourd*. The idea of writing tracts arguing for social equality appealed to him. As Julia tactfully pointed out, Ethan's "special position as a son of the South" made his words all the more poignant, telling, and persuasive. Ethan had to try.

"I am expected in Richmond next week," Jacob said. "I can no longer delay my departure." Jacob looked searchingly into his brother's blue eyes for the answer. "Will you see to Twin Pines in my absence?"

Ethan lowered his head. The steam from the coffee sent wisps over his hands, which held the saucer in his lap. "Jacob, I cannot. Please don't despise me." When he looked up, Jacob had turned his head to the side. Tears ran down his cheek; he bit his lip. Ethan could see that his brother was trying not to weep. "Jacob . . . ," he said, bending nearer. But his brother withdrew, pushing his chair away from the table and turning his back on Ethan.

"Jacob, this war is tearing me apart. Don't you think I want to be the loyal son and brother you and Mother and Father want and expect? Of course I do. But I cannot make a mockery of ideals I hold dear. Jacob, when I was at Harvard I argued as a Southerner against slavery as an institution, regardless of its origin or acceptance. People in the North listened and agreed without hating us. They understood that we need time to change. But the time is now. Time has run out. I can do no more here. Twin Pines is Father's home, and yours, but it's no longer mine."

Jacob wiped his eyes and cleared his throat. "This will kill Father, your leaving now when we need you most," Jacob said softly, without rancor. But his words turned bitter as he continued, "It's a way of turning your back on everything we hold sacred, he and I."

"Everything except God and the Commandments."

Jacob faced him with spite in his eye. "There is no commandment condemning slavery! There is one about honoring thy father, however."

Ethan stood his ground. "I cannot honor him by doing what I know to be wrong, by being too cowardly to do what I know is right. What honor resides in such behavior?"

Jacob was weary of the same old arguments. "We are like this nation, you and I, two forces convinced of the rightness of our causes. Please, leave now, before we come to blows," he said, gripping the arm of his chair. "Don't say good-bye. Don't tell anyone anything. Just go."

Ethan regarded his brother's back, stiff beneath his linen shirt. "What will you tell them?"

Jacob shrugged. "I'll make up a story. I'll tell them that you've gone to Harvard to teach and study ethics." He twirled his moustache, and his mouth curved into a sneer as he asked, "That is what you do best, isn't it? Read and think and ponder what is right and just?"

The sad smile that crossed Ethan's face was almost a grimace. "Actually, I intend to be a man of action, like yourself."

Jacob leaned toward him, frowning. "What do you mean? Are you intending to join Lincoln's army? Is that why you're heading up to Washington, to enlist in the Union army?"

"I'm not that crazy, Jacob."

Jacob heaved a sigh. At least Ethan had spared them that humiliation. Then the thought hit him: For all he knew, he might one day be forced to fire a shot that would take Ethan's life. "Promise me you'll never wear the uniform of the Union. Swear it!" The intensity in Jacob's eyes frightened him; Ethan took the oath, thinking, My work will not require me to wear a uniform, so far as I know.

The brothers parted without embracing.

That night, after the dinner dishes had been washed and put away, and the Parsons had retired to their rooms, Ethan crept out of his room, carrying a knapsack filled with clothes and the Bible, and slipped unnoticed downstairs. In the kitchen, Clara was waiting for him. He followed her out the back door and down the path to the slave quarters. Crickets chirped as they descended the serpentine path, and the stars shone brightly. The half-moon was still too low to cast much light upon the land. Ethan took one long look around, not quite believing that he was leaving Twin Pines for what could be forever.

At Thomas's cabin, Clara rapidly knocked on the door three times. It opened, and they entered.

Alex stood in front of the darkened fireplace, beside his son. Hunched over the bed was a small woman in a dark cotton wrap which obscured her face from view.

Taking Ethan by the hand, Clara led him to the small, wizened woman. "This here's your mammy," she said without a trace of irony.

The old woman looked up at him, her eyes dark and heavy with age and spunk, and Ethan instantly realized what Clara meant. He was to accompany her to Washington posing as her master. He smiled and started to introduce himself, but she grabbed his hand with surprising quickness and strength, and whispered, "God bless you, honey. We goin' to make it."

In that moment Ethan discovered his life's work. The nobility of the calling beckoned to him, and the difficulty of the fight challenged him. He could well lose his life. For all he knew, they could be found out tomorrow, and he might be jailed or beaten or worse.

But the quiet dignity of the black woman before him, herself only the size of a child, inspired him. He knew now that all he and Caitlin had discussed was right: They should do what they could to free the bondsmen and end the war quickly. They would pay a price for their actions, which were treason in the eyes of their families and neighbors. But act they must.

Unlike the other runaways who had passed through Twin Pines on foot, Ethan and the woman, who called herself Old Sarah, would be driven to the train station before dawn by Alex. Ethan would say that he was taking her to Richmond for medical treatment. The North controlled the railroads across the Potomac, and any further travel would bring them close to Confederate forces gathering at Manassas. From Richmond, they would have to make their way to Washington by carriage and boat. The trip would be both arduous and risky, and they rested to store up their energy and determination.

They passed the long hours of the early morning telling stories about Twin Pines, both to educate Old Sarah and to amuse themselves.

Clara, who had been present when all the Parson children were born, recounted stories of their childhood. "Riding his hobbyhorse on the porch, Mister Ethan push too hard and fall, tumble all the way down the front steps. He was no mo' than three at the time. Me and Miss Anna runs to him, sayin', 'You all right, chile?' He say, 'Agin! Agin!' "

They all laughed, and Ethan almost wished they could stay another day and keep talking. He had been on guard for so long that it was a delight to feel that these people were, like him, a part of a great and good struggle.

Then Clara spoke of Charles's fall off the horse ten years earlier. "It done broke his back and his heart," Clara said, and Ethan nodded. Would he be here now if his father were well and in charge? Somehow he doubted it. As overpowering as the old coot was, his father would have ordered him off to Europe or the West at the first signs of his Unionist sympathies. Even in his father's present condition of physical disability, Ethan was half-surprised that Charles had not disowned him for his views and sent him packing.

But bound to his bed like a prisoner, Charles's influence had indeed lessened: His will had weakened. Yet that accident had freed Ethan to be himself ten years ago. Without that horse and that fall in 1851, Ethan would be, as Jacob still was, trembling in the formidable shadow of his father. He was moved to try to believe that it was the goodness of God which had operated to make something positive of the tragedy of his father's accident. But he could not.

Ethan snapped out of his reverie to find Thomas glaring at him. He knew that Thomas had made a similar trip not long before, and had returned against his will to Twin Pines. Clara had made light of the affair when recounting it to Caitlin, assuring her that he would do nothing to endanger them. But Caitlin had expressed to him her worries about Thomas's dissatisfaction. And looking at the heat and anger in his dark eyes, Ethan, too, felt that Thomas would not last long at Twin Pines.

It was time to leave for the train depot. Old Sarah hugged Alex and Thomas, said a quiet prayer of protection for all of them, kissed Clara on the lips, and followed Ethan to the open buggy, which Alex would pick up at the depot later in the day with Thomas.

"God be wif you," Clara whispered in Ethan's ear. He nodded, and they drove off at a slow pace. His heart raced. Could he bluff his way past the fire-eaters if they encountered any?

Next to him on the wooden buggy seat, Old Sarah hummed one Negro spiritual after another. Ethan had often heard the bondsmen singing the sad, mournful songs, but he had never before listened closely. Now, he found the music sweet and stirring, offering comfort to those who had no earthly protection.

The moon was high and pale. The land had never

looked so unearthly and yet so beautiful to Ethan. He felt
that it must be like this when an explorer discovered a
new land: Nothing he would see from now on would look
exactly the same as it did here, even if he came upon an
oak or an elm or a magnolia, whose perfumed flowers
also filled the evening breezes at Twin Pines.

He thought in turn of his parents and Jacob and Martha. He might never see them again. The very thought
ought to terrify him, for it made an orphan of him. Yet
he remained strangely calm, even elated. Some of the faith
which strengthened Old Sarah filled him, too, and they
drove along in alternating silence and song. The bravery
of the small woman's actions overwhelmed him. If the
situation were reversed, Ethan was not certain that he
would be capable of fleeing a master, no matter how cruel.
The sheer terror of living at night with no haven and the
constant threat of capture might easily drive his heart to
burst, he knew. Holding the reins loosely in his right
hand, he looked again at Old Sarah. Quiet now, her
leathery features held a determined set, her lips moved in
silent prayer. For her sake, he pretended to be calm and
confident. At the train depot, where he was known, carrying though with their ruse might be tricky. He sighed,
concentrating again on the empty dirt road before them.
He would know soon enough.

Their journey into Charlottesville was uneventful. As
they trotted up to the station, where the lanterns burned,
Old Sarah grew quiet, and Ethan brought the horse to
rest just outside the red brick building. Tying up the reins,
he told her to wait, and went inside the building. The
first people he saw were two traveling salesmen at the
ticket counter, wearing heavy coats and carrying leather
cases. The only other person in the station was Jim, a free
black who kept the station swept and clean.

Ethan had never been there without seeing Jim. He
seemed to be there twenty-four hours a day, whether
awake or asleep as he was now, with his mouth wide
open and a broom gripped in one hand. Ethan marveled
at how the man could sleep standing up, like a horse. In

the months ahead, he thought with a cynical smile to himself, it might be a good skill to learn.

Satisfied that all was calm, Ethan went back to the buggy for Old Sarah. She seemed pleased to be taking a train trip. "Ain't never not walked nor rode," she told him. He helped the old woman find a seat, then approached the counter to purchase the tickets.

Harris Wilson was a fat, balding man. Ethan knew he supported the fire-eaters, and monitored the traffic through the station closely. He smiled broadly when he saw Ethan coming. "You ain't gonna get much for that one, Ethan!" he joked, laughing in an uneven mule's braying.

Ethan adopted an arrogant smile. He looked back at Old Sarah, then turned to the ticket agent again.

"Ain't selling her, Harris. I'm taking her to the doctor."

Wilson frowned and pushed his wire-rimmed glasses up on his bulbous nose. "Got a doctor in town."

Ethan rolled his eyes. "I know that, Harris. He sees my daddy once a month. She needs special care in Richmond. I need two tickets."

Wilson reluctantly filled in the lines on the tickets and stamped them. "Pampering your colored never paid off for nobody."

The thirty-minute wait for the train to Richmond was excruciating, but nothing unusual occurred. There was just the waiting, Jim's snoring, and the idle chatter of the two white travelers anxious to get to the new capital of the Confederacy to sell insurance. Seated next to Ethan and Old Sarah, they spoke of the profits and opportunity. It struck Ethan as despicable that these two well-dressed men thought no more about the war other than whether it would help or hurt the insurance business. By the time the train rolled in, Ethan was ready to buggy-whip the pair of them.

Once aboard, he settled Old Sarah into the rear of the train, near the baggage, where Negroes free and bonded sat. She closed her eyes immediately; by the time he turned away, she was already sleeping peacefully in her seat.

Walking up to the first-class car, Ethan took a seat by himself and waited for the train to pull from the station.

He looked around at the other travelers, imagining that their curious stares held accusation. The train was lingering in town too long for Ethan's taste. Just as he was about to hail the conductor and inquire about the trouble, the train jerked and squealed, and they were underway. The early-morning sun on the blue mountain peaks in the distance to the west seemed to salute Ethan. Weary as he was, the sight gave him faith.

He had sat well apart from the other passengers, and even as the train made periodic stops along the way, he was left alone. Some hours later, the land flattened as they approached the broad valley of the James River. Crossing the bridge over the great waterway was a stirring experience. Ethan had not expected to see the scores of tents thrown up around the Hanover Junction station, just a few miles before Richmond. It looked as if they were expecting an invasion at any moment. The officers wore a variety of different uniforms, some blue and some gray, trimmed in bright reds and blues and golds. Some soldiers wore plumed hats. For the first time, Ethan was confronted with the South's military might in force. He watched with interest as the soldiers drilled and marched in formations. It was an impressive sight, but of course the might of the North was said to be overwhelming. Why were all these good young men trying to fool themselves into pretending to be soldiers? With the exception of the officers, they seemed country boys, with sunburned necks; why didn't they run back home and tend their farms as they should?

Ethan sighed. He knew the answer. It was because the damn fool boys had a mission, too, however misbegotten. They, too, took risks and were willing to die for their own fool pride, for the cherished glory of the Southern way.

After they crossed the railroad bridge over the James River, the smoke and noise from the encampments diminished. Perched on a bluff like a piece of sculpture, several white marble buildings caught Ethan's eye. The city of Richmond. Half an hour later they had arrived.

At the train station, he left his seat to get Old Sarah, who seemed not to have moved the entire journey. Her eyes were still closed, and her small frame was straight and still in the seat. When he touched her shoulder, she rose with alacrity to join him and step down from the train.

He and Old Sarah drew no stares and attracted little attention as they crossed the bustling station. It was jammed with soldiers in all manner of dress, some looking as if they had just awakened. Overhearing one of them mention something about "awaiting orders," Ethan wondered what kind of orders the man was speaking of. Orders to do what? To go where? Had a battle broken out already?

The vast, domed station was crowded with civilians and soldiers carrying swords and muskets. Ethan stopped a passing newsboy in the chaotic rush of people and bought a *Richmond State Journal*. Quickly he scanned the paper. There had been a recent riot in Baltimore. In response to the riots, Lincoln had ordered ten thousand troops into Washington, D.C. Anti-Federalists had attacked recruits from Massachusetts, and the new soldiers had panicked and fired into the crowd. Twelve civilians had been killed, as well as four soldiers from Boston. Ethan shook his head. Now men were either soldiers or civilians; there was no other choice.

With Old Sarah on his arm, Jacob carried their small bags in his free hand and hailed a coupé, which had doors that closed, offering the privacy Ethan desired outside Union Station. The driver took no special notice of them once Ethan had agreed to his outrageous terms—he would receive ten dollars to drive them to Port Royal. He was relieved that the old fellow thought nothing of driving them the thirty-five miles north.

He must not have been the first to make such a request, Ethan reasoned. He could only hope the man's motive was profit, not deceit. Once in Port Royal, Ethan planned to rent or buy a carriage that would take him and Old Sarah to the Potomac River, where they would have to find a boat and row across to the Northern-occupied capital city. It was a risky venture, but they had no choice.

"The capital is an armed camp," he said to his companion. She had begun to sing again, an old spiritual. Concentrating on the difficulty of this crucial step in their trip, Ethan was unable to find comfort in her sweet, high voice, and the words were lost on him.

He looked frequently outside the windows of the coupé. The entire world seemed in flux. Ethan had never seen so much movement nor heard such a cacophony of curses, oaths, and threats. Men in uniform bullied their way through the long lines of carriages waiting to deposit their passengers near the station. The closed doors of the coupé provided some protection, but Ethan remained tense, breathing more freely only when they had lost sight of the train tracks.

In thirty minutes, they were on the northern outskirts of Richmond. Traffic on the dusty road diminished to a few farmers carrying produce to market and, now and then, a few military men on horseback.

"This world will never be the same," Ethan commented, half to himself.

Old Sarah nodded once vigorously. "Be fo' de better if it ain't," she said quietly, then returned to the spiritual.

They forded the Pamunkey River at an old wooden bridge that groaned under the weight of the coupé. Ten miles farther north, they came upon the more substantial Mattapony River and crossed the muddy brown water near a town called Guiney's Station, where Ethan bought them some biscuits and a tin of meat at the general store.

The next ten miles of rolling hills and pastures brought them to their first destination, Port Royal, where the broad Rappahannock narrowed.

When the coupé halted at the livery, Ethan exited with Sarah and paid the driver. After counting the money, he pocketed it contentedly. The driver rested the horse, smoking the foulest cigar Ethan had ever smelled, and watched disinterestedly as Ethan negotiated the purchase of a horse to carry them to the Potomac.

"That smoke'd keep the Devil away," Ethan complained to the fellow.

"Has so far," the driver replied, contentedly puffing on it. "That horse will never make it," he added.

After a half hour of haggling over a price, Ethan purchased the driver's own horse, which was big enough to carry both of them. He did not question where the driver would find another horse for his carriage; he had obviously pulled this same ruse on others before him. The Potomac was only ten miles to the northeast, and the spotted mare seemed strong, if a little swaybacked. Ethan rode with Sarah seated sidesaddle in front of him; she took up no more room than a child.

They rode undisturbed for another mile and a half before meeting two militiamen on horseback. The two young soldiers smiled in amusement at Ethan's mount as they gestured for him to halt.

"Who are you, and what's your business, sir?" one asked. Ethan guessed the soldier to be nineteen or twenty years old. He had a wispy blond moustache that added nothing to the portrait of immaturity he presented.

"My mammy and I are going to visit relations in Alexandria. You from around here, soldier?" Ethan said.

They both shook their heads. One spoke up. "On that nag, you be lucky to reach the next four corners."

" 'Less you count on walkin'," the other added, breaking out laughing. They spurred their horses, allowing Ethan and Sarah to continue. "Watch out for Yankee patrols!" the moustached boy called out before they had disappeared down the road.

Ethan snapped the reins on the mare, aware of the perspiration that beaded his brow.

"Thank you, Lord," Old Sarah whispered.

By early evening, they had reached a small farm on the southern side of the Potomac, opposite Port Tobacco. There the river was broad but not overly swift, and they

hoped to cross it without much difficulty. From Port Tobacco, a forty-mile ride would take them into Washington.

Stiff and sore from the ride, Ethan knocked at the
door of the farmhouse until a tall, thin man appeared.
Ethan dickered with the man, finally trading his horse for
a small rowboat with oars that the farmer kept on the
riverbank. Thanking the man, Ethan grimly carried their
bags, holding Sarah's arm as they followed a path to the
river's edge.

"I hope he doesn't report us," Ethan said, looking back
every few feet.

"Nuh-uh," Old Sarah agreed, stepping lightly among
the briars.

Ethan checked the rowboat for holes, and to his satisfaction found none. "Miss Sarah, this current could
sweep us anywhere. I can't guarantee success, you understand."

In the gathering shadows of dusk, her face beamed.
"Don't expect no guarantee, Mister Ethan. How does I
git in?"

He helped her, tossed in their bags, seated himself with
the oars, and pushed off. They were lucky; spring rains
had carried a good deal of silt into the Potomac, which
was muddier than Ethan had ever seen it, and the river
was sluggish. He rowed fiercely to keep them in line with
the northern shore, and Old Sarah quietly sang an unend-
ing stream of songs that set a soothing rhythm for his
rowing. Ethan checked both shores frequently. He saw
no one. But he knew that did not necessarily mean nobody was watching them. Night had fallen, and Ethan's
vision was reduced to guessing.

They came ashore in a muddy clump of bushes. Ethan
hopped from the rowboat, his shoulders aching from the
effort, and sank a foot deep into the mud. He helped Old
Sarah ashore and then hid the boat under shrubs and broken branches as she watched.

"Is I free now?" Sarah asked. Her dark, heavy eyes
were glowing.

"Yes, ma'am, I reckon you are."

"You a hero now, all right," Sarah insisted.

Ethan laughed. He was weary and aching from the neck down, and they were still forty miles from the capital. "I surely don't feel like one," he told her. "I just feel bone tired."

They stumbled through the darkness, looking for a light or some indication of the road to the nation's capital. Rounding a bend in the path they had been following, they saw a lantern in the window of a small farmhouse.

"You feel lucky?" Ethan whispered to his companion. He could see her confident smile in the darkness.

"Lord always lucky, Mister Ethan," she said.

Together they walked toward the weak yellow light glowing in the distance.

CHAPTER 17

JACOB WAS DRESSED and packed for a meeting of Virginia state militia leaders in Richmond later that day. He hoped no one would give any thought to Ethan's absence at breakfast; Ethan often read late into the night and overslept the following morning.

As he was stuffing socks and shirts into his knapsack, Martha appeared at the door to his room.

"Sister!" Jacob was lighthearted, almost giddy with excitement. Finally, the pressures of dealing with Ethan's irresponsibility had lifted. Furthermore, it looked as though he might actually see some action any day now, and training was to begin in earnest in Richmond. The task of organizing his bunch of country boys into a fighting unit was just the challenge he needed. Perhaps he, too, like Ethan, wanted—and needed—to leave Twin Pines more than he ever dreamed.

"What is it, Martha?" His smile faded as he stopped to look at her; concern was written on all her lovely features.

She stepped forward and opened his palm, slipping something small and round into it. Jacob looked down to see a small cameo locket, black on white, of Martha herself. "I'm . . . touched. It's lovely."

She backed away, pausing by the door. "Promise me you'll keep it. It will keep you safe and bring you home in one piece."

"I so swear." Jacob found it difficult to say anything else to his sister. He could no longer hug and kiss and tickle her until she was breathless, as he used to when she was small. She was a beautiful young woman now, soon to join a world of her own making, and he had to step aside. It was up to their mother to act as her confidante and guide.

Holding the cameo locket in his hand brought on another rush of emotions foreign and frightening to Jacob. Julia's face seem to embed itself in his mind's eye. Julia, too, would be tested by the war. But why such a surge of desire at the flashing image of her delicate and lovely face?

Jacob vowed not to think of her. Such useless emotions could do him no good. He was certain never to see her again, now that war was a reality. She would never forgive him for fighting to preserve the South's traditions and integrity, if indeed he survived—he was sure. It did not matter how she regarded his actions, he concluded. Whatever the source of his feelings for Miss Keyes, the emotion was best used in the cause and in cherishing the home and family for which he now fought.

Jacob confidently squeezed Martha's locket in his fist, as if the gesture could crush the dangerous emotional undertow that threatened him. He was back in control now.

"What is it you're doing now?" Martha asked.

Jacob concluded packing and closed the knapsack. He looked around the room to make sure he hadn't overlooked anything. Slipping the cameo into his jacket pocket, he buttoned it, then took Martha by the shoulders. "I am due in Richmond today to meet with Virginia's other militia captains. Soon we shall have an army. I might be a general next week!"

She saw that he was joking, but did not smile. "I don't like that talk. Generals often get killed."

"You mean in those French romances you read by the dozen?" He laughed. "In real life, I suspect being a general is safer than raising tobacco. We shall see!"

"Jacob," she said, her voice fluttering, "without you here, I . . . I just don't know about Mama and Daddy. What should I do?"

He almost moved to hold her. But instead he sat on the bed, summoned all the strength he possessed, and explained, "Martha, no matter what, your being here is the greatest comfort Mama and Daddy could ever ask for. Ethan and I are not leaving forever—"

"Then he is gone?"

He had slipped; now she knew.

"I suspect—and this must remain our secret—that your brother has gone to Washington. He as much as told me so, although he swore never to put on a Yankee uniform, thank the Lord."

She nodded, tears springing to her blue eyes. "I am losing both my brothers in one day. . . ."

"No, Martha," he told her firmly. "You're losing no one. We'll return. There's not even a war yet, just talk."

"They have already fought in Alexandria. Daddy told me. It's all the servants talk about, that and freedom."

"They talk about whatever we let out, dear sister," he went on. "It's all they know. Gossip is the coin of the realm in their society, such as it is."

Martha wiped at her eye and snapped her head erect. "Daddy asked to see you. Shall I tell him you'll be right there?"

He shook his head. "I'll see him now. Thank you. Oh, and, Martha, I trust you will write me while I am away?"

* * *

Jacob dropped his knapsack outside his father's door and entered as he knocked. He was surprised to find Charles sleeping heavily. It was unlike his father to sleep late, and Jacob feared something might be wrong. But as he got closer, he saw that his father's breathing was untroubled, and his round face looked peaceful. Jacob decided to let him sleep. Stepping softly to the window, he looked outside.

The view to the west revealed acres of tobacco in full leaf, their green contrasting sharply with the red-and-brown earth. The mountains were all but lost in a heavy blue mist, and dark clouds rolling in from the mountains seemed to threaten rain. Today, I'll be protected from the elements, traveling by train, he thought. But once the war begins, I may be forced to sleep in the rain for weeks on end. Am I strong enough to lead men? What if I panic and fail in battle?

These troubling concerns evaporated with the sound of coughing and wheezing behind him. It took his father a minute or two to open his eyes and focus on his son. His first gruff words were about Ethan. "Where's that brother of yours?"

Jacob held up his hand in a questioning gesture. "I'm not certain, Father. I believe business has taken him elsewhere. So he told me."

The old man flared, struggling to sit up in bed. "Business! Whose business, Lincoln's? What's he up to, son?"

The desperation in his father's gray eyes weakened Jacob's resolve to keep Ethan's secret. "Father, my own conviction—"

"Blast your conviction, boy! Where's he gone?"

Jacob drew back. He could not lie to his father, not about this. "He said he was going to Washington to serve what I take to be the abolitionist cause." Jacob hastened to add, "But he swore never to wear a Yankee uniform. He promised me. He asked me to free the bondsmen. . . ."

To Jacob's surprise, the old man coughed and began laughing, guffawing until he had to lower his head to catch his breath. Anna entered the room, a look of consternation on her face. Seeing that he was in no danger, she straightened the quilt over her husband's belly, then sat in her straight-backed chair.

Anna had had an inkling that something was wrong, and by the time the dishes were cleared from the table, she had established that Ethan had left their home in a definite and unique manner. She found a note on his bed, which had not been slept in.

> Mother,
> I am leaving today. I cannot say when I will return. I love you, Father, Jacob, and Martha dearly. Think kindly of me.
>
> > Your second son,
> > Ethan

Overcome by dread, she had folded the letter and hid it in the pocket of her sweater. She had vowed not to show it to Charles, but he must have read the secret in her worried eyes, for soon after she entered his room, he had sent for Jacob.

Charles spoke to Jacob, shaking his head in amusement. "Did you ever hear such a wagonload of manure? The boy's a damnable dreamer. I guess we should be happy he didn't join up with John Brown and hang up north."

His father's attitude—that Ethan's flight might have come sooner, and at a greater cost to him and the family—did little to relax Jacob. "What do you think he's doing, Father?"

Charles shrugged. "Fetch my tea." Jacob handed him the cup and saucer. He took two sips, shut his eyes, then focused on the view out the window. "I just pray the Keyeses don't ruin him."

Leave it to her husband to mention the pair from Boston, erasing any sense of comfort that might be imagined for her son. Anna knew Charles was right, yet she hated him for allowing her to imagine the worse. "Should we write the Keyeses?" she wondered aloud, but neither her husband nor her son replied. "I suppose it would do little good."

"He's made his bed," Charles said, reaching for pen and paper. "Let him lie in it for now."

Jacob hurriedly said his good-byes. "I expect to be home in two or three days. Units are already forming in Manassas to meet an expected thrust of Northern forces there."

Charles scoffed at the notion. "There are half a dozen creeks and rivers between Washington and Richmond. I don't expect any offensive to be successful, certainly not one undertaken by an army of Lincoln's ninety-day wonders. You tell Jeff Davis to lay and wait and let the Yankees spend themselves just trying to drag all those cannons over that water. Only way to win this war is not to lose it. You tell him. Now, git," Charles scolded playfully. "And don't come home without some Yankee scalps."

"Charles Parson!" Anna snapped. She had had enough of her husband's jibes. "Don't mind this angry old fool, Jacob. He's just mad that he can't join you and get his own head shot off."

After an awkward embrace with his father, who would not look him in the eye, Jacob hugged his mother and went downstairs, where Alex waited with a carriage.

"Got to hurry," Alex said. "Train don't wait for no man."

"Let's go!" As the carriage jolted off, Jacob soaked up every sight and sound of the plantation. "Watch after them, Alex," he said soberly. "They need you now."

"Dey always be needin' me," Alex said under his breath.

In Richmond, a city of forty thousand people, Jacob quickly made his way on foot from the Richmond train station to the new Capitol Building, where he was to ask for General Beauregard, the hero of the Southern victory at Fort Sumter.

Jacob bypassed the many prostitutes hawking their wares at Capital Square, and approached a soldier wearing the uniform of nearby Petersburg. The young soldier pointed him to the building, a beautiful marble palace with a gleaming dome and classical pillars. Inside he found an aide to the general, a robust man who wore a plumed hat and dark blue coat; he directed Jacob to a hallway where dozens of other militia captains waited. Too nervous to sit, he paced as the others smoked and traded bits of information. He was impatient for his name to be called.

"You sign the roster, soldier?" a young man asked. In his lap, the boy held a large, hand-lettered sign reading LOUISIANA.

"No. Where is it?"

The fellow pointed to a desk sitting unattended farther down the long hallway. Upon it, Jacob found a book with three dozen signatures and an ink pen and well. He quickly signed in at the end of the list, adding his regiment and hometown, as had the others. *Parson, Jacob . . . Albemarle Rifles . . . Charlottesville, Virginia.*

The only pleasant part of the wait, which stretched into hours of torment, was the gossip traded freely by the men in uniform.

"Davis is sick and may die tomorrow," said one.

"So is Lincoln," said another.

"Lincoln's son is fighting for the Confederacy." "No, he ain't. He's dead. All Lincoln's boys is dead." "The North is on the march. Richmond will be under siege next week!" "Bob Lee, the man who captured that madman, John Brown? He's sailing to Europe 'cause he can't decide which side to fight for." "No, he ain't. He's Jeff Davis's chief strategist!" "Strategist! What strategy? Don't nobody know what's what! Just looka this mess!"

Jacob had never heard so much scandalous talk spread so freely and openly. These men were from all over the South, from Arkansas to Louisiana, with even a pair of Texans. He was troubled by their accusations. If the war was such a disorganized affair, why bother fighting for the South? But Jacob soon saw through to the motivation for their angry words: They wanted to fight, to win, and to return home heroes. As the afternoon grew late, and shadows lengthened, Jacob dozed off in a corner by the desk.

He came to amidst great commotion. Sleepy, he struggled to attention just in time to see a tall, wiry, handsome man with melancholy eyes and a fine moustache sweep by in the midst of a sea of gray uniforms, gold stars, and brass buttons.

"It's him," someone whispered. But nobody addressed the general. After Beauregard's procession had swept past them, the twenty or so patient officers did not know what to do. He would accomplish nothing that day, Jacob realized. Pushing aside his frustration, he set about getting a hotel room. He would report for duty again in the morning.

Hailing a carriage in the crowded streets proved to be fruitless. They were all filled. But frantic soldiers clambered aboard nonetheless, holding on to luggage racks and even riding the weary horses as if they weren't hitched to the coupés. Shaking his head in disgust, Jacob gave up and walked to the nearest hotel, The John Marshall, and asked for a room.

"Check again . . . in eighteen sixty-two," the clerk said. Several men in civilian suits had a laugh at Jacob's expense. His temper only worsened when he left the hotel and found himself once again on the teeming streets. In every empty lot, tents were haphazardly pitched. He heard from other militiamen that the tobacco warehouses, factories, and all public buildings had been turned into temporary shelters for soldiers. He would have to try one of them, he thought dispiritedly.

Ten o'clock that night, so foot weary that he would have surrendered without a fight to the nearest Yankee who promised him a bed for the night, Jacob laid out his bedroll in a warehouse, squeezing between two husky volunteers from Tennessee. Breathing in the lingering scent of tobacco, he shut his eyes against the noise of poker games and the hooting and singing around the campfires outside, which blazed in the heat of May. The festive mood did little to reassure Jacob, who fell asleep fearing he might pass the war in Richmond trying to see an officer in charge of enlistment.

The next morning, he rose at dawn, ate at a nearby tavern, and from there went immediately to Capital Square. He was the sixth man to sign the book, and at eleven o'clock he met the general's aide-de-camp. A lean, tanned fellow with thinning hair and a faded pink uniform, the aide informed Jacob that Brigadier General Beauregard himself wished to meet him. The news was more than Jacob had hoped for.

Beauregard sat behind a sizable desk littered with papers and books. The general appeared to be angry, tossing papers aside as he searched for something. Two of his aides were nervously shifting through the papers he scattered.

"Where the hell's the map? How do we fight a place we can't find?"

Jacob instantly recognized a map of central Virginia. Stepping forward, he pulled it out from under a pile of papers and handed it to Beauregard, saluting as he did so. The general waved him to a chair. "I'm a Creole, son. I don't stand on ceremony unless I have to." He took in Jacob's uniform with an efficient nod. "Your boots are shined, buttons bright . . . You haven't been here long. What do you want?"

The directness of the question and the piercing look on the general's Gallic features froze Jacob for a moment. Quickly gathering his wits, he cleared his throat and explained that he represented a militia unit from nearby Charlottesville and that he had been granted a commission by the Confederate Congress.

"Fine. Taylor, see to the details." Beauregard turned abruptly from Jacob and began looking over the map with his aides.

As he was escorted out of the vast room, Jacob overheard Beauregard complaining. "Twenty thousand men!

But they're from ten thousand different militia units! Half of 'em can't get from a column into a line!"

In the morning light, Ethan and Old Sarah found their way to the Fourteenth Street, Washington, D.C. address given him by Julia. From the wide, dusty street near Capitol Hill, Ethan looked up at a three-story red brick building with windows as tall as a man, a broad brick porch, and a carriage house in front. Never having seen the Keyeses' townhouse, he was more than a little taken aback by the size and elegance of it. They were dirty and disheveled, and he hesitated approaching the house. Then Ethan spied Julia at one of the windows and waved. They reached the top of the steps just as Julia opened the door for them.

The entrance hall was round, with three large windows overlooking the street. A Turkish rug covered most of the parquet floor. Old Sarah would not enter the town house at first, and when Julia demanded it, the old black woman would not take her eyes off the interlocking vines and flowers woven into the rug.

"You're weary," Julia said, taking in their dirty faces and soiled clothing. "I'll show you to your rooms." She wore a simple green dress, and her hair was pulled off her face in a neat auburn bun. Ethan found her demure attitude curiously ill suited to the luxurious furnishings. She led them through the foyer and into a carpeted sitting room with Louis XIV chairs and a gilded settee that looked so fragile that he feared he would break it if he sat on it. The walls were adorned with paintings, the most noticeable of which was a portrait of Lincoln. Next to it was another portrait.

"That's Harriet Beecher Stowe," Julia explained, following Ethan's gaze. "I met her once."

Jeffrey met them as they were entering a smaller parlor beyond the sitting room. Sporting a wispy goatee and a monocle Ethan had not seen before, Jeffrey looked smaller and more foppish than he had remembered. He had to struggle to suppress the dislike he had developed for his old friend. He was not looking forward to working with him, but his conscience demanded it.

"Ethan! Hail, hero!" Jeffrey cried with bravado. He shook Ethan's hand briefly, then turned to his sister. "Julia, perhaps our guests would like a bath."

Despite the levity of his host's tone, Ethan felt he had to voice a concern that had been worrying him. "What if we were followed to your house?"

"But here at the capital we are amongst supporters," Jeffrey replied. "They know who we are and what we do. Let them try to stop us now, with seventy thousand troops behind us."

He would be damned if he would put up with Jeffrey's avuncular tone, regardless of their dependence upon each other in the work they were undertaking. "You are leading the charge to Richmond, then?" Ethan asked levelly. It was driving him mad with anger. He was spared having to respond to the look of reproof his comment drew from Julia, for a black manservant entered at the ring of a bell and escorted Old Sarah to the kitchen, where she would eat.

The Keyeses had ordered a feast prepared to celebrate the successful conclusion of "Ethan's first mission." As they settled down to roast venison, potatoes, and green beans, Julia asked about Caitlin and all the Parsons. Ethan thought of them, one by one, picturing what they were doing at that very moment. He missed them tremendously already.

"They are very well," he finally replied. "You must understand, it is not easy for me to think of them so soon after my departure."

"But what you are doing will shorten the war," Jeffrey argued, immediately launching into a lecture on the progress of the war, as if in possession of all the facts to come. Why had Ethan not noticed the man's insufferable attitude and oily hair? A June bug would slide right off his head, he thought.

"Is that brother of yours in command of a unit yet?" Ethan knew the question was asked not out of friend-

ship, but with the intent of gaining information. Jeffrey's
question struck him as impertinent, and Ethan ignored it,
concentrating on the venison instead. Jeffrey seemed un-
alarmed, but Julia brooded, repeatedly filling Ethan's glass
with cool water.

"Caitlin wrote to us of your difficulties in deciding
what to do," Julia said after a long silence. "I think I
understand."

"We both do," Jeffrey was quick to add. "It's not easy
to do what you have done. There's no going back home
now, not unless you're under orders—"

"From you?" Ethan snapped. "Not likely."

Jeffrey stood. "Ethan, you have been spiteful and un-
grateful since my arrival at Twin Pines. What have I done
to offend you? Are we not brothers in this great cause?"

Ethan could stand no more of his posturing. Jumping
to his feet, he clenched his fists at his sides. "My brother
is risking his life for a cause he believes in, and at no
profit to himself. It will tear him apart to leave Twin
Pines and know the plantation may very well disintegrate
while he's gone. But he shall do it. As for you, I no longer
feel as I did. It is as simple as that. Excuse me!" Ethan
found little solace as he cleansed himself afterward, allowing the hot water of the bath to ease the aching from
his muscles. Staring idly at the white porcelain of the tub,
he wondered what he had done to feel so terribly wrong
when everything he had done was right. Wasn't it?

The celebration at Twin Pines was twofold. First of
all, the family's elder son had returned from Richmond a
commissioned officer, a major. And second, Jacob had
two week's leave before he was to ride north to Manassas
Junction to join General Beauregard's forces massing
there.

Although only the family was present, Jacob wore his
military uniform. They had gathered in Charles's room,
and Jacob raised his glass in a toast, then added, "I am
grateful that in my absence Twin Pines has not fallen into
ruin."

"It would take us longer than a week to destroy the place," Charles joked. He was proud of his son. They had sat together for hours following his return from Richmond, speaking of the South.

No one mentioned Ethan, Jacob noticed. It seemed to be an unspoken family rule, and secretly Jacob was relieved. He felt much more lighthearted and exhilarated without his brother's taunting presence, and the rest of the family seemed to be calmer as well. His mother had commented that her heart was full with the affection that grew daily between him and his father, and Martha asked him each day if he carried her cameo. Each time he dutifully took it from the inside pocket of his jacket and showed it to her. "I'm not killed yet!" he teased, grinning. She, too, was proud and thought her brother the handsomest man in uniform in the county.

The early summer was hot and dry. With Jacob home, the field hands resumed their labors with little grumbling. Daily, Jacob wrote letters to other plantation owners asking for the names of overseers they might recommend. With most men contributing to the Confederacy's military effort, responses would be few and slow, Jacob knew. He cautioned his father against impatience. He warned his mother, too, telling her not to trust anyone and to write him twice a week. "Keep Alex informed of the field hands' performance," he instructed her. "He can make the others work, when he wants to."

With so many preparations for war and innumerable small tasks to accomplish, the threat of battle became almost a cry, a relief from the ever-building tension of anticipation. Soon, even Martha urged Jacob to "whip those Yankees and send them running home to their mamas in New York City!" With the love and support of his family and the other volunteers of the militia, how could he fail?

On Thursday, the thirteenth of June, President Jefferson Davis declared a national day of fasting and prayer, and Twin Pines religiously observed the day. In the heat, which was already sweltering at midmorning, Jacob drove his mother and sister into Charlottesville. There they gathered with neighbors to pray in the Albemarle County Courthouse where Thomas Jefferson and James Madison had worshiped sixty years before. While Anna and Martha both wore gowns of the lightest silk, their corsets and petticoats weighed unbearably. And in his heavy uniform, Jacob perspired uncontrollably.

The service was long but peaceful, and when the minister had stepped down, Dr. Stuart rose to offer a prayer.

"Lord, we ask that our boys' bullets find the hearts of every invader and send them directly to perdition in the Lake of Sulphur where light is no more!" He began flailing his arms above the podium like a man possessed. "May pestilence and calamity plague the Unionists at every turn. May their crops rot, and their gunpowder fail to ignite in battle! This we pray in your name, Father. Amen!"

Jacob sat quietly, stunned by the vehemence of the prayer. The professor had been unnecessarily harsh. Catching sight of Caitlin, who sat in stony silence and stared steadfastly before her, he wondered what she must be feeling, knowing that Ethan served the cause her father denounced with such violent rage. Did she regret her decision to go against his wishes?

As they made their way to the carriage, Martha looked almost ill. "I never thought about all those young men dying before, not in such a manner. This is terrible, isn't it?" She looked to Jacob, but he could think of no comforting response.

They rode back to Twin Pines in silence, trying to ignore the stifling heat which sent the cows loping to the orchards in search of shade. Once they arrived at the house, Jacob went to his father's room to tell him of the gathering.

"Prayer doesn't win wars; gunpowder and cannons do!" Charles ranted. "What a downright silly thing of dog-faced Jeff Davis to do. I suspect he just wants to save a day's rations for the troops in the field. Alex!"

When the manservant arrived, Charles gleefully ordered lunch.

The long, hot days and nights stretched into a week, and then two. Finally, one blazing morning late in June, it was time for Jacob to leave Twin Pines for battle. Anna and Martha waved good-bye, weeping openly, and the bondsmen gathered to watch. Along with a dozen other volunteers, including Brett Tyler, he rode away into the scorching haze, bound for glory and victory.

"Doesn't he look grand?" Martha said to her mother, who was wiping away her tears.

Anna nodded. "He does indeed. And he will look even grander when he returns."

"A hero!" Martha said, clapping her hands. She searched the group of men mounted at the end of the drive, trying to distinguish which form belonged to Brett Tyler. What would the war make of him? Would it change him into a more gentlemanly creature?

Charles had had Alex move him to a chair by the window, and he watched the group of young men ride away, Jacob in the lead. His heart pounded with pride. It would be good for Jacob to have a war and a victory all his own. That and marriage and a family were the only things lacking in Jacob's journey into adulthood. I'll die happy if he returns a hero, he thought. He regretted only that he was too infirm to join his son and the boys from the other fine families of the area. Hell, he could outshine any of the young pups. Opening his dressing gown, he looked in frustration at his bloated girth and useless legs. For ten years he had not walked a step, nor bedded with his wife. Irritably, he called for Alex to move him back to his bed.

The heat and sun drove everyone but the field hands inside, and soon even they lay down their hoes and found shade. "Too hot for nuffin'," one remarked, and his helper agreed.

CHAPTER 18

IN THE THREE weeks following Jacob's departure, Twin Pines settled into an uneasy rest. Charles railed against the field hands, tongue-lashing Alex almost every day. Alex could only bow his head and accept the blame, and then pass it along to the other slaves.

But the heat and humidity of the July sun and the baked clay upon which they lived proved too mighty a foe to resist. And with war but a heartbeat away and McDowell's Yankee army thirty-five thousand strong poised just one hundred twenty miles away at Washington, there seemed to be little point to nursing along a tobacco crop that would probably rot outside the warehouses in Shockoe Slip. For, as they all knew, the warehouses of Richmond now stocked war materiel and housed weary soldiers from the west and south of Virginia.

Anna slashed her household budget. Meals became simple affairs of meat, potatoes, garden vegetables, and biscuits. Several brass candlesticks were collected and shipped off to Richmond in response to a Confederate call for metal. Despite these concessions, and the adaptation of their life to the war effort, Anna found it hard to believe that they would ever see a Yankee soldier at Twin Pines, unless of course he was captured and in chains.

Charles kept up with all the war news through the Richmond newspapers and various correspondents all over the South, including one in Washington, D.C. Everyone was confident of Victory at Manassas, where Beauregard's army, with Jacob at his side, was every day expecting an attack across a stream called Bull Run and into the little town of Manassas Junction. Confederate forces had stood there ready to fight for a month.

It surprised Anna that so much of what she had assumed would be well-kept army secrets was openly written about in the newspapers her husband received. "Woman, get some sense," Charles snapped at her. "All these figures are poppycock and prattle. Everyone knows that. Both sides either inflate or deflate their strengths, so nobody really knows how many men are where, not even the generals themselves. Their spies just tell them what they want to hear. Besides, moving thirty thousand men at a time is difficult to keep secret, don't you think? Wouldn't you notice thirty thousand Yankees in uniform if they had crossed the yard this morning?"

Anna returned to her needlework. She did not appreciate her husband's sarcasm, but could not ignore the message, either. With the telegraphs and spies abounding, every significant movement of troops—especially on the railroads, which were watched closely by both sides—was easily seen and duly reported, however inaccurately.

"It just seems to me that the papers ought to hush about some things," she complained.

"They'll hush about the outcome if McDowell kicks Beauregard's butt back to New Orleans," he snapped.

Anna retreated to silence. She knew Charles had tired of discussing the war with her, a woman. The waiting without hope of any outcome had wearied her, and now, with talk of a major battle brewing, she was fearful for Jacob. She wanted the fight to begin and end quickly, for both sides to return home. She prayed every night for peace, and awoke every morning to new reports of fighting in and around Manassas, just twenty-five miles southwest of Washington.

Trusting in prayer and the Lord's will, which sometimes conflicted mightily with her own desires, Anna nevertheless could not cease worrying about Jacob, who might be shot at any moment. But she worried even more about Ethan, whom she feared lost to her forever. Her dreams now contained scattered visions of the Apoca-

lypse, with Twin Pines burning to the ground and Charles
and the boys gone. She often got out of bed and prayed
aloud in the middle of the night, asking for God's protection over her boys. But she slept fitfully, knowing that He
did not always answer her prayers as she would have them
answered.

Martha, on the other hand, despised the war, which
simmered and steeped but never whistled for her assistance. "If they are going to fight, why don't they fight!"
she could be heard crying.

She thought soldiers on both sides were behaving in a
beastly manner, refusing to step forth and face each other
like duelists in a fair fight. She was certain that Brett Tyler
and Jacob and the other boys from Charlottesville would
win the day for Virginia, given half a chance. But from
what Daddy had said, Yankees were sly and prosperous,
having more cannons than Napoleon, and more gunpowder than all of Europe had shot off in the last century. At
night, she would imagine a battle scene, with Jacob and
Brett leading a cavalry charge across open fields, their
sabers raised; but Daddy scoffed at her, explaining that
nine soldiers out of ten had neither horses nor sabers.
"Only officers like your brother ride a horse and carry a
saber. And even that isn't very effective against a cannonball!" So she stopped discussing the war with him and
relied upon her mother to supply the latest word. She
ached to lend her talents to the cause, to nurse wounded
heroes back to health, but how could she when war hadn't
even yet begun?

Alex and Clara sat across from each other in their
quarters. Alex's dark face was grim and disgruntled. He
struggled to hold together a fragile truce with the field
hands, but it wasn't easy. Some of them talked about laying down their hoes and plows until the battle was fought.
And Mister Charles didn't do anything about hiring an
overseer. It seemed he wouldn't accept the fact that the

absence of Mister Jacob inevitably sped up the decline of the plantation as a functioning farm.

"I cain't make 'em work if'n they won't," Alex complained. "What I gonna do, throw 'em in the curing barn and smoke 'em?"

Clara understood. "We in a bad place, honey," she consoled him.

They were caught between frightened and unhappy workers and anxious, demanding owners with no one sensible and level-headed to stand between both sides. "I feel tored apart." Alex held up a forkful of greens. "What is dis?" he asked.

"Kale."

"What? You say 'kale'? Kale fo' pigs, not men! Do you see a tail on my butt?"

After dinner, Alex left their quarters abruptly. Clara knew it was more than the presence of the bitter vegetable on his plate that drove him outside. The unbearable heat drove most of the field hands into a stand of oaks and elms well before noon, and some days, little work was done until Miss Anna emerged from the house around dinnertime to shout and wave her apron in a threatening way.

Clara cleared the dishes and took them outside to wash them by the pumphouse. Her heart was heavy with other matters. Thomas left Twin Pines more and more often at night, on foot, returning in the early hours of morning. Clara knew he was attending to one of the Tyler girls, but when she demanded the truth of him, he only smiled. She was so angry and hurt she almost got down the shotgun from the Parsons' parlor wall and blasted a hole the size of a pumpkin in his front door. What was he doin', messin' with that girl? Wouldn't nothin' come of it but trouble.

Alex just told her to let Thomas be. "He soon git enough and let the girl be," he'd told her. But Clara had only glowered at her husband. "What if Tyler shoot him first? What then?"

"Then at least he be free," he said. But Alex knew it was the wrong thing to say.

"I cain't do nuffin' wid him anyway," she said aloud to herself, wiping her hands on her apron and returning to their quarters with the clean dishes. In the distance she saw her husband sitting alone beneath a live oak. "He be your son, Alex. This be on your head!"

The talk of war brought a strange euphoria to the late summer-night gatherings of the field hands and their families. Some nights the singing and dancing lasted well past midnight, and yet no one from the big house on the hill seemed to care or pay any attention. The field hands all knew that had Jacob been there, he would have appeared to remind them that they would have to be in the fields at daybreak, that any bondsman late to the fields could expect to make up the time by working long after dark, plowing by the light of a lantern, if necessary.

But Jacob was not there. Charles noticed some of these changes and described them in long, tightly scripted letters to his son in Manassas. The fabric of Southern society would be worn bare and even torn asunder by the absence of Jacob and the other young men like him. Charles also wrote:

> I have never felt so weak and useless. Never has a summer been so long and so hot. We miss you, son. God bless, and keep an eye out for that scalawag brother of yours.

Ethan wrote once a week from Washington, reporting only that he was living with the Keyeses and hoped to visit Twin Pines soon. He wrote nothing of the war or his work.

In his tent, by the glow of the lamp and the flickering campfires of the other troops, Jacob prayed for bravery under fire. He almost did not care whether he lived or died, so long as he fought heroically. He feared shame more than death.

Each time he met with General Beauregard's staff in the two-story farmhouse they had commandeered for their headquarters, Jacob gained a strong sense of his own shortcomings as an officer of considerable rank. He was inexperienced in battle. The men followed his shouted orders; he was certain they did not know of his doubts. But Jacob could imagine only too easily his failure, losing a battle singlehandedly as he panicked under the boom and smoke of cannonfire and musket blasts. In his thoughts he had surrendered his command more than once.

Jacob sighed as he undressed, hanging his uniform by the flap of his tent. But his sense of duty was strong, as was his will and his stubborn pride. All three dictated that he learn what he could in the short while before the battle, and carry on, doing his best. As Beauregard was fond of telling his junior officers, "You will not be alone out there. We are one army, one living fighting machine!"

But Jacob had his doubts. Watching the men drill under the cruel sun, Jacob began to question the wisdom of his father's request for a commission. Shouldn't he have joined the army on his own and served as a lesser officer, a captain perhaps, instead of acting as an aide to General Cooke, who barely spoke to Jacob? Camp life revolved around routine. He drilled the men each day at the same hour. There were always watch posts to man, laundry to wash, and stews to cook. His men, mainly country boys, could play cards and would gamble the day and night away if he and the other officers did not intervene.

That was another problem for Jacob: The encampment abounded with prostitutes. The rate at which these "camp followers" were able to lure every last penny from some of the inexperienced boys was distressing. Jacob saw his men as they had been a month before: farmers and day laborers barely old enough to be called men at all. Yet he found himself unable to warn them away from the scurvy women.

To further aggravate the situation, the slatterns knew of his efforts to ban them, and inevitably they said something to make him blush and stammer, and in general to make him behave like a fool instead of an officer. Jacob simply could not assume a false bravado around them, for he lacked experience in that sphere of "knowledge." Some nights he was unable to sleep at all, worrying about battle and temptation. He dreamed one night that the enemy was the camp followers. And as he shot one, her blood flowed to his feet and climbed his body, splashing in his loins with a humid warmth that startled him.

Jacob took Martha's locket from the pocket of his uniform, as he did every night, and held it in the palm of his hand. And as occurred all too often, his thoughts drifted from Martha and his mother to Julia Keyes. He pictured her green eyes, her auburn hair, and proud bearing. His contemplations began to take on a less-than-honorable tone, and with a groan he pushed the imagined vision of her breast from his mind and focused on other matters.

Brett Tyler kept popping up, too, often when Jacob felt most awkward. It wasn't that Tyler ever said anything disrespectful—he was too wily for that—but the look in his eyes made Jacob's blood run hot. What bothered Jacob was the way the swaggering private kept his eye on Jacob, as if waiting for a fatal slip. He seemed to be daring Jacob to give a foolish order so the men would turn against him. Jacob could not decide if Tyler had come to Manassas to help him or bury him. But for all his wiliness, Tyler was proving himself to be a decent soldier, lazy but competent.

Weary and anxious, Jacob blew out his candle and went to sleep.

The eighteenth of July was a quiet Thursday. Beauregard spread the area maps on the table of what used to be the dining room of the farmhouse that the Confederacy had commandeered for their headquarters at Manassas. Twenty men clustered around the table to see what he was pointing at, and Jacob had to push aside a captain to get a peek. Before him was a crude map of central and western Virginia. To his shock, he saw that the map had only some of the rail lines drawn in, and those were inaccurate. He spoke up.

"I know," Beauregard lamented, resting an arm on the table and leaning his wiry frame over it. "Get me a good mapmaker and we'll win this war in a week!" The laughter at his comment was scattered and uncertain.

Jacob listened intently to Beauregard's detailed analysis of the scene and his elaborate battle plan. He himself had difficulty following the general's reasoning. How will I be able to explain it to my men if I can't understand it? Sweat poured down Jacob's face. Looking around him, he saw that the other officers were perspiring freely also. They, too, were scratching their heads and appeared to be dazed. Yet the general went on, wholly unaware of his staff's confusion.

"Like Napoleon at Austerlitz," Beauregard bellowed, intoning the French general's name as though he were the Almighty, "we shall flank the enemy before he has even begun his assault. He will be stunned, demoralized, and overwhelmed by our bold maneuver! To draw him where we want him, we will place our men here." The general paused to indicate a meandering line running parallel to Bull Run, a swift, substantial creek, for about eight or nine miles.

Jacob was again struck by the audacity and complexity of the plan. Why not just take up the best defensive positions offered by the natural barriers of stone fences and hillsides, and then let McDowell come to them? Why risk such a ploy? He was in over his head, trying to match wits with Beauregard. "We shall cover all fords and bridges and place our cannons here and here."

Jacob had first seen the Confederates' caissons and limbers earlier that day, old heavy cannons, each pulled by a team of six horses. It had been thrilling to see the might of their arsenal. Yet now he questioned his own ability to manipulate the army's machinery.

"Then, we shall attack across the creek here, swinging

our right over the stream, and outflanking McDowell's left before they have time to organize a resistance. Questions? Are we all clear regarding our duties?"

Jacob considered asking for clarification. He felt lost and only hoped the others couldn't read the panic on his face.

He was then struck by a horrifying thought: What if this hero of Sumter, this elegant man with his European tastes, trimmed moustache, and goatee—what if he were wrong? How many men would die for Beauregard's blunders? The thought was too terrifying to transmit or even to entertain. At least he himself had a position of subordinate authority; he was responsible for only a fraction of the South's manpower. Jacob returned to the general's lecture on strategy.

"Unbeknownst to McDowell and his ninety-day wonders," Beauregard drawled in a Louisiana accent dripping with Creole spice, "our man Johnston will slip away from the Yankee forces of that old fool, Patterson, and board his men on trains at Piedmont, bringing them here, to Manassas Junction, in less than a day. There we have them!"

Jacob again cast his eye around the table at the variety of uniforms representing the Confederacy. In their gray and red and brass and braid, men old and young looked baffled and ill at ease.

Beauregard dismissed the officers with a wave of his long hand. As the other officers were breaking up, talking in small groups, Jacob noticed his own commanding officer, General Cocke. The stocky, bearded man was wearing a small feather in his hat, and on his collar the three stars of a general. He carried himself erect, his sword touching the ground as he stood by the table, frowning down at the map. Jacob approached him.

"Sir. Major Parson."

The general looked up at Jacob with a brief, stern glance, and returned to the map without saying a word. Jacob had not served under the general long enough to establish a true bond, and he resented the disdain with which he was treated by his superior. He was thankful that Cocke was due to leave for Richmond within the next forty-eight hours, leaving Jacob at Manassas as his observer.

"General, if I may . . . ," Jacob began hesitantly.

The general sighed. "Major, I'm sure you have other duties to attend to. If you please, I must attend to the map." He dismissed Jacob but did not notice that Jacob had not left his side.

"Here's where they'll break through." The bearded general sighed. He pointed to a building marked *Sudley Church*, north of the expected battle site and near the unfinished railroad lines. "That's what I'd do."

Jacob backed off, praying that Cocke was wrong.

Jacob was invited by messenger to join General Beauregard and a half-dozen officers for dinner at the Carter farmhouse. The men had just sat down to the meal when a distant thump interrupted their conversations. A second later, a great clatter shook the chimney of the house. Jacob spun in his chair to see a cannonball drop out of the chimney and onto the floor, rolling to a stop at his feet. The look on his face must have been one of astonishment, for a moment later, the room broke into uproarious laughter. Holding up a hand, General Beauregard pounded his fist on the table for silence.

"That, gentlemen," he began, eyeing each man in the room in turn, "is from McDowell. His calling card, if you will. The battle is on!"

As it happened, McDowell's army took two and a half days to drag its brutish way south to Manassas. A brief skirmish farther north discouraged the Yankee general, for several of his best scouts happened to wander into a rebel camp where the soldiers wore uniforms as blue as theirs. By the time the Yankee scouts had recovered their wits, their voices had given them away, and several were shot dead.

The wait was sheer torture. The days were long and

hot, and there was little shade. Tyler hung around Jacob like a terrier, refusing to release him.

"I am your good-luck charm," Tyler bragged. Jacob had just finished drilling his men. He was hot and sweaty and in a foul mood. Turning toward the irritatingly familiar voice, he confirmed that Tyler still wore that ever-present smirk on his face. "I can't let you die," Tyler went on. "If you do, my whole life will be a mess."

Jacob was unable to fathom the seriousness of Tyler's assertion. He had little patience for the man, and no understanding of him. Tyler's manner put him off. But it afforded him some satisfaction that many of the other officers, serious and high-minded fellows, had similar reactions to the rogue. This time he would have to put the man in his place.

Tyler saw the irritation in Jacob's face as he pressed closer to him. *The major is such an ass,* he thought disdainfully. *But I will see him through, and he'll be forced to recognize my help one day.* He had to hand his daddy one thing: With all his drunken barbs and threats, the old hard-ass had forced him to be quick and wheedling and snide. That might not get him into high-and-mighty Parson's good graces, but it would keep him alive—and it would keep Jacob alive, too.

Brett had meant every word of what he'd just said. His future depended upon impressing that Parson ass and bringing him home safe and sound. That way, Brett could expect some kind of reward from Anna and gratitude from Martha. Jacob's survival was Brett Tyler's only ticket to a better life.

Jacob stood nose to nose with the scoundrel, and several soldiers gathered at a distance to watch, expecting a fight. "Tyler," he whispered, "your life *is* a mess, and if my death can contribute in any way toward your continued failure, I will account it a death surrendered to not in vain!"

At Tyler's burst of laughter, Jacob turned on his heel and strode away. All hope for a fight ended, and the men returned to cleaning their guns. The waiting was not good for the soldiers, either, Jacob reflected as he returned to his tent. It left too much time for gambling and arguing over who had the worse duty, the sentries or the cooks. Every soldier hated the lull, for almost all of them would enter battle for the first time. For all their arrogance, he could see that they, like he, wondered what they would and would not accomplish as soldiers. All wanted to hold up their end, and feared letting down his unit.

Yet even as he drilled them and spoke to them about their position and duty, as he mentally reviewed the details of Beauregard's battle plan, trying to absorb every nuance and foresee every possible deviation, Jacob wondered: Could battle really be so orderly and well planned?

He was to find out at dawn on Sunday, the twenty-first of July, that each battle—like each family—had a character and life of its own, existing outside the commands and the fire and the death.

The character of this battle was to be chaos.

Jacob jolted from his sleep at the first boom of a distant cannon. Lifting the flap of his tent, he saw that men were up and running, anxious looks on their young faces. Many officers, including Beauregard, were mounted and riding through the haphazardly swarming masses of men, trying to impose order.

Jacob's first duty was to awaken his men and organize them into a column before they went to take their positions near the stream. Quickly donning his uniform, he rushed to collect his unit.

Despite his efforts and shouted orders, the men would not remain in formation. They wandered dazedly where they would, some taking positions too far in the rear, others wandering up to the bridge, as if to shake hands with the first Yankees to cross it. For once Jacob was grateful for Tyler, who shoved and pushed, engaging in more than one fistfight as he tried to force the men to heed Jacob's orders. They were at last correctly positioned, but Jacob had little confidence that they would pay him the necessary attention when battle ensued.

Jacob never actually saw the approach of the army from the north, for the enemy and their artillery were hidden in a vast dust storm of stupendous scope. The Devil himself could be leading their troops, he thought, and we'd never see him.

"The cannon's about three miles off," an experienced soldier remarked. Three miles away and I'm a target, Jacob thought. What kind of a war is this?

Jacob heard another call to the officers. "To horse!" With Tyler's assistance, he climbed up on the big gray gelding that had been issued him, and rode to the top of a nearby hill, where Beauregard and other officers had gathered. The scene was pandemonium. Soldiers were firing into the dust raised by both sides, and cannons boomed back and forth, replying to each other.

The guns were deafening, and Jacob could hear only half of the general's orders. Suddenly bullets began whizzing by them like hornets. Led by Beauregard, the officers hastened from the hill to safer ground.

As the general had affirmed, the expected main assault along the old road from Centreville was under way. The boom and roar of muskets and cannons and rifles were relentless, and Jacob noticed more than one young soldier ducking behind cover, his hands over his ears. His own gelding shied and jerked, and he had a difficult time keeping his seat. Swallowing hard, he pushed from his mind the unbidden image of his father falling from his horse.

With alarming rapidity, Southern forces spread out along the winding stream were overrun by a concentrated attack near Sudley Church, just as Cocke had predicted. Jacob rode closer, past two surgeons struggling to sew up boys mangled and bleeding and limbless.

With a start of terrified recognition, Jacob realized that he had advanced too far. Not ten yards in front of him was a startled Yankee soldier on one knee, reloading his musket. Jacob struggled to turn the unfamiliar horse, which panicked and reared. He knew that he was about to die.

But just as the soldier stood to take aim, he grabbed

his chest and collapsed. Jacob regained control of his mount and raced back to higher ground, dodging scores of silent bleeding bodies, before one of his own had the audacity to grab his reins.

"Whoa, General!" Tyler cried above the din. "One more charge all by yourself, and I'll never be rich!" He led Jacob into a stand of woods where they could gauge the severity of the damage to their forces. Yankee soldiers poured over the bridge unimpeded and took cover across the stream, on land that the rebels had held for a month as they waited for this chance to match themselves against the North's ninety-day wonders. Now, it seemed, their worst fears were realized: The might of the North was too much to withstand. Rebel soldiers fired and fell back all around them, and a rout was clearly in progress.

"What do we do?" Jacob wondered aloud.

"Want to be a hero, like me?" Tyler asked. The gleam in his eye seemed out of place.

Jacob nodded uneasily. More than to be a hero, what he really wanted was to survive the battle. But he could not admit that, not to Tyler.

"Where are my men?" Jacob asked.

Tyler pointed every which way, nearly completing a circle. "They are widely dispersed, sir," Tyler said with sarcastic formality.

Jacob cursed. What had happened to the battle plan? Where was Beauregard? Jacob could see little through the solid wall of smoke before them which masked the soldiers, the land, and even the stream and sky from view.

"Come with me, there!" Tyler ran off to the east, toward the retreating Carolinians. Ahead of them was General Jackson, rallying his men, braving the fire from the Yankees so nearby. Jacob had heard of Tom Jackson from Beauregard and others who had known him at West Point; he was alternately referred to as a genius and a fool. Jacob watched him, amazed. Jackson sought no cover, waving his sword and urging his men on. Rebel yells punctuated the stutter of rifle and musket fire, and the piercing cries of *"yee-hah!"* seemed to stop the onrushing Yankees in their tracks.

"We sound like demons from hell to them!" Tyler shouted.

Then a stroke of luck balanced the carnage. As Jacob and Tyler watched in disbelief, two enemy batteries allowed a unit of rebels from northern Virginia to walk directly into their midst.

"What the Devil!" Jacob cried, but Tyler understood. "They're wearing blue!"

As the two of them watched, bullets whistling by, the Virginians opened fire at point-blank range, decimating the terror-struck Yankees, who thought their own men were firing at them. Jacob wondered about the morality of the action but couldn't doubt the results. Blue-uniformed soldiers lay bleeding shoulder to shoulder as the Virginians kneeled to reload.

The devastation sowed by the Yankee cannons had ceased. There was a temporary lull, during which Beauregard raced by, a grim look on his chiseled features. The awful smell of cordite from the cannons sickened Jacob; the noise was enough to drive any man mad.

Jacob stood his ground as the Yankees launched one last thrust, pushing their men into the fleeing backs of the retreating rebels. All but Jackson and his men had turned tail. A vast contingent of Northern troops had advanced and was about to flank and trap most of the Southern troops suddenly paused in disarray.

Yelling at the tops of their lungs and riding as if in hunt after a fox, General Johnston and his men raced in, driving back the blue uniforms which scattered before them. Many Yankee soldiers lay down their rifles and ran, the rebel yells sending them across the bridge and the stream in droves.

Jacob heard General Johnston calling out orders to each regiment, urging them on. "Push ahead, boys! Drive them into the Potomac!" Infantrymen came at a trot, picking off scattering Yankees as if they were fleas. Their muskets glittered like jewels in the fierce July sun. Then the cannons were rolled in and quickly put into place and fired into the heart of the fleeing Northern army. The galloping horses that pulled the cannons were lathered and pop-eyed, exhausted.

"Ride that gray into the midst of it and make a scene of yourself, like Jackson!" Tyler urged.

But Jacob felt glued to the hilltop where he and Tyler stood. Jackson was leading his men, not showing off. He wasn't after a medal, he was trying to win the battle and inspire his men. Jacob's shoulders sagged. As an officer, he was useless. He had done nothing but flee and offer the Yankees a broad target.

One rebel soldier after another jumped off the railroad cars behind the main forces and ran screaming into the fray. One boy running by shouted, "We ain't ate nor slept in two days to save your ass!" Tyler waved him on.

Jacob grabbed Tyler and shouted, "Johnston's men!" They had arrived from Piedmont as planned.

Tyler had to laugh. "Well, Major," he began, "what did you expect? He and his buddies from Winchester been ridin' railroad cars for two days to git here and save your butt."

"And yours, too, Private," he reminded Tyler. But Tyler merely grinned.

Jacob lost all track of the hour, and he was shocked to look up and see the sun dipping behind the trees on the hill to the west. The battle had raged all day. For the first time, Jacob saw and heard the cries of scores of men pleading for water. They were suffering from heatstroke and sunstroke as well as injury. Wounded and dead surrounded Jacob. The carnage was everywhere apparent; he could turn in no direction to escape it.

Ahead a big whoop signaled the capture of a large number of enemy soldiers, who were marched to the rear of the Confederate ranks. Then the problem arose: What was to be done with them? The men leading the captives seemed not to know. Jacob's gaze swept in a wide arc. General Beauregard was nowhere to be found, and Johnston was up in front with his weary men, pushing the

Yankees back across the creek and down the road toward Washington.

"Push 'em back to the Potomac!" he heard again. Rebel yells were raised, and Jacob saw panicky Yankees forget to remove the ramrods from their rifles, so that when they fired, they sent a small shower of ramrods into the rebel ranks, like enormous arrows. The rebels laughed and taunted the fleeing Union soldiers, who dropped everything and ran for the safety of the road.

Jacob wasn't certain what they ought to do next. No one seemed to know. Some older officers argued that now was the time to consolidate forces and tend to the wounded, who lay groaning and suffering terribly, in numbers Jacob could not imagine.

Then, just before dusk, to the hushed whispers of "It's the president!" Jefferson Davis himself appeared. A tall, haughty, aristocratic gentleman in a cloak, he surveyed the scene with distaste through his metal-rimmed spectacles, sending immediately for his generals and their staff.

General Jackson, who had withstood enemy fire like a "stone wall," a nickname immediately adopted by his awestruck troops, argued that with five thousand men, he could capture the enemy capital and deliver Mr. Lincoln in chains. Johnston and Beauregard conferred with President Davis for over an hour, while Jacob and the other officers awaited their decision: They would not pursue the fleeing forces.

"We have won the battle," the president stated flatly. "It is unlikely that they shall challenge us again on our own soil."

Jackson, standing near Jacob, made a disparaging face. "Bosh!" the general said under his breath. "They'll be back in a month!"

Then, as Generals Johnston and Beauregard conferred further with the president in the headquarters building, the caring for the sick and wounded began. Dusk fell and spirits rose, especially among Johnston's men, who had performed exactly as they had been ordered, and with great success.

Jacob felt only weary and sick. The blood and death everywhere on the once-peaceful field seemed a sacrilege. Wearily, he rode his gray gelding to Bull Run to give him a drink, and he saw with horror that the water ran red with blood. Dead soldiers from both sides lay stiff in awkward positions both in and near the water. Jacob fought to keep from retching. Surely he had just glimpsed hell.

Looking back over his shoulder, he spotted Tyler. For once the man seemed to read his thoughts and leave him alone. He was helping a physician move the less severely wounded to a makeshift hospital up the hill near the stone house.

He drew closer to a clearing where General Jackson spoke gently with his men. He was reviewing every mistake they had made, and Jacob found himself attracted to the man who wanted to take the war to Lincoln's doorstep. He understood that Jackson wanted to end the war now, before many more men died, before McDowell and Lincoln had time to regroup and call up another seventy-five thousand troops. Exhausted and sickened as he was after witnessing the day's carnage, Jacob agreed wholeheartedly.

He overheard Jackson telling his men, "Hold the line until I relieve you, or until an officer orders you to fall back. Watch the standard; the flag tells you where we are at any time. And don't get too far in front of it unless you want to die a hero." The men laughed, clearly worshiping the general, and Jacob, too, found himself under the sway of the man advocating "right now, not later."

Across the river, in the deepening shadows of evening, a long line of figures was visible, moving slowly like ants toward their homes. They were what Jacob feared he and his men might be one day—defeated soldiers, losers in war.

Dismounting, Jacob joined the men from his unit and struggled until well after dark to gather them together again. To his shock, two of his friends in the 19th were dead, Noah Chesterfield and James Cabell. In the weak yellow light of the lanterns they looked especially solemn, and he wished he could say something to them to ease the pain of their departure. But what could he say? They died soldiering, fighting for their homes and their independence. It could have been anyone in his own unit.

He said a quiet prayer for both of them, asking God to look after their souls and to comfort their families. It was difficult to imagine that the ugly sight was his childhood friends. Noah had always been a good-natured fellow whose greatest pleasures were his horses and his friends.

Just months before hostilities had broken out, Noah had confided to Jacob that he hoped to be a Baptist minister. Now, Jacob thought, you are where you wanted to be, friend, only sooner.

Jacob looked down at the mutilated body of James Cabell. A rowdy brute with a cowlick and a storehouse of dirty jokes, James had been well liked by his fellows in the One Hundred and known for his strength and almost foolhardy temerity, as well as for the practical jokes he relished. This time, Jacob thought sadly, the joke is on all of us.

Jacob scratched his chest where something rubbed irritatingly against it, then located the source of the problem: Martha's cameo. Taking it from his uniform pocket, he had to smile. She had been right: it was a good-luck charm. He wished he had one to give to every man in his unit, to every man in the war, in fact.

Having accounted for his men, Jacob walked slowly to the hospital to visit his wounded. He had only walked a few yards when a deep voice arrested his progress.

"What's that?" Tyler asked.

Jacob realized that he had been flipping Martha's cameo into the air and catching it, like a stone. Without thinking, he tossed it to Tyler. "My good-luck charm. I've had my share. Now it's yours."

Then, turning, he tripped over something. The smile on his face turned to white terror as the bloody mass of hair and flesh rolled with the impact of his foot. Jacob raced to a tree and heaved. The head of a dead soldier was no comfort to any victor, not in any battle. He prayed even more fervently for the sun to set upon this bloody day, that no more young men would die in the murderous twenty-four hours they would all remember as the Battle of Manassas, fought at the stream called Bull Run.

CHAPTER 19

FIVE MILES NORTH of Bull Run, the wagons and carriages carrying dozens of reporters and hundreds of interested onlookers had turned and were making their way back to Washington with the defeated army. A light rain began to fall, and soon the road was muddy and all but impassable. On one jolting wagon sat Julia and Jeffrey Keyes, who, like many others from the capital, had packed a picnic lunch for the day. Beside them sat Ethan.

Fooled by the Northern press, which was convinced of the invincibility of McDowell's force, and the Keyeses' confidence, Ethan had accepted their offer to picnic across the water from the battle. A small voice in his head had whispered, *Don't!* but curiosity had overruled, and he had failed to heed the cautioning voice, perhaps for the last time.

Ethan hunched over in his black frogged coat, oblivious to the conversation in which brother and sister were engaged. His stomach still churned. Indeed, none of them had been able to touch the picnic lunch once the fighting began. The gala send-off for the troops, which had taken place four days earlier in the capital, should have convinced Ethan that he was a fool to follow the Keyeses' advice. For in that regard, Jeffrey rarely failed him.

The scene in the crowded streets of the capital kept returning to Ethan. The march of the soldiers in their gaily colored uniforms had raised cheers by the thousands. Marching bands had kept pace with the soldiers, many of whom could not keep a cadence if they could have heard it above the yelling and the music. They were too young, too "green," in the North's own words. But then, so were the rebels. Or so went the argument—until that very day.

Ethan raised his collar in protection against the rain. It was a shock to him that the Union army was not an army at all, but a loose collection of militia units and volunteers from all over the North. They had worn a dazzling and bewildering array of uniforms. One New York regiment had worn kilts in the parade before President Lincoln and his supporters, although Julia had commented that they would be wise to change the skirts for pants before the battle breaks out. Many regiments mimicked the flashy colors of European armies; some fivescore men marched by in baggy red pants and tight blue jackets with red sashes around their waists and turbans on their heads. Ethan had only seen such dress in a book about Napoleon.

"What excellent targets they'll make," he had said to Julia. The flags of the scores of regiments were varied but of brightly colored silk; Ethan had never seen so many different flags at one time. Of course, there were men who wore simpler uniforms of various shades of blue. And some were gray, very much like those of the Albemarle Rifles, which Jacob led. He pointed out to Jeffrey that those men might easily be mistaken for Southerners.

"Only until they open fire," Jeffrey said with a smirk.

As the long lines of soldiers passed by, he was surprised, too, with the freedom of the individual soldiers; they broke ranks at will, stopping to beg a drink of cider or to court a pretty girl. In the heat and dust, the thousands of men almost seemed to be a mirage, a great imaginary arm off to face an enemy no more real.

Ethan had soon tired of the bands and marching soldiers, the cheers and the circus atmosphere. But the Keyeses had argued that what they were viewing was history in the making, the second great challenge to the survival of the United States of America.

"The first was survival versus the British in seventeen seventy-six and in eighteen twelve," Jeffrey noted in a professorial manner.

Ethan nodded, but he had stopped listening. He thought of Caitlin—and dreamed of her—as he did every day and night. Her eyes haunted him; he was almost tortured by the uncertainty of their color, and recalled them as gray or brown, depending on the light. Caitlin had so many fluid qualities, and yet at the core, was unchanging, like a rock. Ethan felt that he could rely upon her to do what was right, at all costs.

He loved Caitlin, and their love bound them to action many would call treason. Yet she would not confront her father, not yet, and confess her actions and sympathies. And while frustrated by her delay in making her stance clear, at times such as this, when the smells of cordite and burned flesh might well mark the death of a neighbor or friend from Virginia, Ethan was unsure that his sympathies were with either side.

Under Julia's tutelage, Ethan had blossomed as a pamphleteer, authoring tracts that argued for a conclusion of hostilities and an end to slavery. From her he learned that of all the countries in the world, only Brazil sanctioned slavery. His unique perspective as the son of a slaveowner made him a *cause célèbre* in Washington; he could have dined at a different home every night if he chose.

Instead, he and Julia passed most evenings reading and discussing history, with Jeffrey's occasional insights and asides doing little more than exposing his own prejudices. For example, Jeffrey would not believe that Paul sanctioned slavery in the Bible until Ethan showed him the passage.

Ethan's celebrity status as the well-known yet mysterious "Son of the South" writer and abolitionist also gave him the opportunity to speak before church groups and abolitionist organizations. He chose not to use his real name to spare his family embarrassment, but Julia warned him that Southern agents in the capital were aware of his activities and knew who he was.

"Don't worry, Ethan," she told him, taking his hand to calm him. "As long as we just talk and write tracts, we are in no danger, I assure you."

But as she spoke, he wondered if that was, in fact, all they had in mind for him. He had the distinct impression that his work was but a preamble to something else. "Jeffrey and I have been observed for six months now, and never have we felt in any danger. If we did, we would return home to Boston, of that I am quite sure."

In the days before the Battle of Manassas, Ethan was not so sure. He grew more and more concerned that someone would inform his brother or father of the nature of his work. Thus, he insisted upon keeping his real name a secret in his writings and speeches. It ought to infuriate him, he thought, to think that the actions and behavior of which he was proud would earn him the scorn and ridicule of his father and Jacob. But much as the thought of his father's tirades rankled him, he did not want to be the cause of the old man's death.

To his great surprise, sympathy came from a most unexpected source.

"Your work is vital to us, you know that," Julia told him one night. "But I am truly sorry for the position in which our urgings have placed you. I recognize the pain that must come from knowing that your friends and neighbors might well sit on a jury and pronounce you guilty of treason one day."

There was a surprising sincerity to her words, one he had not recognized during her stay at Twin Pines. Meeting her frank gaze, he could not fathom if her words were sincere or if he was simply falling in the same trap that had ensnared Jacob. If so, he would not succumb so easily. She and others like her judged his behavior "brave" and "moral." But he was not so sure of *their* motivations.

And now, with the muddy road jammed by ambulances, gleaming artillery, and stragglers tossing away their rifles and knapsacks as though the war were over,

Ethan questioned all notions of bravery and morality. But
he had no doubt about the gruesome reality of the war.
Beside him the Keyeses had fallen silent. Deep in his heart,
he found some satisfaction in their sober countenance.
The blood and gore and grotesque chaos of the scene had
quieted their cheers.

The rain had waterlogged their picnic goods and
newspapers, some of which carried McDowell's "victorious" tactics in great detail. Once more Ethan found himself a man without a country, with only a past he had
turned his back on and no future at all—unless Caitlin
were to join him. Perhaps he should run back to Albemarle County, swoop her up, and run off to Paris with
her. Amongst the madness all around them, it almost
seemed the only logical course of action.

Ethan turned on the wagon bench as someone
shouted, "The black-horse cavalry!"

Soldiers and civilians alike broke into a panic. "What?
What's all the shouting about?" he asked Jeffrey, who
whipped their horse unmercifully.

Jeffrey ignored him, but Julia, her lips pale and pressed
together, explained. "The rebels' elite cavalry. If they give
chase, we could all be captured!"

"Or killed as spies!" Jeffrey added.

With amazing speed, the rumor swept through the
mile-long twisting column of people. Soldiers dropped
their guns, and some peeled off their uniforms. Everyone
was in a mad race for the capital, for what could be a
last-ditch stand against a Southern invasion of Washington.

As panic spread amongst the thousands of defeated
soldiers and stunned observers, a Confederate shell landed
near a wagon crossing a small stream called Cub Run.
The wagon overturned, tossing its two passengers into
the creek and blocking the only road to Washington. Men
crazed by fear struggled to lift the scorched wagon, rolling it into the water.

By the time their exhausted party reached the capital
sometime after midnight, the scene before the Keyeses

and Ethan had evolved on an almost unimaginable scale of horror. Hundreds of panic-stricken soldiers—Lincoln's famed ninety-day wonders—had changed into civilian clothes and scattered for parts unknown. Invasion fever gripped the city, and a militia of several thousand men guarded the bridges. Gone were the music, the banners, and the bright new uniforms that had decorated the capital just four days earlier. Replacing them was a filthy, bedraggled reality that brought terror to the eyes of every man Ethan saw.

When Ethan rose the next morning, he looked out the parlor windows to see that tables had been set up on Fourteenth Street and all around the city. Soldiers washed themselves, drank coffee, and talked in hushed tones, their eyes red and sorry with defeat. Many slept on the ground, with no cover whatsoever. Washington appeared to have been invaded by tramps.

Over breakfast, Ethan expressed to the Keyeses his reservations about accepting their hospitality any longer.

"What do you mean?" Jeffrey raised an eyebrow, casting a glance at his sister.

"What will you do?" Julia asked.

Ethan took a moment to collect his thoughts. "For the past few weeks we have eaten and spoken and worked alongside each other. And while I believe in the work we have been doing, I sense an overall purpose that goes beyond abolitionist actions." He took a deep breath and directed his gaze toward Julia, who watched him expectantly. "Soon you will ask me for my help again, and in a far greater capacity than mere speechmaking. I can see that I am being groomed for stealthier actions." He could not bring himself to say the word *spy*. "I believe you understand my meaning. Such action is out of the question. Like an awkward courtship, the matter must come to a conclusion." He could hear Jacob's voice echoing in his head: *Fish or cut bait.* Again, he could do neither.

"But what of your duty? Many people are relying on

you!" Jeffrey set down his coffee, his face red with suppressed anger.

Ethan stood and walked to the window, which overlooked Fourteenth Street. "What all those poor men in the street saw, I saw. Yesterday's soldiers are today's beggars. We cannot fight this war in a day. It could last for years. Forever! We must find another way to accomplish our goals. When so many of my neighbors may have died already, I cannot be a traitor."

"Who dares to call you a traitor in my home?" Jeffrey rose, his napkin tucked under his trembling chin.

Julia looked quickly from her brother to Ethan, trying to think of a way to calm them both. Jeffrey would obey her as he always did. She motioned him to take his chair, and he did so. But Ethan was another matter. He was facing away from her, looking out the window, so she addressed herself to his back, speaking softly and convincingly.

"Ethan, you are a hero, both in our house and in this city. If others call you by whatever name, you must decide who's right. Only your opinion matters in the end, am I right?"

He turned slowly to face her. And the woman he saw was stern. Above the high neck of her navy blue gown, her face looked weary and intense, and for the first time Ethan realized what his brother saw in her. In so many ways she reminded him of Caitlin. She was a strong-willed woman with a quick, retentive mind. He had learned in the weeks of his stay with the Keyeses that she sifted thoughtfully through the things Ethan discussed with her, painting a broader picture of slavery and of Twin Pines for her brother, who had little sympathy for Ethan's predicament. She had power and depth. She was unafraid.

But she was among her own people in Washington, those of like mind, even if, like him, she had pulled up roots and gone where danger and glory were ever-present possibilities. Somehow he admired Julia more than her brother. As a woman, she was often considered a mere accoutrement to her wise and educated brother. But Ethan

knew better. She was far superior to him in every important quality, including courage. As Jeffrey gallivanted
around Washington wooing abolitionists with fat purses,
he knew that she had set up and maintained a household,
kept records, written letters by the score to their supporters in Boston, and developed new sources of support—such as Ethan himself.

"I have to leave you and this godforsaken city." Once
he had said it, Ethan felt a great weight lifting from his
shoulders. Leaving the Keyeses and the North, he doubted
he could return home; there, his conscience weighed just
as heavily. To do more for his family would necessarily
mean doing less for himself. It was a Devil's bargain, one
he could not win. More than likely he would be forced
to travel.

Jeffrey exploded, "You little cracker! After all we've
done for you! I treated you like a brother!" He clutched
his fork and knife like weapons, but remained seated. He
would not look at Ethan, who crossed the room on his
way out.

Julia joined him in the parlor soon afterward.

"I understand," she told him. "Really I do." Her hand
on his was soft and reassuring. It might have been Caitlin's. "But please, as a favor to me, wait until tomorrow
to decide. There's someone I want you to meet."

Ethan saw a light in her emerald eyes. She was shielding something. "Lincoln himself couldn't change my
mind," he told her.

She felt the tension in him. "It's not Lincoln. You will
stay until tomorrow night?"

Ethan thought about the scene outside. "With the war
fever what it is, I might be hung if I went out tonight.
Yes, I'll stay."

Julia leaned up and kissed Ethan softly on the cheek,
then left him in solitude, returning to the dining room.

"What was that charade all about?" Jeffrey asked,
wiping his mouth as his sister sat down again opposite
him. The elegance of their surroundings—the rich carpets
and fine furniture—suddenly depressed Jeffrey. Ethan's

betrayal had spoiled the setting of the plot as well as the plot itself. "So he won't assassinate Jeff Davis for us."

"Jeffrey! Stop talking nonsense! As for tomorrow, you'll see soon enough. I must write letters," she said, coming over to her brother and kissing him on the forehead.

"I suppose I am a bit hotheaded at times," he admitted, her hands on his shoulders.

"You are impossible," she chided. "For a coward, your mouth is much too bold."

He waved a fist at her as she walked from the dining room.

With the rest of the day unplanned, Jeffrey perused the newspapers, reading one account after another of the disaster at Bull Run. People called for the dismissal of McDowell, whose "folly" had lost the battle. One editorial urged Lincoln to draft two hundred thousand men and march on Richmond in sixty days, an absurd idea. Jeffrey regretted that for the time being, war news had pushed abolitionist sentiment off the front page of the newspapers. "The price of disaster." He sighed.

In his large, spacious room, Ethan sat before the cherrywood writing table and wrote one unfinished letter after another to Caitlin. They all began with a falsely gay tone and awkwardly described the mingled joy and terror he had felt in observing the battle at Manassas.

But he could not say what he had to. He could not write: *I can no longer betray my father and my family, regardless of the higher moral calling of my betrayal. If God Himself does not speak to me in the next twenty-four hours and tell me to stay, I shall return to Charlottesville on the morrow and we shall escape this madness together.*

He missed her sweet, bright, passionate face terribly, and now sympathized with her plight more than ever. She was not yet willing to break her father's heart, as he had his family's. It was one thing to help slaves to freedom, as she was doing. It was quite another to actively serve the army that might shoot his brother dead. He could not do it.

He slept poorly that night, starting often in response to the stirrings outside his window. A musket fired at one point, and Ethan imagined the rebels marching up Independence Avenue. Hell, he would probably recognize half of the boys on sight. He could wave from the balcony and say, "What took you so long, Johnny?" His body drenched in sweat, his muscles clenched, Ethan rolled over and shut his eyes. But sleep would not come.

In the morning, the tension around the breakfast table was unpleasant. Jeffrey refused to speak, and he would not look Ethan in the eye when Ethan arrived late to the table, bleary eyed from broken sleep.

"News of the defeat doesn't seem to have troubled your sleep," Jeffrey said, his eyes on the newspaper headlines.

Ethan sipped his coffee in silence for a moment, then said, "One man's defeat is another's conquest."

Jeffrey slammed the newspaper on the table. "If that's supposed to be humorous!"

Julia glared at her brother. "Jeffrey! This won't do. This may be Ethan's last day with us. Let us do all we can to make it pleasant and informative."

But after breakfast, Julia unveiled her surprise, asking the maid to show in "Henry."

A black man almost six and a half feet tall entered, ducking his head and casting his eyes upon the rug. Ethan judged the man to be in his fifties. He held a battered felt hat in his hand and wore a cotton shirt and pants that shone from wear. Julia had to coax him to approach the table.

"Now, Henry," she said softly, speaking to him as though he were a child, "just tell us your story in your own words. Don't forget to mention your family."

He nodded. "I told you once, but I tell it agin," he began, speaking in a deep voice that carried the lilt of the Caribbean in it. Henry would not look any of them in the eye, but something about the man seemed familiar to

Ethan, for one saw very few men who were so tall. But he let the nagging sensation go, and listened.

"I runned away, and my master cut off my finger. Den he sell my wife and boy. I ain't never find 'em. I look ever'where. Den I run away again, and de man cut off de toes on one foot and blind me in one eye with lye. Dat my story."

The horror of his story was only enhanced by the simple, unpracticed manner in which he told it. Still, Ethan felt sick to his stomach. Having finished, Henry stood in the middle of the room, hat in hand.

"There is a little more," Julia said firmly.

"Must we?" Ethan said. What was her purpose, he wondered. It couldn't be good for Henry to describe the tragedy again and again.

Julia looked up at the tall black man. He said nothing, staring beyond them and out the window of the dining room. "Tell him who your master was." She spoke to him as if giving an order.

The towering man's hands trembled. Ethan imagined what great power they harnessed, and marveled at how his fear incapacitated the man. "De man was George Stuart of Charlottesville, Virginia. Dey call him Dr. Stuart."

The soft-spoken words sent a shock into Ethan that turned his blood to ice. He found himself trembling in the July heat. "I *have* seen you . . . ," he managed to say.

With a jolt of fear, he thought of Caitlin. He had not realized how cruel the measures Dr. Stuart had taken with his bondsmen were. It was no wonder that she hesitated in telling him of her involvement with abolitionists. What might her father do?

Jeffrey straightened the belled sleeve of his white silk blouse. "So, you see, Ethan, your future father-in-law mutilates human beings and sells their families like cattle. These are the people you do not want to betray."

Ethan knew Jeffrey was right, but found his foppish manner unbearable. He still longed to bash in the runt's head with a candlestick. Excusing himself, he retreated to the privacy of his room. Once he had left the room, he heard Julia's voice excusing Henry, and then the modulation of brother and sister's voices as they discussed something heatedly.

His mind raced with wild thoughts and possibilities. Should he hurry to reach Charlottesville and challenge Stuart to a duel? Should he tell Caitlin about her father? Should he . . . What should he do?

The response that came to him was the one he least expected and most feared: What he most needed to do was to continue the work he'd come to Washington for in the first place. He should serve the cause of abolition, at whatever personal cost to him. A practice so evil as slavery had to be abolished at all costs. He had to accept that or he would never truly be at peace with himself.

With a heavy step he went back to the parlor and announced that he was prepared to serve the cause in any capacity.

Jeffrey flashed Julia a knowing smile. "Good."

"God bless you, Ethan!" Julia ran to embrace him.

"And God bless Henry," Ethan said. He held her lightly, studying Jeffrey over her head with a frown.

Ethan left the Keyeses' home and walked six blocks in the warm night air to the Capitol Building, which lay open to the elements, its dome not yet finished. He waited, smoking cigars, one after another, until a man in a black cloak and a silk top hat asked for directions to Georgetown. Ethan gave the appropriate responses, and the man handed him a folded slip of paper.

Ethan dropped the stub of his cigar, grinding it beneath the heel of his shoe, and opened the paper, expecting to read the name and location of the next runaway he was to help. Ethan struck a match and read: *Enlist in Beauregard's army. Report troop movements and strengths to K in person. Write nothing!*

The note was not signed, of course. Any sort of correspondence was compromising. His hands shook as he blew out the match. For a full thirty seconds, he stood transfixed and unthinking. Then he lit another match and burned the note, watching the ashes of the charred note blow away in the breeze.

A cold sweat suddenly engulfed him, and he shivered in the warm night air. "Jacob would see me hung, if he could," Ethan murmured in distraction. "Daddy will roll over and die. Mama and Martha will never forgive me."

Walking aimlessly down dark and unfamiliar streets, he came upon a tavern. He paused outside uncertainly, but only for a moment.

To the amusement of all there, Ethan drank whiskey and shouted for music from the piano player until the proprietor threw him out just before sunrise.

CHAPTER 20

ANNA WAS HUNGRY, although she would not admit it. With the tobacco cured and shipped to market in Richmond, the Parson estate should have been the scene of plenty. But this year there had been no festival, no holiday. Instead, although the Parsons had sold their tobacco to merchants in Richmond, the tobacco sat in and outside the huge warehouses near the James River, for the war effort superseded any profit motive.

Anna put into effect a rationing plan. She simply told Clara to prepare lighter, simpler meals. Feasts were a thing of the past. Martha complained daily that a mouse ate more than she was served, but Anna would ask to see the mouse. "It couldn't roll under the door, it'd be so fat," she teased.

The situation was apparently even more serious farther south. Charles explained that many cotton growers had refused to ship the cotton after hearing of England and France's support of the North. Some had even burned the crop in their fields rather than see it fall into the hands of their enemy's allies.

But the Parsons faced no such dilemma. They got a good price for the tobacco, considering that a war was being fought in Virginia, and that mountain folk in the west of the state had already threatened to break away and form their own new state, supporting Lincoln.

Such talk was a blow to Virginian pride. Charles could not imagine anyone fool headed enough to leave the Old Dominion for any reason, least of all to band together with a bunch of traitors to form another Yankee state.

"Don't they know that Lincoln wants to be king?" Charles fumed one morning over breakfast. He was reading accounts in the *Richmond Times* that the movement in western Virginia to break away from the Old Dominion was gathering momentum—with, of course, the blessing of the Union. "It's stupid and despicable! To divide this great state like it was the spoils of war! I hope when we defeat them, Jacob and his boys show them no mercy!"

Anna let him rant. She had to if she was ever to press her case effectively. She could no longer keep to herself the worsening state of the estate's accounts. Once he had calmed a little, she began to speak earnestly, begging Charles to hire an overseer and someone to keep the books; Jacob had done both jobs. She worried that this tobacco crop would be their last, for Jefferson Davis had said that loyal Southerners should grow food, not cash crops.

She saw immediately that her words were wasted on him. But then, he had never been one to explain his decisions or to suffer them being questioned, especially by a woman. And most especially by a wife to whom he could no longer truly be a husband. Was all of Twin Pines to pay the price for his impotence?

Charles took a moment between cigars to recount his reasons for resisting her notion to hire an overseer for the plantation. "One, Jacob will be home soon. We'd only have to let go a man we just hired, and that would be unfair to him."

Anna opened her mouth to speak. They might find other duties for him in such a situation, if he was capable. But upon glimpsing his determination, she kept her peace.

Charles raised two fingers. "Two, I don't trust anyone but family. It takes a smart fellow to run this place, and a smart fellow would not work for what we can afford to pay. That means he would steal us blind. Three, if Jacob cannot return soon, I trust that Ethan will. Now go see to the kitchen."

Anna left him sitting in bed with suppressed rage on his face. And as he had so many times before, Charles failed to see that rage mirrored in her own features.

Caitlin looked up from the letter she was reading as her father passed by the parlor. Spectacles pushed up high on his nose, he was lost in concentration. He had received correspondence from Richmond, she knew, for it had arrived at the same time as her letter from Ethan. He would now retire to his library to think and eventually respond to it.

The irony of the situation was not lost on Caitlin. Her father plotted with heart and soul for the devastating defeat of the Union, for the defeat of the cause she believed in and for which she and Ethan had risked their lives. And yet he never so much as looked at her probingly, or asked any questions about the letters she received with no return address.

With a short sigh, she lifted a hand to check that her blond curls were still in place—a nervous gesture. But for days such as this one, when she received a note from Ethan that confirmed their love, she suffered the weeks and months of separation and uncertainty with stoic resolve, worrying constantly that he had been captured. Her father must have noticed that she was often more sullen and remote than usual—or perhaps he had not. He carried on as he had for so many years, terrorizing the field hands and confusing his students—who were many fewer now, due to the war—with his rhetoric.

She often accompanied him to social events and teas at the university, and during their long carriage rides to and from Charlottesville, he spoke to her no more or less than usual. More and more she was able to look upon his indifference as a character flaw, and not merely a criticism of her own shortcomings. He was so sure of his own personal power, so convinced that nothing she might do would break the bond between them.

But he was wrong. Each time she received one of Ethan's letters she realized how brave and bold he was, without wearing the uniform of the South—or the North. And each time, she felt their love strengthen and her pride in him grow. Her fear of disappointing her father was lessening, she could tell. She would have to tell him of her feelings. But each time she summoned her courage and resolved to speak to him, she would recall his face as it had looked when she told him she could not marry Jacob. There had not been merely hurt in his expression, but absolute anger, and anger he had barely managed to contain. She kept hoping that her outwardly appropriate behavior would somehow bring her father's acceptance, that someday he would forgive her for her mother's death. Somehow she could not bring herself to break free of him until he did.

As Caitlin reached to pick up the letter and reread it, a tear slipped down her cheek.

September brought warm, wet weather that turned the roads into bogs and put a halt to troop movements, quieting the war fever that had dominated the summer. Everyone but Dr. Stuart seemed glad for the respite from struggle and death. The professor advocated an assault on Washington led by "Stonewall" Jackson. When he visited Twin Pines with his daughter, Stuart and Charles talked long into the night about the effect of an all-out assault upon the nearby capital of the North.

They said nothing of Ethan, nor of Caitlin, who passed most of her time cheering Martha and sewing jackets and pants for soldiers.

"It's only a hundred miles from your front yard," her father proclaimed. He spoke so emphatically that his stomach shook. He had put on weight in the months since fighting broke out.

"Father," Caitlin commented as she served the tea Clara brought to Charles's room, "it appears that war is good for your appetite."

"Jackson and Johnston could cut off escape, and Beauregard could march into the city with thirty thousand men and take it tomorrow!"

Charles was not so sure. As Caitlin left the room, he reminded his old friend that the Yankees' Army of the Potomac had more men and a new commanding general, McClellan, who had secured western Virginia against the rest of the Old Dominion.

"He's a sly fox, that McClellan," Charles said, raising a bushy brow.

"He's a clay-footed fool!" Stuart did not bother to hide his irritation. "If we had half his manpower, we'd be pushing the Yankees up into Canada today!"

The two old friends liked to talk about the war, one they could not fight. Knowing many of the politicians and soldiers who served on both sides, as they did, gave them extra delight in berating or complimenting a man.

"How's that son of yours?" the doctor inquired.

Charles sat up proudly. He was happiest now when thinking about his son in uniform. "He's a major. Fought at Manassas. Quite a hero, I'm told."

"And Ethan? What of him?"

Stuart's question seemed innocent enough, and in the bright September sun and the sparkle of his room, Charles chose not to believe the worst. But Charles felt no elation as he told Stuart, "He wrote to his mother that he's coming home soon to enlist."

Stuart assumed a serious pose. Hands on hips, he strode around the room that had confined Charles Parson for a decade. Uneasily, he tried to broach a subject he knew Charles would object to discussing.

"Charles, my friend, your farm is gone to wrack and ruin. Wait! Let me finish."

Charles held his argument in check. He looked suddenly away, focusing on the oaks waving in the breeze outside his window.

"If you don't find yourself a crack overseer now," Stuart told him, "this plantation won't be worth spit when Jacob returns victorious from Manassas. You know it to be true. It's time for you to take action. I know a man, Frank Hughes. He comes highly recommended. He's left his native Alabama to join kin here in Albemarle County. Talk to him. That's all I ask."

Charles gave no sign of approval, but Stuart took his silence as assent. Settling with a groan into the armchair facing the bed, he looked up at his sick friend with haunted eyes.

"My friend, it pains me to say this, but I must. Ethan was seen in Washington in the company of known agents of Lincoln's. Spies for the North. Now, unless you can persuade me that Ethan is double-dealing and in fact under the employ of our boys, I am afraid that he will be arrested the next time he shows his face south of Bull Run. The word has gone out to arrest and detain him. Why, for all I know, Jacob himself might be reading the wire this minute. I wanted to tell you face to face—"

"To rub it in!" Charles snapped. "You don't have boys. You don't know what they're like, headstrong and proud. I am not saying Ethan's perfect, but I'll bet my life and this plantation that he's no spy for Lincoln!"

Stuart lowered his head. "For all our sakes," he said softly, "I hope you are right."

Stuart lingered, but no words came, and some minutes later he left. Downstairs in the parlor, Anna could read the disappointment on his face.

"Anna, you must persuade your husband to hire Frank Hughes. Only God knows when this war will end."

Anna paused, setting down her needlepoint. She had not noticed the lines in the man's ruddy face before. "George," she began. "You know I cannot oppose my husband's wishes on this or any other matter. I can, however, essay to persuade him of the errors of his ways, eh?" She smiled at him. "I know you have our best interest at heart."

Stuart did not take well to her joke and switched the subject. "I will never accept her decision not to marry Jacob, not in my heart." His voice sounded defeated; his shoulders sagged.

"Perk up," she scolded him. "You have a lovely daughter, and Charles and I are blessed with a daughter and two fine sons. George, what is it?"

"I can't say, Anna."

But somehow Anna knew. Ethan was in trouble. And George knew about it. Had he told Charles?

An ache in her heart grew sharp. At that moment, Anna knew that her son was in danger. She dropped the needlepoint and stared ahead with vacant eyes. Stuart stepped to her side, then called out for help.

It took Clara five minutes to shake Anna out of her "spell." But Clara understood this sort of trance. The vision of a child in danger was mighty powerful.

Even after she had regained the power of speech and sipped from the glass of water Clara had brought her, Anna still appeared to be lost in her own private realm.

Just as Clara was dismissed from the parlor, Martha and Caitlin came down the staircase.

"Rebels are so much smarter than Yankees," Martha asserted, but as they reached the entry to the parlor, Martha knew immediately that something was wrong. Clara's eyes were downcast; she would not say a word to her or Caitlin as she scurried past. Dr. Stuart, too, was quiet, and he stood stiffly beside Anna. Her mother looked sallow and strangely distant.

"What is it, Mama?" she cried, rushing to her mother's side and sitting at her feet. "Are you ill? Shall we get the doctor?"

Anna shook her head. Her pale blue eyes were blank.

Caitlin looked to her father for a clue as to what had happened. Meeting her gaze, he took Caitlin by the arm and led her into the library across the hall without excusing himself.

Caitlin paced the room, her heels clicking on the pine floor like horses' hooves. "For God's sake, child, sit down!" her father snapped, looking up from a book. "You're worse than—"

Caitlin stopped and set her gaze upon him. "Worse than my mother? Is that what you meant to say, Father? Was she high-strung, too? You've always told me she was perfect."

Stuart held up his hands for quiet, another classroom gesture that riled her. He couldn't face the truth of her words. But he would have the most logical reasons to back his illogical reaction, as always. "That isn't what I meant at all, Caitlin. But please, let us allow them privacy in their own home." He tugged once on his bow tie and ran a hand through his hair, then returned to his book.

But Caitlin would not let it be. She approached him warily, almost as if she were stalking him. Sitting in the chair nearest his, close to the empty fireplace, she asked, "Daddy, why won't you tell me the truth about Mother? She can't have been an angel. I'd like to know—"

Her father jumped to his feet. "She *was* an angel!" he said vehemently. "You did not know her. I did. I loved her! She was perfect. . . ." He turned his back to her and folded his hands in front of him, quieting himself after the extraordinary outburst. Caitlin slowly gathered her skirt and rose to stand directly behind him.

"I am sorry that she died, Father," she said, fighting back tears of frustration. "For you as well as . . ."

He gripped her hand and squeezed. "I know, darling, I know," he said softly. "But she was perfect. You must believe me. She was perfect."

Unlike me, Caitlin added silently to herself. How she wished that her mother had lived, if only so that she would not now feel so responsible and base. I am not God! she wanted to scream. I am on this earth only to do His bidding, not that which you have decided for me in His name.

Why must he constantly force her into the position of living the perfection that his own life lacked? Well, he would one day be left alone. He must make his own peace, she resolved. But even as her mind screamed out at him, she realized that her own sense of peace and serenity would not come easily.

Anna's grip on her daughter's hand was icy and strong, like the current of a mountain stream in spring. But it reminded Martha too much of the chill of the grave, as she had read about it, and as she imagined it when they had attended the military funerals of James Cabell and Noah Chesterfield. The same deep chill had been in the hands of their mothers, too. Martha shivered and reached for her mother's shawl, which had slid beside her on the loveseat. As she tucked the light woolen wrap around both of them, the motion caused one of the candles on top of the piano to go out.

At the fortified entrenchments built by the Confederates at Manassas to withstand the next Yankee attack, a commotion arose at one of the picket posts near the old stone bridge. As officer of the day, Jacob was hailed from his quarters to resolve the situation. He glanced around as he buttoned up his collar and was pleased to see that Brett Tyler was nowhere in sight. Perhaps a lucky Yankee sharpshooter had nailed him in his sleep, he thought. And the thought somehow cheered him. For Tyler alone was witness to Jacob's ineptitude at the first battle.

He strode purposefully down the hill and toward the bridge. Two sentries held a man in uniform, their arms locked around his. The fellow looked familiar and wore the dress of the Albemarle Rifles. Why on God's earth are they holding one of my men? Jacob thought. Perhaps he'd stolen something.

But as he got closer to the sentries, the truth of the matter sent a wave of shock and revulsion through him. Ethan! They were holding Ethan. He had but a few yards to compose himself, and he saluted the sentries, barely able to confront them in a normal voice. "What's he done?"

The taller soldier spoke first. "He tried to bluff his way past us, Major. Claimed to be on a special assignment for the Albemarle Rifles. I knowed it was bull, but I figured to check with you."

The wariness in the eyes of the sentries made Jacob flush. Could they see the lies that raced through his mind? Should he confirm Ethan's story or have him held until later? How could he spare his foolish brother's life if indeed he had been caught spying in the heart of the Confederate army?

"I'll see to him." The sentries released Ethan, who pulled free of them, flashing an uneasy smile at his brother.

"Thank you, sir." At least Ethan was wise enough to say no more. Jacob pulled his pistol and motioned his brother to start up the hill, away from the sentries guarding the bridge.

They marched, Ethan in front, too big and broad for the dusty gray uniform of a private that he wore. Jacob wondered where and how he had gotten hold of it. He shoved his brother toward a clearing beyond the Carter house, which was quiet in the afternoon. After peering around to confirm that they were beyond earshot of the encampment, Jacob lambasted his brother for a full five minutes.

"You stupid ass! I ought to shoot you here and now! How foolish can you be, walking up to a sentry in the middle of the afternoon in a stolen uniform—"

"It's not stolen," Ethan interjected without raising his bowed head.

"I'll thank you to shut up, brother! You say one word and I'll blow your damn foot off!" Jacob was so angry that he stomped around the clearing like a charging bull. He waved his pistol in his brother's face again, but Ethan did not flinch, nor did he look up. "Do you want to send Mama and Daddy straight to their graves? Is that what you want? Because this kind of foolishness will do it, damn it!"

Still out of control, Jacob bit back tears of frustration. He stood in a quandary. If he excused his brother or let him escape, the sentries' report would implicate and condemn him. However, if he allowed Ethan to be held and tried, his brother would no doubt hang. Those seemed the only two choices.

Jacob calmed himself enough to put away the pistol. "Where and how did you get the uniform?" he asked. "Whose is it?"

Ethan knew that if he smiled, the act might cost him whatever slim chance of survival he had. But he could not suppress the curling of his broad lips. "It's yours, brother, from two years back."

He spoke simply and without flourish, but the awful truth of the words and their implication hit Jacob like a brick in the head. His old uniform had hung in the closet since two years earlier, when Jacob had risen in the ranks of the local militia. "When did you—"

"Jacob, you must believe this. I did not take it."

"Keyes."

"You can't blame him," Ethan said weakly.

Jacob shook with rage. "Blame him! I'll kill him when next we meet, in this world or the next!"

The sun dappled in the leaves of the oak they stood under, and somewhere nearby a whippoorwill sang. The familiar smells of coffee brewing and bacon cooking wafted in the breeze. Soldiers playing cards shouted and whooped in the distance; one of them had won a big pot. That they were together in these circumstances seemed impossible to Jacob; he kept waiting to awaken from this terrifying nightmare. It was simply beyond understanding that he, Jacob, the good son, the loyal one, was to be put in the position of judging his brother and deciding, in effect, whether he would live or die. The overwhelming pressure of it broke him; Jacob sank to the ground on his knees, shuddering.

Ethan watched the play of emotions on his brother's

tense, angry face. At first, he feared doing anything, not wishing to arouse his brother's ire further. After a moment, he stood and went to him, gently placing a hand on his shoulder. "God, brother, I am sorry. I am a fool."

"You're a dead man!"

Approaching footsteps shocked them both into action. Ethan came to attention, and Jacob wiped his eyes with his sleeve and turned to see who was coming. He winced. It was Tyler, the grin on his face as broad as the day.

"Well, howdy, men!" he called. "This the spy?" He pointed to Ethan as Jacob ordered him to be quiet. Then Tyler pretended to make a noose with his hands and hung himself in pantomime.

"Get out of here now, soldier." Jacob was ready to court-martial the troublemaker. He had had enough of Tyler's brashness, enough of his witnessing his shortcomings and awkwardness.

Tyler held up his hands, licking his lips. "I will go, sir, but one thing first. I believe I can get us out of this stink with nobody hangin' and nobody in deep crap."

Jacob looked at Ethan, who stood staring at Tyler, his hands by his sides. His brother didn't know any better than he what Tyler was up to. Jacob ordered Tyler to explain. "Simple, sir. I offer the sentries—in your name—a few days without duty and a pass to go home and see their mamas. I'll also tell 'em that your brother ran away in the great skedaddle, and now he wants to run home and see *his* mama before it's too late. They'll understand. I know both boys. They're good soldiers, but they ain't got no more imagination than a trout."

Jacob just stood there with his mouth open—like a trout, it struck him—because Tyler had the gall to open his, mocking him. "That will do, Private," Jacob snapped.

Ethan shook his head in wonder. "Were you born thinking like this?"

Tyler grinned. "All things are possible, sayeth the Lord."

Jacob looked at Tyler. He had never heard that quotation from the Good Book. But then, he thought, it wasn't likely that the Tylers spent much time reading the

Bible. He let it pass. Jacob saluted. "Carry on with your plan, Private."

Tyler snapped a salute and strolled toward the bridge, humming a tune.

"God help me if I don't kill that man before the Yankees do," Jacob admitted.

"He's a fox in the body of a man," Ethan agreed.

Jacob snorted. "He's Lucifer in the guise of an infantry private."

Ethan pulled his tobacco pouch from the stolen uniform and rolled a cigar, offering it to Jacob, but Jacob was not about to let his brother off the hook yet. "You tell me how this came to be and what you plan to do now."

Ethan took a deep breath, lighted the cigar, and blew smoke into the air. "It's a long story," he began.

"You have until nightfall, Ethan. And then you must leave. If you're captured, there's nothing I can do for you, so for God's sake, take off that uniform the first chance you get."

"Agreed."

Ethan spoke passionately for almost an hour, interrupted only by a few questions from his brother.

"I grew up in your shadow, Jacob," Ethan began, almost apologetically, "and you cast a long shadow, Major. Always did. You did what was right and honorable, always told Daddy when you did anything wrong."

Jacob nodded. This brother was so near to him in many ways, yet so foreign in beliefs. He wanted to ask, Are you my brother, really? "Yes, but he still whipped me. And though you choose to ignore his wishes, Father actually respects you more for not minding him so much."

"But he loves you as he will never love me."

Jacob stood and looked toward the horizon, watching the sunlight break through the trees. "That's where you're wrong, brother. Regardless of what I do, I never feel enough love from that man."

After a silence they traded news about their mother and sister. They made no mention of Caitlin.

Then Ethan cleared his throat and asked to explain himself without interruption. Jacob nodded, opening his palms as if to say, "I won't stop you."

"I was always different, you know. You and your friends, Jacob, would be running in and out of the house, bothering Clara for milk and cookies or playing soldier at the stables, but I always felt like an outsider there at my own home. There was always a watcher inside me, observing and noting and judging, even while I was chasing after you. I didn't want this voice and this judge inside me. But it is there, all the same, and it always was. It never let me get away with anything."

"Like a conscience," Jacob interjected bitterly. "As though I did not have one, too."

Ethan shook his head. "No, not a conscience. It's different. It's like having someone else, someone older, living inside of my head." He paused. Jacob was now looking at him as if deciding whether or not he had gone mad. "But you will hear me out, brother. And I am not talking of voices such as those the poor lunatics at the asylum hear. I mean a stern judge, almost like Daddy's voice. And once I began my studies at Harvard, that voice began to tell me that slavery was wrong, that it was immoral to hold other human beings in bondage."

Jacob looked his brother square in the eye, and for the first time he recognized the reason for the gulf between them: They had never really been alike. He could not imagine heeding such a voice, or even hearing it. He was, heart and soul, the life he lived at Twin Pines.

"Now, I'm finally heeding that voice, Jacob," Ethan continued. "You and Daddy can say what you will, but I take the voice to be right and just, and not merely the Devil's tongue wagging inside me."

"I hope you're right, brother. I truly do." And as Jacob walked off to get them both a cup of coffee, Ethan kept his eyes on his older brother. In his major's uniform, Jacob looked as if he had found some clothes that really fit him.

CHAPTER 21

CAITLIN STUART SLIPPED out the kitchen door of the Parson house with practiced ease. The moon was hidden behind heavy clouds that stuck in the sky like mud. She carried only a small parcel under her arm; taking too much food might arouse the suspicions of anyone she chanced to meet. She had specifically waited until late, after midnight, when she didn't expect to meet anyone on the path to the slave quarters.

Suddenly she stopped on the path; she'd heard a noise. She barely had time to gasp before a shadowy figure emerged from the trees, arms open, running toward her.

"Ethan!"

They embraced and kissed. To him, she smelled of clover and magnolia and everything as it was before the war and his experiences in Washington. She had changed nothing about herself; her hair, her taste, her smell—everything was the same, just as he wanted it to be.

"Oh, dear God, Ethan, you scared the life out of me!"

"*Shh!* Where are you going at this hour?"

Once she had explained her task, he promised to wait for her under the oak by the back porch. The breeze from the mountains was cool and sweet, and smelled like no other place Ethan had ever been. There is a smell called home, he thought. An owl hooted in the trees nearby, and something rustled in the shrubs near the house. The usual comings and goings of the animals eased his mind. The creatures were involved in no war other than survival. They didn't worry about duty and honor and shame.

Caitlin returned soon afterward. Another runaway

was en route to Boston. The idea of someone escaping to freedom, escaping from mistreatment and bondage, cheered them. She held his hand, and when he grew quiet and looked away, she knew he had more to say.

"Ethan, what is it? Is it Jacob?" Her eyes widened with fright.

"No, not him," Ethan said softly. "It's news I've learned of your father."

Her grip on his hand slackened. "What? Tell me, Ethan."

"I met a runway, a big man named Henry. He said . . . he said your father had mistreated him. It's one reason I'm doing what I am. When I heard Henry's story, I knew I had to do something. I couldn't pretend it wasn't my fault, when I lived most of my life not ten miles from where the man was caged and beaten."

When he stopped talking, Ethan turned to look at Caitlin. She was crying; her tears fell in drops onto her lap.

"Caitlin, I am sorry. I didn't know whether . . ."

"It's all right, Ethan. You told me the truth. I remember Big Henry. It's Daddy who's been lying, mostly to me and himself. It's all right." Her hands shook with fury as she took his hand again and asked him to describe his capture at Manassas.

"I hate to think of what might have happened if the officer on duty had been someone other than Jacob," Caitlin told him, holding him tighter. "How good of him to let you go!"

Ethan looked at her as if she had gone insane. "He couldn't stand there and let them hang me, could he? Although it took Tyler's wiliness to get me out of there."

"But your brother ordered it."

Ethan let the subject drop. They spoke little more, holding each other in silence for some time before Caitlin turned to go back up the path to the house. "Are you coming?"

He shook his head. "Soon. I want to reacquaint myself with Twin Pines for a moment."

Caitlin left him under the oak, the breeze ruffling his hair. She had forgotten how big he was and how jealous he'd always been of his brother. Running up to the house, she went immediately to her room and got into bed. But she was unable to fall asleep until she heard Ethan tiptoe up the stairs in his stockinged feet and open the creaking door to his room.

In the morning, the house was filled with the sounds of rejoicing. Martha played on the piano, and her mother and Caitlin sang in accompaniment. Out of uniform, Ethan was asked no questions about what he was doing at Twin Pines, nor of his activities in Washington. But after breakfast, when his father asked to see him, the tone of his visit changed dramatically.

Ethan walked into his father's room to find Charles struggling to sit up straight. The sacrifices being made to support the war effort had taken their toll on him. Ethan noticed that he smoked a stub rather than a fresh cigar, and complained bitterly about Clara's cooking. When the old man coughed, his body shook, and he had to catch his breath before speaking.

"You always adored her cooking," Ethan said, looking soberly at his father.

Charles threw up his hands. "That was before this damn war, which would've been over right after Manassas if Jeff Davis knew his ass from his armpit. Letting McDowell skedaddle back to Washington to lick his wounds . . . We might have ended the war right then, in July. That's what George Stuart thinks, and I'm beginning to think he's right."

Ethan hesitated before speaking up. The morning sunlight through the window seemed too bright, catching a thousand floating bits of dust in its rays. "Don't be so sure, Daddy. Northerners may not be as sure of victory, especially now, but they are not giving up. They still have more men, more cannons, more factories, and more ships."

Charles dismissed those arguments with a wave of his

hand. "England and France won't enter this war. And without their sway, the better American army will win, you can count on that. The Confederacy has more experienced generals and West Point graduates than the Union, it's a fact! It all comes down to outfighting the enemy on any given day, and my money is always on the South." He stuck the stub of his cigar in his mouth defiantly; it was too short to light, but he chewed it vigorously.

"I can't argue with that, Daddy, but everyone up north says the same thing about McClellan's Army of the Potomac." He looked outside. With the tobacco harvested and cured, the fields seemed bare. "How was the tobacco crop? Good?"

"It was." His father nodded, then looked at him piercingly. "Your mother and George Stuart think we need an overseer to fill your brother's shoes. Unless you will."

Ethan was taken by surprise, and when he hesitated, his father shot him a look of bitter regret.

"I'm sorry, Daddy, but I haven't come to do that."

"Then what brings you here now? Out of money, is that it?"

Ethan shook his head. "No. I came to see Mama and Martha . . . and you. I came for some advice, too, Daddy."

Charles laughed briefly and sourly. "Advice? You? Never! You came to get something out of me, but what, I do not know."

This cat-and-mouse game was more than Ethan had expected of his father. "You still have the same old fire burning within, don't you?"

"Old fires burn hot," Charles reminded his son. "Have you seen Jacob?"

"No, sir, not since I left." He had to lie. It was too difficult to explain, and telling him the truth might kill him. "Has he written?"

"Every week." Charles sounded proud of Jacob.

"Father, I want to marry Caitlin and take her north to live." Having said it, he waited for Charles to explode.

Instead the old man merely chewed the cigar stub

meditatively. "Have you asked the girl? I can tell you that Dr. Stuart won't cotton to it one bit. Unless she's willing to defy him, it won't happen. Does she want to leave her home, son?"

"I believe so, but I am not sure." The same thought had crossed Ethan's mind many times. He was sure of her affections, but there was something . . . She could not yet confide in him the true reason she remained at Stuart Hall, yet he had to get her away from there. He wanted her in the freedom of the North, away from her father's violent temper, before he returned to continue his intelligence forays.

Charles turned on his son with fire in his gray eyes. "Son, your mind is a hornet's nest, and it's high time you did what I do with a hornet's nest! Get a torch and burn the devils out!" His left hand clutched the bedsheet and quilt, crumpling them into a handhold. It was as if Charles held on to it for life.

"Daddy, please understand me," Ethan began, but his father turned his head, looking out the window. Ethan stood, about to leave. "I'm sorry for all the—"

"Save it, son! Now leave me. Go!"

When he turned at the door for a last look at his father, Ethan saw poised above his father's head a flashing white oval, a reflection of something through the window. The sight chilled him, and he shuddered as he shut the door.

"Look!" Caitlin cried. The blond hair curling out from beneath her hat stirred in the breeze and from the swaying of the buggy on the dirt road. To the left of the buggy, the field hands tended the late-summer vegetables, and above the sky was growing gray and threatening.

Beside her, Ethan followed her outstretched arm with his eyes. A bright red cardinal flitted from branch to branch, his duller-colored mate in pursuit.

"You never pursued me like that," Ethan teased her. "Quite the opposite."

Checking to ensure that they couldn't be seen from the house, they kissed, ignoring the snorting of the mare.

Caitlin pulled gently away, heaving a deep sigh, and looked out over the fields. "Even when we escape the war, such as now," she said, looking pale and perfect in the somber light, "we don't really escape it. It's like the clouds overhead. You ignore them, but sooner or later they let forth the heavens and spoil your day."

The first rumble of thunder sounded from the west. "We'd best get back," Ethan decided. Reining in the mare, he turned the buggy. The wind had kicked up, and it scattered dust in their faces.

"What will we do?" Caitlin said with a forlorn air.

He knew she wasn't speaking of the weather. "We'll do . . . what's right." But Ethan had no clearer idea than she of what that meant in practical terms.

The storm caught them just outside the gate to the yard, and by the time they had entered the kitchen, they were dripping wet.

Anna was knitting socks for Jacob in the parlor two days later when a Confederate soldier knocked at the front door of the Twin Pines, asking for "Mr. Parson." Ethan had gone with Caitlin to Stuart Hall, so Anna told Alex to take the young man up to see Charles.

The young man, who introduced himself as Private Jim Charlton, of Culpeper, was a short, skinny lad with owlish eyes. Charles judged him to be about twenty years old. With a wave of his hand, he invited Private Charlton to sit in the chair, then dismissed Alex. Alone with him, Charles asked his business.

"You got a son in uniform, up at Manassas." The soldier played with his hat and didn't know where to look.

Wondering at the boy's nervousness, Charles replied evenly, "Yes, my son Jacob is a major."

"Oh, no, suh. Not him. The other one. The one what stole the uniform."

The news struck Charles like a lightning bolt in the heart. His chest constricted. What was this charlatan trying to say? In times of war, only spies and madmen put on a uniform that wasn't theirs. "What the hell are you talking about, boy?" His breathing came hard, and the smoke from his cigar filled the room with a stifling haze.

Private Charlton took a deep breath, and his Adam's apple bobbed like a cork when he spoke. "Your other boy, the big one. Me and another sentry caught him sneakin' into camp in the uniform of the Nineteenth Virginia. He ought to a' hung, but your other boy let 'im go. If I tell General Beauregard, both your boys be in boilin' water, way I see it."

The private watched in fascination as the ruddy old man in bedclothes struggled to reach the shotgun leaning against the wall near his bed. "What you doin', old man? Hey, I jes' came for money to keep my mouth shut. Don' make me no bother, but my family ain't rich like you. Hey!"

Charles struggled to lift the heavy twelve-gauge to his lap, breathing with difficulty, and lifted it to his shoulder. He aimed it at the boy, who jumped to his feet and held out his hands. "Whoa! Stop it, you crazy coot!"

Charles sighted the skinny young man with the bulging frog's eyes and pulled one trigger. But the soldier moved with the speed of youth, slapping the gun away so that the buckshot missed his head, crashing instead through the bedroom window. His footsteps rapped on the stairs like a drumbeat.

Alex heard the blast and the sound of shattering glass from the kitchen. By the time he reached the front hallway, the front door had been flung open, and the boy was running down the path, where he hopped the fence and ran full speed down the road. "What de—" Alex hurried up to Mister Charles's room to find the elder Parson gasping for air, his shotgun in his lap; Anna was right behind him.

"Who . . ." he gasped, shutting his eyes.

Alex took away the gun and called for Clara. While Clara ran for water, Alex sent one of the kitchen hands into town to fetch the doctor, and another to Stuart Hall for Ethan.

Charles's eyes rolled wildly in his head, and he was

babbling incoherently about the boys. Anna leaned close, kneeling at his bedside and taking his hand. She called to him, brushing his forehead, which was cool and damp, but he seemed not to hear her. He spoke in desperate whispers. "The boys . . . too fast . . . slow it down . . . Anna! *Anna!*"

The night candles lighted all the windows in the great house, and the bondsmen sang spirituals in deep voices that carried in the wind to the big house like the presence of angels.

Anna sat on the settee in the parlor, barely aware of Martha, who wept uncontrollably beside her. It had finally happened. Charles was dead. She willed herself to feel sad, to feel anything. But she felt as he had looked, immobile and blank. Dr. Sully had been able to do nothing for him, but had given her a potion that was already beginning to numb her mind. Anna could not summon true sadness at his passing. Placing a kiss on her daughter's forehead, she rose and ascended the stairs to her room, unaware of anything but the desire to sleep.

By the time Ethan arrived at Twin Pines, the house was tenebrous and eerily quiet, but for the sound of Martha's weeping and the hushed chorus of the bondsmen.

He ran upstairs to his father's room, where Alex kept vigil. In the pale glow of candlelight, his father's face had lost its robust color and had already taken on the waxy sheen of the dead. Collapsing to his knees, he gripped his father's hand so firmly that Alex feared he might do damage to it, had the man not already died. The bitterness was gone from the old man's features, as was the anger. And for that long moment, Ethan's, too, disappeared. Showering kisses on Charles's forehead and face, he wished he could blow life into Charles's lungs.

It was past midnight when Ethan let go of his father and descended the stairs to the library, where he settled in a leather wingchair.

Alex entered with a brandy. "Should I send word to Mister Jacob?"

Ethan looked up, startled to see the manservant looming over him like a ghost. "Yes, Alex, by all means. Send
a man into town and have him wire Major Parson at
Manassas Junction."

"Yessuh."

Ethan drank the brandy too quickly. The room grew
fluid, and he closed his eyes to still the movement, falling
into an uneasy sleep. One haunting and brief dream after
another brought him face to face with spirits. Each dream
shook him awake, leaving him exhausted and weak in the
leather chair, before he drifted into the next nightmare.

In one dream, his father threw off the burial shroud
and stood, something he had not been able to do for the
last ten years of his life. With the family and slaves gathered on the lawn, encircling the open grave, Charles Parson pointed a finger at Ethan. "You killed me, you and
your cowardice! I never loved you! You're not my son!"

Ethan awoke, drenched in perspiration, liquid guilt
encasing him. He longed to take a bath, now, in the middle of the night, but could not move. Folding his hands
behind his head, he realized with a deep stab of guilt that
his father's death freed him in the way that he wanted to
free Twin Pines's slaves.

His mother had always loved him unconditionally, regardless of what he thought or did. But Charles had been
different. Ethan had always been measured by his father.
And when he had failed, his father had loved him less.
He, and Jacob even more so, had borne the brunt of
Charles's willful assaults upon their characters. But now,
with their father dead, the attacks would cease forever.

Forever, Ethan thought, drifting off to sleep. Again
the nightmares came, and his father leaped from the grave
to choke him. Finally, Ethan gave up on the idea of sleep
and sat in a chair near the library window, listening to
the nightingales and watching for the first weak crack of
light to split the black sky.

At the moment his father died, Jacob was leaning over
the small table in his tent, writing a letter to him, as he

did once each week. The letter began with a tone that surprised even the writer himself.

> *Daddy,*
>
> *I hope you and Mama are well. I am well. We expect more action from the Yankees soon, now that winter has come, and McClellan is in command of their army. If Ethan shows up, don't upbraid him too much. If we turn away from him, where else can he go but to the Devil? Tell him his brother loves him, but doesn't want to see him in this muddy, pestilent hole.*
>
> *Army life is sometimes trying, Daddy. I do my best. Is the plantation in good shape? Mama wrote of her desire to hire a new man, an overseer. Seems a good idea to me. Pay him in produce.*
>
> *I could be here, walking these entrenchments for months, if not years. God help us! Johnston has placed batteries and patrols on the south bank of the Potomac. The river is ours. We're safe, at least from the Yankees. Surgeon tells me we lost 2,000 men in the battle. They lost 4,000.*
>
> *I love you and Mama and Martha. I pray the conflict will be resolved before the year's end, and that we'll all be rejoined for Christmas.*
>
> *Your loving son,*
Jacob

Placing the letter in an envelope, he hurried to drop it in the mail bag in time to be posted that afternoon. Jacob's thoughts were on his family as he walked unconsciously in time with the melancholy strains of a harmonica being played by one of his men.

Jacob's eyes flew wide open as terror flew in on dark, piercing arrows. He gasped at a noise, then realized it was only the sound of his own breathing. He had been dreaming. Touching the frame of his cot, Jacob reassured himself that he was in his tent, that the vision had been only that. In his dream he had seen Ethan, swinging in a noose under the oak outside the kitchen at Twin Pines. With a damp hand he wiped his brow, willing his breathing to return to normal. But try as he would, he was unable to fall back to sleep.

Rising, Jacob walked around the vast entrenchments and camp that was home to twenty thousand Confederate soldiers. Listening to the sound of his boots on the mud and gravel, he marveled at how quiet so many thousands of men could be. Such silence was unheard of during the day. He heard a mockingbird calling a name and dropped under an elm to light a cigar. When would God and man have enough of this nonsense and put an end to it? he thought. Why didn't Lincoln realize he was licked and offer terms of peace everybody could live by? It all seemed so simple and peaceful in the still silence of the night, smoking his cigar, certain that his family was far away and safe.

The next morning, as Alex and Ethan made funeral plans, two letters arrived. One was from Jacob, addressed to their father. It had been written a week before, early in September. Anna read the letter in the parlor but said little. Wordlessly laying it aside, she reached for the laudanum the doctor had left her. She seemed oddly removed, and had evaded Ethan's attempts to engage her in conversation.

The second letter was addressed to Martha. The handwriting was unfamiliar, a wobbly script. Alex took it up to her room, and she opened it before joining the rest of the family for breakfast.

Martha,
I did not write this, but my friend Thomas Buckingham of Petersburg did. He is a lawyer and a soldier. Your brother is fine and well liked by his men. I saved his life once when he got too rambunctious and charged the Yankees all on his own, or maybe he just got lost. Did he tell you?
I'm fighting here for you. I got the locket you gave

Jacob. He gave it to me. It's my good-luck charm. I would like to see you at Christmas leave or before. I hope your family is all right.
Brett Tyler

She saw that he had signed the letter in a stilted, child's hand. Something in the missive stirred her. Folding the letter, she placed it under her pillow, then stared at the pillow casing. Brett Tyler had her cameo. What power that man must have to get it from Jacob, she thought. What was the source of his power? God? The Devil? Or just life?

CHAPTER 22

THE DAY OF Charles Parson's funeral was cruelly bright and sunny. Birds sang in the trees, squirrels chattered and raced around the yard. The world seemed unmoved by the loss of Charles Parson. The family gathered in the parlor with the minister for prayers, and by eleven in the morning, representatives of the government, businesses, and the army had gathered in the ballroom for the eulogy.

Colonel Henry Winston shifted his weight uncomfortably, trying to ease the pain in his legs. An older man stricken with gout, the colonel's duties consisted solely of expressing the Confederate army's condolences at the loss of a patriot or a soldier. He had already been to this part of the state once, following the rout of the Yankees at Bull Run. And before embarking on this second trip, he had confided to an aide that he had attended more funerals than had God.

The minister from town cleared his throat and read from the Old Testament. " 'And into dust thou shalt return.' " He spoke for forty minutes, offering comfort through the series of quotations he'd chosen from the Bible.

Garlanded in black crepe, the ballroom was a far cry from the festive scene it had presented at Christmas. Seated on a couch in the front of the room, Martha and Anna held on to one another. Their grief was apparent in the sobs and tears that so readily spilled from their eyes.

When the minister had finished, Ethan asked for a moment to speak before the pallbearers carried the casket to the hill where the Twin Pines cemetery still stood, where it had stood for over a century, and where Charles Parson's body would now rest for eternity.

Dressed in black, as was everyone but the colonel, Ethan had prepared a short speech about his father. As was the Parson family tradition, a written copy of the eulogy would be kept in the family safe in the library. But now, facing some familiar faces and many strangers hostile to or ignorant of his desires, he was moved to speak extemporaneously, and he dropped the notes upon the table, where they lay unnoticed. In the silence that lasted until he found the right words to begin, people stirred uncomfortably, and even his mother cast him a stern look.

"Mother, sister, friends, and fellows, we gather at Twin Pines today to honor my father, Charles Augustus Parson, a Virginian, a gentleman, and a gentle man. He loved many of us. He respected any man who held traditions sacred and who honored his family and his homeland."

Martha burst into tears, putting a handkerchief to her eyes, and Ethan waited for her to recover before continuing. In the doorway, Alex, Clara, and the cooks bowed their heads in respect.

"My father, who leaves us for a land even greener and richer than Virginia, would be pleased to see this gathering take place. He would be amongst you, shaking hands and offering refreshment if he could. I choose to remember him as a powerful, vigorous man who rode a horse like no other man I have ever seen.

"These last ten years of my father's life . . ." He had to pause to bite his lip. "This last decade of my father's life was a trial, as the minister said. My father fought bitterness as he fought every other evil—wholeheartedly, doggedly, to the end. But we do not grieve for him, for Charles Parson is at peace. We grieve for our loss of him, for the touch and the voice which will no longer reach us. Ours is the loss, Heaven's the gain."

Martha wept unabashedly, her shoulders quivering beneath the black silk bodice of her high-necked gown. Beside her, strangely calm, her mother held her, whispering in her ear. Having finished his eulogy, Ethan stepped away from the table and joined his mother and sister, while George Stuart roused the casket bearers to action. They gathered around the casket, lifted it, and proceeded out the door and down the hall to the front door, Ethan, his mother and sister, and the others following behind.

During the short walk to the family cemetery between the tall pines, Ethan took in deep gulps of air and wiped away the tears welling in his eyes. Much of his burden of guilt had been lifted by his own words. Beside him, his mother held his arm woodenly. She seemed unable to display her grief, and spoke with slurred speech.

He had discussed limiting the amount of laudanum his mother consumed, for he was alarmed by her lack of response. But Dr. Sully had maintained that in her time of grief she was in need of its calming influence.

At the site of the grave, which Alex had dug himself rather than have one of the field hands "put his dirty hands on Mister Charles's restin' place," the mourners circled the pit and the mound of clay, hands clasped. Their silence was accentuated by the song of a bird in the trees. Overhead a crow cawed, as if to shoo the gathering from his home. From the kennel behind the house, the hounds howled eerily, as if smelling death and signaling their own sorrow at the loss of their seldom-seen master.

The minister stepped forward to utter a brief prayer.

Then George Stuart and the others lowered the plain wood coffin into the earth. The finality of it hit Ethan hard, and he reeled, almost losing his balance. He would no longer have his father to hate—or to love. He looked across the circle of mourners to Caitlin. She wore a veil, but her eyes shone through, and in them Ethan found some comfort. He could not stop shaking.

George Stuart told someone, "He was a fine and strong man, a real Virginian." Ethan thought the implication was clear: not like his son over there, Ethan, the coward and traitor.

Anna and Martha led the sad and quiet procession back to the house, where a table of food and drinks had been prepared. Even in times of sacrifice, with scarcities a reality, a feast was laid on the long tables in the ballroom, and gallons of punch and whiskey came forth. Yet the gathering could not have been mistaken for a true celebration, for the dress was somber, the tone hushed and serious, and there was an absence of music.

In Manassas Junction, the wire sent to Jacob arrived just as his father was being lowered into his grave. The delay, as the messenger explained in response to Jacob's raging question, had been caused by confusion resulting from the flood of messages wired to the Southern army each day. Jacob felt like a naked man trapped in a snowstorm without shelter. The messenger who handed him the cable had not read it, but looked up to see the young major turn pale and stumble away from his tent in a fog. "Major!" he called. "Hey, Major! You all right?"

Jacob walked without purpose for miles, past tattered camp followers washing clothes, and startled sentries who let the dazed officer pass unquestioned. Jacob felt suspended in time, no longer a soldier, or even a man.

He wandered across the creek, which flowed muddy brown now—the blood shed at Bull Run had long since washed away—and stumbled up the road that had been the scene of the Yankees' humiliation two months before. Looking up, he marveled that the sky could remain blue

and the earth firm underfoot without his father's seeing
to them.

To Jacob, his father was kin to the Old Testament
Jehovah, ever present, ever wise, and as powerful as any
man had a right to be. Even injured and bound to his bed
like a prisoner, Charles Parson had exerted influence on
the world, more so than either he or Ethan could ever
hope to do. Jacob felt orphaned and cheated, as if God
had decided to play a cheap trick on him by waylaying
the wire until it was too late for him to attend the funeral
and to see his father before he was laid to rest.

He paused to lean against an elm tree, considering
taking a leave to return to Charlottesville. But why go
now? he asked himself. Daddy is already buried. He
would want me to do my duty above all else, even above
comforting Mama and Martha.

He found some solace in the uniform he wore, the
sight of which had brought a smile to his father's face.
Without Charles, Jacob was his own man. He feared failure and death now more than ever.

For the next day and a half, Jacob spent much time in
bed, rising only to drill his men. The surgeon looked in
on him once, telling him his lethargy was similar to the
state some soldiers slipped into after fighting their first
battle. Jacob had no appetite, no desires. He lay in bed,
staring at the roof of his tent for hours at a time. Only
Tyler came to visit him. He would stay and chat for hours,
as if Jacob were fascinated by the story of Tyler's first
love affair or the time he killed two quail with one shot.

The day after the telegram was delivered, Tyler set
down Jacob's cold coffee cup and made a space for himself on the cot. "Parson, you beginnin' to bore the hell
outta me."

Jacob paid him no mind.

"How am I gonna be a hero and marry that sister of
yours if you set here on your tail for the remainder of the
war?" But even that outrageous question aroused no answer. Tyler shot Jacob a look of concern. "Fine com-

manding officer you are, Major. Well, if you ain't gonna get up off your ass on your own, I'll find some other way to make it happen." Without any further comment, Tyler left the ailing young major to his own amusements.

Late that night, as Jacob lay awake and unheeding in his cot, two men burst into his tent and grabbed him, stuffing a sock into his mouth. They wrestled him out the door flap and dragged him down the hill to the creek. One fellow, a large man with a beard, held Jacob's ankles while the other hooked his hands under Jacob's armpits. Together, the two men swung him like a pendulum.

They mean to toss me in the creek! Jacob thought. Summoning all his strength, he kicked and swung and twisted his way free, pulling the sock from his mouth and charging the two kidnappers.

"I'll have you hung!" Jacob swore in a fury. But the appearance of Brett Tyler from behind a line of fortifications brought a light of insight into Jacob's musty mind. He understood that Tyler had arranged the seizure to jolt him out of his funk. He ought to take out his pistol and shoot Tyler dead on the spot.

"I could have you locked up for this, Private!" he snapped, seething.

"Yessuh! You surely could."

His smile was infuriating, but Jacob could not carry through with his threat. Instead, pulling his jacket closed, and with some dignity, he marched back up the hill to his tent, so weary that he collapsed into a dreamless sleep as his head touched the cot.

One morning, a week after Charles's funeral, a wide-shouldered, wiry man of middle height and years rode up to the gate at Twin Pines. He announced himself to Alex as "Mr. Franklin Hughes, calling at the request of Dr. George Stuart." Alex took the man's hat and an instant dislike to Hughes. The man's downturned mouth was thin and pressed into a sneer. He seemed to have tasted bitter fruit at an early age. Alex feared such men. As he full well knew, if Mr. Hughes were hired as overseer, he could vent that bitterness on the field hands as he pleased.

Anna heard the man give his name from the parlor, where she sat knitting another pair of socks. She sent them to Jacob regularly, but understood that he was distributing them to other, poorer boys who served the cause. Mr. Hughes sounded a little rough around the edges, but he came highly recommended, and they could ill afford to wait for another applicant. Twin Pines was adrift; the hands had grown lazy. Ethan had indicated that he would soon leave. She needed a strong individual to shoulder the burden of running the estate.

A moment later, Alex entered and introduced Mr. Hughes. He was not a tall man, but walked with a cocky lift in his boots that hinted at his eagerness to jump to the task. He had long, wavy brown hair, and his thick moustache was speckled with gray. His tanned face was lined and seemed somehow older than his body. He wore a starched white shirt, a black tie, and a short formal coat, also black. His pants were worn to a sheen. Anna knew at once that Mr. Hughes had dressed for this important occasion and that the man was down on his luck.

She greeted him kindly. His steel blue eyes resembled her husband's, and with that recollection came a flood of memories and regrets she struggled to control. Hughes kept his vision downcast.

Ethan entered the room and shook hands with the shorter man in a perfunctory way, then bid him be seated.

"Might this be the son who's running the place?" Hughes asked. He had a deep bass voice out of proportion to his size which seemed to carry like the roar of a lion.

"He is. But only temporarily," Anna replied. "That's why we requested that Dr. Stuart send for you."

"He is a fine man, Dr. Stuart," Hughes put in. "Knows how to handle the boys in the field."

Ethan was appalled that Hughes spoke not directly to him, as the man of the house, but to his mother; it was a blatant show of disrespect. The man had been referred by Dr. Stuart. In all probability, his idea of proper means of "handling the boys in the field" did not concur with his own. More than likely, Stuart had made Hughes aware of his sympathies concerning the bondsmen. Hence his present lack of manners.

In a curt voice, Ethan asked about Hughes's past employment. The man was slow to reply, producing a letter from his coat pocket. Ethan scanned it, then handed it to his mother.

"It's a glowing letter from a Colonel Fischer in Alabama," Anna commented. "He says it was with great regret that he let you go, so that you could be nearer to family."

Hughes shook his head. "Yes, ma'am. I got kin up this way, in Tidewater. A brother and cousins. Hope to see them after the tobacco harvest."

Anna could see that Ethan had taken a dislike to the sharp little fellow and wondered why.

Hughes bowed his head in Ethan's direction. "I could not help noticing, sir, that as I rode here on this fine day, there's crops in the field and weeds waist-high. Why ain't your field hands workin'?"

Anna turned to Ethan, who replied, "We have been in mourning, Mr. Hughes, for my father. I am afraid the affairs have slipped somewhat."

Hughes stepped in, but trod lightly. "I'm sure a gentleman such as yourself has other duties to attend to. As overseer of Twin Pines, my sole concern would be workin' the hands and makin' a profit for the family."

Anna smiled. She liked the man's common sense, his lack of pretension. "Would you care for tea?"

"Ma'am, with all due respect, I would care to run this estate at a profit, with a strong and free hand." He turned toward Ethan and added, "Meanin' no disrespect to you. Have we a deal?" He extended his hand. Hesitantly, Ethan took his hand and shook it. Hughes's hand was rough as a rock, and powerful and tanned like leather.

"Now, to work!" Hughes said, rubbing his hands together. "Suppose while we have tea, you tell me who does what around here. And who *don't* do what. That's important, too, right? First off, who is that insolent giant that met me at the door?"

As Anna explained and answered one question after another, Alex listened from the open kitchen doorway. "Don' like the sound of dat!" he said.

"Pooh!" said Clara, elbow deep in dough. "We be rid of this banty rooster in a month. You'll see. If I has to, I put hot peppers in his boots!"

Alex usually bowed to her in all judgments, but a nagging voice told him to watch out for Mr. Franklin Hughes.

It took Frank Hughes longer than he himself expected to begin the painful process of rebuilding the decay which had set into Twin Pines. It was dry rot, he thought as he toured the plantation. Weeds had stunted the growth of the corn and squash, so that now the crops would never reach their optimum size. Many of the hoes and plows were not functional. But his worst enemy was not in the equipment or in the fields, but in the complacent attitude the slaves had taken on under the direction of the son he knew to be an abolitionist.

First, he roused the field hands at sunrise. Cracking a whip with practiced ease, he faced them, demanding twice the work and threatening "twice the punishment."

No slave at Twin Pines had ever been beaten or mutilated. This new threat of harm puzzled the bondsmen and their wives. "What he gonna do?" a woman whispered to her husband, a field hand, "burn down our corn twiced?"

Hughes bedeviled and puzzled all the field hands for weeks. The stocky man was always there, sometimes stepping out from behind a hoe to catch a lingering field hand the moment he stopped to wipe the sweat off his brow or sit and catch a breath. He had a nose like a hound for trouble, and would walk like the Almighty Himself into the slave quarters to break up a fight. "I'll hang you dead here and now!" Hughes would shout, and they all believed him.

"Mama," Ethan pleaded with his mother, who sat across from him in the parlor wearing a black mourning gown, "it's clear to me that Mr. Hughes is digging gold here, too, not just corn and potatoes."

It disturbed him to witness his mother's lack of good sense when it came to the new overseer. He had seen her as she watched Hughes from the porch, or spoke with him about items that needed to be ordered from town. Ethan did have to give the man credit for one positive change in her behavior: Anna had stopped taking the laudanum. Her slurred speech and memory lapses had become a thing of the past. But was she so relieved not to have to worry about the estate that she was willing to put her faith into such a man? It was enough to make him wish her mind were cloudier. "Father is only a month in the grave," he concluded. "It's a disgrace."

Anna had retained her calm demeanor as she listened to him. She and her son had formed different opinions of Mr. Hughes in his first two weeks of employment at Twin Pines. From a distance, she had kept her eye on the short man, and it was obvious to her that he had taken the situation in hand. He had Charles's spirit and gumption, and had managed to instill a discipline in the bondsmen that had been lacking for many months.

She repeatedly denied the attraction she felt for Hughes, refused to recognize that in his presence she felt unaccountably attractive and youthful. In his own rather unfinished manner, he was a hero and a savior.

Her mind was made up. "Mr. Hughes has never said nor done an ungentlemanly thing," she gently told Ethan. "And I trust him with our plantation until Jacob returns from the war."

"Let me find out more about Mr. Hughes," Ethan insisted, but she waved him away.

"I must write your brother, who, by the way, approves of Mr. Hughes." Anna did not mention that Jacob also wrote that she should watch him like a hawk and never sign anything over to him without Jacob's seeing it first, regardless of the cost or the delay.

* * *

Hughes had his way, and the farm produced more vegetables than in any previous year. The slaves complained, but they always complained, Anna reasoned, in good times and bad. Hughes became a legend. Alex told Clara that some of the field hands believed that the white overseer "Never sleep, never eat, never pee. He just work."

Clara scolded him for listening to such nonsense, but Alex himself began to believe it. The man seemed unnatural in his passion for work, and there was a cruel light in his eyes. More than a few bondsmen called Hughes "de Devil's nephew" behind his back.

One chilly day early in the fall of 1861, one of the field hands, a tall, handsome buck named Arthur, refused to work, saying that his back pained him badly. Hughes did not believe him.

"Get up and out of here, or I'll kick in your door and whip you!" Hughes threatened, pounding on the wood slat door to the field hand's cabin.

None of the hands had yet challenged Mr. Hughes, and Arthur feared being the first. But none of the Parsons had ever doubted Arthur when his back flared up. They had accepted his claim, and even sent poultices for the swelling.

"No, suh," Arthur was bold enough to say. "I sick. Cain't work today. No, suh."

Hughes reared back and kicked in the door with a crash. Seeing the larger man lying on his pallet, Hughes grabbed him by the collar and dragged him into the dusty yard in front of the cabin. The slaves gathered to watch, too frightened to protest, as Hughes picked up his whip from the flower garden where he had laid it. He gave Arthur one last chance to get to the fields. Arthur shook his head, saying nothing.

Hughes shook out the whip and snapped the first blow, stinging Arthur's thigh. The man yelled and scooted away. Hughes hit him again, causing the field hand to topple.

"Get up and take your place in the field!"

Arthur stared at Hughes, who cracked the whip again, wrapping it around the seated man's side.

Ethan was in the library reviewing the ledger when he heard the whip crack. His head had shot up, reddening as the sound of the second blow came to him through the open window. It was the third crack that brought him running through the open passageway to the rear of the house and out the door of the kitchen. He stalked down the path and stood face to face with the overseer, towering over him.

But the overseer stepped around Ethan and drew back the whip, ignoring him. Ethan reached out and firmly grabbed the whip, holding on so that when Hughes snapped his wrist, he nearly broke it. Uttering an oath, he spun and raised his fist.

"Drop it," he told Ethan.

"This is not your plantation, Hughes," Ethan said, retaining his grip on the whip. "You would do well to remember that."

Hughes did not back down. "And it ain't yours! Your mama gave me the right to do as I please, and I please to whip some sense into this boy!"

He jerked the whip again, freeing it from Ethan's grasp. Ethan charged him, but Hughes sidestepped him and stuck out a foot, sending Ethan tumbling in the dust. Furious, he got up and flew back at the man, but Hughes ducked, ramming his head into Ethan's stomach and knocking the breath out of him. Ethan sat on the ground, trying to catch his breath as Hughes calmly drew back the whip and let it fly once again, this time tearing Arthur's shirt. The black rose unsteadily. He had had enough. With the help of two others, he made his way toward the fields.

Hughes did not smile or show any sign of triumph. Instead, he walked over to Ethan and offered his hand.

"An overseer can't never be showed up in front of col-oreds."

The Tyler girls were hungry, and their father was in no mood to hear their whining. "Go marry a rich man," he taunted, "instead of beddin' with some colored from the Parson farm." William Tyler drank so much that his appetite for food had diminished to nothing, sparing him the hunger pangs that plagued his daughters and their mother. With Brett gone to war, and the family unable to hire even a free black, who would work for next to nothing to farm for them, the Tylers had only the girls to farm.

So they lived on potatoes and roots and a chicken once a week. There was no hope of things improving until Brett came home.

Even Dora May, who had faced nothing but hard times since marrying the spoiled, drunken William back in 1839, had seen nothing like it. She had resolved to go to Mrs. Parson and ask for help, but this was an action her husband would not allow.

"I'd sooner starve!" he shouted when she'd hinted about it.

"We *is* starvin'!" Dora May replied. But she had received a broken nose and countless bruises over the years for crossing her husband, and so did not carry through with her threat.

Dora May knew that Sara was meeting the son of the house servants from Twin Pines. One moonlit night she had seen them embrace beside the barn. It had turned her stomach to see her daughter with that nigra. And yet Dora May could not scold her, for what Sara sought in the arms of a colored boy was love and warmth, something no one in the Tyler house was likely to provide.

There seemed to be no solace from their plight. They had no land, no food, and they feared they would soon be surrounded by an enemy even worse than William.

"Stop yer whinin'!" William had snapped at Sara one

evening. "Who d'ya think we are, the chosen people? We Tylers, and nothin' more. This ain't no holy land!"

But the women ignored him, waiting until he fell silent, and in the light of a candle, they sat around the bare kitchen table and softly spoke of Brett. They all agreed that their savior in this world was Brett. They all believed it—the three girls, Dora May, and even William. They prayed for his safe return, for if he were killed, they would have nothing. He had sent but one brief note that only William could decipher. It said:

> Ain't no hero yet but I saved Jacob Parsons neck once. When I git paid I will send money. Look for it.
>   Your son.

The girls and Dora May looked at the letter and reread it every night. It was like scripture, holding out the promise of food and hope to them.

Ethan's plan formed itself so easily that it frightened him. After Hughes shoved him in the dirt, and then tried to act like a gentleman about it, he resolved to leave Twin Pines once and for all. He hated the man, was convinced that he wanted to woo his mother and either wrest control of the plantation from Jacob or assume control if Jacob were killed in the war. Yet every time he broached the subject of Hughes's evil intent, Anna shushed him.

"I will hear no evil spoken of Mr. Hughes," she said time and again, like a refrain. Ethan feared that the man had cast a spell over his mother. And he himself could not undo it.

So he resolved to leave Twin Pines earlier than anticipated, to serve the only just cause he had found and, if need be, to die in the process. One afternoon in late September he rode to Stuart Hall to tell Caitlin of his decision.

As they walked in the formal gardens behind the white Georgian estate, Caitlin kept her eyes on the path beneath her feet. She had known he would leave, had known he would ask her to accompany him. Tears filled her eyes when she finally turned toward him, absorbing the cut of his tall, muscular body, and the pleading look in his blue eyes.

"I cannot leave, Ethan. Not yet." There was the look of disappointment, as she had known it would be. "My work here is still important," she hedged. "Aid such as that which I can provide is vital. There are not many in my position who are willing to help the cause."

He knew there was something else, but the pain in her eyes begged him not to press her, and they walked on in silence.

CHAPTER 23

THE TRAIN WHISTLE blew a lonesome wail, like a dying beast in its last throes. Wearing the gray of a Confederate captain from Virginia, Ethan stepped onto the platform at Manassas Junction under the watchful eyes of a score of soldiers standing there.

"You boys ever sleep?" he asked one of them. The young man, a private with a crooked grin, just shook his head.

"Your orders, Captain?"

Ethan took a deep breath before turning to face a tall, thin corporal.

Reaching inside the pocket of his coat, he withdrew a folded piece of paper and held it toward the officer, who read it under the light of lantern held by his aide. He whistled and handed it back to Ethan. "Thank you, Captain."

Ethan snapped a salute he hoped was correct and requested a horse to ride to General Beauregard's camp.

After some squabbling over who would have to give up his mount for the night, Ethan was handed the reins to a tired mare tied up in a stand of pines beside the station. The corporal pointed the way to camp.

"He's mighty young," one of the soldiers commented.

"So are you, Shelton," snapped the corporal, and conversation hushed.

Ethan rode on the dirt path through the quiet woods to the sound of a hoot owl warning him to turn tail. He hadn't stopped perspiring since the train had pulled out of Charlottesville hours earlier. His first confrontation with authority had gone well, but other challenges faced him. Bone weary from the train ride, he let the gray mare mosey at its own laggard pace, taking in the stars and the cool, clear air.

Just a mile from the train depot, a dark figure jumped into the center of the road and aimed a musket at his head. "Halt! Who goes?"

Ethan's heart leaped into his throat. Regaining his speech, he saluted and introduced himself. "Captain Ethan Palmer, with orders to see General Beauregard." Again he went through the routine, his pulse racing and his palms clammy. But again, he was waved on with a salute.

The first sign of the campfires was a mere flickering in the tall pines, like the ghostly light from a falling star. Then, as he came around a bend in the road, he came upon the vast army encampment itself, its trenches and tents cluttering the hillside. Part of his mission was to estimate enemy strength, but there were more tents and fires than he could ever hope to count. Those figures would have to come from Beauregard's staff, Ethan decided. His own guess could be wildly high or low.

The third sentry post was at the western edge of the army's camp.

"Will the captain require lodgings?" asked the guard. Ethan replied that yes, he wanted a bunk and a tent.

"You will have to share with one of the other officers, sir."

Ethan nodded his assent, stilling the fear that crept

over him. Some of the One Hundred were serving here, he knew. He could easily be discovered and placed under arrest. What if he was shown into Jacob's tent, or that of an officer who knew the Parsons? Discovery by a Char- lottesville boyhood friend could prove devastating, not only testing their sense of duty but forever tarnishing the Parson name throughout the South. People would forget his father and remember only "that Yankee spy caught and hung at Manassas."

Ethan ran grave risks every moment he wore the uni- form of the Confederacy, carrying out his bluff. But he was driven to succeed.

Good fortune shone on him. He was brought into the dusty, cluttered tent of a captain from Georgia who was fast asleep. Quickly stowing his things, Ethan stepped outside the tent. When he asked the guard to direct him to General Beauregard's quarters, the guard pointed out the stone house up the hill.

Ethan walked to the house, which was ablaze with the light of lanterns and candles, and peeked in a window for a split second. He saw a half-dozen men in gray uniforms of varying degrees of decoration looking over a lamp at papers on a long table. Jacob was not among them. To- night might well be his best opportunity to find out where General Johnston planned to strike next. He could get out of the encampment with the morning's light, before an embarrassing and dangerous encounter might occur. Steeling his strength, he walked toward the steps which led up to the front door of the house.

"Parson!" an unfamiliar voice called out. Ethan froze, then turned slowly to face the caller.

The man was an officer from a Mississippi regiment.

"My apologies," the man said, flustered. "You look just like Major Parson from Virginia."

Ethan nodded and smiled. He boldly saluted, walked past the two sentries outside the headquarters building, and opened the heavy oak door to the house.

The small group of men hunched over the map did

not look up to see who had entered. Their conversation was animated and intense.

"I say we hold the high ground here, on the bluffs," the man Ethan took to be General Johnston concluded. He had the moustache and the gamecock jauntiness of the famous warrior. "We move up the guns and wait for the Yankees, holding the higher ground, and also control passage on the Potomac."

The others gave their approval. Standing uncertainly just inside the door, Ethan listened, then moved quietly nearer, trying to get a look at the map. What bluffs? Where?

He stepped closer to the table, staying behind the officer nearest the map, and peeked over the shoulder of the shorter man. The map showed northern Virginia; he recognized Manassas right off. The bluffs appeared to be about twenty miles north, near Leesburg, along the banks of the Potomac. Now the question was, were Confederate troops in place already or were they only en route? Was there time to counteract them? He must find out.

He decided to slip back outside and question the officers.

"Who the hell are you?"

Ethan sucked in a deep breath, spun, and saluted. "Captain Palmer of Virginia, sir!" He prayed that no one recognized him from his previous capture or questioned his resemblances to Jacob. He was well aware that his brother might enter at any moment.

"State your business, Captain." The man was wiry and wore the uniform of a general; he was looking Ethan over closely.

"To serve the Confederacy, sir!" Ethan said with all the bluster he could manage.

General Johnston relaxed. "At ease, son. We're all here with the same Godly end in mind. Who's your commanding officer?"

Ethan had to be careful here. His story could be checked out at any time, and a wrong answer could be the last one he ever gave.

"I serve with Major Parson of the Nineteenth Vir-

ginia, sir!" Sweat rolled down Ethan's face. He said a
silent prayer, asking for mercy.

"Good officer," Johnston said to one of the older men
beside him. "Thick in the seat but well liked. What brings
you here?"

"The major seeks a more active role in counsel," Ethan
blurted out. It was all that came to mind. If Jacob got wind
of this tonight, Ethan would be a marked man before he
even left the encampment.

To Ethan's surprise, Johnston and his advisors chuckled. "Oh, he does, does he?" the general said. "Well, tell
him the next time we get into battle to try to stay with
his standard and lead his men instead of riding off to
Timbuktu! Tell him to take counsel with his brigadier
general, son. That's how it's done in the army." All the
officers roared with laughter, and Ethan smiled uneasily,
unsure of how to respond.

"Well?" Johnston asked. "Nothing more? Dismissed!"
Ethan stood at attention but did not yield. He had to
discover the location of the bluffs. "Sir, the Major re-
quests an active role in the action at the bluffs."

This request took Johnston by surprise. His bushy
eyebrows lifted, and his smile faded quickly. "What on
God's earth would I do with another virgin regiment at
Ball's Bluff? Get the hell out of here, Captain! Now!"

"Yessir!" Ethan saluted and left hastily, forgetting to
make a military turn as he spun. The room was eerily
quiet as he shut the door.

Outside in the cool night air, he heaved a sigh and
stepped past the sentries, shaking.

"Back home the sky goes from blue to red to black in
twenty minutes," one sentry bragged to the other young
man.

"Sunset ain't no race," the other replied in a south
Georgia drawl.

Ethan escaped to the shelter of a stand of pine trees,
not two hundred feet from Johnston's headquarters, and
sat at the trunk of one. He almost did not believe his good
fortune.

Another man, a young private, joined him, offering a smoke. Ethan declined.

"Lot on your mind, sir?" the boy asked.

He wore neither cap nor gun. Ethan judged he couldn't be more than sixteen, and was thin as a rail.

"When they gonna attack again?"

Ethan shrugged. He must say or do nothing that could reveal him in any way. This unlikely-looking hero could know Jacob.

"I never fought before," the boy went on, spitting tobacco out of the cigarette he had rolled. "I hunted coon and rabbit back home in Valdosta, but it ain't the same. Been there, sir?"

Ethan shook his head.

"My daddy's got a farm there. Pigs and hens, cows, corn, onions, and tomatoes the size of your head. Big sky down there. I get hemmed in by these mountains up Virginia way."

Ethan was tempted to shoo the boy away, but he feared arousing attention. And the boy's words were touching. He turned his eyes anxiously to the stone house, but all seemed quiet.

"Where you from, sir?" the boy asked.

Ethan did not want to give away much. "These parts."

"A Virginian? It's right pretty. You got a lot to be proud of." His voice cracked. He was just going through puberty, Ethan realized. The boy was homesick and surely younger than he'd first thought. Ethan yearned to take him by the shoulders and say, "It's okay, son. You're probably going to live through this and get home to your mother." But he could not say that or anything more than he had to. Because if he relaxed—if he were to be himself for only an instant—he might let slip something that would reveal his mission. Ethan was on guard with each gesture and word.

"Beauregard somethin', ain't he? He looks like a general, huh? Second in command now to General Johnston, they say."

Ethan nodded.

"I didn't know about the women. I thought the soldiers cooked and did the washin' and such." Ethan wondered if the boy knew of the other services some of the camp followers provided, like sex for money.

"But they ain't for me. I promised my mamma I'd stay pure till I get home."

"Good for you," Ethan said softly. He kept his face in the shadows and turned away from the boy so that even if he wanted to tell somebody about their conversation, he would not be able to describe the officer he spoke to, other than to say he was a tall, husky Virginian who didn't talk much and refused a smoke.

"War ain't what you think, is it, sir?" the boy asked. A falling star made a dying arc overhead, and Ethan followed the fleeting arc sadly. "I figured to face a Yank and call on him and plug him, but I didn't see nothin' but smoke. Cain't shoot smoke."

Ethan was startled by the passing of two soldiers. The men glanced at them, but did not pause. They were arguing about poker, from what Ethan could hear, and who owed what. Their laughter trailed as they walked down the hill in the direction of Bull Run.

"Most I want is to do myself proud and be a man, like my daddy. He died in Mexico."

The boy was stirring up emotions he could not afford to awaken, not now. Ethan knew it was time to move. He got up and brushed off his pants before waving goodbye.

"Good talkin' at you, sir!" the boy called. Ethan left him smoking a cigarette under the pine. That boy belonged behind a plow in Valdosta, Georgia. Damn war, Ethan cursed softly to himself as he walked away. He was all the more committed to getting this information to the Keyeses as soon as possible and to doing whatever he could to ensure a Union victory with all possible speed.

It was unlikely that he could gain any more useful information, especially in the daylight, when more men would be up and about. Any of the One Hundred, or Jacob himself, could spot him. Jacob had made it clear:

Treason was inexcusable. If Jacob caught him in the uniform of a Confederate officer now, Ethan would hang.

He must leave and ride to Washington with what he knew, hoping that the information was vital. Perhaps Lincoln already knew about the batteries and men being moved to Ball's Bluff. But if not, Ethan would be there to tell him.

He requisitioned a horse from the corral, saying that General Beauregard himself had approved the act, and was saddled and mounted in ten minutes. Judging by the moon, which was high in the sky, it was just after midnight. He would reach Washington before morning—or not at all.

Jacob stirred in his sleep. He awoke bathed in perspiration and trembling as if from great effort, but could not recall any details of the dream. It had something to do with a battle—there had been smoke and the boom of cannons. He felt the familiar fear and wondered yet again, Can I do this? Am I a leader of men at war?

No divine answer would show itself. Jacob sat up and placed his stockinged feet on the bare earth. He stood and opened the tent flap. No burning bush. There were only the silhouettes of tents and trees against the flickering light from the fires. Unlike Moses, he would have to wait for another, and probably subtler, sign. Would he guide his men and inspire them next time in battle? Or would he panic and ride to safety, or simply fail to organize and lead his men? His fellow officers all said conflict was looming and would surely take place before winter, when bitter weather made a Yankee assault unlikely.

His father would have known, with unswerving conviction, how he would perform even before his first battle. Soon, Jacob would face his second, and he still was unsure whether or not he possessed the necessary courage. Only time—and the Yankees—would tell.

He found it impossible to go back to sleep, and lay awake in bed recalling every detail of daily life at Twin Pines. He knew exactly what the fields looked like now, with the corn harvested and the squash and pumpkins ripening. The earth would be a vivid red now in the early light as dawn inched over the horizon. Soon, Clara would rise and build a fire in the kitchen.

Then Jacob thought of his father, always an early riser. But his father was dead and buried. The sunrise would shine not upon the old man's weathered face but only upon his grave. He thought about obtaining a leave from Johnston or Beauregard. He could be back at Twin Pines in a little more than a day. He could see his family and visit his father's grave.

But duty required his presence. He ought to get to know his men better, to drill them, and to practice the art of war, as much to satisfy himself as to help them. Besides, he found Beauregard unsympathetic and distant, as the general's hero, Napoleon, must have been. What did he care for the sorrows of one officer in an army of thirty thousand men?

Jacob rested and waited uneasily for reveille. Perhaps the music of the bugle would raise his spirits and inspire a more martial spirit. At the very least, the new day demanded much attention and effort, and for those demands on his mental and physical reservoirs of energy, Jacob was grateful. He said a brief prayer and closed his eyes.

He had just fallen asleep, the burning emerald eyes of Julia Keyes smiling upon him, when the bugler blew the first notes.

Ethan rode unchallenged on the road to Washington, the scene of the grotesque retreat of the Union army two months before, which the Southern press had dubbed "The Great Skedaddle." As the light of day broke in a thin line over the horizon, Ethan spurred the horse, wondering when he should stop to take off the Confederate uniform. Before long, it could get him shot.

Around a bend in the road where the Potomac was out of sight to the east, Ethan found his way blocked by a pair of men in blue. Pointing muskets at him, they demanded to know his business.

Ethan knew they would never believe the truth, but it was his only hope. "I have word of the enemy's movements for Mr. Lincoln," he told them.

One of the men hooted. "So you're Mr. Lincoln's man at Manassas, huh?" he sneered. "Must be a mighty burden to bear, the fate of the Union on your shoulders and all."

His companion roared with laughter, almost dropping his gun. Then, snapping the body upright, he leveled his musket at Ethan and ordered, "Get down off that horse. Now!"

Ethan judged the odds of convincing these soldiers that he worked for Lincoln's intelligence agents to be about one thousand to one. The look in their eyes was murderous. He had to act quickly. Letting out a wild yell, he spurred the horse and made her rear. As the pair of soldiers parted to avoid the kicking hooves, he hunkered down and kicked her past them. Slipping to the side, he grabbed the saddle horn in one hand and hid under the belly of the galloping beast. Two shots rang out. Both missed, raising dust along the road behind him. He barely heard their oaths over the thundering hooves and kept the mare at a gallop until he was safely out of range. Slowing the horse, he got back on top and began to peel off the Confederate uniform.

From there Ethan rode undisturbed to the southern edge of Washington, where he was met by a Union patrol just after dawn. They detained him, questioning him at length. Eventually he was accompanied through muddy streets smelling of sewage to a warehouse that had been converted to military quarters near the commercial center at Seventh Street. By noon, the Keyeses were contacted, and an audience with Lincoln himself was arranged.

Ethan was uncertain of the purity of the Keyeses motives and still torn to be in their employ, but he could not suppress his excitement as their carriage rolled to a halt in front of the White House.

Daddy must be rolling in his grave, Ethan thought as he gazed at the impressive structure, gray in the afternoon light.

He had been reading Lincoln's speeches since his debate with Stephen Douglas in 1858. Like many of the young men who had been his acquaintances at Harvard, Ethan reasoned that the new Republican party, which owed few favors to anyone, might be the best hope of sensibly settling the issues of secession and slavery. Now, it seemed, such issues were beyond settlement, except upon the battlefield. But Ethan still longed to meet Mr. Lincoln, whose wisdom he had admired for the three years Ethan had followed his progress.

"This old place needs a good coat of paint," Jeffrey said, noticing Ethan's preoccupation with the shabby appearance of the home of the United States' president.

"It was burned to the ground in eighteen fourteen," Julia added, looking up at the balcony overhanging the first floor.

"I know," Ethan said. He regarded her serious face in exasperation. "I have studied history on the university level, you know."

He realized, of course, that the man he was about to meet was his family's greatest enemy. And Ethan's intent was not to challenge the man or to hurt him, as his father would have demanded, but instead to pay him homage.

"Don't be frightened, old boy," Jeffrey said, tossing an arm around Ethan and leading him between the pillars and up to the door where a large contingent of militiamen in baggy red pants stood guard. One of them checked their papers and then passed them through the entrance.

Their footsteps echoed on the floor. As they followed one of the guards, Julia took Ethan's arm and whispered, "What you are doing could save a thousand lives. Maybe more. Keep that in mind."

He tried to thank her, for that was his motive—to shorten the war and ensure that slavery died with the fa

of the Confederacy. He wanted the fall to be as fast and
gentle as possible, but he now recognized that the South
must lose the war and be torn asunder. A moral impera-
tive dictated the collapse of the union of slave states.
Ethan prayed that it would occur soon, before too many
young men on both sides died.

They entered a foyer with a curving marble staircase
and a ceiling as high as a cathedral's spire. A black man
in formal attire appeared to take their coats, and led them
to a couch beside the bottom of the stairs.

"The president will send for you shortly," he told them
before disappearing with their wraps.

Jeffrey peeled off his white gloves. "I wonder who will
be there. Hay? Seward? What do you think?"

Julia's eyes, too, shone with anticipation, glittering like
emeralds. When her brother stood to greet a Union officer
who passed, she bent near Ethan and asked, "How is
our brother? Well, I trust."

Ethan was taken aback; he did not know what to say.
Should he tell the story of Jacob's rescue and pardon? "He
is well. A major at Manassas. Bull Run, the Yankees call
it."

She smiled. "I'm well aware of what we call it."

Another black manservant came down the stairs and
asked them to follow. Ethan's heart pounded in his chest,
pushing against his ribs and lungs.

At the top of the stairs, the trio followed the tall black
man to a door at the end of the hall. They halted as he
rapped and entered, announcing them.

Julia kept a tight grip on Ethan's arm as they entered
the parlor where the president greeted visitors. He saw
no one resembling Mr. Lincoln, but a heavyset young
captain wearing eyeglasses approached them. Shaking
their hands, he introduced himself as Captain Lyons, then
led the party into an office, where survey maps of Virginia
and Maryland were spread upon a large table.

Bent over one of the maps with his back to them was
the president. Lincoln wasn't quite as extraordinary in
appearance as Ethan had expected. The president turned

to greet them, casting sad, deep-set eyes upon them, and the lines of a smile formed upon his pale face. Ethan glimpsed the giant, just over six feel tall, with a gangly, awkward build. He felt small as he extended his hand and the president took it; Lincoln's hand wrapped almost completely around his own. His were surprisingly smooth hands for a rail splitter.

Lincoln urged them to take a seat and dismissed the half-dozen officers who were in attendance.

"I am shopping for a general to win this year," Lincoln told them with a sad smile. His voice was higher than Ethan had expected it to be, with the lilt of backwoods Kentucky in it. His blue eyes were underscored by dark circles. "Too many Indians and two few chiefs is just as bad as the other way around."

After inquiring about their health, the president turned his attention to Ethan.

"So you are the brave young man we are all indebted to. Thanks to the information you provided, we have rushed a reconnaissance force to Ball's Bluff, led by Colonel Edward Baker. We expect his report in a matter of days."

"Bravo, Mr. President!" Jeffrey exclaimed. "That is grand news!"

Lincoln shook his head. "No, that is no news at all," he said soberly. "A positive result, on the other hand, that would be news. I am inclined to give McClellan a free hand, though it concerns me that the general is most familiar with the war in the west, while we here in Washington face the Confederate capital only a hundred miles away. But I reckon he knows what he is doing." Once again he faced Ethan. "Now tell me about yourself, young man. Where are you from? Have you any brothers in the war?"

Under the gaze of the president and his companion, Ethan explained with honesty the uncomfortable position in which the war had placed him, concluding, "I must either betray myself or my family." He lowered his head and was surprised to feel a powerful grip on his shoulder a second later.

"Son, you did not betray anyone. When this war ends, and I trust in God that it will end soon, there will come a day when your family will understand. There will come another day when they will approve. We must all pray to live that long."

Ethan felt blessed to be so addressed by Mr. Lincoln. He could find no words to express his gratitude, and his eyes filled with tears as he imagined that great day of public and private reconciliation.

"I'm certain you are correct, Mr. President," Jeffrey said in order to fill the awkward silence.

Lincoln soon showed them to the door, promising to send a messenger to them to relay news from Ball's Bluffs. "Beware out there," he warned them all in mock seriousness. "Spies abound!"

Squeezing past the officers who waited in the parlor outside Lincoln's office, they were soon outside in the warm October sunshine. As they walked to their waiting carriage, with the crisp sweet odor of firewood in the air and the world polished by the newborn hope Ethan felt in his heart, he almost broke into a jig. He now had the highest confirmation that he was honorable. He swore an oath of loyalty to Mr. Lincoln and prayed that his family might one day be reunited in love, and that his name on their lips would be spoken with pride and compassion.

They paid no attention to the cab which had followed them and waited on Fourteenth Street as they opened the door and entered.

CHAPTER 24

A CHILLY FALL rain cast a shroud over the autumn day, and the Keyeses and Ethan had settled into the parlor for tea when they were notified by an army courier that despite Ethan's information, Colonel Baker had blundered badly, walking into a Confederate trap. He and several of his men had been killed.

The death of Colonel Baker, a United States senator raised a storm of protest in Northern newspapers; the *New York Tribune* called for an attack on Richmond President Lincoln's first response was to call for more than a hundred thousand new volunteers; his second, to back General McClellan's cautious stance.

Jeffrey was furious about the news. "With the information Ethan gave them, Baker and his men should have surprised the rebels and wiped them out!" he exclaimed over their dinner of veal and potatoes. "Now people are beginning to believe that one rebel can outfight ten Yankees. It's a dangerous attitude to foster. I agree with the *Tribune*. It foments delay and procrastination when we should be advancing upon Richmond like Napoleon army!"

"We?" Ethan asked cryptically. "Have you an army in your drawing room?"

Jeffrey ignored his sarcasm. "One more such fooli maneuver, and we shall never free the slaves!" he seethe

Ethan looked over at Jeffrey's ruffled red hair and disgruntled face. It was when he said such things with genuine passion that Ethan almost forgave his dandy friend for being haughty and supercilious. For Keyes had been one passion: the abolition of slavery in the United States

Jeffrey was in danger, too, for his face and house were well known to Southern agents who would like nothing more than to injure the fast-talking, self-assured young man from Boston.

Ethan found himself drawn to confide in Julia, who possessed all the character attributes hailed in a man yet often feared or demeaned in a woman. She was invariably well informed, sympathetic, wise, and supportive. However, unlike most men, she was also kind and gentle. She passed hours counseling Ethan. In their talks, Julia asked about Jacob, and this curiosity and concern for her brother surprised him. With the war a reality, as was evidenced by the rise of the price of cotton to twenty cents a pound, how could she imagine that she and Jacob would ever meet again? Why would such a sensible being hang on to a dream that would never come true in her lifetime?

Yet she did, or seemed to, and whenever he spoke of Twin Pines, Julia would listen, fascinated. She asked probing questions that often had little to do with slavery and much to do with Jacob Parson.

Word came in November of 1861 that Ethan would soon be sent on another mission, most likely to Kentucky, to scout General Johnston's position near Paducah. Could he hold the bluffs? Would he be flanked easily? How many troops did he really have? President Lincoln was losing faith in Pinkerton, whose reports to General McClellan consistently inflated the size of enemy forces, thus discouraging aggressive action on the part of the North. Lincoln wanted a pair of eyes there he could trust and, as he put it, "a man who can add two and two and get four." He put trust in Ethan, whose information concerning Ball's Bluffs had been accurate, despite the poor result of Baker's mission.

Ethan had traveled the eastern United States extensively, but had never been west of Virginia. Kentucky was foreign to him, though he knew of course that both Jefferson Davis and Lincoln had been born there.

He thought of Caitlin, too. It ran against his better judgment to move farther away from her than he was already. In Washington, there was some chance that she would join him, but now she could not do so, were she to undergo a change of spirit, until his mission was completed, perhaps months later. His nights were spent in sleepless agitation.

A shadow fell across the lamplight illuminating Ethan's desk, and he looked up from the tract he was writing to find Jeffrey standing behind him.

"What is it, Jeffrey?"

Disappointment was evident in his face as he revealed that Ethan would not be sent to Kentucky. "The president feels that as a native of Virginia, you are too valuable here, where the war may very well be decided."

Ethan let out a rebel yell that startled Jeffrey and brought Julia up the stairs from the parlor. Taking her in his arms, he led her in a jig around the room as she and Jeffrey exchanged glances of confusion.

"My friend," Jeffrey said, a note of amusement in his voice, "I wonder if you shall ever decide whether or not you want to be a hero."

Soon Ethan could think of nothing but returning to see Caitlin and marrying her, George Stuart be damned. He wrote her as much, and late in November received her reply, which he opened with trembling hands:

> My Dearest Ethan,
> My heart and my prayers go out to you. Yes, yes, yes! I will marry you, wherever and whenever you choose. I can no longer hide my feelings from Daddy, not when each moment is so precious and time so short.
> Daddy grows more bitter each day. I heard a terrible howling from the slave quarters last week and found a man staked to the ground and branded on the calf. He would not tell me who did the terrible deed, but I suspect Daddy's overseer. I confronted him, but he refused to answer my inquiries. Daddy leaves the room when I bring up the subject. Even here in my own home there is no respite and no reform. The institution must

*be abolished or it will linger and taint us all for another
generation or more.*

   *My beloved, I trust your judgment. I shall be here,
I am and shall always be yours.*

                                            Caitlin

After rereading the letter twice, he told Jeffrey and
Julia that he must be excused from service for a week.

"Why?" Jeffrey asked. "Have you lost your nerve
again?"

Ethan ignored his comment, unable to stop smiling.
"Caitlin and I are to be married!"

Julia hugged Ethan and kissed him on the cheek. "Does
her father approve?"

"He doesn't know," he replied. "We may be forced to
elope. Perhaps we'll honeymoon at the White House. Can
you arrange it with Abe?"

Laughing, Julia again congratulated Ethan. But when
he expressed his wish to pack and leave for Charlottesville
immediately, she counseled caution. "Remember, Ethan,
you are a known Southern agent. Your face may be on
posters. You cannot ride the train into the heart of the
enemy's country—"

"But it is my home!" he shouted, red-faced.

"No longer." Jeffrey stood to confront him. "You have
no home, not until this damn war is over. You are an
orphan, Ethan. Surely you understand that by now?"

The rage left Ethan in a moment of insight: Jeffrey
was right. Now that he had met Mr. Lincoln and all but
sworn an oath to aid the North, he had no home. It was
a chilling revelation, and he collapsed heavily into a chair
as it struck him full force.

Quickly going to him, Julia knelt beside Ethan and
took his hand softly in hers. "My brother is too stern."

Ethan slowly shook his head. "No, he is correct to be
blunt. We can't dance around every issue affecting my
work. The fact is, my brother might well be forced to
hang me. It is possible," he added when she began to
protest. "Unlikely, but possible in this war."

She wisely left him in the gathering gloom of the evening, leaving him to his thoughts. But that night as she lay in her bed, she listened for him, determined not to let him go until he was properly prepared with papers and a different identity.

It took Jeffrey two days to acquire identification for Ethan, who was now to call himself Arvil Pearson, a textbook salesman from Maryland who would be traveling to Charlottesville and the university.

"Thank God you don't have that corn-pone accent some of your friends do," Jeffrey told him, pulling textbooks into a carpetbag. "These are the tools of your new trade. Carry them proudly. If anyone asks, don't be shy about showing them, but don't be too obvious, either. And regardless of what happens—even if Jacob points you out—never admit to being Ethan Parson! Understood?"

Ethan gladly registered the warnings. He was fully aware of the foolishness of his personal mission. Julia and Jeffrey spent an hour warning him against virtually every customary act. "If you see someone who knows you—and you *must* see them first—turn away. Duck into a room, turn a corner, anything . . . but get away!"

"No false whiskers?" Ethan jested. But they did not laugh.

"Speak when spoken to," Julia cautioned. "If you meet someone from Maryland, tell them about your travels up the eastern seaboard. Don't allow yourself to be pinned down on where you were born or grew up. The friendly fellow across from you on the train could be an agent as well, working for Mr. Davis. Say as little as you can without appearing uncivil."

"Stop only to rest the horses, and if ordered to do so by the military. Stop for nothing and no one else!"

"I shall miss your assistance with the tracts I am writing," Julia added at his leave-taking. "Your help has been most valuable to me." She paused, eyes downcast, then added, "Please give my best to your family."

Ethan embraced each of them. They had given him a

good sum of cash and a letter of credit for emergency use. "Just in case you are forced to flee to Europe or Canada," Jeffrey said. He started to say something more, but Julia put her finger to his lips.

"We shall meet again. Godspeed."

"Don't do anything stupid," Jeffrey added, a grin on his face.

Ethan thanked them both again before slipping out the door and into the chill of the late-November night.

He found the journey to be exceedingly pleasant. While his guard was always up, Ethan found time to relish the stark beauty of the countryside as winter came upon them again. He made his way without difficulty across the Potomac to Alexandria and to the carriage that would carry him to Charlottesville. Mist hung like ghosts in the trees and along the riverbanks, and at dawn the mountains turned a pale blue that was barely discernible. The discomfort of travel—the noise, the hard wooden seats, the smoke—was nothing compared to the sights.

As he had expected, there were soldiers at every town. And from the windows of the carriage he saw plenty of men marching and lounging in camps. The threat he had felt in Washington dissipated somewhat, and he almost relaxed as the carriage he had hired left Alexandria.

Manassas was buzzing with soldiers; they were everywhere, inspecting bags and faces with great care. The officer who inspected Ethan's carriage looked him over but asked no questions. He seemed bored by the procedure. Ethan remained still, allowing himself to breathe only as the carriage jerked to a start, leaving the vast Confederate army behind. For once, he gave little thought to his brother. Instead his mind was focused upon Caitlin and the happiness they would share. The sun soon rose, and its rays, weak but warming, hit his face like a promising kiss. He had the strong sense that his trip was blessed.

In the solitude granted him by the journey, Ethan settled into an uneasy calm that belied the turmoil

swirling inside him. Caitlin had said she would defy her
father, but he knew that arrogant bastard would put up
a fight, and it wouldn't be a fair one, either. With a deep
sigh, he looked out the small open window at the pale
brown earth and the leafless trees sweeping by, as if in a
sad, dizzying dream.

Laying his head back, he shut his eyes for a moment,
imagining Caitlin in a bridal gown. The sight pleased him.

CHAPTER 25

ETHAN DESCENDED FROM the carriage at the familiar brick
train station in Charlottesville. For the first time since he
could remember, Old Jim was nowhere in sight. Things
had changed. With a brief look to reassure himself that
there were no familiar faces, he walked around the corner
to a stable, where he hoped to rent a buggy. Ethan was
relieved to discover that the owner was new to the town.
He had moved from Orange when the Confederate army
bought all his horses at what he called "prices I wouldn't
offer a man of color without hidin' my face in shame."

The stable owner had no carriages, but he found a
horse he would let Ethan lease for five dollars a day, an
outrageous sum, plus a fifty-dollar deposit. That took
most of Ethan's cash, but he had the letter of credit in
reserve.

Storing his bags alongside the saddle, he mounted the
tame brown mare. And as he set off down the road to
Twin Pines, he learned immediately why Jeff Davis had
passed up the mare; she plodded along as if each step
might be her last. Ethan sighed with frustration as he
eased himself into her slow pace.

The eight-mile journey to Twin Pines was filled with

new sights. Some of the smaller farms had fallen fallow, apparently left untended by sons gone to war. Ethan passed few men, either young or old; they were all in uniform. He felt the women looking at him with accusation in their eyes, and he understood. With their sons and husbands and brothers in uniform, why was Ethan not with them? In the big, wide-brimmed hat and heavy coat he wore, no one seemed to recognize him, and he was careful to keep his eyes lowered as much as possible.

As he came to the site of his confrontation with the fire-eaters of nearly a year earlier, the New Year's Eve when he might very well have been killed, Ethan was overcome by a strong sense of place. It was as if roots buried deep within the earth snaked up and grabbed hold of him.

Mixed emotions of fear, love, and regret overwhelmed him as he rode the last two miles to the farm. What were the feelings of his mother and Martha toward him? How much had Jacob told them?

It was midafternoon when he rode over the rise and caught sight of the white frame house on the hill. Passing the scattered farm buildings at a slow walk, he saw several field hands trimming trees and carrying brush; they showed no interest in him. The house looked grand and unchanged. As he rode nearer, however, he could see that the trim needed painting, and the windows rattled too freely in the brisk November wind.

No one was there to greet Ethan when he arrived at the scene. Where is Alex? he wondered. Jumping off the mare, he tied her to the fence in front of the house. After taking one last glance around the ground, Ethan opened the gate, walked to the front door, and went inside.

At the sound of the door opening, Alex appeared through the open walkway from the rear of the house. His dark face took on a frown when he saw the unexpected visitor, but in the next second he broke into a wide smile.

"Well, I be!" he cried, delighted. "Come in, Mister

Ethan!" He started to call out, but Ethan put a finger to his lips.

"Let me surprise them, Alex. Are you and Clara and Thomas well?"

Alex grinned. "We fine, sir. Yo' mama in the parlor with Miss Martha and Mr. Hughes."

Ethan frowned. This was the first he knew of Hughes's being admitted so freely into the Parson home, and it did not please him. He looked at Alex for some further explanation, but his stern black face shed no clue as to how Twin Pines was faring under the direction of the overseer. Throwing off his hat and coat, Ethan dashed into the parlor.

The trio had been playing whist, and his entrance had jarred Martha from her concentration.

"Ethan!" Martha cried. Jumping from her chair, she ran into his arms and kissed him repeatedly on the cheek. She was as lovely as ever in a blue gown he recognized from the year before, but she was pale and thinner than he remembered.

Anna rose slowly, excusing herself from Mr. Hughes's presence as Ethan turned to embrace her. She smelled of cinnamon and honey, and wore a gown of gray trimmed with white lace, rather than mourning clothes. Over her shoulder he saw Hughes's face. He looked smug and at ease, as though he were used to spending time in the house, and he was regarding Ethan with a disapproving scowl.

Anna gestured toward him, including Hughes in their reunion. "You remember Mr. Hughes."

Repressing the revulsion he felt for the man, Ethan extended his hand. Hughes was slow to rise, and when he did, he clasped Ethan's hand weakly and briefly. Ethan no longer denied the sensation that this man despised him. "Is there no work to be done today, then?" Ethan asked Hughes.

He looked to Anna first, as if wondering whether an explanation was due Ethan, and after she nodded, said "The Lord counsels resting on the seventh day."

"Are you a religious man, then, Mr. Hughes?"

Looking quickly from her son to Mr. Hughes, Anna intervened. "Mr. Hughes has worked the hands very hard the last few weeks, well after dark. Today is their reward, a day off."

"And what price have they been made to pay for this respite? I trust none of the field hands has been mistreated?" he asked his mother.

She lowered her eyes. "Not to my knowledge."

"No bondsman working at Twin Pines has received unjust punishment," Hughes asserted.

Ethan bristled, clenching his fists. Had his mother and sister not been present, he might well have challenged Hughes then and there. His mere presence galled Ethan, but he kept his peace. After all, if he himself had undertaken the responsibility, rather than leave Twin Pines, Hughes would never have set foot in their house.

"We are so surprised—and so pleased to have you home!" Anna exclaimed, perhaps a bit too enthusiastically. Ringing for Alex, she asked him to bring them some sherry. They took seats, Hughes and Ethan in chairs which rested at either end of the sofa, where Anna and Martha sat.

In the moment before Alex arrived, bearing a tray with four glasses and a decanter of sherry, an awkward silence settled over them.

"Did you have a pleasant journey?" Martha asked, seeking to fill the deepening void between them.

In different circumstances Ethan might well have burst out laughing at the forced quality of her voice and manner. But the state of affairs turned his stomach; he was a stranger in his own home. Before the others had been served, he reached for a glass and drained it. Hughes clearly disapproved of the breach in etiquette, as well as of Ethan's past and his sudden arrival. He took deliberate caution in handing the small glasses to Anna and Martha before serving himself. They waited uneasily.

"I should like to propose a toast," Martha began.

Cutting her off, Hughes said, "To the Union!" raising

his glass high. From the side of his eye, he watched Ethan for his reaction.

Ethan sat stonily, still holding his empty glass and staring straight ahead. However, Hughes pressed him, asking directly what his sentiments were.

"My sentiments?" Ethan repeated, surveying the man critically. "In my own home, you ask me a question you have no right to ask and expect an answer? It is you who should answer for your behavior."

"I am no spy!" Hughes shouted, jumping to his feet. The sherry in his glass spilled onto the rug, but Hughes seemed not to notice.

In the tense seconds which passed, with Ethan squaring off against Hughes, the overseer saw the collapse of all his carefully laid plans. He could not back down from a fight with Anna's son. Yet to beat the boy and risk losing her trust and affection would be a grave error.

He had arrived at Twin Pines with nothing, and in only a few months he had come to within an arm's length of a pot of gold and the Parson woman's hand to boot.

There *was* an obstacle: Her sons stood in the way— both the coward who waved a fist in his face now and the loyal buffoon off at Manassas whom he had yet to meet. He had to win them over or force them out the door with Anna's assent.

Ethan stood, glowering at the smaller man. "And I am not on trial. This is my house, Hughes. You are nothing but a hired whip!"

Hughes would not back down. "This house belongs to Miss Anna while Mister Jacob is away! Ain't one inch of it's yours!"

"Frank, hush now. And, Ethan, you be quiet, too. Please! Isn't this war providing enough fighting for all of us?" Anna looked anxiously from one man to the other, but the square-off continued. Taking a deep breath, she spoke sternly to the overseer. "Frank, you had best go now. Ethan is my son, and I wish to spend time with him. Go on."

Hughes paused a full five seconds before setting his

glass on the table and excusing himself. When he slammed
the door the walls shook.

"Does he come to the house every afternoon?" Ethan
asked. Anna did not reply, but looked into her sherry
glass.

Martha swallowed the last of her sherry with an audible gulp. "Did you hear about Ball's Bluff? Isn't it grotesque? All this death and dying, and people call it a
victory!"

"Wasn't what grotesque? That three rebels were killed,
or six Yankees or two thousand men, like at Manassas?
Martha, it's terrible every moment, this war, and we don't
help by prolonging it with this interminable waiting. Do
you understand that? We have to make peace now, by
any means."

Their mother looked at him in shock. "What do you
propose?"

Ethan shrugged his shoulders. In that moment he
could not tell her what he really prayed for: The dissolution of the Confederacy and the end of slavery, which
gave power to sadistic brutes such as Hughes. "A peace
conference between Davis and Lincoln, I suppose."

"Mama says Jeff Davis is flawed and Lincoln is bloodthirsty," Martha chimed.

Ethan's face turned red. "I have met Mr. Lincoln, and
he is no more bloodthirsty than Christ Himself," he said
quietly.

Anna gasped at the blasphemy. "Ethan!" she cried.
Standing, she fled the room in tears.

Ethan stood to follow her, but Alex blocked the door,
scowling.

"Let her be, Mister Ethan," he said.

Ethan saw that he was right. He should not have blas-
phemed. Returning to the parlor, he saw that Martha had
poured them both another glass of sherry, which he took
gratefully. As he drank, he realized the significance of her
gesture. Dazed, he set down the glass and gazed at her;
he wanted to at least establish a connection with his
younger sister, but he could not speak as he wanted to,

so great was his frustration. "The war isn't turning you into a Tyler, is it?"

Her nostrils flared, and the look in her blue eyes was colder than the air outside. "You have a way with words tonight, Ethan. Just what do you mean?"

"I am sorry. It was in bad taste. I was just wondering if you often drink two glasses of sherry at one sitting."

"I've drunk more," she said with pride.

"When? Where was Mama?"

"Here. With me and Mrs. Hughes."

Ethan was aghast that they would sanction her drinking spirits in such excess. What had come over his mother? Was she so struck by that banty-rooster Hughes that she was blind to her daughter's dangerous habits? "Well, don't do it anymore. You're too young for alcohol."

He could no longer dream of Twin Pines without Hughes butting into the picture. The snake was an integral part of their lives. Lord, if something happened to Jacob, he thought with horror, Hughes might well run the place.

"Where do you stand with Hughes? Do you get along with him?"

Martha stood and crossed to the fireplace, where she gazed pensively into the blazing fire. "He's a good man. Quiet. Says what he means. He treats me nicely."

Martha did not mention to Ethan that Frank Hughes was cruel to the bondsmen, driving them too hard and forgiving not the slightest oversight or violation. He had even scolded Alex for talking to his son before Thomas's quitting time.

Keeping her gaze fixed on the fire, she would not look at Ethan directly, for she was angry with him. He had abandoned their mother and her. All the men had abandoned them with never a thought to their loneliness, but only of the war, the everlasting war. Since his and Jacob's departure, she had found herself lonely for attention. And if her brothers weren't there to provide it, at least Mr Hughes was. Recently he had begun treating her with kindness, as if he were a distant uncle trying to make amends for years of silence.

Yet a voice within Martha told her not to trust the man. This warning she would not share with Ethan, not yet. But there was something in Hughes's eyes when he looked at her mother—when she turned her head and reached for a teapot or her needlework—that frightened her. It was the look of a wild dog entering the henhouse late at night. Whatever she had read of romance and courtship, and what she had seen in her almost twenty years, convinced her that Hughes was not a nobleman disguised as a Gypsy vagabond, but the heartless, grasping Gypsy himself. Hughes frightened her, and she worried for her mother, who responded more to his wiles each day.

Ethan watched her back with interest. It was new, this determined set to her back and shoulders—there was more to it than a spoiled demand for attention. She would not tell him anything more. Yet his nagging fears would not relent. "I don't trust him, Martha. And you shouldn't, either. Mama's . . . she's not herself now, with Daddy gone. You have to help her."

She turned to face him, and in the light, her young beauty was spectacular. She glowed. "How? By doing what, exactly?"

"Don't let her get any closer to him. Keep him at arm's length. Watch him, whatever he does, and tell Jacob."

"Write him, you mean. We don't know when he's coming home."

"Yes, of course. I know."

Apparently she had heard nothing from Jacob of their encounter at Manassas. He hoped it would remain so. There was enough sadness at Twin Pines. But his visit was meant to change that, he reminded himself. "I came to marry Caitlin," he confided.

Martha's face shone with joy. "That's wonderful! Will you live here or at Stuart Hall? I will so enjoy having Caitlin as a sister-in-law!"

She broke off, glimpsing a hesitation in her brother's manner. "What is it, Ethan? Are you in trouble?"

"Martha, I doubt that Caitlin and I can live here once we marry."

"You mean at Twin Pines?" she asked, a perplexed frown creasing the white skin of her forehead.

"I mean in Virginia. I . . ." He could not find the words to explain. "I suspect we shall live in Washington for the near—"

"That damn Jeffrey Keyes!" she screamed, jolting Ethan from his own pensive thoughts. He was completely surprised and more than a little shocked to hear his sister's outburst. Jeffrey had, after all, been a minor figure in the drama of life at Twin Pines.

"Why do you curse Jeffrey?"

She buried her face in her hands, and her black curls shook with her crying. Going to her side, Ethan held out his handkerchief, and she took it, still crying. She used the square of white linen to wipe her eyes and blow her nose, until gradually her tears stopped flowing. "He's a sneak. You told me to watch Mr. Hughes," she said, facing her brother squarely. "Well, I am telling you to watch *him*—closely."

He watched her attentively. Martha was often given to outbursts of one sort or another, but in this particular instance, Ethan was almost afraid to discover the truth. But he did not have to fear learning her secret, for she would tell him nothing. That new determination again.

"Where will you be married?" she asked firmly, closing the topic of Jeffrey Keyes.

Ethan had given it little thought. He merely shrugged.

"You must do it here! Say you will!" she urged him. "This house could benefit from some happiness and good cheer."

If he knew Dr. Stuart, it would not be as easy as Martha proposed, but he could not bring himself to disappoint her. Ethan made the promise, not knowing whether or not he would be able to keep it.

He had not eaten since leaving Washington, and

suddenly he was famished. Excusing himself, he went to the kitchen, where Clara prepared him some ham and potatoes. He ate greedily as Clara filled him in on the local gossip, and was relieved to learn that Hughes had whipped only one man and that the slaves found him to be a stern but fair taskmaster, if something of a puzzle.

"I don't know what makes him tick," Ethan told her.

"Miss Anna make him tick!" she insisted. "But what do he want?"

As afternoon slipped into evening, they pondered that and other questions. Clara seemed at ease with every topic except her son, so he steered clear of asking more about Thomas. Ethan's guess was that the young man might soon ride the Railroad north to freedom.

CAPTER 26

ETHAN SET OFF for Stuart Hall the following afternoon. As he rode in discomfort along the road to Richmond, clouds boiled on the western horizon, skimming the mountain peaks, and a storm seemed imminent. He kicked the mare to go faster, but she only balked and turned her head. Ethan cursed the stable owner who had dared charge such a price for the nag. She wouldn't go any faster unless he got off and pushed her.

Stuart's house man, Noah, met Ethan at the door of Stuart Hall and ushered him into the warmth of the parlor. A moment later, Caitlin appeared in the doorway. She wore a pale blue gown and looked lovely.

She laughed and embraced him, and as he bent to kiss her, inhaling her perfume with all his strength, he told her, "I have missed you so!" Dr. Stuart be damned, he thought, tasting the sweetness of her mouth.

"And I have missed you, Ethan! I dream of you every night." She had a look on her face that was both saintly and devilish, prompting him to ask more about her dreams. But she would not explain. "Perhaps once we are wed, not before."

Releasing her, he walked to the fire, rubbing his hands together. "Caitlin, that's why I've come. Will you?" He turned to face her gravely. How he'd yearned for her these past months. "Will you do me the great honor of marrying me?"

Her mouth opened slightly. Nodding wordlessly, she ran to him and threw her arms around him. "Yes, of course I will! I shall marry you today, tomorrow, and every day until I die!"

For a fleeting moment he thought to beg her not to mention dying, but he knew she was soaring in spirit, as he was. "Can you hear the beating of my heart?" she asked. "It's racing."

"Mine won't stay where it should, either," he admitted. "This happiness is too much!"

He felt her draw away from him. "What is it, Caitlin?" he asked, searching her smoky eyes.

She gazed at him lovingly, boldly. "I must tell Father now. I'd like you to wait here."

She did not smile, and Ethan saw that a determined set had come into her features. Ringing for a house servant, she ordered him to bring Ethan some refreshment; then left him alone in the parlor.

Caitlin found her father bent over a law book in his library. He looked up over his reading spectacles to see her standing solemnly in the doorway. Crossing the room to stand by him, she spoke to him in a voice of firm determination. "Father, Ethan is here. He's in the parlor. Father, I want to marry Ethan. I must. I should also like your blessing—"

"Don't ask me for my blessing! You cannot have that!"

Stuart put a hand to his spectacles. He had exploded, acted without thinking, and that was unlike him.

He wasn't sure how to express his disapproval without losing his daughter's obedience. In the classroom, he always knew which pose to strike to suit his purpose, but with her he had never known. Setting his large hands on his hips, he rocked on his feet, his eyes boring into hers. "I cannot approve the match. Caitlin, you well know that Ethan Parson is a traitor to our—"

"I deny such an assertion!" she interrupted. "Father, as a professor of law, you ought to understand the concept of presumed innocence!" It was a desperate ploy, for she knew that under her father's definition, Ethan had no doubt behaved treasonably and deserved the rope. Yet she had to cast doubt upon his assumptions.

"You have chosen the wrong damn Parson!" he shouted at her.

The force of his voice stopped her where she was. The fire in his eyes was hateful. It was what she had always feared, and yet she remained calm.

As she opened her mouth to respond, Ethan appeared in the doorway to the study. Running to him, she put a finger to her lips and motioned him to retreat down the hallway. "Please, Ethan, give me another minute," she whispered to him.

"You tell your father that he is not God!" Ethan hissed, his hands clenched with rage. Caitlin's face was anguished, and she could no longer contain the tears in her eyes as her father appeared beside her like a bull from the chute.

"I heard that!" Dr. Stuart said, shaking his fists at Ethan.

Caitlin tried to calm her father, whose face was contorted and red with anger, but he pushed her aside and drew back a fist. Ducking the punch, Ethan shoved the old man backward, and with a cry of surprise, George Stuart lost his balance and fell to the floor, stunned but apparently unhurt. His face was red with fury as he struggled to right himself. Caitlin went to him, but he waved her away and tore her hand from his arm. "Get out! The two of you! You are no longer my daughter!"

"I am!" Caitlin insisted. "You know I am!" Ethan tried to leave with her, but she pulled in the other direction. "Look at us, Father. Look at us and see us as we really are. We are—"

"You are out of my will! Penniless! Let Lincoln support the two of you!" He would not let her attend to him, but shouted for Noah. When the manservant appeared, Ethan took Caitlin by the arm; she was trembling.

"Come with me now. You can see your father tomorrow."

With one last glance at her father, she relented and went with him, pausing only to get her coat and gloves. But despite the warmth the wraps provided, somewhere in her heart she felt a deepening chill.

Caitlin ordered a carriage to take them to Twin Pines, leaving word with Noah that she and Ethan would be wed two days hence at the Parson estate, and that Dr. Stuart was welcome.

He held her tightly against him all the way to Twin Pines. She spoke not a word, and as they approached the house, he hugged Caitlin even closer, causing her to gasp. Or was she crying?

The ceremony took place on a crisp, sunny day, with only Martha and Anna witnessing the nuptials. And although their signatures naturally had no legal force, Clara and Alex also attended, Clara in the crisp cotton dress she wore to Sunday service, and Alex in his best suit.

Ethan stood before the fireplace, the rotund minister, Reverend Bowles, by his side. He had begun to fidget, tugging at the tight starched collar of his white shirt, but one look at his bride, when she appeared, wiped away all concerns except that of marrying her and making her as happy as possible.

She wore one of Martha's gowns of flowing white crinoline trimmed in white lace. Entering the parlor on Anna's arm, with Martha behind her, supporting the train she herself had made the previous afternoon, her brown eyes were luminescent and brimming. With her feet hidden from view by the floor-length gown, she seemed to float like a swan to Ethan's side. She held out her gloved hand, and he took it. It was so light and trembling that he impulsively put it to his heart. She turned to him and smiled with a serenity that laid to rest his gathering fears.

Together they faced Reverend Bowles, and both spoke their vows, saying, "I do," with conviction. With a simple prayer, the minister pronounced them man and wife.

Martha and her mother wept openly, and Clara, too, wiped away tears, but Caitlin and Ethan stood dry eyed and smiling, staring into each other's eyes even after they had kissed and the minister had left their side. Ethan's happiness was great, tempered though it was by the war and his own fear of arrest. His heart was full when he looked over Caitlin's shoulder and out the parlor window to the hillside.

But his gaze landed not on the enormous pine, but on the overseer, who stood there, dressed in a dirty coat stained with manure, spitting a long stream of chewing tobacco in a brown arc across the grass. Ethan's grip around Caitlin's shoulders tightened, and misunderstanding his gesture, she looked at him earnestly and spoke.

"I'm so afraid," Caitlin whispered in his ear. "What if something happens to Daddy? He wouldn't let me explain about our work or—"

Ethan put his finger to her lips. "Caitlin, my love," he began, "the life we have chosen will not be easy, not from this day forth. But I love you and I trust you and I rely upon you to do the same for me now. We are two moons in search of a sun to orbit."

She nodded and squeezed his hand. "I'm frightened of the future, too. But you are wrong, husband," she said softly, looking out the window to the east, in the direction of Stuart Hall. "We have a sun to orbit, and it is you."

Later, as they sat to eat cake and sip punch, Caitlin's spirits revived. Her smile was dazzling. No longer did she seem concerned that she wore a borrowed dress and carried the curse of her father with her, rather than his blessing and presence. When Ethan asked her about the transformation, she smiled and said, "Later, husband. We have no secrets from now on."

Just after dark, the newly married couple excused themselves, climbing the stairs to Ethan's room.

"I always imagined a honeymoon in Paris," she said, teasing him. "Talk French to me."

Ethan had to laugh. "I never learned it, darling. There are not many great French theologians. Will Latin or Greek do?"

Shutting the door to his room, Ethan bent and kissed Caitlin deeply. The room had been scented with rose water, and on the bed lay a lone gift—sweetbread from Clara.

Pulling gently away from her, he reached into the pocket of his vest and pulled out a small box. "Here," he said, handing it to her. "I have something for you."

Caitlin's mouth opened wide in surprise. "Ethan!" she exclaimed softly. "However did you manage—"

"It was no easy feat, believe me." Taking the gold band from the box, he took her hand and slipped it easily onto her narrow finger.

"It's lovely. I don't have a thing for you." She was almost in tears.

Breaking away from him, she asked Ethan to turn his back and count to five hundred.

He did so slowly, listening to the arousing sounds of skirts rustling and Caitlin grunting with effort. "This dress . . . takes two people to . . . get on," she explained in a hurried whisper.

"I'll help!" he volunteered, but she shushed him.

"And keep your back turned. Eyes on the wall!"

The candles lighted throughout the room cast flickering shadows on the walls, and Ethan watched them, mesmerized, as Caitlin removed one skirt after another.

"I am ready to be seen." She had never before spoken

to him in such an alluring tone. The secret world that marriage created between husband and wife had begun to form itself. This was the dawn of the first day.

He looked at her standing before him in all the glory that was Eve's before the Fall. She was a perfect creature, so beautiful that all at once Ethan felt unworthy. Shyly he looked away.

"What is it? What's wrong?" She stepped closer, placing her hand on his shoulder. He turned and lifted her chin with one hand, finding it cold to the touch.

"You're freezing," he said. "Get under the quilt." She did, and soon he, too, had undressed and lay beneath the covers on the cool sheets, shivering and expectant. Her bare thigh became warm next to his.

"Are you pleased?" Her voice was soft and childlike.

"Yes! Yes! I'm . . . overcome. Caitlin, you are so beautiful. I'm afraid to touch you for fear you'll break, like crystal."

She laughed at him. "Your ideas! I'm not crystal, Ethan. I'm flesh and blood." She rolled over onto him, and he felt the full, soft warmth of her breasts brush against him. "Aren't you?"

"Oh . . ." Before he could reply, her kisses sealed his lips. But the unspoken *Yes!* was in his heart, and she sensed it. Their passion grew white and hot, blinding as the sun. And it burst like a falling star across the nighttime sky, leaving a trail of illumination and awe.

"You are the woman of my dreams," he whispered afterward, brushing her hair from his face and eyes.

"I dreamed of you often, husband," she said, trying out the word again. It seemed to fit Ethan, and she was pleased. "I realize now that all that was missing from my dream was you."

Their kisses awakened new and prolific spirits of fire within them. The heat seemed inexhaustible.

Jacob was homesick and cold. Christmas was just a month away, and the Yankees dallied as if they had all the time in the world to march and train. As Tyler said,

"What are they waitin' for, an invite to the wedding?" The newspapers and messages they had intercepted all seemed to indicate a different kind of struggle than anyone had predicted as little as two months before. Northern strategists spoke openly of a war of attrition that could last for years, a notion once scorned as ludicrous. Years of this mud and cold and disease, Jacob thought. A man would go insane.

He ached to hear his mother's voice, to tease Martha and hear her laugh, to taste Clara's sweetbreads; these deep and abiding pleasures were denied him by the war. He felt foolish in the wee hours of the morning, playing soldier like a boy. He was no warrior. One look at his broad bottom and thick waist revealed that much. But once the sun rose, and the army awoke with it, the Parson pride emerged, dazed but intact, and he carried out his duties with precision and vigor.

Only the hope of a substantial leave at Christmas kept him from falling into deep despair. That, and the knowledge that many others in the vast camp must have felt the same. Yet no one ever spoke of it. He heard sad songs over campfires, songs of home and loved ones, but no one ever talked about the things which haunted his sleep, and prowled his mind like beasts of the night.

Tyler once suggested that he visit one of the camp followers, a slattern who sold more than soap, and Jacob had nearly slugged him. But sometimes he felt that lonely, that he could have found a moment's solace in her arms. He noticed that Tyler did not take his own advice, preferring instead to socialize with the card sharps and mouth-harp gang, telling one tall tale after another. Jacob actually had begun to hope that both of them might make it through the war alive, although Tyler's losing a limb or an eye might teach him some humility and slow him down a bit.

Jacob pulled up his blanket, trying to remember what his bed at home felt like. He found himself picturing Julia Keyes at their parting. Had she said or intended more than he recalled? When the war ended, could they ever hope to meet without bitterness? He tried to set aside such fanciful notions, but the lovely lady from Boston kept turning up like one's reflection in a pond—slightly unfocused but familiar.

Perhaps, he thought, my misguided brother was right about one thing: Follow your heart. I wonder if I might volunteer to undertake a mission to Washington, perhaps just after the New Year.

Brett Tyler twitched in his sleep like a hound dreaming about cornering the fox. But the fox in his dream wore a gown, and her name was Martha Parson. In the dream, which he had experienced over and over for weeks, he was drowning in a pool of dark, swirling water. Martha stood on shore, looking in his direction but not seeing him. He waved and shouted for help, but she could not hear him. Her eyes looked through him.

As so many times before, Tyler awoke choking, a drowning man in a sea of uniforms and dirt and cold, clear air. He pounded the ground in frustration, praying that she not marry until he had one last chance to see her. He knew the first thing he would tell her—and it was sure to scare her or shock the daylights out of her. "I can be kind," he would tell Martha if he ever got the chance. "I can love you good."

Far off down the hill, some unnerved soldier had picked up his mouth harp and begun playing "My Sweetheart Waits." Tyler hummed along, wishing she might say to him: "You have a chance." Those four words would change his life, he knew, binding him to her like Adam to Eve, the only two people on earth.

Anna Parson could not sleep. She was haunted by the disapproving presence of her husband, who now hovered above her in a manner so cruelly denied him the last ten years of his life. It was almost amusing that, dead and buried, he darted about, embarrassing and worrying her at every turn, in a way that in life he never had. No longer dominated by Charles, she was adrift. The last six months had cost her her husband and two sons, both gone to war and never to return "her boys," but as independent men. She resented the calendar. The dates themselves had betrayed her: the day that Jacob joined the army; the day that Ethan went away; and of course, the day that Charles died. What was it about Franklin Hughes that vanquished all her reserve? From the moment she set eyes on the man, who was cocky and ill educated but strong willed and attentive, she felt as if she had taken a giant step backward into her youth. She had the chance to live her life again, with a man who could walk and work the plantation—and hold her in his arms.

That was it: Hughes was her youth, the evoker of her romantic nature. She knew better than to trust him, but knowing had nothing to do with how she felt around the brassy little fellow. If she could just persuade him to back down in front of Ethan and Jacob, all would be well, for a while at least.

She did not like widowhood and found little honor in it, much as she loved and served Charles. When he died, the sickness had died with him, and with it went the nurse in her nature. What was born anew in her was the passionate pilgrim trudging relentlessly in her spirit, searching for a holy heart that lived for love. Charles could never abide by such ideas; he had dismissed them as poo. But Anna knew better now: She knew that there was a man with such a heart, if she could only believe him.

Just before dawn, she awoke from a light sleep with the strong sensation that her husband lingered in her room. Charles was smiling at her, and she returned the smile. Then he wagged a finger, warning her. She sat up in bed, but Charles had gone. She was alone, and the floor was cold on her bare feet.

Ethan awoke and left the bed. When Caitlin stirred, he turned briefly to assure himself that she had not awoken. Shivering in the cold air, he went to the window that overlooked the pines which gave their name to the Parson land. Bathed in moonlight below them was the new grave and the simple headstone. What would Daddy think now? he wondered.

If he was to be honest with himself—and he had to be now, involved with spying for the North and wed in a union his father had found unacceptable—he had to admit that Charles would have been as outraged as Dr. Stuart was. He would have sent them packing, too, as soon as decency allowed. In the still night air, he could hear his father roaring, "I won't have him caught abed in my house, not even if he's shot and killed Old Abe!"

The fire was dying, and the room was growing even colder. He looked at Caitlin, his bride, his future, his life. She lay sleeping serenely, royally, and he marveled at her strength. To defy Dr. Stuart was no mean task. He made a promise to see to her welfare first, at whatever cost to himself. And what if they were to have a child soon? The thought sent him into a panic.

Slipping under the quilts that Clara had piled two feet high on the bed, Ethan nuzzled closer to Caitlin, who rewarded him with a sleepy kiss and a hand on his chest. Finally he fell asleep with a prayer on his lips and more hope in his heart than he had a right to expect.